YELLOWSTONE SHIFTERS

GREG MARCHAND

Yellowstone Shifters

Greg Marchand

RHETASKEW   PUBLISHING
UNITED STATES OF AMERICA

COVER AND
INTERIOR DESIGN

© 2021 - Flitterbow Productions

All characters, settings, locations, and all other content contained within this book are fictional and are the intellectual property of the author; any likenesses are coincidental and unknown to author and publisher at the time of publication. This work and its components may not be reproduced without the express written permission of the author and Rhetoric Askew, LLC.

ISBN-13: 978-1-949398-50-2

© 2021 – Greg Marchand
and Rhetoric Askew, LLC
all rights reserved

To a red-haired woman named Linda, who had the resilience to raise two stubborn boys on her own and not kill them in their sleep. How she accomplished this, and countless other miracles, I'll never know.

Thank you, Mom. This one is for you.

PROLOGUE

DEEP BELOW THE Rocky Mountain spines, within the bowels of the earth, something turned. Swells of mantle magma moved against the outer crust, and colossal masses of rock plates slipped against one another. Gases laced with metal elements seeped from one corridor to the next. Crevasses and passageways opened, and parts that had not moved in millennia began to shift.

Far above the stir, tucked into a mountain draw, a broad horse barn quietly warmed in the buttery sun. The whispering Wyoming breeze swept through the open valley, tickled the pasture blades, and met the weathered barnwood. Horseflies teased at twitching horse flesh as rays of light lasered through the wall slats.

The largest animal, a white, gray-spattered stallion, gave a low nicker as young James and Elliot unlatched and heaved open the swinging doors.

As the hay dust gently swirled around them, the boys held a healthy dispute between friends.

"This one. He's the best horse! Papa said I can ride him next year when he's seven, just like me." Elliot, big for his age, with khaki skin and fine, black hair to his shoulders, approached the stout stallion in the middle stall. As he stroked its fleshy snout, the horse blew a swell that lifted his onyx hair.

James brushed a shock of hair from his pale face to assess the horse. His jade irises were unimpressed. He critiqued, "Who, Badger? Badger's not the best horse."

"Yes, he is. He is the strongest horse ever."

James looked up at his larger friend. "Yeah, but he's just like you; big and slow."

Elliot grabbed his smaller friend by his collar and said tartly, "Oh yeah? You wanna bet I'm slow?"

James clutched Elliot's big wrists, set one foot back, and leaned forward. "Yeah, I know you're slow. I bet you a hundred dollars I'm faster than you."

For a moment, neither backed down, and each held their challenging stare.

The gathering breeze thrust its way into the barn, forcing the unlatched door at the other side to swing open. The door swayed to a rest, and for a moment the sounds of the foothills filled the barn—magpies in the field squawking in competition over rabbit carrion, a nearby stream burbling where its descent through the draw met flatter earth.

Just then, horse dung thudded onto the ground, and Badger's muscular rump let out a loud spurt of gas. Elliot was the first to drop his grip and succumb to laughter.

James teased, "Ewww. He *is* just like you, Eli," then giggled as he sprinted away. Elliot lugged after him.

The nimbler James leapt onto a hay bale, said, "Anyway, Coyote is the fastest. That's why he's the best horse. He could beat Badger in a race any day of the week."

With James's help, Elliot stepped onto the same bale of hay.

It was time for the first of their daily contests.

Elliot steadied himself, and asked his friend, "Ready?"

James nodded. "Yep."

Together, they counted, "One . . . two . . . three!"

The boys launched themselves from the hay bale like Olympic long jumpers. As their feet planted and the two toppled over, the first tremor occurred, going unnoticed by the playful duo.

The earth's tectonic plates below them rubbed and fault lines jostled. Tens of miles to the north, the Yellowstone caldera rose from its slumber like a hibernating grizzly bruin.

They recovered and read the results in the dirt. James's superior leaping ability once again held true, and he proclaimed his victory. "I win."

"You got lucky. Let's go again."

"All right, *Eli*."

"Stop calling me that. I mean it," Elliot said archly as his brow furrowed.

The irked expression seemed to take James by surprise. "Are you okay?"

With confusion tightening his dark eyes, Elliot said, "I feel funny."

James gave him a sideways look, then remounted the bale. He said, "Okay, fine. This time you can count down. It doesn't matter to me."

Elliot joined his side atop the hay, and said, "Fine. Ready?"

"Uh-huh."

"One . . . two . . . " Elliot shoved James clear off the hay and leapt. "Three!"

The boys tumbled haphazardly, as if the landing were the most entertaining part. James stood and dusted off his dingy t-shirt. "Hey, not fair!"

Elliot grinned mischievously.

Suddenly the second, more powerful tremor shook the ground.

This one did not go unnoticed. The boys idled, dumbstruck by what they felt.

Hanging gourds continued to sway from the rafters, and the horses paced nervously in their stalls.

As the barn's frame resettled, a seismic surge rearranged the underworld. Geothermal features within Yellowstone and the region began to spurt and spew. Mud pots boiled vigorously, while unseen hot springs flowed. Hot pools surged—some emptied.

The boys stood quietly, waiting for the next shake. A paralyzing quiet overtook the barn—it seemed every creature within earshot had vanished and the murmuring breeze had fled.

The boys and animals froze, as if a tyrannical thunderbird had just landed on the barn's metal roof, perched in anger, seeking to render flesh and steal souls.

That's when Elliot leered at James, and James at Elliot, their tender faces quickly turning to scorn.

As they met in the middle of the barn, Elliot shoved James to the ground and towered over him. Elliot's dark hair draped around his eyes, which seemed to blacken entirely.

A fierce intensity rose inside of James, and a wolfish growl rumbled inside his throat. He scurried to his feet, narrowly avoiding Elliot's hands as they reached for his neck. He lunged at Elliot, and the two struggled.

Within the grapple, Elliot managed to lock in a bear hug from behind. He squeezed James's lower ribs, forcing him to fight for air. James thrashed ravenously like a caged dog and freed himself. He snagged Elliot by the wrist and sunk his teeth in, puncturing Elliot's radial artery, and the blood began to flow.

Elliot screamed furiously.

Badger's hooves batted the stall gate.

Elliot backed away and examined his wrist as it spurted blood.

Freshly enraged, Elliot charged and speared James into the ground. He straddled James, and the two pummeled each other with closed fists. Elliot quickly acquired a grip around James's neck with one hand. James choked for air.

Badger, Coyote, and the others neighed and thrashed against their wooden enclosures.

Showing his teeth, Elliot shoved dirt into James's mouth. When he ran out of dirt, he used loose straw.

Color receded from James's face as his resistance weakened. His punches withered to slaps—then to nothing at all.

Elliot's blood painted both boys, and its flow wasn't slowing.

Elliot lowered his hands and slouched with the onset of faint.

James lay motionless.

The ground shook again, this time much more aggressively.

A woman's voice shouted from across the property in the direction of a large farmhouse. "Boys?! James! Elliot! Where are you?!"

PART I
INFECTION

CHAPTER 1

A NARROW TRAIL, used by intrepid hikers and those on horseback, threaded through a southern glen in Yellowstone National Park. The path had been engraved over time by other creatures as well, hoofed ones: the occasional lazy buffalo on his migratory route, mule deer five or six at a time, or a bull elk searching for his cow—his nostrils to the wind, discharging his screechy bugle to the far reaches of the park. Nearby, meadow lilies swayed as the bees launched from their blooms, and pine martens chattered to one another as they busily cached their September seeds. The glen was one of countless slices of heaven found deep within Yellowstone's two million acres, locked in the tranquility of its remote location.

Yet, a sense of beauty and danger conjugated here, knew Kyle Fenn, and journeying such a trail meant playing the odds, preparing for anything. Breathtaking alpine ridges and snowcapped peaks, produced by ages of subterranean turmoil, stood over stretches of scorching-hot geysers and fragile patches of ground above immense magma reservoirs. Such was the dual nature of the slipping weather patterns; shine and bliss here, wind and hail there, snow one second and God's light the next.

Where the placid path began to climb the boulder-strewn foothills and overlook a lay of scattered forest, Kyle rested on one knee. The breezy young man leaned his elbow against a lodgepole pine and watched Nicole Bowman as she surveyed the elevated view. His eyes lingered on her honey-brown hair that lapped over her pack. She stood with her thumbs tucked beneath her shoulder straps, her pale-brown skin glistening in the sun.

Beyond her was a roll of dark clouds. The distant thunderheads created a wall across the geyser basin, and inclement weather barreled their direction.

Those legs though, he mused. Nicole called them her "thunder thighs," as she'd always been ashamed of her slightly larger bottom half. That was nonsense, he'd told her, and she was a ten from head to toe.

"Annie!" Nicole's strong voice reverberated through patches of alpine evergreens and rolling hills until it escaped through a clearing and into the silent valley. "PeeWee!"

Kyle crept up behind and pinched Nicole's thigh. "Nice set of lungs you got there."

She whirled and slapped his shoulder. Her chestnut eyes were wide, "*Kyle James Fenn!*"

"I couldn't help myself."

Kyle had a natural lift at the side of his top lip that showed when he spoke. It was an involuntary feature that could almost be taken as a smirky snarl, except that when he smiled fully, it was swept away by an affable face.

Like a pitcher on the mound, Fenn raised the bill of his Red Sox hat, and studied the dark horizon. He straightened back his black hair, tucking it behind his ears, then returned the fitted hat to hold it in place. He pointed with his chin. "There's a storm coming."

"No shit, Sherlock." Nicole said. She sighed. "They've been gone an hour. Where the hell are they?"

He adored her frustrated scowl and loved the sound of her voice. On rare occasions, if he listened closely, he could hear the remnants of her childhood speech impediment—once, as she tried to step out of a canoe while Kyle held it, she had exclaimed, "I'm going to fall in the water if you don't hold the damn bo!" —meaning "boat." She had let Kyle know of her discontent for the subtle articulation errors—the result of a mild hearing impairment—but he saw it as a lovable feature, even a turn-on at times.

He said, "Let's wait a little longer. Those clowns will catch up."

"They better get their asses moving. There's about to be a torrential piss and pour." Nicole adjusted her bean-shaped, skin-toned hearing aid with her fingertips. "What if they're lost?"

"Don't worry, the dining guests at the *majestic* Yellowstone Lake Hotel won't notice if we get back a day late . . . or a member short. It'll just be some other faceless cook screwing up their orders."

She shoved his chest. "That's not funny."

As it does before a storm, the air had calmed in the valley. A similar serenity surrounded Kyle each time he was near Nicole. He considered himself "one lucky redneck" as fate had aligned their paths this summer. The park's setting was fertile ground for the two seasonal employees to find what Kyle considered to be love, or something close to it, as they searched the mountains and themselves. Conceivably, this could have all been a dream; his strange and enchanting summer with her in this otherworldly park, the spark in her eyes each time they reached a mountain view and soaked it in, how she was able to lay her head on his shoulder, reach right in and clench his beating heart.

It was no dream, however, and she was as real as the reaching peaks surrounding them and the crystal, meandering stream cutting the valley floor. He was never known as the most patient person, and it was almost painful waiting for the day she'd say it back to him—the "L word."

He locked onto her eyes as she searched the trees for their friends.

Finally, she noticed Kyle's longing stare and a grin stretched across her face. "What are *you* looking at?"

"My hot Virginia city-girl." Kyle circled round and hugged her from behind. He cooed in her ear, "*Heey good-lookin', waaatcha got cookin'?*"

"Would you stop?" Nicole weakly resisted. "What is that, something you Tennesseans sing to your sisters at night?"

"Come on, sing it with me. You were in the school choir. Jump right in."

She rolled her eyes. "Our coworkers have vanished. You might want to focus on that."

Kyle said, "Why did you want those two to tag along anyway? I mean, they're good people, but they're kinda weird."

Directly overhead, thunder shook the sky.

"Kyle, I don't like this."

Crack

A massive lightning bolt powered down from the heavens and split a cedar tree a kilometer away. The blackening horizon rumbled, and Whitebark pine trees nearby bowed in the gathering wind.

Kyle grabbed Nicole's arm. "Come on."

PeeWee suddenly appeared on the trail behind them. "Yodelay hee hoo!" He waved them on. He was shirtless with a joint in his hand. His bare white chest was accented with a small patch of hair in the center, and a tweaky-eyed owl tattoo covered his side. Dirty-blonde hair dipped down his back.

"I think he wants us to follow him." Nicole broke away from Kyle and headed toward their co-worker.

Fenn mumbled to himself, "Okay. Guess we're just gonna get stoned instead of finding shelter . . . that's cool."

He buckled his pack's waist belt and followed Nicole. He shouted, "Can you really trust a man with a mullet? Honestly, though?"

"**HEAVY AND SOAKING** curtains a stout storm, you are a solitary drop

Headlong sojourning fall without a thought, your end seems fated or bought

All the while, it plagues your mind, what leads your destiny?

Leaving a city sodden, its underlings sieged

Or . . . "

Annie, whose co-workers called her Annie-A because her last name was hard to pronounce, sat cross-legged, reading aloud from a damp notebook. Her straight hair was the orange hue of a red fox and it concealed the sides of her face.

Kyle, Nicole, and PeeWee were keyed in to her every word. Outside, the hills drank of the buckets that cascaded from the sky, but within the granite overhang, the group of friends were safe and dry.

A small fire lit their faces as dusk set in.

"Holy shit, you wrote that—just now?" Kyle couldn't find a real meaning behind Annie's dictation, but it sounded profound.

Nicole slapped Kyle's knee and shushed him.

Annie continued,

"Or . . .

Delight a raindrop knows no beginning

Deride men that seek their never-ending

For we are sent on our way, a star amidst a galaxy

And told our deeds will soon pay, our tolls against our fallacies."

Annie closed the notebook and slid it into her pack. Her gaze moved over the others with marijuana-induced, drooping eyes.

PeeWee sat up from his laying position and clapped. "Bravo, Annie-A!"

Kyle and Nicole joined his applause.

Annie smiled abashedly, her eyes in the dirt, clearly pleased by their praise but too modest to acknowledge it.

Nicole was curious. "Is this what you guys were doing the whole time we were looking for you? Just sitting under here?"

PeeWee pulled a mandolin from behind him. He settled in and began to strum. "Yep. That, and jammin' a bit."

"I didn't know you played," Kyle said.

"If it's got strings, my old ass can play it. Twenty years of playing in bars. Like Creedence said, 'If I only had a dollar for every time I had to play while people sat there drunk.'" He paused, then released a quick smile. "Wait. I *did* get a dollar every time. Hm. Well, you get the gist of it."

"Old's a relative term, man. Forty-five isn't old, not *really*," Annie said. She seemed to have a permanent grin, and her nose wrinkled when she wanted to emphasize a word.

Kyle snorted, "Y'all been smokin' this whole time, too? You look a little uh . . . you know."

PeeWee chuckled. "You two were so far ahead, and a hell of a storm was coming, so we just shimmied under here and rolled a few. Thought we might as well sit here and watch it come by. It's what any normal guy and gal would do, right?"

Kyle raised his eyebrows. "Normal?" He teasingly tossed a twig at the mandolin player.

PeeWee swiped the stick away as it landed in his lap. He replied, "We just like to live while we can, you know?" He winked at Annie, and she nodded. "I kinda like to go where the breeze takes me. That's my kind of mantra, man. I've been through so much shit in my life . . . you know what I mean? You ever been through shit, like some real bad shit, that you don't ever want to remember?" PeeWee looked down at his graceful fingertips as they strummed away.

No, Kyle thought. Nothing in his twenty-three years that he could recall had ever been too much for him—probably because he knew how to deal with his problems, unlike these potheads.

Kyle just smirked.

PeeWee offered, "Go ahead, get you a toke. Chill out. There's plenty to go around. Or are you too good?"

"Last time I did, it got me kicked off the team," Kyle replied.

"What team?" Annie asked.

Kyle used to swell with pride when people would ask about his sports life. Now he slouched. "I played shortstop in college. Me and my buddies got busted one night at a party. Cops found the weed. Coach was a real holy roller and kicked me and two other guys off the team."

Annie's eyes ballooned. "Wooow."

"That's how I ended up here. And I really thought I had a shot at the next level, but . . . "

"That's a bummer, man," PeeWee said.

"So, I said, 'Fuck it,' and hopped on a bus for The Stone." Kyle glanced at Nicole. She was privy to the whole story—he'd laid it on her one night after rum and Cokes at the employee pub, raving that his release from the team was the worst day of his life and how he just wanted to know his place in the world now. He put up a solid front to others, but he knew that she knew better—that deep down he had a lingering fear about his future, doubts about his own worth.

"Well, you're in good hands now." PeeWee gestured to Nicole with the headstock of his mandolin. "Looks like you come out on top, despite all that."

Kyle nodded at Nicole with a warm grin. "I think so."

AFTER DEVOURING THE cellophane-wrapped sandwiches and granola bars they'd packed form the employee dining room, PeeWee started a soft bluegrass tune.

The other three stared blankly into the campfire.

The pine needles and sagebrush cushioned the raindrops as they met the earth and began their downhill journey to their waterfall meccas. The mountainside and its critters were tucked in for the night, and the brilliant stars waited behind the storm clouds. The tired hikers adjusted to a more comfortable position and rested their overworked joints and muscle tissue.

Annie tilted her head back and guzzled the last of her beer can. She kept her half-baked eyes skyward, searching the night's canopy as the clouds started to part. It seemed her poetic mind wandered in a sweet, childish way as she took in her surroundings.

She took a drag from her joint. "Hey guys, not to be too cliché, but you know this is how scary movies start, right?"

"Ooh!" PeeWee mused. "I like it."

"It *is* grizzly country." Kyle noted.

Nicole added, "And timber wolf."

PeeWee stopped his strumming. "And mountain lion." He grinned under his overgrown goatee, then continued playing.

Annie wondered, "What if we're just hiking along tomorrow, and a geyser just shot up out of the ground and threw us all into the air?" She demonstrated this by extending her arms skyward, gracefully like a ballerina.

PeeWee leaned back on a log as he played. He said, "Annie-A, honey, did you stuff a little somethin' extra in that doobie?"

"Don't worry about the geysers," Nicole reassured Annie. "We're more likely to get attacked by a roaming park ranger, armed with his self-righteous possession of marijuana tickets."

Annie said, "I just get the feeling that this is all too perfect. Don't you? How can we have it this good? Something's not right. I mean, I look at you guys and I get a weird feeling."

"A weird feeling?" Nicole asked.

"You guys look like heroes stumbling into danger, like something's waiting for you right around the corner and you don't know it yet. It just doesn't feel right, man. It feels like a bad movie where we all get ripped to shreds by a boogie monster." Without missing a beat, she said, "Furthermore, I realize how drunk and stoned I sound."

"'Cause she is." PeeWee said.

"Yeah, I'm just messin'." Annie clumsily withdrew a bundled tent from her pack and started to unravel it. "I just want you guys to know I love you. You *are* my heroes. I mean it. I love you guys."

PeeWee replied for the group, "We love you too, girl."

Annie's kind words seemed to remind PeeWee of a different song when he stopped playing and collected a silent rhythm, bobbing his head. After a few beats, he began a clean, melodic picking, a lick that seemed to sorrowfully mope out into the nasty rain, dejected, its head hanging low.

"Is that 'Whiskey' by 'Trampled by Turtles'?" Nicole asked after a moment.

"Yup."

Nicole left Kyle's side and sat next to PeeWee. Like waiting to leap into a moving jump rope, she found her entrance and lent her soft voice.

The lyrics spoke of heartbreak, and a turn to whiskey to get through an overwhelming problem. As she sang, Kyle watched her face intently. Though her elegant, trained singing voice was alluring, he could sense something wasn't right. He saw it in her eyes as they reflected the flickering flames—they trembled in the slightest way.

Nicole looked Kyle in the eye as she sang the next few lines.

Before she shifted her gaze back to the flames and continued her rendition of the song, Kyle swore he saw her start to tear up.

Never again that night did she look him in the eye.

AT DAWN, KYLE woke to the sound of prancing hooves.

Just outside his tent, a small herd of mule deer were grazing, and two fawns bounced friskily as they broke in their new legs.

When he rolled over and found Nicole at his side, he was once again taken aback by his good fortune. Not many people could say they'd ever shared his experience— waking up in the middle of a stunning hike in this "World's First National Park," having harmoniously shared the night with the mighty creatures, being one with a raw nature unlike anywhere in the world, and the kicker—sharing it all with the girl of his dreams. When would his luck run out with her? Surely one day she'd slip through his hands, fly back to heaven.

He thought of the crazy circumstance that had led him to cross paths with her. After dismissal from his baseball team, he'd been haunted by the question, *Now what?* His modest town's factory would have welcomed him with open arms, but too many like him had spent their entire lives within its walls, and if he wanted the most out of this fleeting life, he would have to "roam." This gut emotion pulled him from the green grass of home and dropped him here to discover the world. In a pleasant twist of fate, though, he discovered something much more powerful than the joys of roaming—he discovered her.

Exhausted from the eight-mile journey, Nicole was switched off. He admired her slightly pointed ears that she always tried to hide beneath her hair. Her mouth gaped a bit, adorably, as she was lost in a dream. It was comforting to see her face content after her teary expression last night. Kyle had spent a few sleepless hours staring up at the corner of the tent, stewing over the odd message she seemed to be sending him from across the campfire. Nicole was never one to hold back her thoughts, so whatever it might be, it appeared she chose to keep it to herself. He would honor her choice and leave it be, though it took a lot not to ask her what was wrong. After all, maybe there was no message—perhaps he was overreacting.

He zippered out of the tent and stood up straight to stretch. He watched through the subdued light of dawn as the deer herd's grayish figures abruptly froze, noticing his sudden presence.

One turned to bolt away, and almost simultaneously the rest followed.

He found a log and sat alone at the dead fire to steep in the approaching sunrise. Frosty dew on the surface of the three tents twinkled in morning's first glow. Nicole slumbered in Kyle's Coleman tent, PeeWee snored loudly from his, and through her half-zipped tent door, Kyle saw Annie lying in the fetal position, sleeping hard.

Kyle twisted the release on his propane burner, releasing a ghostly *hwoo* sound. He flicked his pocket lighter at the gas beam, and it ignited.

Ahh heat. Instant coffee was nigh, and he couldn't wait for the brown liquid to warm his insides, make him forget about the chilly air at their elevated location.

He adjusted the flame until its blue hue changed to orange, then set a tin of water over the burner.

He raised his head to greet the brisk Wyoming morning. A special kind of silence lingered on the mountain side—a kind of cold quiet that had become his favorite part of these hikes.

Between Nicole and these surreal moments, he wondered if the way he viewed the world, and more so, how he behaved in it, was changing. He had softened in a way, it seemed. He'd been called incorrigible in Tennessee, even a bully once—the accusations had taken him by surprise and had merit upon reflection, though he would never concede it publicly. It didn't seem like others viewed him as such here. Here, people just called him dude or bro and took him for what he really was: harmless when left alone. Perhaps Nicole and the park had sank into his skin, dampening his brash tendencies. His Tennessee-self had proudly boasted, when asked, that he'd never lost a fight, and it was mostly true. Now, his brags were of his longest hikes, how many wolves he'd spotted, how beautiful Nicole was.

He dumped a package of coffee crystals into the steamy tin cup and noticed the peaking sun. Then he could see that a better view seemed to be just uphill.

He turned off the burner, grabbed his coffee, and left to investigate.

Sure enough, a mountainous expanse met him as he stepped around a bundle of trees. The sun crested the ridge on the opposite side of the valley, sending a grayish-pink glow across his mountain's east face. There was nothing like drinking in a Yellowstone sunrise and the feeling of an entire mountain beneath his boots.

Kyle gently blew the steam rising from his cup. Then came a voice.

"Hey." Nicole suddenly appeared behind Kyle, wrapped in a flannel throw.

"You sleep all right?" Kyle handed Nicole the hot beverage. "Careful."

"Thanks." She sipped. "I'll never get used to these sunrises."

"Right? The guys still asleep?"

"I think I heard a tent zipper a second ago." She reached the coffee tin out to Kyle.

When he took the cup, he noticed her hand trembling.

She drew in a deep breath and shakily exhaled. "Kyle. I don't know how to say this."

He saw her lip quiver.

Something was wrong. He asked softly, "What is it?"

"Mom's got cancer."

He stepped closer to her. "Oh my God. Are you serious?"

"They were hoping it wasn't, but . . . it's bad now. I put in my notice last week."

He reached for her arm, and she turned away.

"I can't—we can't do this anymore." Her tears pooled as the rising sun lit her subdued brown irises.

"What do you mean?"

"This, us, we can't be together anymore. I'm going home."

"I'll come with you." It startled him how quickly he said those words.

"It's not that simple."

Kyle rubbed his temple. "Wait. When were you going to tell me this?"

He knew the answer by the desperate look on her face: when she could find the courage to tell him.

Kyle threw the tin cup to the ground. The metal clanked against a boulder, and the brown beverage painted the rock. "What about staying for the winter? You were supposed to be here with *me*! Remember?"

Nicole began to sob.

Kyle instantly regretted his selfish words. "Wait."

Suddenly, a frantic whisper came from the trees. "Hey, hey, hey. Guys." It was PeeWee. "There's a *fucking* bear at the *fucking* tents."

The couple quickly abandoned their quarrel and raced to PeeWee. He was hunkered behind a tree. He said, "Look at that big son of a bitch."

A large boar grizzly dug at the campfire, scavenging the ash for charred marshmallow remains. Searching the campsite for hidden food, it upended the log sections they used for seats, issuing groans of disapproval.

Though they were a distance away, Kyle could still hear its nasally huffs as it hunted for breakfast. Then it dawned on him. "Where's Annie?"

"She's not with you guys?" PeeWee gasped.

Nicole wiped her still-damp cheeks, and said, "No, where the hell is she?"

"*Shit.* I don't know. I got out of my tent and saw her tent flap was open, so I thought she was off, taking a piss or something. That's when I saw a goddamn bear coming, so I split."

As the grizzly knocked over Kyle's propane burner with its nose, Annie's head emerged from the dark entrance to her tent. Her face turned dead pale.

Nicole desperately whispered. "No, don't run Annie, don't run. Get down." Then Nicole raised her voice and waved her arms. "Hey bear, over here!"

Annie ran.

Annie's flight startled the bear, and it gave chase.

Nicole bound forward. "No! Hey bear, hey bear!"

PeeWee quickly did the same, joining her side, blaring at the bear.

Kyle froze.

The grizzly took Annie down. Annie couldn't scream— she could only make a choking noise as it bit her face.

She went limp, and it shredded her ribcage, then peeled a flap of skin from her shoulder.

Kyle spilled over and vomited. Morning's coffee sprayed from his mouth and splatted on the ground.

PeeWee and Nicole stopped running when the bear lifted Annie by her thigh and thrashed her lifeless body.

Nicole screamed, "Hey motherfucker!"

It stood on its hind legs to see Nicole.

Steam rose from Annie's open wounds.

Nicole yelled again, half-crying, "Go the fuck away, you fucking asshole!"

Just then, a disturbing and gut-turning groan of finality left Annie.

The bear returned to the ground and looked over the young woman, sniffing every inch. Its hot breath swirled around Annie's body. It clamped its jaws around her neck and lifted.

Annie was done.

Calmly, the bear dropped her lifeless body. Blood flowed from it jaws and down its drooping bottom lip.

PeeWee was the only one who could speak. "Go! Just fucking go!" He javelin-tossed a stick in the bear's direction.

The grizzly grunted and whuffed as if it was thinking.

Eventually, it turned shoulder and retreated into the thick of the forest.

Nicole ran to Annie. Kyle followed behind her but stopped to dry-heave.

PeeWee collapsed to his knees and wept with utter surrender.

As Kyle looked away from the fresh mauling, he saw a trickling stream. Last night's rainwater traveled its path and met with a meadow creek in the clearing. The crystal water, bound for the Grand Canyon of Yellowstone, lapped and gurgled round the rocks, traveling with absolute indifference for Kyle's spinning head, for the evisceration, and for Kyle's new and unwanted bachelorhood.

CHAPTER 2

AN EMACIATED MOUNTAIN lion lay in a flat circle at the top of a hill, its tan skin drooping between its ribs and pelvic bone. Porcupine quills pierced its muzzle like matador spears in a bull's shoulder—a sign that it had gotten desperately hungry. It was almost hidden within the dry ground and cover of sagebrush that spread around it. The harsh Yellowstone winter hadn't even arrived, and already the big cat appeared to be starved.

At the foot of the large hill, dozens of tourists crowded a paved pullout on one side of the two-lane road, congesting traffic as far as the eye could see in both directions. Their many tripoded cameras were aimed at the doomed cougar—cameras that had monitored the situation for a day and a half. Folks from every corner of the planet—Chinese, European, Thai—conversed excitedly in their separate sub-groupings, updating each other on the status of the animal.

Seasonal law enforcement officer Henry RedMoon had heard from the Wildlife Management division that the dying cougar raised its head once yesterday. That was the only time it moved the entire day, and it hadn't moved since. The division also said it was considering what to do with the cat since it had gained a dangerous amount of attention. Where there were too many cars, accidents increased, and where there was a soon-to-be carcass, predators increased—mix the crowd with the extra predators, and they'd have a dumpster fire on their hands.

RedMoon knew what "considering" had meant. It meant permanent removal.

Standing in front of the line of cameras, Henry's duty was to contain the visitors where they were. His straw-colored, wide-brimmed hat shaded his dark eyes, and his gray and green uniform concealed his Native American skin. He was broad-shouldered, clear-eyed, formidable. He watched their movements sternly, more like a special agent or drill sergeant rather than a friendly ranger. His fellow officers, especially the full-timers, often informed Henry that he lacked the charisma the Park Service preferred its officers to possess and demonstrate.

RedMoon didn't flinch when the rifle blast came from a high position over the distant bluffs. As the shot rang out, the entire crowd ducked.

The tourists gasped and cursed. Parents reached for their children.

Henry smirked under his hat's shadow. *Guess I forgot to warn you*, he thought.

The shot echoed through the mountain meadows and across the geyser basin.

There was another blast that scattered the crowd.

Quickly there was another.

RedMoon heard the dull *thud* of the third bullet finally entering the cougar, ending its misery.

Henry rolled his eyes. It took three attempts to hit a clear, unobstructed shot with an immobile target and no wind—*what a disgrace.*

A large woman wearing a safari hat and sunglasses had her face in her camera's viewer. She squealed, "Oh my God, they shot him!"

She relayed the information to her cohort of on-lookers, who were now experts in mountain lions and mountain-lion habitat.

"Her. It was a female, ma'am. They're removing the lion for everyone's safety. They'll be by soon to retrieve her." Henry stepped forward and gestured toward the road with his palm. "So, if you don't mind, we'd like to start clearing the road."

The woman responded, "Well, that's fucking terrible! Why would you do that?"

"Like I said, it's for your safety."

"This is total bullshit. I paid damn good money to be here. I deserve to see this thing, even if it was dying!"

Henry approached the woman and said acidly, "You deserve nothing."

The woman stepped back.

RedMoon flinched as he recognized his father's anger rising in him. He hated when that happened—he was not his father. But, this woman—he couldn't stand the sight of suburban trash like her.

"That lion would rather be eaten by scavengers than be gawked at by you *aliens.*"

"Alien? What the hell is your problem?"

"Take your camera and leave before I arrest you for traveling into a restricted area."

"I'm not in a restricted area." She planted her hand on her hip.

Her cohort nodded in agreement and stood their ground.

The rest of the crowd turned to the confrontation and quieted to hear Henry's response.

Henry removed his ranger hat, revealing his rough, and sand-colored face. His narrow eyes were perched atop high cheek bones, the irises so dark it looked like he had no irises at all, just two huge pupils—a distinguishing RedMoon trait.

He said to the small band of rebels, "Fine. I'll let you stay here and watch them remove the poor animal, and you can continue spouting your self-righteous nonsense about how beautiful she is and how much you know about the mountain lion population in the park . . . if you can do one thing for me."

The group shifted nervously, though their chins remained high in defiance.

"That mountain lion up there has more than forty different names in English. If any one of you—" he caught himself. "—you *folks*, can give me just one of those names, besides 'cougar,' I'll let you stay."

The angry woman scratched her paunch. She looked at the others.

An embarrassing hush cascaded over them like a sinking, shameful fog.

He raised his voice like a marine drill instructor, "Come *on*. There are forty damn names. You can't think of just *one*?"

He circled them, looking into each of their faces, getting no response.

In a pouty retreat, the woman and her companions slowly gathered their cameras, told their kids to come along, and walked to their SUVs.

The rest of the crowd followed behind.

As they were leaving, he counted on his fingers and taunted, "Well, there's the catamount, the puma, the Nittany lion, the panther . . . "

A grin almost raised on Henry's lips. "What? Oh, come on. Isn't that why we're all here—to learn?"

Just then, RedMoon's shoulder microphone squawked, "Hodges to RedMoon."

Henry squeezed the Motorola mic. "Go ahead."

"What's the situation with the cat?"

"It's down. Visitors are leaving."

"Already?"

"Yep, nice group, real cooperative. Good thing, too, my shift ended three hours ago."

"Heading back?"

"Leaving now. Be there in thirty."

REDMOON ENTERED THE ranger station at the park's south entrance.

"Another late day?" Fellow seasonal officer Hodges leaned in his rolling chair behind a scarred counter. The bridge of his nose jutted forward, giving him a face like an axe. The gangly man had his reed-thin legs stacked on top of a printer. His mustache was poorly kept, dipping lower on one side of his mouth than the other, and it caught Henry's eye every time he talked. The skewed facial hair, Henry would think to himself, complemented Hodges' overall ineptitude as a ranger. The lead ranger for their district often paired the two, to Henry's chagrin. It was obvious that their pairing was so Henry could correct Hodges' missteps. They'd been called to Moose Falls once when visitors were illegally jumping from the head of the waterfall. Henry had led Hodges on a hidden route to surprise the divers. When they'd successfully snuck to within feet of the water, Hodges overzealously sprung forward, slipped on a boulder, and rolled his way right over the falls, his arms flailing, barely keeping his head above water after landing. A visitor had to dive in and assist him out of the water at the base of the falls. Henry still cited the divers, though Hodges had made it difficult to do so with any kind of dignity.

When Henry removed his cruiser keys from his belt, his eye spotted a new public service poster near the front door. The image was that of a grizzly with its mouth cranked open in a powerful display of fury. The message across the top read, "Hike smart. Conceal your food. Make noise. Carry bear spray." RedMoon studied its teeth with intensity.

Hodges repeated himself. "Another late day, Henry?"

RedMoon was transfixed on the bear.

"Ah, don't worry about that guy," Hodges said. "That's just one of those tame bears they keep in the West Yellowstone sanctuary. Look how fat he is. He's probably posing for bacon."

Henry shot Hodges a sharp glance.

"You're a rough guy, RedMoon, you know that? About as charming as an army tank."

Henry strode across the wood floor and set the car keys on the counter.

"I filled the cruiser with gas. I'm going home."

"Do you really drive an hour and a half to get home?"

Henry began to walk away. Hodges threw up another question like a curious six-year-old.

"Is it true about your family? You know, like, you guys don't use electricity and you're filthy rich? It's two thousand and three, you know, it's okay to be on the power grid."

RedMoon didn't answer.

"Do you guys really have Przewalski's—you know, those endangered Russian horses or whatever?"

Henry gritted his teeth as he reached the door.

"Someone told me you guys are only allowed to marry women from the rez."

He turned to Hodges. "Why don't you get your feet off the printer?"

RedMoon's glare burned a hole through Hodges.

"All right, jeez."

Henry said, "Hodges, I'll have my own district one day. You might want to think about that and how you conduct yourself around here."

Hodges perked up. "So, you applied for the Mammoth District?"

"Goodbye, Hodges."

As Henry closed the door behind him, Hodges called out, "Take me with you. I'll transfer. Henry?"

CHAPTER 3

KYLE DRAGGED ABOUT his day in the Yellowstone Lake Hotel kitchen, unable to shake the image of Annie's body from his mind. He gloomily pondered his own existence, in almost every moment, on others' faces, on cans of tomatoes.

He stared blankly at the six-pound can. "Peeled and Diced."

Ugh, did they have to use those words? Living with the vivid memory of an innocent woman, really a girl, being ripped from existence wasn't what his former self would have imagined it to be. It wasn't a "cool story." The only words that he felt described it were "the worst" or just "fucked up." The experience made him question everything he thought he believed about the so-called gift of human life. Sacks of monkey meat were all we were, he supposed—apparently, bags of flesh that can be easily torn into. What good was a soul with such a vulnerable shell?

Furthermore, he questioned what sense there was in having a heart—so you can give it to someone who'll stomp and shred and dice and bite at it, too?

Just then, a few gravel stones clanked against the storeroom window, and Kyle snapped to. As he shook his downbeat thoughts aside and peered through the windowpane, he saw Nicole watching him from the parking lot. She dropped the rocks, looked at the bus as they loaded her bags, then back at Kyle.

He threw his apron over the counter. "Hey Chef, I'm taking lunch."

With a thick New York accent, the pot-bellied chef said, "But we're about to pick up any minute."

"Not my problem."

The chef remained speechless as Kyle exited the kitchen. He tossed a rubber spatula in a mixing bowl and raised his hands. "I'm the executive chef for a five-star restaurant and he tells *me* when he goes on break."

When Kyle stepped out onto the back steps, Nicole was waiting.

"I just wanted to tell you goodbye," she said.

Kyle sat on a step. He watched an Osprey glide on a thermal over the massive lake. "I just don't get why you won't let me come with you. I can help you."

"But you just met me, Kyle."

"I don't write poetry. I don't sing or play an instrument. Is that it? Too hick for you?"

"Kyle, I'm more than grateful for you offering to come. It's too hard for me to explain."

"For once you're the one who can't express their feelings. That's something."

"It's just something I have to do on my own. These should be the best days of your life, right here. I'm not going to take that from you. Just don't wait up for me, okay?"

Kyle pulled out his greasy pocket notebook.

He avoided eye contact as he handed her a pen. "At least give me your address. I'll send you pictures from the hike. The general store said they should be ready in a week or two. I think I got a few with Annie and all of us together."

Kyle scooted the dust off the step with his food-stained shoes. He pouted, "Don't worry, you don't have to give me your number. I know how breakups work." Although he'd never been on this end of one before.

"Are you still staying for the winter?" She asked.

"Yeah."

Nicole wrote down her address. She looked at the pen and bit her lip. She continued writing. Once finished, she handed the notebook back to Kyle.

"You should consider talking to the guidance counselor they offered us. I did. I know you don't want to hear it, but it's no one's fault that she's gone, Kyle. Annie wouldn't want any of us to think it was."

Kyle stared out at the lake. "I'm good."

She was stiff, though a storm of emotion played across her face. She took a deep breath. "You'll make some girl really happy one day—someone more deserving than me."

Nicole bent and kissed Kyle's forehead. As she walked to the bus, she wiped her eyes.

Kyle looked at the notepad in his hand. He opened it to read her words.

You have the courage to follow your gut and to be true to your heart. That's why you're beautiful. I never said I loved you, but I always wanted to. Nicole.

He looked at the bus as it drove off. The windows were too tinted to see inside. *Shit.*

He mumbled to the wind as it sailed her away, "I love you too."

GUESTS EXCITEDLY BUZZED about the century-old hotel as Kyle moped through the grand lobby in his white chef jacket and checkered pants. It was lunch break, but eating was the last thing on his mind. He felt abandoned, but he knew he had no right to blame Nicole for doing what she must. It wasn't fair, not being allowed to hate her. All the smiling faces around him—the healthy couples with their perfect lives, their perfect relationships, their perfect kids, on their perfect vacations . . . Screw them for having the ones they loved.

He noticed the size of the crowd was thinning these days as the season was wrapping up for "The Grand Old Lady of the Lake." In the regal foyer was an art display consisting of wildlife and nature paintings. The artist was there, creating a colorful portrait of a bull bison for a guest. A grand piano sat near a tidy bar. A professional pianist tickled an elegant wild west tune—her ornate tip bowl brimming as appreciative guests listened from their sunroom rocking chairs. Kyle pondered what all of it would look like in a few weeks' time when the hotel closed and he was still here to cook for winter road crews.

A whiff of elk medallions and lobster tail coming from the dining room kitchen reminded Kyle that his break time was limited, and the rest of the kitchen staff was probably scrambling right now, wondering where he was. Then he smelled the puttanesca sauce he prepares for the specialty pasta dish—he could pick out the aroma of the kalamata olives he sautés and the cabernet he simmers down each morning.

Kyle snorted at this.

At one point in time, he could change the carburetor on a '75 Chevy, bale hay, and bury fence posts all day. He studied his soiled, white uniform. *Look at me now. I'm goddamn Chef Boyardee*, he thought.

For the first time, Kyle felt ashamed. He sighed with frustration as he wondered what the hell he was doing with his life. What good was being in Yellowstone now, when she wasn't there to experience it with him?

The sight of a perfect, cookie-cutter family disgusted him just then—a man in a collared shirt and his beautiful wife, their three well-mannered kids, all with gorgeous smiles posed for a picture next the painter as he worked. Right before the photographer said 'three', Kyle casually and swiftly reached his long arm out and displayed his middle finger behind the father's right ear.

The camera flashed, and Fenn slipped into the main hallway, hurrying away with a sly grin.

The joy of mischief quickly faded, however, as his sullen, freshly dumped mood resurfaced about halfway down the hall.

He ambled along further until, he spotted an exit at the hallway's end where he could get some fresh park air. The chatter of the lobby guests faded away until all he could hear was the cushioned sound of his own steps. The aged wood below the Navajo-inspired carpet gave a little under his kitchen shoes as he walked along. The hallway was so wide, Kyle thought perhaps a herd of buffalo could pass through. The walls were a neutral dark with an occasional painting depicting the free and open western frontier of old, one canvas showing the long and canary-yellow hotel with its pillared façade nestled lakeside in a cradle of hunter-green forested mountains. There were black and white photo reprints of U.S. Army soldiers at what was Fort Yellowstone in the 1890s at the northern entrance to the park—others of the servicemen outside tacked-down canvas tents at Theodore Roosevelt's camp as he'd visited the park. Other frames with grainier quality were of indigenous peoples outside teepees, tending to buffalo hides. It was as if the age-old building begged of Kyle, "Remember when?"

Funny how the building was abruptly present with a different personality when no one was around. The hotel was just a piece of his world when others were present. But when he was alone in the building, it was as if he was part of *its* world, like all eyes were on *him*.

Kyle thought of turning back, so he wouldn't be late, when he heard voices.

One guest room was open. Kyle peaked inside.

Two college-aged girls, in housekeeper polo shirts, sat on the bed watching television. They ate vending machine granola bars and drank coffee. One braided the other's hair.

"Damn. Wish I had your job," Kyle said from the doorway. His lip raised on one side, making his casual joke look like a brazen remark.

One girl shushed him.

The other girl said with a Polish accent, "We are watching this crazy man on the TV."

"Who?"

"A scientist man," she said.

The American pointed at the television with her chin. "This archeologist guy who lives in Paradise Valley, Montana."

A portly man with a graying beard spoke behind an auditorium podium. A few in the audience rudely booed him.

The Polish girl was amused. "Yes, he is mister *monster* man!"

Kyle tilted his head. "Come again?"

She clawed the air in front of her face. "*Raaarh!*"

CHAPTER 4

THE SEATS OF Clarion Hall, at Montana State University, were filled with spectacled scholars and university students fulfilling their mandatory participation hours. Fliers in their laps read "Native Tribal Conflict Within the Greater Yellowstone Region: Truth to the Folklore by Dr. Donnan MacLeod." The conference topic was Human History of the Rocky Mountains. The participants sat awkwardly silent as Dr. MacLeod lectured to them from the wide, empty stage. He was a condensed, blazered man with a barreled belly. His blocky salt-and-pepper beard was mostly salt, giving him the appearance of someone who was only a few years away from wearing a red suit and granting children's Christmas wishes at the local mall.

A projector screen behind MacLeod showed two columns of bulleted text; one had the heading "Wahota Tribe," the other, "Yohawnee Tribe."

His Scottish-tinted voice echoed throughout the dark facility. "Losing your children and elderly to a cruel winter because it sprang so quickly is one thing. Imagine losing even your strongest members to an invading tribe—men who turned to beasts—now that is something truly terrifying."

He squeezed a remote in his hand and the next slide of his PowerPoint appeared on the screen—an artist's rendering of animal-hide-wearing men surrounding a Russian Brown Bear of epic proportions, a spear in its gut, the dark-headed men firing arrows at the beast, it roaring with rage, a geyser in full fume in the expanse beyond the bear. "And what terror—"

The crowd shuffled. MacLeod's bright but sallow eyes shifted behind his frameless glasses at the crowd's unrest.

In the audience, a man leaned over to mumble to the woman next to him, "He's the one I meant to tell you about—he found his wife buck naked in their car with a valet driver."

She whispered, "A *valet driver*?"

Eavesdropping students behind them snickered.

"He's never been the same since. He's totally lost the science in his work. He taught at the University of Washington—Native American History, Archeology, Anthropology, Oral Traditions, you name it. He used to be the head of his field, a very accomplished field researcher, but now—well, he gets on these rants about werewolves and ridiculous nonsense. It's quite self-denigrating when he speaks. Sad to watch, honestly."

She shook her head, "Unbelievable. Is he—"

"Drunk?" The man nodded and rolled his eyes.

MacLeod continued, "I know, I know, this is where dear ol' Donnan jumps the rails, but hear me out." He instinctively felt at his breast pocket where his whiskey flask rested inside. A flair of silver-flecked brown hair fell from his brow. "What terror, knowing the power said tribe possesses and all you can do is run. They sneak into your camp by the light of the full moon, gut your children, cut down your warriors by the *dozens*. You flee, and they let you. They let you because they know that when they find the remainder of you in another month's time, they get to grow their fur and kill again."

A group of men chuckled in the crowd.

"Ladies and gentlemen, colleagues, set aside your preconceived notions about my research. I stand before you and posit that the myths and legends I speak of are real—they *hold water*. Regions above seismic hot zones produce eerily similar lore from those who inhabited those lands. There is a meeting of three energies in these areas, one of geothermal, one lunar, and one of the living—a dynamo of awful consequence."

A suited man pretentiously stepped onto stage. *Here we go again*, MacLeod thought.

He had seconds. "Whether you believe the myths or not, entertain the idea. Do today's militaries not spend boatloads of their nation's funds on matching other nations' combat technologies? Have men not been at each other's throats since the dawn of time? Doesn't evil *always find a way?*"

The boos pummeled him.

The man politely gripped the elbow patch of Donnan's blazer. MacLeod leaned to the microphone. "Ah, yes, the shepherd's crook is here to clear the stage. Well, I suppose that's all for today, sadly."

As the two exited the stage, MacLeod pulled his arm from the man's grasp. "Relieve yourself of my jacket, you wee Jessie, or I'll show you what an old Royal Navy boxer still has in his tank."

THE CUBES SWIRLED as Donnan set aside his snifter of whiskey. The clicking of his chubby fingers striking his laptop keys echoed throughout the spacious chamber. His desk was as large as a queen-sized bed, though he only used a small portion of it. One wall of his study held rows of books so high he'd installed a rolling ladder to reach its upper volumes. The glow of the screen splashed his face in the low-lit room. A fire burned and snapped in the stone belly of the wall across from the researching ex-professor.

MacLeod wiped his mouth. He almost drooled at what he queried:

"State of Wyoming, 2002 Census" *Click.*

"Fremont County" *Click.*

"City of Dunoir" *Click.*

MacLeod moved to the edge of his leather chair.

"RedMoon."

"1 RedMoon Lane." *Click.*

"Sid RedMoon, Self-Employed, Horse Husbandry, Horse Trader"

He jotted in a leather-bound notepad. The top of the page was labeled "Wahota Lineage."

He scribbled:

Sid 65, Larinda 67. Sons Wymon 34, Vic 30, Henry 27.

MacLeod leaned back in his desk chair and stroked his beard. Lifting his glasses, he rubbed his exhausted eyes and yawned. He clutched his whiskey glass, closed the laptop, and left the study, which was separated on an upper level of the home.

As he waddled into the main-floor kitchen that opened to a large living parlor, he flicked on a light. He suddenly wobbled as his now rushing blood distributed the alcohol. Several sets of reflecting eyes aloft in the shadowy living room watched his movements—taxidermal glass eyeballs of three mule deer, a full-bodied bobcat, and a bull moose head staged ostentatiously about.

He flipped on another light, and the stunning chamber became animated. It resembled something found in an in-flight tourism magazine. The furniture was arranged perfectly, but was dusty, unused and seemingly staged. Tan leather couches faced each other under a glowing chandelier crafted from elk antlers. The mounted deer and bobcat, their poses frozen in time, seemed to revere the higher-placed moose head. The moose's dewlap dipped over a tall fireplace big enough for Paul Bunyan to walk through. The towering living-room windows framed the town of Gardiner, Montana and the chimerical northern mountains of Yellowstone under a clear, starry night.

MacLeod refilled his glass and added ice from the freezer. He took a sip and clumsily set the drink down onto the marble top of the kitchen island, sloshing the liquid onto a stack of opened mail. He cursed, "Aye, you're a wee scunner!"

He started to soak up the spill with a towel but saw that the ruined papers were his overdue bills. MacLeod resentfully flipped the towel onto the stack and swept them aside.

Another swig.

The alcohol was hitting the spot now. His beverage heated the inside of his stomach and zipped through his veins, melting his mind into contentment. Donnan knew it was only a matter of time before the contentment wore off, making way to darker thoughts, but he ignored the fact.

As he swayed slightly, he lifted his glass of whiskey and shuffled out of the kitchen and into a small hallway.

Before turning the doorknob at the end of the hall, he stopped to view a framed photo on the wall. In it, a busty woman in her forties squeezed a Pomeranian pup while MacLeod planted his lips on her cheek.

MacLeod sloppily impersonated a woman's voice, "No Donnie, you don't need a 401K! You're so brilliant! People love you! Retirement plans are for amateurs. Buy me a yacht instead."

He sighed as a tear trickled into his beard. *I loved you, you evil—*

MacLeod opened the door and stepped into the four-car garage. A mock road sign was nailed over the parking spot nearest the door. It proclaimed, *Spot Reserved for Sherri MacLeod. All Others Will Be Towed.*

He gave a pouty wince at the empty parking spot and tiny wire dog crate nearby.

Another sip and the glass was empty again.

On a shelf next to him was a vase with dead daisies slouching over the sides. A faded and curled sticky note barely clinging to the vase welcomed Sherri home.

His stomach turned yet again at the realization that she was never coming back. Each day, he wondered if this was how he'd live the rest of his declining life—in a perpetual mad routine—curse her picture, see her empty parking spot, see the dog crate, check the flowers. Drink. Cry. Drink.

He scanned around, realizing he'd forgotten to bring fresh water. Donnan looked at the glass in his hand, then dumped the ice into the vase.

MacLeod swayed harder. He stepped back on one heel and stabilized his backward lean. He whimpered as his face tightened, "Just come home."

Pulling his cell phone from his vest pocket, he dialed a number and put it to his ear.

A woman answered. "Grand Canyon of Yellowstone, Canyon Hotel Reservations, this is Sherri speaking."

MacLeod opened his mouth, but nothing came out.

"Donnie, is this you?"

He didn't answer. He knew she was probably checking the caller ID right about now.

"I told you to stop calling me. It's over—get that through your goddamn head, you fucking alcoholic."

He hung up and returned the phone to his vest.

In a sudden flash of rage, MacLeod spiked his snifter into his garbage bin. Shards of glass ejected, one slicing across his forearm. He slammed the bin lid shut three times with increasing force.

Like an angry child, he dropped his arms to his sides and breathed heavily. This was the part of his routine that he knew sometimes went south.

MacLeod stormed back inside. He opened a kitchen drawer and retrieved a Smith and Wesson MP Shield nine-millimeter pistol, gripping it tightly.

It was black and clean, heavy in his hand.

His breath sputtered suddenly like a frigid blast of air rose up his spine. He revisited the idea of ending it all.

Tears streamed down his face.

Not in the kitchen, he thought.

MacLeod dragged himself to a living room couch, his shoulders slumping defeatedly. He laid the gun on the coffee table and curled into a ball on the plush couch cushions.

For the next two hours, he cried and shivered until he eventually fell sleep.

CHAPTER 5

WINTER'S FIRST FLAKES pinwheeled from the sky and melted into the oil-stained streets of a dilapidated neighborhood in Blacksburg, Virginia. Dead weeds rose from the snow through sidewalk cracks, and shambly houses struggled to keep the heat in. Children with unkempt hair, too young to be outside alone, played on a large truck tire. Some circled a swing set, its chains rusted and seat straps long since removed. They pelted each other with balls of muddy snow and hurled profanities at a malnourished stray hound as it sought their attention. Mean mugging teenagers and vagrants entered and exited an abandoned house, which had its windows boarded up or knocked through entirely and a bedraggled couch on its porch. Above it all, white clouds billowed endlessly from a midtown factory, pushing into the atmosphere a heavy steam from the plant's constant toil.

In a one-bedroom house with a metal roof consumed by rust, Nicole Bowman's mother lay in bed as cancer consumed her body. The shrunken woman's spirit never dampened, however, as Nicole sat by her side and held her hand. Nicole knew her mother wouldn't show her pain in front of her no matter how much it hurt, how much it dragged her through hell.

"I'd tell you not to worry about me, Nikki, but I know you'll do whatever you want. You're the most stubborn thing on two feet I've ever known." She smiled weakly and squeezed Nicole's hand. "And I've known some real jerks in my time."

Nicole understood who she meant by "real jerks"— Nicole's father.

Nicole didn't reply, only caressed her mother's forearm. The subject was too sensitive for Nicole—if she talked about his abusive ways, she'd feel that familiar urge to find him and kill him in his sleep. Only in a perfect world could she do that, though, as he was currently behind bars.

Her mother continued, "Sometimes I wonder if you realize just how stubborn you are. Do you remember why you decided to take singing lessons when you were a little girl?"

"No, Mom."

"Your speech problem. Back in school, in the fourth grade, a kid teased you about the way you talked."

"Is that right?"

"Speech therapy at the school cleared that up, but that wasn't enough for you. You had to go above and beyond. You promised me one day you'd be a famous singer and show them 'meanies.'"

"Oh my God, I forgot all about that." That memory had been crowded out by other events that had happened to Nicole at that time. That was the fourth grade, the year she learned to stick up for herself, the year a girl had called

Nicole "Mulatto Molly," to which she'd responded by pushing the girl off the slide. No one dared call her that after that day on the playground. That was a day she'd never forget.

"You were spitefully determined. You made me so proud when you sang. Made me cry every time."

"Is that why you always sat in the back?"

She nodded.

"What would you like me to sing to you tonight?"

"Honey, you could sing any song in the world, I'd still love it."

"I think some Loretta Lynn sounds good. What do you think?"

"Oh, you know I love her."

Nicole held a cup close to her mother's face and let her drink from the straw.

"Thank you, Nikki." Her mother asked, "Hm, why don't you go by Nikki anymore?"

"I don't know. Nicole just sounds more respectable, I guess. I started going by Nicole in Yellowstone, and it felt good. I felt more grown up."

"There you go with that stubbornness again. People will still respect you naturally, because you're a sweet girl. You don't need to change your name—just be you. I bet none of your Yellowstone friends know you grew up in a neighborhood like this, huh?"

"No."

"Be proud of who you are, the woman you've become despite all this. One day, promise me you'll actually let someone love you for who you are."

Nicole couldn't argue. It was all true. "Okay, Mom."

"And promise me you'll go back."

"Go back where?"

"To Yellowstone, when I'm gone."

"Mom—"

"No, no. Being out west in them mountains has been so good to you. I could see it in you every time you came home between seasons. You're right to get out of this shit hole, so why do you keep coming back?"

"I didn't want you to miss me."

They shared a warm smile.

Nicole stood up from her cot that served as her bed next to her mother. "I'll be right back."

Nicole entered the cramped kitchen and sat at the small dining table. She put her face in her hands and fought back tears. *Why Mom?* The woman was an angel in Nicole's eyes. She struggled to understand why cancer had to find such a tender and loving person to feed on. She did everything she could to keep smiling in front of her mother, but how long could she continue to watch her fade like this?

To make things worse, she'd received a letter just this morning from the utility provider stating that service would be cut off in ninety days as the payments were already six months overdue. In it, the provider stated their deepest regrets and offered contact information to community outreach services, each of which Nicole had already sought help from and failed.

There was no one else to turn to. Her mother's side of the family had a habit of dying early, and only very distant cousins were still alive. Nicole's father was of no help as he and most of his family were in prison. Not that she wanted anything to do with the deadbeat. He probably didn't even know about all this, and she didn't care. Neither did her mother.

On the table were unopened letters from Kyle. It was hard enough leaving him—likely reading that he still loved her would only add to her anxiety.

Looking at the address written in Kyle's handwriting, her mother's words of advice ran through her head. She was right—Nicole did have hang-ups with allowing people to love her for who she was. There was no way she was going to let Kyle see where she grew up, so she foolishly denied his help.

Nicole had left Kyle with the notion she was strong enough on her own to handle this—a notion proving not so true. The regrettable truth revealed itself more each day—that someone was there for her, someone who would've moved heaven and earth in her name, but she was too proud to let him into her world.

She felt the letters. One was thick with photographs. *Annie!*

Nicole resisted opening the envelope. Not only would she have to ignore Kyle's words, but who knew how she would handle seeing pictures from that hike? She was strong, but not nearly as strong these days.

Just then, her golden retriever, Cujo, nudged his snout under her arm.

She stroked his soft head. Greying hair surrounded his kind eyes, which seemed to know something wasn't right.

The poor dog had rarely seen her since she started working in Yellowstone. She had been Cujo's best friend since he was a puppy, but for nearly a decade, the dog only got to see her twice a year. She felt regret for abandoning him every time she saw his slobbering jowls and doe eyes, though he never seemed to hold it against her so long as he got his ears scratched.

"I know, buddy. I love you too." She rubbed his ears, but he continued to stare at her. She projected her own thoughts onto him and heard his voice in her head.

She rolled her eyes. "All right, I'll open it."

Nicole opened the envelope. She carefully removed the two photos, leaving the handwritten note.

The first picture was a portrait taken by Kyle. He had interrupted Nicole while she set up the tent. *God, I look like a total bitch.* She remembered at that moment she had been rehearsing her breakup speech, desperately searching for the best way, and time, to tell him. Seeing him so content watching that sunrise, she initially thought her breakup wouldn't hurt him nearly as much. What terrible timing it was though, in hindsight.

She flipped to the next photo. Annie hugged a tree. Her porcelain cheek squished against the bark. She had no idea just how precious those last moments were. At least Annie didn't have the dread of knowing her last days were upon her.

With that thought, Nicole dropped the pictures and rushed back to her mother's side.

CHAPTER 6

A FULL, BLOATED December moon rose above the snowy mountain ranges that run northeast to southwest within the Absaroka and Washakie Wildernesses, just east of Yellowstone Lake. At this time of year, all life seemed to have vanished from the alpine lake situated over seven thousand feet above sea level. Its one hundred and thirty-six square miles made a desolate, cold void whose surface was frozen over. Wildlife no longer drank from its rim nor dove into its belly for a meal—and they would not for several months.

Daylight hours were now fleeting and grayed by a persistent, creeping fog as the bitter cold continued to push its way into the region. Anything that had planned to travel south or crawl into a hole was far gone by now, and the scarcity of prey animals within the harsh winter realm dispatched stealthy predators to travel about the mountain in search of a kill. They skirted around the geyser basins lest they slip into a lava-hot geothermal feature like a mud pot or hot pond and succumb to an excruciating death.

The mammoth Yellowstone Lake Hotel was closed, hunkered down for another brutal winter season that would soon see even more snow. The lake location was a few hours' drive from the only two open locations; Mammoth Hot Springs at the north entrance and Old

Faithful Snow Lodge to the south. The scattered cabins and accompanying Lake Lodge had closed earlier in the fall—all remnants of food removed, pantries scraped clean, not a morsel remaining that could draw unwanted attention from cold season scavengers.

Eventually the post office room for the location had closed shop, and Kyle was forced to stop writing to Nicole, to lose hope of ever getting a return letter. He regretted not asking for her phone number before she left, although he doubted she would want to speak to him as a simple return letter was already asking too much. At times, he thought it was as if she was glad to be rid of him. Why, though, would she write those words before boarding the bus? *I never said I loved you, but I always wanted to.* Those words were a thorn in his side, *Then why didn't you?* Maybe he could try writing again in the spring when the mail service returned. Maybe a lot of things would look up for him when the season shifted.

For now, Kyle's days running the hotel kitchen to feed the road crews dragged on at a snail's slither. When he was off, there wasn't much to do as temperatures were harsh and snow blanketed every trail, and many of the roads to get to them. Only a few employees remained at the location. With the crowds gone, Kyle had been pleasantly surprised to find that two bull elk had inched ever closer to the facility. For a few weeks, they had occupied a pasture between the cabins and Kyle's dormitory and allowed Kyle to watch them. He sat and stared at them, sometimes for hours. Now, he couldn't even enjoy their presence since the sun was already gone by the time he was off work. He could only tread carefully to his dorm each night on the lightless foot path of hardened snow and hope nothing prowled.

On this night, Kyle's cabin fever was at full tilt, and he found himself giving in to his curiosities. He'd wondered too many times what the inside of the hotel would be like now that it was closed, and he often found himself peeking over the swinging kitchen doors into the dark sea that was the dining room and its open threshold into the rest of the hotel.

After stealing a flashlight from the kitchen office, he braved those swinging doors and the darkness, and helped himself to the mysteries of the resting building.

The moon and stars shone through the bare windows, giving the place a ghostly gray appearance. The sounds of the pianist and guests were absent from the foyer and sunroom. Furniture was stacked and covered in sheets. The liquor bottles were gone from the bar, and the dining room behind him was vacant and clean, with the chairs stacked neatly along the back wall.

The old building slept—its halls lifeless. The night's breeze was laced with tiny pellets of ice that tapped against the windows as he passed each open room, the round glow of his flashlight nervously scurrying across every surface.

He shivered and tried shaking off the uncomfortable sensation of being watched.

Just then, something big knocked against the exit at the hallway's end, like someone had thrown a pumpkin at it.

Kyle jumped. *Jesus!*

He gathered himself and walked to the exit.

Something spoke to Fenn. But it wasn't a voice—more of a feeling.

No, that wasn't it. A whisper? What was it?

He needed to know, and against his better judgement, he decided to follow the unseen lure.

Kyle opened the door and entered the bitter cold. He swiveled his light in the direction of the lake to find the moon had cast a pale blue veil over the water, across the banks, and upon the far mountain ridges, miles upon miles away.

Kyle, his hands shaking now, wandered down a gentle, snowy hill dotted with rabbitbrush. The bare vegetation brushed his pant legs as he tromped headlong toward the lake's frozen shore.

Just before the stony beach, Kyle found a dark hole tucked under a rock overhang. The slick reflection of the black obsidian circling the hole drew him near.

He felt the rock—it was smooth with sharp edges, as if sheered by mechanical force.

He folded forward, making himself as small as possible, and crept inside.

After the short crawl, the space opened up, and he was able to stand. His light met the pearl-gray walls of the cave, and his nasal cavity was instantly filled a muddy, dank aroma. The rock surrounding him was produced by old lava flow; the melted then cooled form of granite known as rhyolite. This geological tidbit was a "fun fact" that was drilled into his head on every park tour he'd taken that summer.

The cave felt like it shouldn't have been there, like an unnatural formation created by an alien race. He heard water as it trickled through an unseen crevasse. The frigid wind whipped at the cave entrance—a location he wouldn't let out of his sight as he began to have a bizarre feeling of being nowhere.

As his light moved along the cave wall, a drawing suddenly caught his attention. At about chest level was a rudimentary eye carved into the rock, with a circle engraved around it. Another was to the left, and near it was a design with two arrows pointing at each other. Between the opposing arrows was a single black dot.

He moved his light again. There were several more of these two petroglyphs positioned at all heights, on undersurfaces, around edges of rock face. What he found spoke of another era.

Kyle searched further, struggling to keep his hand from shaking. A pulling force steered his attention away from his body, which told him he was cold and vulnerable.

On another wall he found more symbols. These were painted in red: a broken arrow, three triangle tops resembling mountains. Then, next to these, at the most practical spot to leave a message, was a paw print with five toes and claws and a cross. Kyle's breath shortened—a stick symbol of a man lying horizontal, then a paw print with four toes and claws. After the print was a squiggly line like that of ripples on the surface of water, then another broken arrow and mountains pictographs.

Something swiped broadly across his leg as if a dog had run by.

He turned quickly.

Nothing.

His heart raced, thumping against his breastbone.

He looked at the ground in front of him. *It's just a breeze. These caves are weird like that.* Although he'd never been in a cave in his life.

He played his light over something that was laid out on a flat slab of rock. *Oh God, don't tell me that's a dead body.*

The wind at the cave opening stopped.

The trickling water ceased.

Taking a closer look, he saw it was in fact a body—a very large skeleton. By the looks of its long structure, the skeleton must have been seven feet tall or more, and not so human. The bones of the legs were strikingly long. The humerus, radial, and ulna of the arms were also grossly long, like the those of a gorilla. A stretch of skin still remained under one of the femur bones. He pinched the large bone and lifted to see it. Thick, brown hair clung to their follicles, the leathery piece of flesh curling at the edges.

A tremendous feeling that there was a perversion of the natural order of things washed over Kyle.

He stepped back, pointed the light toward the head, and flinched.

There *was* no head.

The whole discovery had been creepy enough already that not finding a head was actually comforting. What would he have done if some guy's skull was cryptically sitting there with its jaw missing like those movies where they find the missing body in the attic?

Just then a hellish growl emanated from one corner of the cave.

Kyle darted away from the sound and tripped over a bulky object.

He got to his knees and cast his light onto what tripped him—the skull. It lay on its side and was the size of a Harley-Davidson engine. The upper jawbone extended out a few inches from the eye orbitals, and the temples ascended in a V shape, stretching to the top of the skull as if its creator wished to mold a baleful expression. It possessed two pronounced canines, like white daggers, matching those on the hefty bottom jaw. This portion was detached, sitting upright next to the upper skull, wide as it was long.

Despite its defeated arrangement, the remains shot an electric surge of fear up Kyle's neck.

He'd seen enough.

He scrambled to his feet and attempted to bolt for the cave opening, but something gripped him.

He let out a strangled cry and he tried to run, but his legs wouldn't move.

Something powerful rattled his inner core as he witnessed a foggy figure, a black and nefarious mist, manifest before him. His skin crawled and turned pale when he sensed an aura of malice slowly swirling around the misty apparition.

In a flash, the presence shot at Kyle and imprinted itself onto him.

He fell flat on his back, and his mind's eye floated.

He saw, spewing from his hands, the whirling souls that had once been residents of Yellowstone and its surrounding lands throughout past millennia. He heard voices coming to him—voices that he somehow knew came from as far away as the Bitterroot and Absaroka Ranges. In a flash of frightful visions, he saw raw and disturbing scenes—stories from the ground that had never been told. He was injected with hardships and unspeakable occurrences that those mountains had hosted over the centuries. He saw a man wrapped in fur, fighting off cold and eating from a boy's blue corpse. He saw one man butcher another, then dance around his body. He saw two wolves take down a young woman in the rushing snow.

Who were these people?

These visions seemed to be a welcoming parade to a sacred and unwanted brotherhood of murderous or tortured souls.

Evil's grasp was upon him.

Suddenly, he found himself in an inexplicable land of darkness and twinkling snow—the silence thick. He somehow knew that he'd foregone time and space.

Laying on the frozen ground, hurt and desperate, he was unable to move or escape, as if a nasty venom coursed through his veins.

For what seemed like several minutes, Kyle watched a bighorn ram from the corner of his eye. The ambling, yet curious ram made its way to Kyle's side. It finally looked down at him with flaming eyes. The sky above it rotated and turned from an inky black to an orangish cast with blinding yellow streaks that screamed like tormented children.

Deep in the ram's eyes, Kyle saw the reflection of a timber wolf charging for it. The ram fled, and the wolf suddenly appeared, snarling over Kyle. It bit his shoulder and shook mercilessly. He felt as though his arm would be ripped from its socket. His heart stopped beating, but he remained alive. He screamed, but his voice was sent into a void by a cosmic vacuum.

He again saw ancient acts of violence and hardship from the mountains. A desperate man lay on the ground, bleeding out with a spear in his chest. A Native American family was scattered among the rocks at the base of a cliff, their hands bound. The mother was still breathing but lay motionless, her eyes wide open as she bled profusely from her ear.

Then Kyle experienced a creature, a man beast. It ran amuck on two legs, slaughtering children, men, and women. It slung the red guts of one from its claws, then attacked the next.

Kyle desperately jerked his head side to side to shake the visions.

In a wink, he awoke in pure terror, gasping for air.

He quickly got to his feet to flee but tripped again into the darkness. As he pushed himself up, he had a copper-like taste at the back of his tongue. He gagged at the flavor, but pushed forward, wriggling back out of the cave. When he was free of the terrible cavern, he crumbled to the rocky sand and vomited.

He encouraged himself. *Get a grip Kyle!*

Suddenly, he heard a deep and primal howl from a nearby hillside.

Kyle ran westward up the bank, through a patch of forest and thick snow. He focused on the warm light of the distant dorm lobby where sanctuary awaited him.

He heartened himself with tears in his eyes. *Don't look back. Run, goddammit!*

BY SUNRISE, KYLE'S room was empty. Fifty miles east, his red Silverado pickup sped through the eastern exit, the park's majestic peaks fading behind him.

CHAPTER 7

CROW-HAIRED HENRY RedMoon scooped coarse sand from the snowy bank of a babbling brook and allowed it to slide from his half-clenched fist. He felt the pellets slip through his fingers—jasper and agate grains that had been extracted from the rocks, beaten and battered, drowned, swirled, crushed, carried, processed by the river system, and finally deposited in this very place for him to find at this very moment.

His tan face lifted to the cold wind and he returned a black Stetson to the crown of his head.

He inhaled deeply and closed his eyes. He felt the sand's journey, acknowledged and surrendered to its voice. He found that everything of the earth had its own voice if you only let the spirits guide you to it.

This brook was the site on RedMoon Ranch where it happened—the day he and his family's trajectories started to separate.

A vision of that disturbing and pivotal event from his childhood entered his mind.

She was eight, like him. Her family lived on the other side of the mountains and was wealthy, like his, her smile full of wonderment and naivety, like his. The pale skin of her hands, however, was unlike his, a refreshing new experience, and soft to the touch when she let him hold it earlier that day. Her white-dotted, tangerine sundress swayed as she skipped about at the edge of the thick cedar forest, a daisy bloom in her straight, golden hair. His strict father, Sid, had allowed the girl to visit the farm this day, something out of character for the silver-haired RedMoon patriarch. Outsiders never visited, never stepped foot on RedMoon land. Even local hunters knew the eight hundred RedMoon acres well and steered clear of their boundaries. Henry's mother, Larinda, had protested the girl's visit, for which she had received a strike across the cheek from Sid's hard hand.

Henry's mind took him to the moment it happened on that dreadful evening. The girl had removed her tennis shoes and was splashing her toes in the cool stream. The clear water originated in the mountain snowcaps and flowed into the low pasture from the forest floor. She was a shouting distance away from Henry, and he could hear her sweet laughter as it bounced off the stand of cedar trunks next to her.

Dusk had settled in quickly, he recalled, and oddly, Henry's parents had not called for him.

A sliver of setting sun had just slipped beyond the arid, summer horizon. She glowed in the fading light with her orange dress. Henry had watched her in between his efforts to create a fire for her. He'd recently learned to start a fire with a long, flat piece of wood with a groove through the center and another stick he rubbed vigorously through the groove. His shoulders fatigued as he desperately tried getting the smoke to rise from the wood, but no amount of fatigue would be too much if he could impress her—give her warmth, be her great protector.

One plume of smoke had just emitted from the sticks when he heard the charging through the underbrush, behind the forest's edge.

He looked for the girl again but could barely see her. The night had grown thick, and her angelic glow now dimmed as would a dying firefly.

Her blood-curdling scream at that moment had stuck with Henry his entire life.

He remembered how her long, bright hair had whipped around when she turned her head from the forest to him and shrieked, "Henry! *Help!*"

He remembered the vague and haunting shadow dashing through the woods. The beast moved like liquid fog, darker than the dusk, slaloming between the cedars closer and closer to her. Large branches snapped so loudly that their echoes reflected off the raised granite walls to the south. Swift thuds increased in speed—

Henry snapped back to reality.

He sighed and focused his eyes on the horizon. A few swollen clouds dotted the cyan sky. His jaw muscles tensed.

By the day's end, his resolve will have been tested. Today, he planned to tell his father of his desertion. He was leaving the ranch, daring to become the first RedMoon to strike out on their own.

Tomorrow, he would leave for Gardiner, Montana, to begin his permanent position as a lead ranger in

Yellowstone National Park. He would break history within his family's long, long tradition of keeping to themselves—a move that did not align with Sid's governance.

Sid had vehemently opposed Henry's decision to enroll in the three years of training, class work, and seasonal hire—telling Henry countless times that he'd never make it through to a full-time position anyway. Sid never did bestow much confidence in Henry formally, though Henry knew better—knew his father saw Henry's competence but hated his son for his contumacious nature. When he was young, Sid would instruct Henry to brush the horses—Henry would insist that it was a waste of time, a job best suited for his dull brothers, and refuse. Sid would say, "Bring me that saddle," and Henry would bluntly say, "No," no matter how many beatings Sid laid upon him. Sid would order Henry to harvest the hay, but he would resist, and saddle break the colts instead on the basis that he was better at it than his older brothers—and he was. Henry knew he was better at nearly everything than Wymon and Vic. He was cleverer too, and had to be if he was to avoid their wallopings, the earliest of which was so fierce that young Henry had actually urinated on himself.

Henry knew he had been a stick in Sid's craw, as Sid held the most important position in the extended family—that of patriarch. The notion of seeing eye to eye had been thrown out years ago in their unstable relationship, but Henry cared not. What was right, was right—and what was wrong, was exactly that. Henry would lead a just life, even if it meant turning his back on his family. They were the ones, after all, who were the killers, and the ones content to abide by Sid's cruelty.

TRAVELING THE WELL-TRODDEN horse trails, Henry visited other memories that he would have to take with him. The memories would need to last, as his father would surely banish him from the ranch.

Rocking gently in his saddle, he skirted the western seam of a small, snow-covered valley. After his horse walked him up a rolling hill, he halted to study the fanning buckbrush, sporadically dropped into the earth there by its Creator. It was there he'd taught his nephew Phoenix, Wymon's son, proper archery technique. Wymon was an impatient father, an inflexible and harsh man like Sid, and learning from him was beyond difficult for Phoenix. Henry would sneak Phoenix off to this valley and help the boy perfect his shot. He recalled how he had helped Phoenix learn to lace his boots when he was no more than four years of age—Phoenix had run to him later that day, after accomplishing the task himself, and squeezed Henry around the waist with genuine gratitude. From that moment on, he was there for the boy and raised him as if his own.

Henry cracked a warm grin at one side of his mouth for a beat, then gave a click to his horse.

"I SHOULD CUT you down where you stand." Sid RedMoon's black eyes and weathered face held a sternness as cold as the Wyoming dirt in February. He sat upright in his leather chair, straight as a statue, still wearing the day's long-sleeve, button-up denim shirt—the small buttons were pearl, the shirt's tails tucked tightly behind a thick belt. His chest puffed proudly, and his trim abdomen was the only part of him that moved, the only part of him that seemed to show emotion. Every strand of hair on his head was a streaming silver, and it graced both sides of his upper chest with all the reverence of an ancient Egyptian deity.

The den was small yet dignified. Lamp shades were fashioned from animal hide and cast low light across the wooden floors. Paintings of the previous heads of house lined the walls. Sid's hand-painted portrait was ominously present above the mantle.

Sid continued, "For decades, I have kept this family safe. We have shielded our livelihood from those vultures, those worms, and you wish to be one of them?"

Sid then said in the Wahota language, the equivalent of, "Henry, you foolish child, have I taught you nothing?"

Henry stepped defiantly toward Sid. "The Wahota *cannot* keep the old way. It is primitive, sinister, and will only plant seeds of retribution, from the living *and* from the spirit realm."

Sid stared straight ahead.

Henry pointed at his father with all five fingers together like an axe blade—like his instructors did at basic law enforcement training. "It will be the end of us, you *have* to know that."

"You are too weak to understand, my son."

Henry raised his voice further, "This family will *collapse* under your leadership if you do not change our way. I even heard you are considering forbidding education for the children?!"

A heavy door swung open, and Vic walked in, followed by Wymon. Their boots pounded heavily on the wooden floors as they glared at Henry. Both had the same broad shoulders and swaying onyx hair with a deliberate, steady gaze. Behind them came Phoenix. Their procession looked to be the same person declining in age: Vic being the biggest of all the RedMoons, then Wymon a foot shorter, and Phoenix a spitting image of the two in their adolescence. Noticing the resemblance had always made Henry smile, but he couldn't now. Henry was defying his father's rule, making his exit known, delivering his bitter farewell.

The ever-forward Wymon immediately sensed the tension. Glancing at both his father and Henry, he asked, "What's this? Father?"

"Your brother was just leaving."

Wymon and Vic's eyes darted as if they knew something was awry. They kept quiet, though, in their father's presence. Henry knew if it came down to an altercation, his brothers would ultimately fight on Sid's side like obedient, mindless canines.

Henry stepped to the door his brothers and nephew had just come through. When his eyes met Vic's, Vic slouched his huge head and stared at the floor.

Henry lifted his black Stetson from the prong on the wall and turned the doorknob. "To answer your question, *Father*—you taught me the natural virtues of our land and love for family. But most of all . . . " he thought, then answered sharply in Wahota, " . . . self-reliance."

Henry laid his eyes upon his brothers one last time, then perched his dark and dusty hat on his head. He looked at Phoenix and kept his emotion from showing on his face. Seeing Phoenix for the last time, he knew, would be the hardest part.

Henry looked away. *Sorry, kid,* he thought.

CHAPTER 8

AN INDUSTRIAL-SIZED table saw abrasively buzzed in a long, rhythmic fashion, setting a busy tone in the factory as it divided boards into their precise dimensions. One man circled a pallet of neatly stacked, unadorned cabinetry with a large roll of plastic wrap, bundling the freight for transport. Two workers, one at each end of a kitchen countertop, carried the freshly cut piece into the open back-end of a semi-trailer. Every employee moved with a purpose, effortlessly, a product of years perfecting their daily routine—every employee except Kyle.

After a few weeks there, Kyle still wasn't catching on. He seemed not to care for the fact, and this irked the foreman.

Kyle's goateed boss barked from inside his humming forklift, "I said move the damn pallet, boy. Move your ass!"

Kyle stood stock-still, glaring up at him. His arms rested at the sides of his six-foot frame in a clear sign of defiance. Dark rings circled his sunken eyes. His uncombed black hair covered his brow, and his teeth clamped inside his frowzy mug. Kyle's clothes were hanging from his thinned-out body, and he had an ill-omened look about him, as if he had no fuse left.

The fingers in his gloved right hand involuntarily twitched.

When the foreman shouted the command at Kyle again, three co-workers wearing safety glasses and power drills on their hips took notice.

Kyle didn't move. He calculated that, with two well-placed steps, he could quickly be inside the forklift cage with his boss, crushing his skull on the thick metal enclosure.

He removed his gloves and dropped them to the floor. Raising his right hand to rib level, he clenched and unclenched his fist. The bones in his hand felt heavy.

When Kyle's glare met his supervisor's, the boss's eyebrows loosened, and his ears seemed to fold back like a frightened dog. He turned pale in an instant, as if Kyle were the grim reaper in the flesh.

Kyle clung to the single shred of restraint that resided deep inside. He turned and strode directly to the time clock, punched out, and handed his tape measure to a confused coworker.

He shoved open the warehouse door, allowing the midday Tennessee sun to come beaming in, and left the cabinet factory for good.

KYLE'S SILVERADO MOTORED across a dusty road flanking a barren cornfield. The burbling red pickup traveled the wintry, quiet countryside and came to a stop in a gravel driveway.

Kyle's residence was an extra farmhouse, more like a shack, that belonged to Art Scanland, who lived just up the hill. Art needed someone to feed his cows and to do a few odd jobs when they arose. He was an elderly man, a salty veteran of the Korean War who'd lived on his own for decades. But with his age came lack of mobility, and he desired to keep his farm operational as long as possible. Aside from the endless odd jobs, Kyle's only dues were a mere fifty dollars a month.

Fenn had been too proud to move in with his parents after leaving Yellowstone. Besides, he didn't want to answer questions about how he'd been. A darker force had seemed to pursue him since that night in the cave. He couldn't tell them that. Nor did he want to tell them there was something slow and deliberate corrupting his mind, pushing him ever closer to the edge. Oftentimes, he found himself staring into space or breathing heavily for no reason at all. And there were the random voices in an unknown language—some Native American dialect, he assumed—that would occur at any given moment.

The strangest part—a sense of violence, dread, sorrow, or any combination thereof would accompany them. He'd managed to ignore it all at first, but like a distant yapping dog, the voices and emotions were incessant, eating at him.

He drank to quiet the occurrences, to help him sleep, and to help him forget about Annie. She'd been attacked by a monster, and he'd just stood there. Why did he just stand there? The others ran to her, but he couldn't. What was he really made of? No wonder Nicole didn't think highly enough of him. Why *would* she want a coward to be the one she was supposed to lean on while her mother fought for her life?

At other times, he was filled with a burning irritation toward people—just any other human who was around. It was overwhelming at the factory and ruined his concentration there. Living far from 'town' and other people helped with that. Though on one markedly rough day for Kyle, Art's daughter happened to visit from the city. She had given Kyle a once-over that told Kyle he wasn't right. He thought he'd stifled any visible annoyance he might have shown at her presence. The professionally dressed young woman thanked him cordially for "looking after Pops," but her eyes said, *Just stay over in your little shed, away from my Daddy, please.* He almost swore he saw her lift her nose as if Kyle reeked of something.

Kyle killed the engine and sighed. He rested his elbows on the steering wheel and placed his palms over his forehead.

Where would he work now?

Could he even hold another job once he got it?

What the *fuck* had happened to him?

Here he was, living in seclusion, a semi-psychotic, an ex-coulda-been baseball player, a drunk, a loser, a *coward*, and now—a quitter.

Last summer, he was on top of the world, quite literally, in those Yellowstone mountain ranges, but now . . . now he was a low-life failure with no one but a crotchety old man as his companion.

Better get inside, he thought, *before Art-hole sees me and makes me do some unnecessary bullshit.*

HIS FACE MOISTENED with sweat and his body twitched as he slept. Moonlight crept in through the rough-hewn window frame. Kyle's room was silent, save the occasional twig scrape against the distorted window glass—the outreaching of a silver oak planted too close to the house.

Kyle jolted up in bed.

He gasped for air.

In the corner of the room lurked a dark figure.

Kyle quickly pulled his lamp chain, and a warm glow filled the empty corner.

Another long night.

He clenched a bottle that sat on his nightstand and took a painful drink.

Just then, he heard the ruckus of flailing chickens coming from the coop outside.

Something caught his attention and he walked to the window. A set of glowing eyes paced the wood line nearby, then disappeared.

BLOOD SPLATTER AND feathers decorated the insides of Art Scanland's chicken coop.

Art poked his metal cane at the hole torn through the chicken wire in the back. "Same motherfuckers as last time. That makes six times this year, goddammit!"

Scanland's face always had a drooped and irritated expression, sunken eyes—one of which strayed to the side, above his wiry, grayed mustache. He had a way about him that Kyle knew was different from other people—he said what he felt and meant what he said in a way only a bitter war veteran could. Art's way was that of someone who'd seen too much, watched too many friends die right before his eyes—killed brutally and in undignified ways on foreign land.

Fenn often wondered how someone who'd been through a war like that could come home and find it possible to live a normal, socially adapted life. It must have been difficult enough being only one of three black Ashton, Tennessee citizens and facing racial bigotry in certain circles of the community. Despite being a tyrant of a landlord, the man was owed so much. The things he did for his country—he deserved a lifetime of fishing from an ocean beach somewhere, left alone, to sort through and smooth over his scarred mind. Fenn gathered that this secluded farm plot that Art toiled every day since the Korean War was his island, his retreat, and the reason he never returned to 'society'. It was this need for seclusion, if anything, that connected Kyle and Art, though Kyle doubted Art ever realized that.

Kyle was bent over inspecting the coop for Art. "There are two in here. Pretty dead, I'd say. The rest are all gone."

"They took a baby calf I had in the fall, too. Been tryin' for two years to shoot them damned coyotes. They're lucky my eyes ain't what they used to be."

Kyle believed that. "So, it was coyotes that did this?"

Art shot a disgusted look at Kyle with his good eye. "Yes, it was coyotes, you dumbass. Scoop them two up and give 'em here."

Kyle shook his head and did as instructed.

Despite Art's abrasive exterior, Kyle could read the helplessness in his rough eyes as he'd taken another loss. Maybe Art saw his fallen comrades in the dead livestock, he mused, in that they were being taken from him and he couldn't stop their killers, couldn't save them. Art did act particularly scowly about these occurrences.

The pain that Art must have kept inside made Fenn furious at the coyotes, preying on a helpless old man—a crotchety one, yes, but an honest one.

Art continued to glare at Kyle and said, "You know, you look like shit. You've looked like shit since the day you got here."

"Yeah."

"Yeah? Yeah, what?"

"I just got a lot on my mind lately." Kyle looked out over the gentle hills and the cows as they lowed and grazed about. He took a deep breath. "I'm dealing with some stuff."

Art just stared cockeyed.

Kyle hesitated, but his urge to talk about his problems was intense. "I've had some real bad luck recently. I do what I can, but sometimes it's not enough. Sometimes I wonder if I'm going to be able to keep on dealing with it. I think there's something wrong with me."

Art continued staring, showing no sympathy. He waited a beat then said, "What—you think you're goin' to get some wise, old black man to set ya straight, huh?! Give you some kinda great wisdom, huh?"

Art laughed heartily, something Kyle had never witnessed.

Kyle said, "I just—"

Scanland interrupted, "Clean this *shit* up and get the cows in. I got shit to do, boy. Come on now."

CHAPTER 9

NICOLE SHUT THE front door behind her and dropped her purse and keys on the couch. Somehow it seemed colder inside than outside, making her shudder. She hurried to the thermostat and raised the temperature.

Waiting for the fossil of a furnace to produce some heat, she rubbed her hands together and bounced on her heels. It would be a good twenty minutes before it would be comfortable enough to remove her puffy coat.

She wanted out of her clothes. For twenty days straight, Nicole had come home from her waitressing job in the same basic garb: black slip-resistant work shoes, tight and faded jeans—too long in the legs, with the bottoms frayed and wet where her heels dug in, an apron around her waist that smelled of French fries, and a V-neck top that revealed just enough to get an extra dollar or two from the ogling schmucks on lunch break from the local mill.

She unzipped her puffy coat and leafed through her apron pockets. Her fingers pulled several bills from somewhere in the bottom. Tallying her gains, she counted seventy-three dollars.

Not bad, she thought. *But not enough.*

Nicole shifted her attention to the Renaissance Bronze cremation urn on a high shelf. She knew the price of the urn would crush her for a stint, but this was her mother—she was worth every penny.

The day her mother died, Nicole had walked straight into the funeral home and ordered the nearly three-thousand-dollar option. The urn was her last homage to her mom, and Nicole would settle for no less than the perfect vessel to hold her remains. On a deeper level, though, it was Nicole's way of defying death, spitting in its face. It was a means by which she flipped her middle finger to the low-income life her mother had to live and to the abuse the woman received from Nicole's father. It satisfied Nicole every time the urn shimmered at her—knowing her mother was separated from this unjust world in a dignified manner.

Following her routine, she stepped into the bedroom. She removed her headband and untied her ponytail, releasing her lush yet crumpled hair to fall across her shoulders. The hair ties she wrapped around her wrists.

As if someone in the room had suddenly said, "Let's pray . . . ", she folded her hands and stared blankly at her mother's bed. She was stone-faced—tears did not fall. There were no more tears left, as if her body lost the ability to make more. Day and night, she'd cried, bawling for so long that a red irritation developed at the rim of her eyes—marks still visible today.

The sheets and blankets were clean and neat, the pillows arranged in a perfect line. She slept in the bed each night, drifting off to sleep to the smell of her mother, only to wake up to the stark reality of her absence each morning. To combat the harsh feeling, she would immediately get out of bed and meticulously straighten the sheets and blanket, primp and tuck, make it proper and honorable—another *Fuck you!* to the cancer, to the loss, and to all the behaviors that could accompany depression.

Fuck you! —the new mantra she used to replace the initial, *Why me?*

Nicole had grieved all right, but maybe hadn't accepted it quite yet. She knew her mother was gone, but she could still feel her.

Nicole closed her eyes.

Her mother's voice still flickered about the room, asking Nicole if she'd seen the weather report on the news, or calling for Cujo in her sweet tone. It was as if her mom could be right there in front of her at any moment, sitting on the bed with the TV remote in her hand. Nicole stirred these little memories and pictured her there as clear as day.

When she raised her eyelids, though, that nothingness swept across the bed—a cruel, unforgiving reality that kicked her in the gut. Giving in to the darkness of that reality wasn't an option. She knew suffering was certain, but she'd never let the memories fade. Her mother, who'd shielded Nicole from her father and took on three jobs at once to give Nicole every opportunity possible, would not be forgotten.

Suddenly, her cell phone buzzed in her pocket.

She saw the caller ID. It was Sandra from work. "Hello."

"Hey, girl."

"Hey, Sandra."

"You make it home okay?"

"Sure did."

"Just checking."

Nicole smiled. Her fellow server was a thoughtful person, the only one who actually talked to Nicole about her loss. The divorcee was her mother's age with a son and daughter of her own, so maybe it was her motherly instinct to want to care for her, Nicole thought.

Sandra asked gently, "Look, I know you're trying to make those big bucks and all, but when's the last time you went out?"

"Like, to a bar?"

"Yeah!"

"Well, honestly, I don't remember."

"Come out to The Den with me Friday."

"I don't—"

"Oh, come on, come on. I think it'll be great for you."

"I was going to try to pick up another shift that night."

"Drinks are on me, girl."

"Well . . ."

"Let me tell you, there is no shortage of good-looking men at that joint. And some even better-looking women if you smell what I'm stepping in. I'm just saying. Not that I'm looking . . . " She whispered, "I am," then giggled.

Nicole snorted.

Sandra pressed, "Come on, just come out this one night, just once."

Nicole knew Sandra was right. Nicole had been so determined to get that urn paid off, she hadn't thought about finding some social normalcy.

"All right. I'll be there"

"Great! Fun starts at nine."

"Just remember, you're buying."

"Yeah, yeah, I got you."

LIKE A LARGE bird feeder, the downtown Blacksburg, Virginia establishment drew a diverse group of guests. It was upbeat enough to attract the local Virginia Tech students, upscale enough for white collars after work, and progressive enough that even a few hippie types frequented.

Sandra's strawberry roots still showed along the part, but the rest of her hair was dyed black, framing her pale face. She motioned Nicole over with a wave—her many bracelets noisy and unbridled. "Hey honey, how are you? You look gorgeous. I didn't know you cleaned up so well," Sandra complemented.

"Thanks. Haven't been out in forever, but I managed to find at least one outfit." Nicole had her cinnamon-hued hair down, and she readjusted it after she took her stool at the table. She wore a chartreuse green blouse and tight, black pants—the pair she thought were best at hiding her thighs.

Sandra was sporting a blouse resembling a white pirate shirt.

"You know, I always thought of you as being, like, a tomboy when you were a girl. But seriously, you're beautiful." Sandra leaned over the side of the table. "Wow, look at that ass. My goodness. Last time my ass looked like that, Reagan was president. *Jesus.*"

"Did you bring me here to stare at my ass? At least buy me a drink first."

"Already on it." Sandra slid a wine glass to Nicole and lifted a yellow bottle. "Are you a fan of Moscato? You look like a Moscato kinda gal."

"That works for me."

Sandra's goofy demeanor was a breath of fresh air. It was good to feel a connection with another person again. With the terrible turn her life had taken in recent months, she'd pulled inward, forgotten how to be one in the crowd—to be normal.

Nicole thanked Sandra for the wine and sampled it. Though there were plenty of conversations and laughter in the bar, it was oddly quiet.

Nicole said, "Didn't the sign on the door say it was karaoke night?"

"It's only nine. I guess after people start getting hammered, somebody will eventually sing."

The DJ texted on his cell phone, getting paid to do nothing at the moment.

Nicole surveyed the crowd. She spotted an older, well-dressed woman with gray hair in a ponytail and an exaggerated smile as she entered through the front door. She was greeted by several people and escorted to a table of friends near the front of the stage. Those at the table stood to greet her.

There was an executive feel about the woman, like she was used to people smiling and laughing heartily at anything she said.

"Oh, look!" Sandra said excitedly. "There's the owner of Mountain Lake Hotel. She was here last time for open mic night, just hanging out. I bet she's got cash coming out of her ass."

Nicole felt a bit excited when Sandra said the name of the hotel. It was more precisely the Mountain Lake Hotel and Conservancy, the site where they shot the film *Dirty Dancing* in 1986. The movie was a favorite of Nicole's. But it was her mother's absolute favorite movie, her "number one," as she called it. Nicole glowed, remembering how her mother would cry when Patrick Swayze delivered the classic line, "Nobody puts Baby in a corner."

Sandra saw her reaction. "I know, Swayze, right? Oh Lord, what I wouldn't do to that man."

Nicole sipped her wine. She looked at the stage, then to Sandra.

Sandra perked up. "What?"

"How's your baritone?"

"Huh?"

Nicole leaned forward. She did an over-dramatic impression of something she'd heard in a movie once, "I've got—a—plan."

Sandra seemed to have no idea what Nicole was up to, but played along, "You've got—a—plan."

Nicole said, "We've got—a—plan."

WHEN SANDRA AND Nicole were the first ones to walk onstage, the resort owner and her friends hadn't even noticed—no one had. Even the DJ had to be interrupted when they wanted him to play their chosen song.

"Hello, is this thing on?" Sandra tapped the microphone and it squealed a tick.

Nicole whispered, "Yes, it's on. Shh, stop it."

Nicole instructed the DJ which song to play: "Time of My Life" by Bill Medley and Jennifer Warnes. He did so, then went back to his cell phone.

The music began, and Nicole used her index finger to shut off her tiny hearing aid.

Sandra tucked her chin comically and sang the opening lyrics deeply, impersonating Bill Medley.

All eyes in the crowd looked their way. A few sitting at the bar chuckled.

The resort owner took notice and flashed a thumbs-up to them, giving them her big, charismatic smile.

Unexpectedly, the crowd's stare created a nervous tension inside Nicole. She hadn't expected that. Performing on stage was something she was familiar with, having sang in the high school choir and performing solo pieces for the drama club. During her three semesters at Virginia Tech, which spanned as many years because of her time spent in Yellowstone, she'd also sang with their theater group. But there was something different here, something subconsciously blocking her.

Mom, she mused.

Her mother was the reason she was nervous. In the back of her mind, she worried that she wouldn't perform the song to a standard worthy of her mom.

She acknowledged the hidden fear and confronted it. In an instant, something comforted her—let her know that it was all right, that she could let go. She felt a presence tell her, *Let me hear you.*

A liberating joy ran through her veins, and she raised the microphone just in time to belt out Jennifer Warnes' part of the song. Her voice was sultry sweet.

You could've heard a pin drop were it not for the bulky, black speakers playing the instrumental and background music. Bargoers ogled with astounded, gaping mouths, pleasantly surprised by Nicole's pitch-perfect voice.

The beat in the song pulsed, then a group at the other end of the stage started to clap in rhythm.

Nicole could see the resort owner's eyebrows rise all the way from the stage. She looked at her companions in disbelief.

Sandra's ridiculously deep voice tromped again through the microphone. The loose arms of her pirate shirt dangled as she danced her arms side to side.

Then, Nicole nonchalantly raised her microphone and rang out her part again. Her impression was dead on.

The resort owner stretched her arms out wide, her fingers splayed, like a football coach whose kicker just won him the game.

As Sandra and Nicole proceeded through the song, bargoers trickled two and three at a time onto the dance floor.

Before long, everyone was dancing or singing the lyrics with the two ladies on stage, including the owner of Mountain Lake Hotel and Conservancy.

"IT'S NICOLE BOWMAN." Nicole started to rise from her stool, but the Mountain Lake Hotel owner stopped her.

"No, no. Please." She warmed Nicole with a wide smile. "It's a pleasure, Ms. Bowman."

"And this is my coworker, Sandra."

She shook their hands.

Sandra batted her eyes at the ponytailed, well-to-doer.

"I'm sorry to interrupt you ladies this evening, but I couldn't help myself. That performance was remarkable."

The woman folded her hands.

"I'll just get straight to the point, Ms. Bowman. My hotel could use a voice like yours. Are you currently employed—may I ask, without being completely intrusive?"

Sandra bounced in her seat and clapped her hands. She said cheerfully, "Yes, you may. And yes, she'll take the job. She'll do it, she'll do it."

CHAPTER 10

THE WATERS OF the mighty Yellowstone River slid down the highlands of Wyoming and snaked through Yellowstone Park. Traveling in and out of Yellowstone Lake, then falling over four hundred feet, the majestic waters coursed through the enormous yellow-brown canyon into the heart of the park, then finally flowed north into Gardiner, Montana. Before making its way easterly and joining the Missouri River, it trickled and gushed around smooth stones in front of Henry RedMoon's new Gardiner apartment.

As the new District Ranger of the park's most northern region, RedMoon should have been provided company housing at Mammoth Hot Springs just inside Yellowstone's north entrance, in the historic turn-of-the-century military and government housing. Instead, park housing was full, so he was temporarily placed in the Gardiner apartment five miles north.

As RedMoon inspected his new place, he heard a lovers' quarrel break out between his new upstairs neighbors. They stomped the length of their floor, one threatening the other, that one stomping away, the other following, then back the other way.

Henry felt crowded by the bright walls of his temporary apartment. The small living quarters smelled of fresh paint and new carpet. There was a light shining every five to ten feet. He squinted and turned off all but one. There was so much electricity running around him still, it caused a constant buzz in his head.

He'd experienced these modern conveniences before in law enforcement training and schooling. The lack of fireplaces baffled RedMoon. He'd always reeled at the outside world's utter dependence on electricity.

Only one feature amongst the furnished living room, kitchen, bedroom, and provided appliances held his interest—the coffee pot. Coffee was Henry's vice, though he knew there were worse things a man could be weak for. Even now, his mind was on his empty coffee mug.

As he waited for the last percolating drops to fall, Henry pulled back the thin curtain of the living room window and admired the Yellowstone River rolling by. Beyond the river, to the south, would be his domain, where District Ranger RedMoon earned his money and would have to earn his respect.

District Ranger RedMoon. He loved the sound of that.

Gazing at the northern peaks of the park, his previous anxiety about whether what he was doing was necessary, whether he was betraying his family or was doing the right thing, smoothed over. This was where his life outside the family would begin. The residents of Gardiner were his people now.

Most folks in the town were as white as a sheet of paper—relative to Henry any way. They were pleasant people, and there were only around a thousand of them, but it was the population density that was striking to RedMoon. In Gardiner, everyone knew everyone, save for the tourists, and there would be a great deal of those from spring through fall. The restaurant folk knew the ranch and cattle folk, who knew the hotel owners, who knew the highly paid chefs, who knew the backcountry outfitters, who knew the lower-income hospitality workers, who knew the elitists living out in the neighboring Paradise Valley, and so on. It was only a matter of time before RedMoon started to know "who was who" in this mountain town.

TWO MILES WEST, on the other end of Gardiner, Russell Hatfield parked his El Camino on the side of a high road and stepped out to have a Marlboro Red. He sat on the hood, took a Zippo lighter from his dirty jeans, and lit the end of his cigarette. His forearms, covered in a mess of tattoos, lay across his big stomach. His Marlboro perched between his lips in the thick of his bushy goatee. He had a full head of shoulder-length blonde hair. Pronounced wrinkles stacked across his brow, which nearly hid his drooping eyes, giving him the look of a Shar Pei dog.

The man exhaled and focused his attention downhill. The late morning sun to his left accompanied the brisk air of a new Montana day as he watched the children of Newkirk Elementary enjoying a playground romp. They struggled on the monkey bars, chased each other around in endless circles, and screamed excitedly. The youngsters seemed oblivious to the grand view of Sepulcher Mountain and Electric Peak that stood over them at around ten thousand feet in elevation. Oblivious to the cold as well, most of the kids discarded their coats. The children couldn't care less about the pristine mountain country that they grew up in, Hatfield noticed, only about who was the fastest on the playground, or the smelliest.

Russell's unflinching attention was set on one little girl—the one in a puffy red coat with brown fur on the hood. He watched intently the adorable tyke's every move—with whom she interacted, which bouncy ball she played with, how she responded to the teachers' instructions.

Each morning he was off work, he'd eye the recess and the same little girl meticulously, the girl in the red, puffy coat. His inner-city upbringing was one that taught him how to be tough in an unforgiving world and how to hurt people before they could hurt him. He brought this same intensity into the protection of the girl in the red coat—his daughter, Maddie. She was the only thing gentle about Russell Hatfield, and the only thing truly important in his life. But she was in the care of her mother, who kept the child from him. His criminal background and what he did to his ex-wife had made it too easy for her in their divorce and custody case.

Russel finished his smoke and threw the butt to the ground just as a car pulled off the road near him. An Asian man dressed in a button-up shirt and a sweater vest, wielding a large camera, exited the likely rented car and began to take photos. From their position, one could capture great shots of Montana mountain ranges accented by small-town American living.

Russell despised a great deal of people, tourists being near the top of the list.

"Hey!" Hatfield walked over to the man and snatched the camera from his hand. With the other hand, he grabbed the foreigner's collar and escorted him back to his car.

Throwing the car door open, he tossed the man's camera inside and pushed him in by the forehead.

He slammed the door shut and pointed down the road. "Drive, asshole!"

He knew the tourist had no bad intentions, but that didn't matter. The scumbag was too close to Maddie with his camera. The foreigner was lucky enough to leave without being hurt—that's how Russell saw it anyway.

CHAPTER 11

AT EIGHT FORTY-FIVE in the morning, Harper's Barber Shop had four customers—one in the barber gown, the others sitting in the metal waiting chairs, reading the local newspaper. A small refrigerator sat in the corner, with a sign taped to the front: SODAS-50¢. On top of the fridge, a small antenna TV played *The Price is Right.*

The only one who noticed Kyle when he entered was Bob Harper. The gray-haired man had his collared shirt tucked in and his pants hoisted to his belly button, scissors in hand. Harper had been Kyle's barber a few times in his younger days. Surely, he knew of Kyle's falling out with his baseball team over a measly marijuana possession charge—the whole self-righteous, Bible-thumping town knew it.

When the loud bells hanging from the door finished their racket, Harper had his chin tucked, looking over the top of his no-rim glasses at Kyle unenthusiastically. Harper's eyes examined Kyle's disheveled hair and unshaven face the same way someone would look at a stinking, muddy hound that had tromped into the house.

Yeah, he knows, Kyle thought.

"Mornin', young man," Harper said.

"Mornin'." Kyle took his seat.

With an ear-piercing, brash voice, the fat man in the barber gown continued his conversation, "Yes, I believe I'll have t' stay a while. I've been nothin' but blessed by this town since I took office. We've got a right, fine staff and this town's a' makin' a turn for the better, I say." The new mayor apparently had no other business to tend to on a Wednesday morning more important than getting his head dolled up. Bits of hair accumulated on top of his jelly bowl belly that moved when he spoke.

"Mm-hm," agreed Harper.

"Jimmy's boy just made County Clerk, don't know if ya heard. A bright, young man. He's got himself a right promisin' future, too, if he keeps his head on straight."

"Mm-hm," Harper appeased.

The mayor's eyes were on Kyle, "Yes sir, that's what this town needs more of—upstanding, sober young men who care about their community and are willing to work for it, willing to serve."

Clearly, even the mayor knew who Kyle was.

Pathetic, Kyle thought.

As he circled the barber chair, Harper shot Kyle the same condescending look as when he walked in.

Kyle clenched his fist as irritation surged through him once again. He had decided last night to do something about his cursed life. Something needed to change—he just didn't know what. In his search for some kind of clarity, he thought coming to town for a proper haircut would be the first step, then, who knew? Maybe he'd go see his parents, have a hot meal with them, seek out old friends. Maybe, eventually, he'd even put down the bottle.

But here was Bob Harper, a man who'd never left town yet acted as though he knew everything, berating Kyle with judging eyes. And the mayor, thinking his weightless words mean anything to anybody, thinking he was a big fish—he was nothing.

What the hell did they know about Kyle? Nothing.

Each time they laid their eyes on him was like another dump of lye on his skin. Kyle felt himself giving in to the living, vengeful emotion that stirred within him.

Suddenly, his self-control slipped like a tectonic plate.

He shot up from his seat—the metal chair scraping loudly backward and against the wall, seizing the attention from everyone in the room.

Kyle's eyes zeroed-in on Harper, once again locked in a death stare, envisioning how best to attack his offender. Harper had stepped back from the chair, wide-eyed, staring at Kyle.

The fear that he created this time pleased Kyle. At this moment, he saw that this could be an untapped resource that gave him power, this idea of letting go and lashing out. He didn't know quite what it was about himself that scared them so, but it was empowering.

"You got somethin' you wanna say, Bob?"

Harper simply shook his head.

"Didn't think so. You can stop givin' me the stink-eye then. You don't know shit about me."

After making his discontent clear, he lingered to let it set in and to allow any rebuttal or someone to back up Bob.

The mayor puffed his chest out as if preparing to speak. Kyle stopped him, "What, fat boy?"

No reply.

The barber shop patrons were worthless old hypocrites who sit around gossiping all day, the way Kyle saw it. A voice inside him urged Kyle to turn violent and hurt the old barber and everyone in the room.

Instead, Kyle stepped across the room, took an RC Cola from the fridge, and faced Bob Harper. Without losing eye contact, Kyle opened and drank the entire can at once and casually dropped the empty can to the floor. He let out a drumming low belch that seemed to morph into a growl as he stared Bob down.

Smirking, Kyle withdrew another can from the fridge and slowly walked out.

Standing outside the shop entrance, Kyle took in his surroundings. The day was bright and new. Intoxicated from lack of sleep and now, from lack of concern for others, he decided that today would be his day—to do what, he still wasn't sure. He had just insulted his small town's "pillars," and soon everyone would know about it.

If he had a chance at regaining respect here, he'd just lost it.

But this was wickedly liberating.

A HALF-MILE FROM the barber shop, a friendly baseball game ensued between a dozen high school-aged boys. Kyle had been roaming, with no destination in mind, when he came upon them. He was slightly amused at his barber-shop antics and was waiting to see what would happen next. It all felt like a twisted dream to him anyway.

"HEEEY boys!" Kyle rang out sarcastically. "What we got *here*? A little ball game, huh?"

The group stopped what they were doing.

He walked through the fence gate and toward the batter. Kyle hadn't played any manner of baseball in forever it seemed. Maybe it was time he reunited with his old love.

Without asking, he pulled the bat from the boy at the plate and took up a batting stance. He gave a few warm up swings. "Come on, Pitch. Let's go. Gimme some heat, boy!"

The pitcher, still confused, looked around.

Someone from the outfield spoke up. "That's Kyle Fenn. Hey, let him hit."

Kyle pointed the bat at the outfielder with gratitude. "Everybody, look sharp! I'm 'bout to blast this shit to the moon!"

The young man at the mound readjusted his Mossy Oak hat to its proper position. He wound up and gave him his best straight ball.

Kyle let the first pitch through and smiled at the pitcher.

On the second pitch, however, he focused and delivered.

When Kyle hit the ball flush, an energy within him released quickly. Instead of hearing the *crack* of the bat, he heard the sound Annie's femur made when the grizzly snapped it like a twig.

He buckled to his knee.

It felt like a punch in the gut when the repressed memory of her attack came back.

He raised his head.

There was Annie's corpse on its hands and knees, eye-to-eye with Kyle. Her arm reached for him, the bicep muscle hanging from the bone, and weakly tugged at his shoulder.

She pleaded, "*Help.*"

Kyle scurried backward, and the vision vanished.

A cold sweat broke out over his face, and his pulse raced.

He could sense a deep and manipulative presence feeding off the fear he experienced seeing her mangled face. The dark, internal presence instantly reemerged, like a mummy stirring inside a sarcophagus.

"Are you all right, man?" A boy in a catcher's uniform was kneeling where Kyle had seen Annie. Startled, the catcher raised his face mask, got to his feet, and stumbled backward.

Kyle got to his feet, bolted for the outdoor bathroom. At the porcelain sink, he splashed water on his face. With hesitation, he checked his reflection in the dusty mirror. Behind his hanging hair, Kyle's face was moon-pale, his eyes shining with brindled bumblebee colors.

AT THE EDGE of town, on the corner of an intersection, Fawn Creek Baptist Church stood with its towering stone exterior and ornate stained-glass windows. Kyle arrived at the corner of the building and slowed from his sprint.

"Are you okay, son?" a man in his sixties said sweetly from the church's back steps.

Kyle dry heaved, then turned his head to the man. "Pastor Clemens."

"Kyle? Kyle Fenn?"

Clemens closed in and put his hand on Kyle's shoulder.

"Pastor, I can't shake it. It's in me. It used to be only when I closed my eyes, but now it's when they're open, too."

"You are all right."

"*No*, I'm not all right."

Kyle stood up with Clemens' help.

"Come now. Calm down. Find your breath and look at me."

Clemens examined Kyle, cocking his head to the side with empathy.

"I know what you're going through, Kyle. Let me be your guide."

"No, you don't know. It's not what you think. I—"

"I want you to come to the service Sunday night. Please. You know your parents are still faithful to the church—they'll be here.

Kyle's eyes softened and nearly teared up at the thought of his old self, the days when all he had to do was wake up and play baseball, when sleep wasn't something he feared, when he had a future to look forward to. How he longed for that kind of peace again.

Clemens said, "Give me a chance to show you the Kyle you remember."

CHAPTER 12

BUT I'VE RUN clean out of money," Donnan MacLeod pleaded into his cell phone, beating the meat of his hand against the kitchen counter to express his desperation. "I've got nowhere else to go. I am telling you—I am neck deep. I had to sell all my stocks, the RV—I am going to lose the goddamn house within the year if I do not find income."

"The board granted you a severance . . . " A man on the other end bit off his words as his patience grew thin.

"Aye, it's next to nothing."

"I'm sorry. You can't just show up to your classes half-drunk and expect to keep your job. I've turned a blind eye too many times. I warned you time and again."

"I'm the most decorated professor to ever step foot in that university. I can just serve a suspension, then?"

"You assaulted another professor and called your female students 'whores.' You can't undo that, Donnie."

"I've always been there for you, haven't I? Haven't I always been a good friend? I recall 'twas a nephew of yours I made sure passed his exam that time. Yes?"

The man sighed. "Yes, but that doesn't come close to the shit I've done for you. The shit I've had to sweep under the rug."

"What *shit*?"

"I'm not explaining myself again."

"I've got no money for Christ's sake!"

"Then swallow your *stupid* pride and sell your damn house! It's enormous!"

MacLeod didn't answer.

The man let out an audible sigh, then said, "Look Donnie, we just finished dinner, and I need to tuck in the kids. I gotta go."

The man hung up.

"But, you—"

Donnan flipped the phone shut. He gaped out the small kitchen window as if the man were out in the backyard somewhere. "You ungrateful *shit*."

The laptop on the kitchen island beeped to life as MacLeod hastily opened it. He signed in, his forehead still furrowed.

Donnan's despair sharpened as he read his notice of loss on the semi-legal gambling site, caribbookie.com, based in Antigua and Barbuda. His ten-thousand-dollar wager that Hibernian would win over St. Mirren in the Scottish Premiere League, a nine-to-one favorite, had flopped. His hard-earned and dwindling money had been placed on a fierce game played in the cold January mud of his homeland—money that now electronically bounced around the sunny Caribbean somewhere between bookies and their banks.

Gritting his teeth, he cursed himself. "Pure barry!"

The trashcan sailed across the kitchen floor as he punted it in anger. Crumpled, microwave dinner boxes and empty whiskey bottles were cast out across the tile floor and into the living room.

He paced about, breathing heavily. A heavy swig, this one straight from the bottle, would help.

He returned to his laptop and angrily pecked the keyboard. Twenty thousand: Aberdeen over Dundee United.

After running his hand down his beard, he clicked Submit.

Donnan slammed the laptop shut, pushed it aside, and turned on the living room television. The behemoth screen, mounted over a declined level of half-circled couches, fuzzed to life. The light from the television screen cast a glow onto the dark living area. The local news recited its umbrella network's keywords for their intro: "We are proud to be your leading source for what affects our community."

The nightly news ran through a few seconds introducing the current top stories as night fell upon MacLeod's grand estate. After zoning out for a few minutes, Donnan entered the living room area and visited his display case—another dangerous routine. He flinched at his reflection in the mirrored backing as the case's internal lighting highlighted his face. The corners of his mouth drooped, and his cheeks moved as he nervously chewed at his gums.

The man in the reflection was jumpy, desperate.

He gently opened the display door. His bloodshot eyes glazed over the blue and yellow graduation regalia worn only by distinguished professors: the velvet-trimmed honors sash and tam cap. A large purple W with dark gold trim was embroidered on the back of the gown, proudly representing the University of Washington.

He pushed his spectacles up the bridge of his red nose, then wiped the dust from a framed certificate. It read, *University of North Carolina, Master of Anthropology, Concentration in American Indian and Indigenous Heritage and Unwritten Histories*. Wedged in the corner of the frame was a faded photo of a young MacLeod in a black cap and gown, three *summa cum laude* honor cords laying over his stout shoulders. He posed in the photo with a flexible smile behind his full brown beard, a ribboned scroll in hand. On one side of him was a middle-aged Native American woman in professor gowning. On his other side was Sherri.

He felt a deep remorse slice through his heart once again, and his eyes welled up.

MacLeod returned the frame to its position next to another, much larger frame. The bigger one was made of stained cherry oak and had two compartments: one displayed an eight-by-eleven document, the other, a small rock hammer. The document inside was issued by The Archaeological Institute of the Americas, for "Prestigious Lifetime Achievement."

MacLeod's soul collapsed at the cold reality—all these keepsakes meant nothing.

No one cared.

Without closing the display, he retreated to the couch and sank into its cradling embrace. The couch was his last stop—where he went when there was nothing left. Recently, however, the couch felt less like a sanctuary and more like a cushy coffin.

He stared blankly at the coffee table. Light from the newscast flickered off the metal slide on the nine-millimeter.

The pistol beckoned him.

Amongst the background news talk from the TV, one word suddenly shot through MacLeod like an arrow in the back.

RedMoon.

The news anchor read, "Earlier this week, Yellowstone swore in its next full-time law-enforcement ranger. The park has seen a two-fold increase in visitors each season for the past three years. This has caused a greater demand for law-enforcement officers, and the Park Service has added higher-level positions in response to this demand. With Officer Hamilton moving up to the newly created North Regional Ranger position, Officer RedMoon, who hails from Dunoir, Wyoming, will take over as Mammoth District Ranger at the park's north entrance."

On the screen, Henry RedMoon stood statuesque next to the Park Service Superintendent of Yellowstone National Park. He had a serious, intense look on his face as he stared into the camera. The Superintendent spoke of the honor, dignity, and the prestige of wearing the badge, being a full-time law officer, protecting the precious land that was Yellowstone, while dutifully serving its visitors as well. He also spoke about diversity and its benefits—an unwarranted and self-serving attempt to bolster his future constituents, MacLeod assessed.

Henry's chest swelled with pride as the swearing-in proceeded—his hands behind his lower back, his uniform fresh and starched, his new badge gleaming, his black hair cut tight on his head.

He looked ready for action.

He looks, twenty-seven years old, Donnan thought, and had Wahota written all over his face.

CHAPTER 13

A SERIOUS MOOD settled over the crowded congregation at Fawn Creek Baptist Church that January evening. The sun descended slowly behind the barren cornfield horizon, casting a citrusy glow across the Tennessee sky. Most of the town was ready to settle in for the night, to get their rest for the demanding Monday morning ahead—but not before evening service.

As Kyle entered the back door, the pastor motioned him to the front pew.

Fenn's eyes were daunted, sunken, with dark circles around them. His mouth stayed slightly agape, and he lightly wheezed. Sweat gathered on his clammy and greenish skin.

Kyle noticed Art sitting at the back of the room where he was perched like a hawk, needing to see everything and everyone in front of him. His black Korean Veteran baseball cap rested tall on his head. When Art caught the sight of Kyle, he immediately gathered his cane. With his eyes glued to Kyle in a furtive look, he exited through the back door.

Kyle's parents sat at the front, saving an empty seat between them.

Clemens had told him to be there at five. Kyle looked at his watch having trouble focusing—it was twenty till five.

A curious question entered his mind—why was everyone already there?

It hit him. He'd been deceived.

By the looks on his parents' faces, he now understood this was their righteous interdiction for their apparent alcoholic, loose-cannon son—bringing a lamb back to the fold.

Again, Kyle fumed inside with that wild anger: *Clemens, you narrow-minded, backwoods, hillbilly fuckstick. I'm not an alcoholic. I don't need a fucking intervention; I need an exorcism.*

Kyle glanced around the building, studying its walls, its wooden rafters, the fading light coming through the windows. Images of it all engulfed in flames raced through his mind, the people screaming, those *idiots* choking and clawing each other, trying to get out.

Suddenly he envisioned his parents in the burning building too.

He squinted his eyes shut and shook the visions.

He stepped forward.

The congregation cooed a gentle song of praise as he walked the center aisle and sat between his parents. He placed his elbows on his knees and looked at the carpet in front of him, his black mess of hair obscuring his eyes.

As the song ended, the town shut their hymn books and sat down.

In a soft voice, Clemens began, "Good evening and welcome everyone. Thank you for joining us this evening as we celebrate God's love for us and continue to worship Him in fellowship and praise, amen."

After telling a brief bromide story of a shepherd who searched for a lamb, the pastor gradually walked to the side where Kyle sat, and said in his gentle voice, " . . . and in dire times, we find ourselves wondering from His flock, questioning Him. 'Where have you been, Lord? If you love me, why have you left me?'" He now faced Kyle. "God never leaves His children. It is they who leave Him."

Shut up, you stupid son-of-a-bitch, Kyle thought. His heart beat violently, threatening to crack open his chest.

Kyle could see the pastor's loafers as he stood in front of him.

Clemens' voice came more aggressively, "Let us not *deny* our sins. The Lord is waiting for us, each one of us, to confess ourselves, to *let go and stop our unrighteous behavior."*

The pastor touched Kyle's shoulder.

The touch felt like a jab from an electric cattle prod, and something inside him erupted.

With a beastly huff, Kyle stood, clutched Clemens by the throat, and yanked him close. He glared menacingly into the pastor's face.

A growling threat came out of Kyle. "Come on, preacher man. I'll take you to hell with me."

Kyle's father reached his arm between the two.

Several members of the congregation closed in on Kyle to diffuse the situation.

Kyle released the preacher.

As his father tried flexing his arm around Kyle's neck, Kyle pivoted and shoved his father over two rows of pews. He landed on two elderly women, the bulk of his weight crushing one, while his bracing hands met the other's face.

His mother screamed, "Son! Please!"

Kyle felt his back arch unexpectedly.

He forced himself to stand straight again, then pushed his way out of the church.

Art stepped aside as Kyle busted through the front door. Kyle stopped and turned to Art, breathing heavily like he'd just ascended six flights of stairs. Something unexplainable ran through Kyle's mind, like an instinctive fear for Art's safety, that forced him to blurt out, "Don't go home tonight." Art's hard face didn't argue, and he simply nodded.

A GROTESQUE FORM of Kyle circled Art Scanland's chicken coop under the spotlight of the moon. Art's new chickens scrambled and clucked loudly at his presence.

Bristly black hair had sprouted down the center of his back and his skin slowly blackened, as if being scorched by an unseen flame. Drool seeped from his jaw, which extended down between his clavicle bones. His lips curled back, revealing lethal canines. A mess of teeth like glass shards lined the inside of his mouth. He exhaled huffs of hot air rhythmically, like the chimney stack of a steam train gaining speed, its inner workings laboring with great effort.

In minutes, his form was monstrous in size, with no semblance of Kyle left at all, except that it had black hair. It dwarfed the two-level coop.

Its legs, now, were those of a dog. A slight hitch accompanied its gate like a newborn calf that tries to find its footing for the first time. The mud gave beneath the heavy, clawed feet. The sound of crunching and still growing bones was muffled beneath thick and impenetrable skin.

Soon, its shoulders and chest were weighty, beefing and spasming with a controlled rage. The black hair continued to emerge, thickly over its hulking shoulders, down its long legs, and lightly into the crevasses of its sinewy body.

Its jaws then widened, pulling its teeth back to slanted ears, as if the natural lift on one side of Kyle's upper lip just minutes ago was now punctuated, and spread across the entire snout.

The creature lifted its nose to the wind and turned its massive head to the wood line.

A guttural growl rolled up its chest as it glared at sets of glowing eyes gliding along the forest floor. When anxious whimpers and yelps came from the woods, the thing's pointed ears tucked back, and it lowered its belly to the soil.

It was coiled, intense, and a yellow gleam shown from its angular, malicious eyes. The beast crept forward, powerful and low to the ground like a brand-new, jet-black Corvette ZR1 rumbling off the assembly line.

THE DESOLATE COUNTRY road was silent, except for the hissing of a car tire as it deflated. A 1987 Grand Prix rested on the side of the moonlit pavement, the rubber tracks beginning in the right lane, zigging left, then streaking abruptly to the right shoulder. The only light provided on the rural road was that of the pronounced full moon.

A thin woman in a long parka kicked the rear bumper and huffed. She pulled out her cell phone and dialed.

A voice answered, "Patty Cake's bakery."

Her smoker's voice was frustrated and pointed. "Hey, it's Patty."

"Well, a good early morning to you."

"Yeah, not really. I popped a tire. I'm gonna throw on a spare."

Patty checked her watch. "I'm thirty minutes out, but it'll probably take me another hour, unless I get lucky and someone comes by to give me a hand."

"What happened? You okay?"

"Yeah, I'm good. The fuckin' opossum's okay, too. Should've just drilled the son-of-a-bitch."

"I'm sorry. Well, do you want—"

The call was cut short.

"Goddamn reception," Patty cursed.

She popped the trunk with her key fob and fished through the contents. She uncovered the spare tire, jack, and a tool that doubled as a crowbar and lug wrench.

Rolling her eyes, she removed her parka and threw it into the trunk.

She pulled her hair back into a ponytail, lifted the tire out, and rolled it to the side of the car.

As she turned to retrieve the rest of the tools, a shadowy apparition loomed on the ground next to a standing, dead maple. The tree's crooked and leafless limbs hailed the crisp moon. The maple's shadow covered most of the figure. When it shifted its weight, Patty flinched.

She faced the object and jutted her head forward. "The hell is that?"

Two yellow eyes appeared within the dark mass.

Patty froze.

It slunk further back into the shadow.

Her hands began to shake. "Is someone there?"

No answer.

She cautiously stepped back around to the trunk like a cat, careful not to make any sudden movements. It was only thirty degrees outside, but sweat still formed on her face.

She retrieved the lug wrench-crowbar and peered back at the tree.

The figure was now standing next to the maple, slumped and enormous.

Patty spoke, "Hey, I can see you. Come out from there—this shit ain't funny." She raised the crowbar in her hand so it was visible.

Still no reaction.

She raised her hand in a half-hearted wave to the figure.

Then those eyes appeared once more, cutting through Patty.

"Look, I don't think you know who you're messin' with. Quit fucking around. As a matter of fact, I'm calling the police."

She pulled out her cell and pretended to dial nine-one-one.

She said, "Yes? I need the police—"

A dark-haired creature, three times her size, drove her into the ground.

The crowbar and cell phone bounced and slid across the asphalt.

Patty screamed and threw her forearms in front of her face.

It roared at her with the strength of a lion, its devilish head vibrating, saliva spraying from its horrific jaws.

The creature bit into her leg and dragged her down an embankment. The baker continued to wail in horror as it pulled her across an empty soybean field. She dug her fingers into the soil in a futile attempt to pull free from its grip.

Finally, it dropped her, thrust its claws into her gut, and slashed her abdomen open. With two more digging swipes, her shirt was shredded away, and her intestines and stomach spilled out.

Patty's screams subsided, and her eyes glazed over.

The creature's head was now covered in blood all the way to its pointed ears. After ravaging her lower torso, the thing bit down on Patty's face with tremendous force. Its canines punctured her skull, and her mandible audibly snapped like a chicken leg between a husky's pre-molars.

AT SEVEN IN the morning, Art's daughter hugged him tightly. "All right then, Pops."

Her words escaped her mouth as puffs of water vapor in the cold air, then disappeared.

He blandly reciprocated. "All right then."

She beamed, "This was fun, Daddy. It really was. Anytime you want to stay with us, *please*, just give us a ring, okay?"

Art lofted a smile and kept it there until she had reentered her Lincoln Navigator and drove down the crackling gravel road.

He stepped up to his front door, shuffled for his keys, then opened the ancient door lock. That's when something drew his attention.

As he peered down his long porch, something made him backpedal, knocking over his primrose plant.

In the Monday morning mist, where the concrete walkway met the end of the porch, was a pile of fur, blood, and fangs.

The old farmer went inside, took an old .308 rifle from his closet, and returned cautiously to the porch.

He limped toward the meaty pile with his rifle aimed and his head on a swivel.

Four canine carcasses lay at the end of his porch. The carcasses were coyote and had battered heads and blood-matted hair around the necks and abdomens. The larger ones had broken limbs laying the wrong direction. One was nearly torn in half, the white of its ribs protruding through the skin.

SCANLAND DROVE HIS riding mower down the hill to Kyle's house.

Kyle's truck was gone.

Art stealthily entered and checked the place, keeping his rifle out in front of him, his index finger hovering over the trigger.

Kyle was gone, along with all his clothes.

Art stepped onto the front porch and sighed. He put his rifle back on safe and cradled it in the crook of his arm.

He spoke to the horizon. "What the hell got into you, son?"

PART II
THE SAPPHIRE POOL SOLUTION

CHAPTER 14

THE PICTURE FRAME windows looked out over the rolling Virginia mountainside at dusk. Winter had relieved the trees of their foliage, but the deciduous woodland was thick, creating gray expanses that fused to a murky ocean of Appalachian waves.

On the other side of the glass was a dance hall—a prom-like atmosphere stewing as low lighting emitted from dim chandeliers spaced along the long walls. Facing a stage were spectators dressed formally in ties and dresses, murmuring quietly in their seats.

A single overhead light suddenly lit the stage. Moths circled and dove into its heavy beam like kamikaze pilots.

Stage-side, within the shadows, Nicole stood behind a microphone. A hefty man in a suit and tie with his own microphone waited next to her, swaying to his own silent beat. She and the man exchanged grinning nods.

Nicole patted her thigh with the same nervous anticipation she had the other three times she'd performed here at the Mountain Lake Hotel. It was a familiar and welcomed anxiety, though. She lived for the thrill and the pay was outstanding.

The man commenced the ballad in a deep voice.

Then, a striking man in a black, tight-fitting collared shirt entered the stage left. His short sleeves hardly covered his shoulders, and his shirt buttons at the top were flamboyantly undone. A woman in a light-pink feather of a dress entered the stage right. The couple began their performance, moving slow and deliberate, like two exotic birds facing off in a mating ritual.

The song's rhythm picked up. Nicole enjoyed that part, because that was always the point when the crowd started to get into it. From her semi-hidden position, she observed their excited faces.

No sooner had she belted out her first line, when a sight at the back of the open room made her heart stop. She gasped, and the music continued without her voice.

A set of double doors at the back of the facility had just flung open, and in had stumbled Kyle Fenn. In contrast to the audience members, his hair was unkempt, his dingy clothes hanging off his frame, his shoulders slouched with fatigue. The paleness of his skin was a curious one, like he'd been lethally bitten by a copperhead and had emerged from the deep, Virginia woods to find he'd made it to heaven and this gathering of happy souls.

She locked eyes with him as he looked desperately to the stage.

Nicole instantly knew from his troubled face that he needed her, that he had come for her.

Kyle collapsed with an audible *thud*.

Without hesitating, Nicole cleared the stage and went to him.

The male singer looked wide-eyed at her as she fled. He continued the song, filling in her part. Between lines, he whispered loudly to a stagehand, "What the hell . . . "

As she came to Kyle's side, a few guests were there fanning his face.

She scooped him up to a seated position. His eyes were lost.

Nicole patted his cheek. "Kyle! Wake up."

He spoke, but his words were garbled.

"Kyle, what's wrong with you?"

Finally, he said, fatigue tainting his words, "I'm sorry." He was gaunt, sweaty.

"Are you sick? Do you need a doctor?"

"No, no. I'm okay. I just needed to see you. I'm just really tired." His eyes started to close again.

"Help me get him up." With help from the guests, Nicole carried him to her car, where he instantly fell asleep.

THE SCENT OF dog breath and someone else's home brought Kyle into consciousness, and he found himself nose to nose with a lapping golden retriever.

He sat up and squinted. Memories from yesterday began to swirl in his head.

The sound of spatula on skillet came from a nearby kitchen.

After charting his surroundings some more, he got to his feet and followed the golden to the kitchen.

"Hey," Nicole said, almost whispering, as if a loud sound might cause Kyle to crumble to pieces. "Come here and sit down."

She helped him to the kitchen table.

Nicole sat next to him.

They stuck to each other like magnets. He reached under her arms, and she wrapped herself around his neck. They embraced like they were falling from the sky with only one parachute.

A full minute passed before either let go.

Nicole straightened Kyle's hair and pulled fuzz from his sleeves. Kyle finally noticed the sky blue sweatshirt that fit tightly across his chest and arms. The word "PINK" was embroidered across the front.

Nicole giggled, "I'm gonna need that back when you're done with it."

He smiled. "I was in bad shape, huh?"

"How are you feeling?"

"What time is it?"

She nodded at the wall clock. "Three in the afternoon. You've been passed out since seven last night."

Grabbing his wrist, she asked, "Kyle, what happened to you? What's wrong? Were you drunk or something?"

"Nicole, I'm so sorry. No, I wasn't drunk. I—I didn't know who else to turn to. It's just, a lot of crazy shit has been happening. It's hard to explain. I don't know where to start." He exhaled, bone-weary, then rubbed his face.

What was he supposed to tell her? That some kind of ghost injected itself into him in a cave, that he heard voices, that he experienced violent urges, couldn't sleep, and drank to try to cope?

Was he supposed to tell her that he had woken on his back porch, naked and painted in blood, with no recollection of that night? His entire drive from Tennessee had been spent trying to remember—and trying to stay awake. An explanation for why he came to see her had never formulated.

He hesitated.

Nicole said, "It's okay. How about eating some food first?" She lightly pinched at his meatless ribcage. "You look like you could use some."

Kyle sniffed, "Is that sausage?" For the first time in weeks, the thought of food was welcoming.

As she got up, she grinned. "I thought you would want some."

Nicole prepared a plate of pancakes and sausage, poured a glass of orange juice, and brought them to the table.

Kyle immediately shoved forkfuls of pancakes into his mouth.

"Wow. You *were* hungry."

He nodded and quickly consumed two sausage links. Grease dribbled down his unshaved chin.

Nicole asked, "So, how did you find me? This is pretty stalker-ish of you to just show up at my place of employment. That's how it starts, you know, psychos murdering their exes."

He replied with a food ball under his cheek, "You weren't home, but your neighbor told me you were at that mountain hotel whatever place."

"So, you drove all the way from Yellowstone to see me? I don't understand."

"No, I went back home in December."

"Why?"

He didn't want her to know about the cave—not yet. "I just couldn't take it anymore, being in the park. Drove me crazy a little bit." He wasn't lying, he reassured himself, just withholding information.

"So, did something happen in Tennessee?"

"Yeah, kinda. Home and I didn't agree. I don't think I'll be going back there for a long time. I've made a few enemies there, including my parents."

Nicole leaned in, "Is it Annie? Is that what's bothering you?"

Well, there's way more to it, he thought, *but* . . . "Yeah, I guess you could say that."

There was his alibi.

"It's called PTSD, Kyle. You're not alone. I really struggled with it too, but my counselor really helped. We can get you help too."

Kyle paused, suddenly recalling what he had seen in the living room when he awoke. He looked over his shoulder through the kitchen threshold at an urn high on a shelf, then back at Nicole. He pointed across his body, and looked at her.

She said, "Yeah, that's Mom."

"Nicole, I'm so sorry." He rubbed her arm, and she nodded, forcing a smile.

He said, "It's beautiful. Really, it's . . . " He searched for the word, but he was no poet. "It's bad ass."

Nicole's half-smile turned into a full-arching display of pride.

He ate the last bite of pancake, then asked, "So, you're a paid singer these days?"

"Not really—well . . . " She looked down at the table abashedly. "Yeah, I guess I am. Part-time, though. I serve tables full-time."

"Oh my God." Kyle suddenly realized he didn't recall anything after seeing her on stage. "I saw you singing, but I—"

"You passed out. Your head bounced right off the floor. You looked like absolute garbage, so I took you home."

"Oh, no." Kyle deflated. "You're not in trouble, are you?"

"No, I'm sure it's fine. My boss is super chill; she'll understand. I'm just glad you're all right. I was honestly happy to see you. I've missed you." She smiled warmly and handed him his orange juice.

As he took the juice, Kyle saw a shallow bookshelf next to the table. On top were several pieces of mail, including a few of his unopened letters.

Nicole said, "Kyle, I'm sorry, I wanted to write you back, I just had a lot going on."

"No. Don't apologize. I probably wouldn't have opened them either. I was an ass. It wasn't my place to tell you what was right or how to handle things. I can't imagine having to deal with what you did."

"I wanted to handle it on my own. That wasn't exactly easy, and . . . I regret not letting you come with me." Nicole straightened her back. "But there's more. I made Mom some promises before she left. One promise was to be proud of who I am, so, here it goes. Yes, I left to take care of Mom on my own, but even more than that, I didn't want you to see where I grew up."

"What?"

"I know. It was shallow, but I'm just not proud of—" She grimaced and held her palm up like she held an invisible hors d'oeuvres platter of slugs, "this."

"Wow. Really?"

"I know. Shallow."

"I don't care about any of 'this.' I wouldn't care if you grew up homeless. I wouldn't care if you were secretly an axe murderer."

Nicole raised an eyebrow.

"Well, maybe I would."

They both beamed at each other.

Kyle's eyes began to drift as if he hadn't slept at all.

"You tired still?" Nicole asked.

"I'm tryin'."

ONCE KYLE HAD finished eating, Nicole led him into the living room and had him lay on the couch. She sat with his head in her lap. "Your hair's gotten so long," she said.

"Nicole, ever since I left the park, I've been having these weird visions and hearing voices. I can't eat or sleep. I even lost my job. I thought I was going to kill my boss."

"That doesn't sound good, Kyle. You mean, like, you were literally going to kill him?"

"Well, no, not actually."

She gave him a silent look of concern as if to say, "Are you sure?".

"Sorry. I'm being overdramatic," he said. "Really, I'm fine."

After a beat, she suggested, "The mill here is always hiring. They're dying for help, I heard."

"Really? Are apartments cheap here?"

Nicole ran her fingers through his hair. "You seem to like this couch. I could use a roommate."

Kyle asked slyly, "Just a roommate?"

She laid a kiss on his mouth, then said, "We'll see."

Kyle looked up heavy-eyed.

Nicole peered thoughtfully out the window. She asked, "What did you mean by visions?"

Kyle's voice started to fade. "They're all just . . . bad. Sometimes, I feel this rage. Something's happening to me."

She chuckled. "Well, maybe *you're* the axe murderer here."

Nicole looked down at his weary face, and he was fast asleep.

CHAPTER 15

"STANFORD? YOU'RE KIDDING," The bartender said in a high-pitched voice. He braced his arms on the bar as he leaned forward, his dish towel laying over his shoulder. The afternoon sun shone through the large windows of the Green Goose Saloon of Gardiner, Montana, accenting his bright blue eyes and wispy, red-tinged mustache. "So, you're a truck driver with a degree from Stanford. Now, that's something you don't find every day."

Russell Hatfield's elbows swallowed up two places at the bar. He raised his beer to his lips and swallowed, then wiped the froth from his bushy goatee. Finally, he confided in the bartender, the only person he really trusted, "Yep, Political Science major. Well, I left my senior year, never got that degree." He looked straight ahead at the wall of liquor bottles and said gruffly, "They gave me the boot."

Before the bartender could ask why, Hatfield said, "Well, Frank, I didn't really see eye to eye with one of my classmates."

Frank cringed. "What happened?"

Hatfield clenched his jaw as he remembered the event. He said through his teeth, "Jim, *fucking*, Walters . . . "

Frank snorted. "You don't mean, Jim Walters, like, the son of our beloved Senator Walters?"

Russell glared at Frank. "Yes, that's exactly who I mean. One day, we had a dispute—"

Frank interrupted, "Oh wow. You know, I just saw on the news the other day the Senator's making an appearance at the Cody Rodeo in May. His wife will probably show, too. She is *gorgeous.* I mean, for her age, she's stunning. Oh, and their little girl—so—precious." He picked at his fingernail and grinned, "A hundred bucks says the kid isn't his. What is he, like, sixty?"

Frank suddenly noticed Hatfield staring him down and flinched. Hatfield growled, "Don't *fucking* interrupt me."

"Yes. You're right. I'm sorry." Frank dropped his nail-picking, shifted uncomfortably. "So, what about *your* little girl? Are you ever going to get custody?"

After a moment, Russell conceded to himself that he must have let his situation with five-year-old Maddie slip to Frank one day as beer flowed through him. He could see that happening.

"New rule," Russell said. "No more talk about Maddie."

"Okay Rus—I mean, sir. No more." Hatfield had rules for Frank and number one was never call Russell by his name, just "sir". He'd informed Frank that he doesn't need his name being used, that he had plenty of enemies that could show up any given day, looking to settle scores.

"Ah, look at me. I'm on one today. Sorry, Frank."

"No harm done."

He's a weakling, but a damn resilient one, Russell thought. He considered all the shit he'd given Frank over the last year or so, from yanking him around by his collar one day, to demoralizing him in front of other bargoers for "liking boys". Russell's turn toward violence and anger was like a switch, especially when drinking, and Frank took the brunt of it. Hatfield wondered if one day he would have one too many drinks and actually hurt the kind bartender.

Russell noted, "Ain't we just the happy couple? Goddamn, Frank, I swear, if I wasn't such the ladies' man, I might be inclined to shack up with you. You're a pretty man, I'll give ya that."

Frank uneasily wiped down the taps.

A crooked grin emerged on Russell's weathered face. "You know what, Frank? I like you. You're all right. You're probably the best barkeep in town."

Frank had been a safe ear to receive his deep-seated issues. He was a quivering man, one who wouldn't dare betray him, something Russell found useful. Russell had done some unspeakable things in his life and he needed to brag about them—someone needed to hear it. Frank was the perfect safe to throw his secrets into and spin the wheel shut.

"Would you like another beer?"

Russell finished his mug and slid it to Frank. The barkeep took the mug to the tap and began to fill.

"Anyway, as I was saying, before you . . . " Russell's disgusted look returned to his face. "I was saying, Jim Walters, that piece of shit . . . we got into it in class one day and I had to knock his teeth out. He spouted that capitalism helps grow the middle class. I told him only a dumbass believes that bullshit, that it's a lie the 'haves' cook up so they can keep capitalism alive and keep the money and power on their side of the table. It's only a matter of time before the one thing that keeps our capitalistic society from collapse becomes broken."

"What's that?" The mug overfilled, and foam gushed down the sides. Frank jerked the glass away from the tap. "Shit." He dried it and placed it in front of Hatfield.

"Tolerance. Or, you might call it "naivety"." He said "naivety" like there was no chance Frank had ever heard the word before.

When Frank wrinkled his brow with confusion, Russell rolled his eyes. Hatfield said, "The tolerance of the have-nots. Tolerance for the sinful amount of wealth that the few hoard from all the rest. They hoard it and force the rest to help them do it. They do it by creating this illusion of power over them. The 'haves' need the separation of wealth—it's what keeps their wealth growing. One day, that tolerance will break, and power will shift. Like I said, power is an illusion. It's what I told Jimbo Walters right before I clocked him. I told his privileged ass, "Who's got the power now?""

Russell took a long pull from his beer mug. He loved the sound of his own logic. He pushed the point of his index finger onto the bar, then wiggled it in Frank's general direction. "It's kinda like what we got between us, right here. Power is an illusion. You think I have the power. I'm big and strong, so you let me push you around. But what's to keep you from pulling out that revolver you got stashed in the cabinet over there and turning the tables on me?"

"But I don't have—"

Hatfield just raised his eyebrows. Frank shrunk.

Hatfield said, "I'm completely vulnerable to you right now—I'm unarmed, always am." This was an outright lie, but Russell wanted to make a point, so he bent the truth. "But you, you tolerate it because you think I have the edge. You see?"

Hatfield glanced at the mirrored backing on the wall in front of him and admired his brilliant face. He could almost feel how uncomfortable Frank was, like a wave of heat coming from him. Then, Russell suddenly felt sorry for the little guy, even if for a fleeting moment. He changed the subject. "I ever tell you about what I did in Jackson Hole?"

"No. Don't believe so."

Hatfield lowered his voice and wrapped his large hand fully around his mug. "Well, you know that economic symposium they have every summer down there—where the world bankers, power players, and politicians like Senator Walters get together and sip their champagne, pretend they're outdoorsmen, finger each other's buttholes?"

"I have heard of it. I can't say I've heard about the latter part, however."

"There's only one thing I hate more than my ex-wife for keeping me from Maddie—" He paused, realizing he'd just broken his own rule about not mentioning his daughter. He shrugged it off. "The only thing I hate more is a bloodsucking politician. God damn scumbags—right and left of the isle, don't matter. That's what crooked means anyway, right? You lean left or lean right of what's true . . . "

Russell took a swill, belched without opening his mouth, then continued. "Anyway, a few summers back, I started paying them a visit." He sat back smiling, proud of his work. The big man slurped his beer and wiped his mouth again. "The first time, I caught them with spike strips when they drove out to their mountain spa resorts. Their security detail, the drivers, you should've seen the look on their stupid faces. They were helpless."

Frank was intrigued. "Wow, where'd you get spike strips?"

"At the Nunya store."

"Nunya?"

"Nunya damn business. Are you *sure* you want to interrupt me again?"

Frank closed his mouth and returned to wiping the bar.

"So, the next summer, I found out where they went fly-fishing—well, where the guides caught the trout for them." Hatfield turned his big head side to side like a great-horned owl, searching the room for intruding ears. "While they were out grab-assin' in the river, I served some Molotov cocktails to their vehicles, blazed their shit up. Dumbass security drivers were down there trying to fish, too. They had no idea I was there."

"They were showing "naivety", so you took advantage of them," Frank said proudly.

"Now you're catchin' on."

Frank wiped his hands in his towel. He peered out the front windowpanes of the bar in deep thought. "About your comment earlier—if I did, actually, use that revolver on you, you know, to gain the power like you said . . . wouldn't that just get me nowhere? Like, it wouldn't actually help me, because then I'd be in jail for murder or assault, right? That wouldn't give me much power, would it?"

Russell felt his heartbeat pick up and his ears got hot. Frank was right, and on another level was squashing his analogy and, possibly, his philosophy altogether. He never knew if Frank was seriously stupid or just messing with him. He looked into Frank's eyes to try and figure this much out. He couldn't.

Hatfield huffed, said, "Frank, you are the single dumbest person I know." His repulsed face matched his degrading words. Hatfield huffed again.

Russell stood and pulled out his wallet. He asked, biting off his words, "What's the total?"

Frank checked the tab and said flatly, "It'll be twenty-seven fifty."

"You mean ten bucks." Hatfield gave a murderous look to Frank and laid a ten on the bar. "Because I have the power, so I name the price."

Frank stammered, "Yeah, ten bucks is good."

"Ten bucks, what?"

"Right," Frank said. "Ten bucks, sir."

Before turning away, Hatfield snapped. "Frank, you're almost as stupid as my ex-wife's fiancé. Maybe you two can get together and spout your bullshit to each other."

"Who's that?"

"Jimbo *fucking* Walters."

THAT NIGHT, FIVE miles south, Donnan MacLeod sat alone in his Toyota ForeRunner. His buggy eyes were fixed on the exits of the Mammoth District Ranger Station, waiting for a glimpse of this District Ranger Henry RedMoon—a Wahota in the flesh.

MacLeod's vehicle was alone in the parking lot.

The cold bore down on the northern Yellowstone location at fifteen degrees below freezing. Exhaust fumes lightly rolled from the truck's tail end, and the engine burbled in the frozen silence.

When Henry RedMoon walked out the back door, Donnan froze.

There he was again. *What an amazing sight*, Donnan thought.

This was the third time MacLeod had spotted him, and again, he didn't know how or if he wanted to proceed. Did the RedMoons know MacLeod was onto them? If so, he'd be putting himself at great risk.

But Donnan wanted so badly to interact with Henry, to ask him what it was like, to look into his eyes, to breathe in this incredible man.

MacLeod stayed put, knowing instinctively that he needed to keep his distance.

The Smith & Wesson sat between Donnan's legs as a measure of safety.

Donnan pondered—could he just run him down with his truck right now, take him home, lock him up, and witness a changing firsthand?

He threw off the ridiculous idea. *Come now, Donnie.*

As his mind was lost in thought, MacLeod's foot slipped off the brake and depressed the gas pedal.

The motor revved.

RedMoon glanced in MacLeod's direction, then continued walking toward the corner of the building.

Donnan inhaled as if he'd just surfaced from a great depth. After a moment, MacLeod gathered himself.

RedMoon turned the corner, and MacLeod put the truck in drive. This time MacLeod would trail him, see where he lived.

After Donnan rolled forward a few feet, Henry suddenly returned around the corner, treading briskly toward the ForeRunner.

RedMoon leaned forward as he marched, daring the truck to advance further.

"*Fuck!*" MacLeod jerked the wheel around and sped away. As he looked in his side mirror, he saw RedMoon leer at his back bumper.

Luckily, MacLeod had remembered to remove his plate.

CHAPTER 16

THE ROAR OF a lumber crane rebounded off the Smoky Mountains as the huge machine hoisted chained logs, forty feet long, and placed them on the conveyer system. Inside the mill, Kyle and a coworker pushed a sixteen-foot log section back and forth through a seventy-two-inch vertical blade. The long cuts roared like a tyrannosaurus, vibrating the metal roof. The two men moved with ease, in choreographed steps, exchanging the oak pieces between their gloved hands as they separated the wood into clean-edged boards.

Pulling the final boards out of the saw and sending them onto another conveyer, Kyle gestured to his co-worker. He tapped his wristwatch, then pretended to curl forkfuls of food into his mouth with his hand. His companion mimicked the forking motion, then flipped Kyle the middle finger.

Kyle returned the gesture and smiled heartily. His face was clean shaven and beamed with energy and color. He hit the kill switch to the saw, and the loud noise ran away like a turbo jet leaving the airspace overhead.

When it was quiet enough for conversation, the co-worker asked, "You going to the diner?"

"Yeah, you hungry?" Kyle asked.

"Yeah, but—"

Kyle cut him off. "You're hungry? Then eat *shit.*"

His cohort grinned. "Tell Nicole I said hi. Tell her she still owes me for last night."

Kyle punched the man's shoulder on his way to the exit.

AS HE REACHED his truck, Kyle removed his thick gloves and tossed them in the bed. He stopped and enjoyed the sound of the machines, the cranes, all coming down from a loud, constant buzz to the peaceful quiet of lunch break. It reminded him each time that he was surrounded by pristine Appalachian wilderness. The wooded mountains were not the Rockies of Yellowstone, but had their own charm. There was a comfort here, a safe feeling. Yes, there were black bears, but they were docile animals. Other than copperheads or water moccasins, it was a wild that he could handle, that wasn't out to kill him or people he knew, wasn't waiting with a hidden, evil cave for him to become ensnared in. The same could be said of Blacksburg residents and the folks who were part of his daily routine. Unlike Ashton, Tennessee, there were no snakes in his new microcosm, no hidden agendas. No one knew him, and he liked it that way.

Kyle could keep this routine for a lifetime, work this job eighteen hours a day, not just for his own benefit, but for something much more precious—supporting the woman he loved. Nicole was a healer, he presumed, a being sent from the heavens. She was his rock, seeing him through an apparent second growth spurt, healing his wounds, eradicating his reliance on alcohol, and silencing the demons in his head.

He and Nicole generally worked the same hours, except for her occasional performances at Mountain Lake Hotel. In these last three weeks, it seemed the simplicity of his comfortable life revolved around three anchors: Nicole, work, and eating. He loved hearing Nicole compliment him on his increase in weight—she radiated with pride when he recently informed her that he'd gained fifty pounds. Kyle's rapid return to his natural weight was remarkable, and he credited Nicole's cooking for it all. His girl loved to feed him, and he loved to eat.

NICOLE SET A steaming plate of spaghetti in front of Kyle. His empty salad bowl was stacked on top of a ranch-smeared plate that once held chicken fingers.

"Excuse me, miss, this food is just terrible. I'm going to need a discount or something."

Nicole collected the plates and playfully shook her head.

"All right, I'll settle for a neck rub instead?" Kyle waggled his eyes at her, then flexed his pectoral muscles under his T-shirt—left, then right, left, then right.

She rolled her eyes. "Just stop."

"I dig chicks with tats." He glanced down to the small tattoo near her ankle. It was the word *Mom* with an elegant feather merged into the font.

"I guess you slept well," Nicole said.

He corralled the noodles as they fell from his mouth.

"Haven't heard you grunting in your sleep in a while."

Kyle swallowed. "Thank you?"

"I gotta get back to work. Can you feed Cujo as soon as you get home this evening? I totally forgot to this morning."

"And you wonder why he likes me more."

Nicole turned. "Not on your life."

Kyle threw his finger up. "Hey, before you go, let me get a pen."

She left him one and tended to another table in the busy diner.

Kyle pulled a postcard from his back pocket and clicked the pen.

He addressed it to his mother in Tennessee. Today was Wednesday, the day he sent her a postcard with a friendly, *How are you?* and, *Doing great here!* Each time, he'd artfully dodge her requests for him to come home and visit or at least give her a phone number. None of their postcard communications had touched on their unfortunate event at church.

Seeing Nicole go through the loss of her mother urged Kyle to reach out to his own. Kyle longed to forget his past, but his mother deserved to know that he was okay. Maybe today he'd give her their home phone number as Nicole had suggested.

He decided it could wait.

Kyle signed the card, and as he slipped it back into his pocket, he watched Nicole taking an order at a table with an elderly couple.

How long would he keep those bizarre occurrences to himself and not tell Nicole? Maybe he'd keep them hidden until he was as old as the man giving Nicole his lunch order. Maybe the old fella had secrets of his own, from ages ago—truths locked away that would have ruined a good thing at the time with the woman across from him. Maybe if he'd confessed those secrets, they wouldn't be where they are today.

Some things are best forgotten, he supposed. What did it matter anyway?

But something did matter.

He'd written off his black-out episode in Ashton as a simple case of an alcoholic who'd gone home, gotten lights-out drunk over a "family quarrel," then woke up the next day not knowing what had happened.

That was all wishful thinking, and he knew it. Even raving drunks don't wake up naked and covered in blood.

Or maybe they did.

He desperately wanted to believe all was well, but deeper inklings told him otherwise—the same inklings, perhaps, that had blurted out of him at Fawn Creek Church, telling Scanland, *Don't go home.* Why had he told him that?

Kyle tried yet again to remember exactly what had happened once he returned home from the church that night three weeks ago. He could see himself opening his front door.

... breathing heavy, felt hot, ripped my jacket off ... the loose cabinet knob when I pulled it open, grabbing the bottle and chugging it, skipping putting it in a glass, crying at the kitchen table, beating the table with my fists, then scratching it ...

Another memory then surfaced. He saw himself at the bathroom sink—his face grimacing in the mirror. His jaw— his jaw hurt like holy hell, like a heavyweight boxer had landed an uppercut to his chin.

Had he been in a fight?

No, he didn't remember a fight. That would've been something easy to remember.

Then,

dogs gnashing their teeth, squirming beneath a great force, his force ... Some kind of dogs, were they, no, they were, coyotes

He saw flashes of bloody scenes. They were like quick camera flashes in the dark,

fur, teeth, a struggle—there was whimpering.

Kyle pulled himself from the memory, and fought to catch his breath. He sat up straight, shook his head, then gulped down his black coffee.

He'd just gone further down that rabbit hole than he ever had before.

This was why he didn't do this. Nothing good could lie down this path. The memories were best left under lock and key.

He told himself it was just some kind of anxiety messing with his brain. Perhaps Nicole was right—maybe witnessing Annie's mauling had really screwed him up.

His stomach turned, however, as he considered the next issue. The Ashton event was one thing, but what happened in that cave, and what followed?

Yes—*followed.*

God, Kyle, shut up, he told himself.

Kyle looked again at the old man Nicole had been serving. He searched the man's eyes—they dumbly measured the walls. Taking a sip of coffee was the man's next arduous task. He reached and jiggled the cup as he lifted it, sipped, then returned the cup slowly, sloshing it a bit. He shakily and unnecessarily shifted his spoon's position on the table, then returned to his stupefied stare at the wall beyond the old woman.

At least Kyle's life wasn't mindlessly boring, he thought.

CHAPTER 17

A FEW DOZEN residents filled the Green Goose Saloon's tables and booths. The bar-and-grill restaurant was long, like the mercantile shops or saloons of the late 1800s. It was a modest meet-up for the common folk of Gardiner, as opposed to one of the many high-dollar establishments nestled within a lodge on the mountain side, accessible only by driving up switchbacks.

Only once before had Donnan MacLeod walked into the saloon, affably known by locals as "The Goose." Sherri had dragged him along with her and her friend on an art gallery viewing extravaganza in town. After three hours of the nonsense, he'd cut out and strolled into The Goose for a beer and a scotch.

Tonight, MacLeod had sat in a corner booth, his eyes prowling, hunting for a sign of Henry RedMoon. He knew park rangers at the north district were sometimes housed in Gardiner. If that were the case, and if RedMoon were a social drinker or even hungry at this hour, this is where he would be.

MacLeod spotted a handful of Yellowstone employees cutting up at the bar and visiting the pool table from time to time—Mammoth Hot Springs concessionaires who descended a few miles of winding, cliff-teasing roadway from the north entrance to get here. They were an isolated bunch, an interestingly animated flock, MacLeod noted—here for a moment to enjoy a slice of almost-normalcy, then scampering off, back up into the mountains and to their life of Yellowstone adventure.

"Another whiskey, sir?" A chubby female server with a large tray of hefty angus burgers and steak fries threw the question at him in stride, too busy to stop.

"Yes, uh one moment—" MacLeod reached for her.

She turned to him on her heels.

"This is a silly question, but I'm looking for a friend. His name is Henry RedMoon. He's a new ranger for the park. Has he been in here at all that you know of? I was just in town and thought I'd surprise him. I'm an old friend. Sorry to say, I don't know where he lives or how to contact him."

"Sorry, never heard of him." Her waist was turned away, waiting for a signal that he was finished with her.

"Very well, thank you."

Donnan sighed. He tilted the last sip of his whiskey down his throat and opened his laptop.

Booting up and opening his internet browser, he typed in an address, *1 RedMoon Lane, Dunoir, WY*. He brought up the aerial satellite photos of the RedMoon property again and eyed it with pure fascination.

"Here you are, sir." The waitress sat his whiskey next to him. They were quick. *They know an expensive drinker when they see one,* Donnan thought.

Without looking away from the screen, he said, "Thank you, dear."

He pulled a drink from the glass, keeping his eyes on the map. He zoomed in and prowled their property, feeling like a devious eye in the sky.

Then, an email notification popped up in the bottom corner of the screen. It was from his former department head at the University of Washington.

Was he going to ask MacLeod if he'd sold his house yet? Donnan thought. *That prick.*

MacLeod pulled it up and read curiously.

As his former boss informally offered MacLeod another speaking opportunity in Missoula, Montana, he urged Donnan:

Donnie, I do this out of respect for you and your tenure here. However, if you go nuts again, throwing out nonsense about ancient evil and crap, I'll pull you off stage myself and that will be the end of us. Please don't make me do that. I know you need the money, so please don't ruin this. I pulled a lot of strings to get this for you. Just stick to your field work and share your brilliance. Do the lecture, take the honorarium, and let that be your re-entrance into the archaeological community's good graces. If someone asks about your recent outbursts, just play it off, feed them something about the power of AA or something, they'll love you for it. Hell, it may even improve your image, give you a pity vote. Let me know if you want the gig . . .

MacLeod rotated his glass by the rim as he read the email two more times. This lecture, he thought, could be his one, last chance to convince the world of what he knew.

MacLeod would have to lay out all his cards, though. He would have to present the government census records he'd found detailing how the Wahota tribe in northwestern Wyoming had officially assimilated and legally assigned themselves the RedMoon name. He could show them the archeological footsteps of the Wahota that routed from the geothermal hot spot known as Kamchatka Peninsula in northeast Asia, where the evil began, across the Bering Strait, south through Canada, into Yellowstone, then to Dunoir, Wyoming. And the kicker, at the end of his lecture, he'd show them the photos of the morbid and enormous skeletons he'd found on two Wahota digs that coincide with the Wahota/Yohawnee myths. When he'd found them years ago, he knew he needed to gather more evidence before going public. That ace in the hole was still there.

His career was tumbling, along with his bank account.

Now was his shot—his time for glory.

He weighed the danger in releasing the RedMoon name. The RedMoons would not be happy when he accused the family of years' worth of local murders.

Donnan's convictions collided. His mind shifted between both ends of the decision, the potential consequences sloshing over both sides.

As with every decision, large or small, Donnan filled his belly with whiskey once more.

He set the glass down, and Sherri showed her face again, slipping her way into his drunken mind.

Donnan clicked on his home security application. Six camera feeds shown on the laptop screen—two rows of three. He focused solely on the feed in the top left—the one he had them install first, six months after she'd left him and over three years ago from today—the camera over Sherri's parking spot.

The spot was empty, of course.

Each time he saw the oil spots on the concrete pad and her car missing, his growing rage became more concentrated, and his mad desperation deepened.

MacLeod clenched his fist and pursed his lips.

He replied to the email, thanking his friend for the opportunity and inquiring which hotel he should book.

CHAPTER 18

KYLE'S SILVERADO STOPPED at the curb in front of Nicole's house. When he killed the motor and the heater stopped, he could already feel February's chill coming for him. It crept through the tiniest crevasses and passageways of the truck, targeting his warm-blooded body, seeking him out, fueled by some unseen and malevolent force that wanted nothing more than to torture him, consume him, eat through to his bones.

The oddest thing was, although he could physically recognize the cold on his skin, it wasn't cold. It was like he knew it should be affecting him, but it didn't—no more than recognizing the feel of his jeans touching his legs. Both sensations were equally insignificant. This was strange—Kyle was a southerner, a Tennessee lowlander who would have normally been shivering right now.

Fenn's cell phone rang. The caller ID flashed: *Nicole Work*.

He picked up. "Hello."

"Hey, it's me. I'm running late."

Kyle glanced at her empty parking spot, which was two dirt paths striping into the short front yard. "I see that. You guys get busy?"

"Yeah. I think I should be done within an hour."

"Want me to get something started for you? My shells n' cheese is pretty kick ass."

"No, no. Don't cook *anything*."

"Jeez, a simple 'no thanks' would've been fine, but . . . "

"No, I have a surprise for you tonight. Well, for us. I got some free stuff. Don't eat anything. It's going to be awesome!"

Kyle snarked, "Do I need to shave my legs?"

"Just shave your face."

"But I was just starting to like my man-beard." Kyle rubbed his scraggly facial growth, examining the thinner areas in the rearview mirror.

Nicole remarked, "What other kind of beard is there?"

"Well, there are circus-lady beards."

Nicole chuckled. "I didn't want to say it, but you forced my hand—Kyle, your beard is . . . eh."

"Eh?"

"All right, I gotta go. See you in a little bit."

"Smooches." Kyle hung up.

When he finally took his foot off the brake, his knee brushed his keys. The jingling sound was enhanced inside the closed cab, reminding him of his mother. As a kid, whenever he'd acted up, she would pull to the side of the road and shut off the car. In between the tongue-lashings that were a mixture of stern authority and motherly love, the silence inside the sealed vehicle was remarkable. He couldn't remember one word she ever spoke in those moments, nor understand exactly what he did wrong, but the quiet pauses between her thoughts as she decided her next words had stuck with him.

As Kyle went to pocket his phone, he noticed he had a voicemail. He dialed in to listen to it.

Halfway through the message, his fingers began to tap his thighs. He shifted in his seat and felt his palms sweat.

In the voice message, his mother informed him that Patty Cakes owner, Patty Feltner, had been found murdered, ripped up like an animal in a field the night before he'd left Ashton. She didn't insinuate anything with Kyle's involvement, but concern tinged her words. The police had waited until two days ago to release the details, and it was the biggest news the town had seen in decades.

Kyle ended the call.

He closed his eyes and tried to remember what happened that night. Where were his clothes? What was the blood smeared all over him? Did his violent flashes have anything to do with the blood? Whose blood—"

He stopped himself. *Just quit it, that's absurd.*

Kyle snorted at himself. *Yeah, that's ridiculous*, he thought as he exited his truck.

After walking briskly up the frozen yard, Kyle unlocked the front door.

With one step inside, he heard a whine.

Cujo averted his eyes from Kyle, whimpered, and scurried to the back door.

"Cujo, come here, boy."

The dog scraped wildly at the base of the door.

"Hey, quit that!" He stormed over.

Cujo turned to him and bared his teeth. He spread his front paws out on the linoleum and bent his back legs, ready to spring.

"Whoa now!"

Kyle stepped back, and Cujo bolted passed him, banging against the kitchen table. The retriever scrambled out the open front door and disappeared.

TWO HOURS LATER, Kyle's right hand was placed on the small of Nicole's back.

A thin man in black slacks and a turtleneck eyed them stoically. His voice cadenced them along, "Two and three and four . . ."

Kyle twirled Nicole by the wrist and the two separated to opposite ends of a wooded floor similar to the floor of a basketball court. A large window overlooked the greenery of Mountain Lake Hotel's back lawn. Mirrors were wall to wall.

The "surprise" with "free stuff" that Nicole told Kyle about over the phone was an all-inclusive "Dancing, Dining, and Dozing" package. The deal was a gift from the owner, a token of gratitude for the exceptional singing Nicole provided to the hotel's biweekly, (formerly monthly) dances—for the extra profit her performances produced. First on the agenda—dance lessons.

For the fifth time, Kyle and Nicole sprinted to one another and Nicole dove at Kyle's head.

This time he caught her. He pushed her to the sky by the crests of her pelvis, her arms outreached like a soaring eagle.

Kyle bowed out his chest, his brow clenched as he held his focus.

The stoic man applauded just as a full audience would.

"Yes! Yes. You two! You *are* Baby and Johnny. It's incredible."

Kyle kept Nicole aloft. He could hold her there all day, he thought. This was all he wanted out of life, was to help her reach the sky, and he purposefully held her there to nonverbally send that message.

With Nicole still in the sky, he walked her over to the instructor.

Kyle boasted, "What, like this? Is this how I do it? How long do I hold her here?"

The dance instructor rolled his eyes, "Okay, Swayze, you can put her down now."

Nicole tittered and said, "Just don't put me in the corner."

SID, VIC, WYMON and his son, Phoenix, sat high-postured on horseback, hidden in a high copse of white birch trees, watching the activity of two white men on the other side of a narrow valley. Their hair was as long as the horses' tails, dark as night, except for Sid's which was completely silver. Their profoundly dark eyes were intense and fixated like a pack of timber wolves eyeing a fawn elk. Their buckskin-toned and stout Przewalski horses looked the same direction, as if mind-melded with their riders. Both man and horse exuded a uniqueness and rarity of bloodline within their respective genera.

The sun sank halfway behind the rugged Wyoming horizon. Patches of snow and the white aspen trunks around them started to glow as twilight set in.

Sid called to his grandson, "Phoenix. Come."

The boy brought his horse next to Sid's.

"There, in that stand of pines. Do you see them?"

"Yes, Grandfather." His voice was juvenile, yet husky. Phoenix looked across Sid to see his father, Wymon. Wymon kept his eyes on the men in the distance.

The two white men carried boxes into an abandoned RedMoon hay barn. One man carried a lantern inside. After a moment, a warm light arose between the gaps in the boarding. At first, the men had been looking over their shoulders with every step, but by now, had become complacent.

Sid leaned to Phoenix and shot his arm out straight, guiding Phoenix's gaze. "That peak there beyond them—you see it?"

"Yes, Grandfather."

"Our land runs all the way to that peak," Sid made a Z gesture across the horizon, "and just as far in both directions. Those men have chosen to intrude on our land. Do you know what they are doing, Grandson?"

"No."

"Making drugs to sell for money."

"But drugs kill people."

Sid met eyes with Wymon. Sid smiled showily, "And where did you learn that, Phoenix?"

"From you, Grandfather."

Sid continued looking at Wymon. He said, "The outsiders are *spiritless*," biting off the last word. "They care not for the animals and the land that give us life. They take and take, and they'll take us, too. That is why we cannot become like them, nor become *one of them*. We must keep to ourselves and guard what we have with tooth and claw. It is *why* we keep our talents sharp."

Sid addressed the boy, "Your talents, wise Phoenix, have just arrived."

Sid ordered Wymon and Vic back home, and the two stoically sauntered off.

When they crested the ridge and vanished down the other side, Sid addressed Phoenix. "This night you will remember the rest of your life. This night is your right of passage. You will do it alone. Do not hesitate. You carry with you a great responsibility—a great honor. When the time is right, reach for it and it will come to you. Let it flow through you and harness it."

"But last time I couldn't. I won't—"

Sid thrust his face at the boy. His upper canine teeth slipped over his bottom lip, and he said harshly, "You will."

"Yes, Grandfather."

Phoenix clicked his tongue and started his decent.

Sid turned for home.

The sun disappeared, trading shifts with the brilliantly bright full moon.

ELEGANT, WHITE SHEETS covering the tables reached all the way to the floors of the ritzy dining room. Grand chandeliers sparkled in the high ceiling. Servers in cummerbunds and bowties buzzed in and out of the kitchen doors with silver trays.

Kyle was just telling Nicole, as they waited for their order, how his decision to find her a month ago was the wisest decision he'd ever made.

When Nicole's steak and Maine lobster tail was set in front of her, tears suddenly filled her eyes, and something happened around her mouth—her cheeks rose to smile, but the edges of her mouth frowned. She looked like a toddler whose toy had just been stolen.

"Is everything okay, ma'am? Is this not your order?" The confused server held her hand to her chest with concern.

Nicole laughed awkwardly and said in a pitchy voice, "No, it's perfect. It's amazing. Thank you. I've just been through a *lot* lately, and this—oh my God." Nicole wiped her eyes and laughed again.

Kyle winked at the waitress. "She *really* loves the surf n' turf."

The server said, "Wait a sec, aren't you the singer for our dances?"

She nodded.

"Holy cow. You're amazing. You sound exactly like Jennifer Warnes. We can hear you all the way from the greeting table. I walked over and saw you last week. You've got a great voice!"

"Thank you," Nicole said.

When the waitress left, Kyle cupped Nicole's hand and said, "You going to make it?"

"Yeah." She sniffed, "It's just—"

"I know. It's all right." He knew it wasn't the surf n' turf—it was what it meant. She'd struggled a lot, for a long time, fiercely. Things were looking up. It was okay for her to exhale, finally—and cry if it helped.

"Thank you, Kyle, for everything."

"Nah, I don't do much."

"You came back into my life right when I needed you the most. You're like . . . my hero."

"I'm happy to be here."

But he was no hero, he reminded himself. He was a coward who'd lost control and ran to her. It was Nicole who was the hero.

"You ever miss Yellowstone?" Kyle asked. Maybe the time was now, since he'd just reached "hero" status, to let her know about the cave. She deserved to know why he showed up looking the way he did—to let her know that it had nothing to do with Annie's mauling and everything to do with that cave.

"I really did right before you came here. Now I don't care as much. I'm just happy being around you. Do you ever think about it?"

While she responded, he imagined himself explaining all of it to her—from the cave, to going home, to the drinking, the anger, to striking a preacher, to the blackout night and subsequent coyote visions, the blood. If they were to be together, she had to know everything.

But, he concluded, there was no way he could tell her. It sounded like something a psychotic would say, or a lie concocted by some half-witted stalker thinking the stalkee would be none the wiser.

No, *hell* no, he couldn't tell her.

"Kyle?"

He'd zoned out. Then, "Yeah? Oh sorry. What was that?"

"I asked if you ever considered going back to the park."

He was nervous. Kyle had a feeling deep down, a ball of anxiety in his stomach like there had been the time he was dared to jump from an eighty-foot cliff into a quarry lake in

Ashton. It was the feeling of knowing he was about to do something stupid, or something amazing. That *something* compelled him deeply, and if he would only close his eyes and go, the amazing could be achieved. That amazing thing would be Nicole finally knowing and understanding the very real pain and fear that had gripped him.

He had to tell her.

Kyle's heart raced, "Nicole, I need to tell you something . . . "

He clutched his water glass and took a drink to wet his suddenly dry mouth.

Kyle then felt a cold-hot flush run through him, and his heart thumped.

As if stepping out of his skin, Kyle felt himself at Art Scanland's house. He had a quick memory flash of him pacing outside Art's house, putting his nose to the windows, his hot breath fogging the glass.

"Kyle?"

"Huh?"

"Your eyes, what's up with your eyes? They're like, yellowy." She pushed her head forward, staring closer into his eyes.

Kyle noticed his hand was clenching the tablecloth below the table. "Uh, I'm just going to use the bathroom real quick, okay? Be right back."

He kissed her forehead and walked toward the bathroom.

For some reason, he knew he needed to get himself outside.

Bolting out onto the back deck of the hotel, he told himself he was fine—to just breathe some fresh cold air and *chill out.*

I'm trying goddammit!

He gripped the wooden railing and huffed.

Four women chatted on the deck.

Kyle suddenly baulked at them like a cobra giving a warning strike, "Go the fuck inside!"

They didn't argue—only retreated inside with frightened and disgusted looks on their faces. The last woman to re-enter the building said, "Fuckin' jerk," and flicked her half-smoked cigarette at Kyle.

Kyle stared at the hot ember of the cigarette as it landed next to his boot. He picked it up, stuck it in his forearm until it blackened out.

There was no pain.

As he looked down at his growing fingers, he instantly remembered the same had happened at Scanland's house.

Kyle placed his hands on his face and felt it contorting.

Nicole's scent suddenly reached him, though she was well inside. His protruding ears sensed she was approaching the back door.

Run, just run!

Kyle launched himself over the railing and landed twenty feet below in the well-cut lawn.

As his quadriceps bulked, and his toes burst through the front of his boots, his last thought was to get himself to the wooded mountain slope, and clear from sight.

Halfway to the slope, Kyle slipped from control and his possession took the wheel.

It dashed across the well-lit lawn and would have made it to the wood line had the mother of two in a nearby parking lot not seen his morbid form and screamed in horror.

The family's heat signatures in an unlit parking lot radiated in its vision.

The half-creature was within a stone's throw of the family in seconds, bounding on all fours, shredding through its clothing.

The mother quickly pushed her kids into the van and got herself inside. She shook violently as she pulled out her cell phone and called for help.

The glass in the passenger-side window shattered as the hideous thing rammed the van.

The children's screams echoed off the rolling hills of leafless timber.

It returned to a bipedal stance and swung its arm through the window. The remaining glass shards sprayed as the creature swiped at one of the young boys. The nails sliced through the boy's back as he scrambled to the back of the van. The mother pounded the creature's arm with a large, plastic dinosaur.

Suddenly, it picked up Nicole's voice. "Kyle? Are you out here?"

It swung its head back to the deck of the hotel restaurant. The creature's jaw jutted out further. It shook free from the split boots, which had been hanging to its feet only by the laces.

Its fibulas and tibias cracked and grew in length. The legs bent backward, and its eyes bulged. Hair sprouted at the flanks of the neck and up its rounded shoulders. A choking noise came from its throat like the sound of someone stuck in one, long dry heave.

A battle raged inside the man-creature. It pivoted its head back and forth between the van and the wooded slope. After a beat, the horrid creature took a few strides toward the forest, then looked back over its shoulder at the woman who had started the vehicle. Finally, it turned and fled into the mountains.

PHOENIX REDMOON'S BUTTON-UP farm shirt and jeans were folded next to a distinguishable, leaning pine tree, along with his leather boots. He crept naked in the moonlight toward the rundown hay barn. His feet were as silent as owl wings as he stalked across the pine needles.

Slinking to the side of the barn, he watched them through the spaces between the old wood. The two intruders shuffled about inside the barn, speaking quietly, blotting out the low lantern light as they worked.

A tall man with a beard that reached his bottom rib unloaded a cardboard box. He pulled out a plastic strainer, cellophane wrap, and a large glass jar with a spout on the side, and placed them on a fold-out table. He searched through a plastic bag of Sudafed tablets, shallow glass bowls, and lithium batteries. He whispered to the other man, "I thought I told you to bring the spatula."

The other man, also tall, with wavy red hair, was pulling a white coverall suit above his waistline. He replied, "It's on the table, jackass."

A whisper fight started.

The bearded man said, "Don't call me jackass, ginger dick."

"I swear to God, I'm going to screw your sister so hard when we get back—"

Bearded Jackass held up a hand to stop him. "Shh, shut the fuck up." He crept to the wooden door, withdrawing a pistol from the front of his waistband.

The door creaked as he opened it with the muzzle of his shiny revolver.

Phoenix snuck in from behind, moved as a shadow, unheard by the two, and scaled the ladder up to the loft.

Ginger Dick continued struggling with his white suit. "What, you hear a boogie man?"

Beard replied in a whisper, "Shush, keep your voice down. There's someone out there."

"You afraid the big, bad RedMoon gonna getcha? Fuck the RedMoons, buncha wild, mangy dogs. I ain't scared of them."

Phoenix's face tensed. He took a knee and closed his eyes, concentrating deeply.

Beard agreed with Ginger, "Yeah, fuck them." He squinted one eye and aimed his gun at an invisible man. "I'd love to shoot one of them red niggers right between the eyes."

The loft floor buckled.

Splinters of wood fell as the ceiling strained under the sudden presence of something enormous. That something huffed loudly, like a working Clydesdale horse.

Bearded Jackass raised his pistol to the noise, his hand shaking as if he had a sudden onset of Parkinson's. He cried, "What the fuck was that?"

Thump. Thump.

Ginger scurried to get away from the overhead threat, stumbling with the suit still around his legs, knocking over the lantern.

Leaf and straw litter ignited.

Thump. Thump.

A hole burst through the ceiling, and a huge hairy limb with claws continued to strike the wood.

Thump.

Beard fired desperately at the thing, emptying the six-shooter.

The thumping stopped, and the gunshots reverberated off the hugging rocky ridges.

The sound of fresh flames gaining fuel *whooshed* like whips of wind picking up.

Before the men could run for the door, the beast crashed through the ceiling, landing on their level just beyond the firelight.

There was one large glob of black within the shadows.

When the dark figure seemed to stand, its head disappeared through the hole it had created.

It crouched and moved forward.

Inching closer to the light, it opened its jaws.

White fangs and jagged teeth were now visible, and two eyes reflected the growing flames.

Its jaws opened wide and blasted the men with a roar as powerful as the back blast of an Abrams tank.

Ginger wet himself in his suit. Jackass ran for the exit.

As Beard swung open the wood door, Ginger's scream was brutally cut off by the wet, ripping sound of dismemberment and butchering.

Beard made it fifty meters when the beast trounced him.

It pinned Beard face-down and clawed ravenously, straight through his back, until his thoracic cavity was void of lungs, liver, and a heart.

IN THE VALLEY below, emergency and police vehicles raced through the highways with sirens blaring, but on this high ridge, the Virginia woods were silent. A National Forest Ranger rode a lofty, acorn-colored mare in search of a white male, mid-twenties, six-feet tall, possibly armed, named Kyle Fenn.

The ranger rode high in the saddle with a wide-brimmed hat. The Beretta at his side blinked with a metallic glint in the moonlight. A thick, hunter-green forest service coat insulated him from the night air.

The ranger's horse suddenly halted. The mare lifted her head and rotated her ears like satellites searching for a signal. She snorted anxiously.

"What is it, Lucy?"

He slowly withdrew his Beretta and thumbed backed the hammer.

Without warning, the horse backpedaled, putting the man on top of her neck.

They traveled this way for a few beats, then splashed into a wide riverbed only a foot deep with mountain water.

"Whoa! Easy now."

He regained his saddle, holstered his pistol, and stroked Lucy's neck.

The horse slowly backed up to the middle of the river, her hooves clacking against the river rocks.

They waited silently there, the clear water dribbling over the dark stones. The twinkling reflection of the full moon danced on the water's surface. The high-reaching and bare branches of oaks loomed above the banks in the starry sky, framing the nervous scene.

Lucy's breath, which was visible as rhythmic billows of steam when they entered the water, gradually calmed to smaller puffs that vanished quickly.

The law officer leaned forward and said in a quiet voice while readjusting the reins, "See Lucy Girl, everything's fine."

He pulled the reins and turned her around. "Let's get out of this damn crick bed."

Lucy carefully negotiated the river floor and nearly reached the other side when she again stopped and employed her satellite ears.

For a moment, they both remained still and listened— just quiet, trickling water, one bluster of wind, a few troubled crows in the distance.

The silence was broken then, by a splash.

Something large had entered the river.

Horse and rider turned and faced a hairy creature in the water, standing erect near the opposite bank, the side of its body highlighted by the moonbeams.

With its striking yellow eyes directly on them, it lowered its long arms to the water and began a quadrupedal walk toward them. Its doggish snout snarled, showing a mass of pointed teeth strung across wide jaws.

Its tongue flicked from side to side behind its teeth like a caged viper.

Lucy reared back, throwing the uniformed man to the shallow water.

As he landed awkwardly on his back, his ranger hat fell and drifted away with the stream.

In an instant, the beast was in front of them and lunged at the horse's throat. As it pulled her to the ground by the neck, Lucy thrashed and neighed in distress.

The ranger jumped to his feet and scrambled into the wood line. He hid behind a wall of upturned roots at the base of a fallen tree and pulled his pistol from his hip.

The shaky ranger peeked around at the river. The man-beast crouched over the defeated horse, her back leg still twitching. The creature's skin was steaming, as if its hairy skin was breathing.

The ranger whispered, "Shhhit."

As he let out his quiet curse, the creature's pointed ears perked. It stood slowly, turned, and locked eyes with the man.

It paused and tilted it huge head slightly. Its crazed eyes seemed wickedly curious, and it licked its chops.

Color faded from the ranger's face.

The beast's ears lowered back, and malice squeezed its brow.

The officer stepped out from behind his cover, his pistol ready.

His face was blank, and his eyes were empty as if his soul had already fled.

With its eyes on the man, a deep growl began in its chest, like the sound of a bathtub draining. A ridge of spiked hair stood on its back, and a sneer displayed on its bloodied snout.

The lawman raised his weapon, but it was too late.

The creature sprang forward and tackled him to the ground. It bit down on the man's neck and head. Its mouth covered the officer's entire face, preventing him from breathing.

The man kicked and moaned. He scratched at the beast.

The creature gave a shake, and with one violent jerk, the ranger was relieved of his head.

CHAPTER 19

DISTRICT RANGER HENRY RedMoon drove home from work, feeling somewhat numb from an uneventful third shift. He'd volunteered to work last night's nine-to-six shift, which drew curious looks—why was a lead ranger pulling an all-night shift? He claimed he wanted to get a real feel for how things operated on all shifts at his post, and he did. But moreover, Henry knew he wouldn't be sleeping and figured he may as well be doing something to redirect his mind—to keep it from stewing over his family.

He'd taken the shift from Officer Hodges, saying Hodges looked like he needed some time off—to which Hodges had whooped with gratitude. Hodges was like a puppy, and RedMoon didn't have the heart to shake him from his heels. That youthful enthusiasm was what had led RedMoon to reluctantly grant Hodges' request to work under him at Mammoth. Hodges needed supervision, after all. However, if Hodges didn't stop calling Henry "boss" all the time, RedMoon might have to change his mind and relocate the man-child.

On his way to his apartment, Henry had noticed the Green Goose Saloon was open for breakfast. He'd calculated that the local establishment could be useful, a place to gather helpful information. Something weighed on his mind—the mysterious person in the Toyota ForeRunner who had been watching him at the office.

Who was he? Or she? He never got a good look, though the bulk of the person and the wideness around the face suggested a male. He assumed this person was a local, either a park employee, or someone living in Gardiner, as the ForeRunner had waited for him outside the station sporadically for a few weeks—longer than any park visitor would be staying. From what Henry had gathered, The Green Goose looked to be Gardiner's watering hole, where he might find some answers. At the very least, he might find his favorite new place to have breakfast, or find coffee he approved of.

After switching into civilian clothes, Henry drove his black Jeep Wrangler back to the saloon and parked along the sidewalk. Only a few other vehicles lined the snowy street. At one end of the sky, a full moon had faded to gray, and at the other, the beaming sun crested over Electric Peak. The fresh light beat down on the sidewalk, but Montana's winter didn't allow for a melt. These days, Henry's breath was visible round the clock.

RedMoon pulled in one last breath of clean morning air and pushed open The Goose's front door.

Only two tables were occupied—an older gentleman in a long-sleeve shirt and vest, his cowboy hat sitting crown-down on the table like a proper rancher would have it. Two well-to-do women sat chatting at another table. Henry thought the women looked like they were fueling up for a long day of shopping the art galleries and clothing shops.

What else is there to do around here being dressed like that? he thought.

Sliding out a stool, Henry nodded at the blue-eyed, red-mustached bartender, and placed his black Stetson crown-down at the bar.

The barkeep glided over. "Morning, stranger. What can I do for you?"

The bartender was quite pleasant. He had such an agreeable aura about him, that Henry even felt inclined to befriend the man, though that wasn't usually his nature when it came to strangers.

"Coffee."

The bartender said, "Black," not as a question, but a statement.

He poured a mug from the pot and set it in front of Henry. "Are you having breakfast this morning?"

"Sure."

Handing Henry a menu, he said, "You got a name? Don't believe I've seen you here before."

"Henry RedMoon."

"It's a pleasure to meet you, Henry. I'm Frank."

They shook hands.

A sleepy-eyed waitress with a cushy face was punching her fingers at the digital register that also served as the clock-in. She said, "Hm, that's weird."

Frank joked, "What? Is the clock mysteriously ten minutes fast and you're late again?"

"Shut up, Francis."

Frank cocked his head. "Really? Can't come up with anything better? Need your coffee, honey?" He poured a mug and dramatically placed it next to her.

"I meant, I recognize that name." She looked at Henry. "Did you say RedMoon? Henry RedMoon?"

Henry nodded. "Yes, ma'am."

She went back to poking at the screen. "There was a man in here the other day, said he was an old friend of yours." The waitress stopped typing and hung her head. "Ah shit, I wasn't supposed to tell you. He said he wanted to surprise you. Asked if I knew a 'Henry RedMoon.'"

"Is that right?" Henry casually sipped his coffee but was more than interested. "Do you remember his name?"

"Eh, no I can't recall. I know he looked like the guy from *Jurassic Park*, the, uh, rich old white guy who owned the dinosaurs." She pointed at an imaginary person and said dramatically, quoting the movie, "And the only one I've got on my side is the bloodsucking lawyer!" She snorted at herself.

Frank said, "You mean the man at the corner booth Friday night?"

"Yeah, with the beard."

"That was Donnan MacLeod. You didn't know that was him? My God, girl." Frank turned to Henry and rolled his eyes.

Henry hid his reaction behind the menu and changed the subject. "I'll have the Bronco Breakfast. Please."

"You got it." Frank took the menu and started to the kitchen.

Henry stopped him. Knowing his question would sound odd, still he asked, "You, uh, have any pine nuts?"

Frank raised his chin and shot Henry a confused look, but said, "Yeah, we've got some that we garnish the trout with at dinner." He winked at RedMoon. "I'll hook you up."

And when Frank got back, Henry thought, he could tell Henry where he might be able to find this old friend of his—this, Donnan MacLeod.

DOWN THE STREET, in the empty parking lot of the Gardiner Shopping Plaza, Russell Hatfield's eighteen-wheeler rumbled loudly as it came to a stop just in front of the long, one-story building. His route the next few days would take him south to Salt Lake City, paralleling the western faces of the Teton Mountains, then west to Portland, Oregon to drop a load of coffee beans and bulk flour. He killed the engine, rolled down his window, put a cigarette in his thick lips and lit it. The brisk morning air quickly filled the cabin and was cold against his exposed skin, but his awareness was concentrated elsewhere. He glared at the double-door entrance to an office, the sign above reading: *Montana Republican HQ.* The windows were drowned out with red, white, and blue signs, most blazing the words: *Re-Elect Walters for Senate, Montana's Man.*

As he waited patiently, he thought about the long trip ahead. He knew that, yet again, he faced hours upon hours of stewing over the downturn his life had taken the last few years. After the divorce and restraining order, his ex-wife had moved her and Maddie here, thinking he wouldn't follow. *What a selfish bitch*, he thought as he eyed a picture on the dash of him and Maddie on a swing set together— his ex-wife scratched out of the photo.

He wanted so desperately to have Maddie back in his life, but there was no taking back the day he first laid his hands on his then-wife, nor the next two times. His temper had gotten the best of him when he discovered she had secretly been in contact with Jim *fucking* Walters, son of Republican Senator Monte Walters. Their love triangle had started at Stanford, where, if Russell hadn't assaulted Jim in class over a political dispute, Russell wouldn't have been expelled and probably wouldn't be sitting here behind the wheel of a tractor trailer as a means to earn his income.

His suspicion of her and Jim's hidden, but now open, relationship was verified by what he saw last month at a Senator Walters re-election celebration rally. Jim was there, with his pressed blazer, Lego-looking hair, silky smile, and his arm around her waist. To compound Russell's anger, Maddie was also there, huddling at Jim's leg.

Remembering the sight of his ex at the rally reciprocating to Jim a warm look that lasted too long, and Maddie playing with her doll that Jim probably bought her, Russell spit from his window. He turned his gaze back to the building to find a Cadillac SUV pulling into the lot. It parked in front of the republican HQ office. Russell flicked his butt through the open window, then quickly rolled it up, concealing himself inside the tinted windows.

Out of the SUV stepped Jim Walters in a long-sleeve shirt and tie, a leather satchel slung over one shoulder. Russell gritted his teeth. *"Fucking snake."*

Walters walked directly in front of the semi and flipped through his keyring as he approached the headquarters' door. Hatfield turned the ignition and revved his engine, causing Walters to jump and pivot. Russell chuckled as Walters tried looking through the tinted passenger window.

After shaking his head, the senator's son returned to unlocking the office door.

Russell threw the truck into gear and pulled on his air horn, without releasing it, dispatching a constant blow as loud as a cruise liner docking into port.

The refined, clean-shaved man lifted his shoulders and ducked his head. His satchel dropped to the snowy slush at his feet.

Russell bore down as he pulled away and forced a massive plume of black smoke out of his vertical exhaust pipes that trailed behind him and washed over Walters. He released the airhorn, then looked into his side mirror. It brought him displeasure that he couldn't see Walters inside the smoke, probably coughing, swearing, and gagging.

Next time I'll have my Camino, and I'll paint the pavement with your guts, he thought.

CHAPTER 20

KYLE WOKE TO the roar of a moving train.

Sitting up from a lying position, the deafening rumble overhead instantly pressed on his aching brain. He sat on a rocky surface, staring up at crisscrossing metal beams. After a moment he pieced it together—he was under a train bridge where it met a steep ravine slope. He looked down at his naked body and took in a sharp breath. He was covered in smears of congealed blood—again.

And again, he couldn't recall where he'd been or what he'd done.

Nicole. He remembered her voice. He heard her words, *Kyle, are you out here?*

Out where?

He suddenly remembered he'd been on the back deck of Mountain Lake Hotel. They had dinner. They were talking about Yellowstone.

Kyle searched his memory, but his mind was uncooperative, like trying to start an old sedan in the cold.

Putting his hands over his stomach, he suddenly felt nauseous. He noticed a lingering, metallic taste of blood at the back of his mouth, and it made him regurgitate violently. When he did, he nearly lost his footing and slipped into the gorge that the bridge stretched across.

A small, isolated ledge of earth was all that kept him from falling. How the *hell* did he get here?

Kyle wanted to yell for help, but the train was too loud. Besides, he knew he probably shouldn't yell for attention. The blood—*the goddamn blood*—what was it?

He ejected that line of thought and started to feel around for hand and footholds.

The train passed and silence returned.

Two exposed roots and three half-sunken boulders were just enough for him to grasp the support beams of the trestle and climb onto it.

When he stood on the bridge, all he could see in either direction was woodland mountainside.

He spotted a stream not far away and went to it, scrambling over a few boulders until he was at the bank. The blood came off easily in the clear water, washing downstream as ominous, scarlet clouds.

Something odd, though. This was February, wasn't it? The water should've been freezing.

Kyle splashed it on his face and chest again. There was nothing cold about it.

Another quick look around and Kyle gathered he was still in the Appalachians. That was just about all he could tell.

WHEN HE CAME upon the backside of a Big Lots department store, he recognized the outskirts of Blacksburg.

Kyle left the train tracks, descended the hillside, and snuck to the open bay at the back of the warehouse.

A crew of three workers had just finished their smokes and headed back inside, leaving Kyle free to pick through the overflow stock of jeans and flannel shirts. He snagged some underwear, a pair of boots, and socks as quick as he could.

Retreating behind a dumpster, he pulled on the jeans—too big, but wearable—then inspected his bare feet. The coarse granite nuggets and tarry planks of the tracks had been rough treading. The souls of his feet were red. However, he thought for sure he'd find them bleeding.

They didn't bleed, and they were oddly absent of pain.

PEELING A FLATTENED, mesh hat from the street, Kyle popped it open, bent the bill, and pulled it low over his eyes. He continued down the sidewalk, keeping his head down to avoid being recognized.

How did he know that blood wasn't someone else's? If he'd lost that much blood, shouldn't he feel weak? Or at least have a wound? On the contrary, he felt strong as ever—and it was as if he barely breathed, like he had the resting heart rate of an Olympic freestyle swimmer.

Hiding was his best plan of action until he could figure all this out. But where?

Kyle wandered the sidewalks of Blacksburg's outskirts, lost in thought as he stewed over last night and the Ashton event. They were too similar to be a coincidence. Why had they happened? What triggered them? He and Nicole were talking about Yellowstone right before this one happened—maybe that was it?

Maybe Nicole was right. Did he actually have PTSD from Annie's death on a deeper level of his subconscious?

No, that didn't fit. It didn't explain the randomness of the events, the hours-long blackouts, the blood . . .

Kyle read the next green road sign. Foxtrot Road—the long roadway that eventually passed through Nicole's neighborhood. It was probably another six miles, he estimated.

As he turned the corner, he noticed a newspaper stand. He read the headline: *Mother of Two Attacked, One Ranger Dead.*

Within the first lines of the article, Kyle read that police were looking for "twenty-three-year-old Kyle Fenn, who may be missing."

Kyle's heart stopped, and dread set in as he continued reading.

The article gave his description and a phone number to call with any information.

So, that was it—he could just come out of the shadows and everything would be all right. He was only a missing person.

He chewed the inside of his cheek.

He knew that wouldn't be possible.

They'd pin the murder on him for sure.

He kicked the ground. *Why can't I remember what happened?*

Kyle spotted a police car from the corner of his eye, ducked, and raised the collar of his flannel jacket as if a cold wind had gusted by.

Walking the opposite direction of the patrol car, he was haunted by his mother's recorded voice, telling him about Patty Feltner. Though there was no direct evidence that it was he who did anything to these people, there was no evidence that it wasn't.

I gotta get out of here, he thought.

Kyle needed to be some place he knew well, a place where the whole population didn't know him or wouldn't be searching for him.

He kept walking with his head down.

Kyle had problems—big problems. His mind reeled as he tried coming up with solutions. He could go into hiding, but for how long? He'd seen stories where killers change their identity and live for decades that way.

But could he really pull that off? Did he want to live like that?

This couldn't be happening.

That fucking cave. It was the start of all of this.

Kyle fumed.

You just had to go into that fucking cave, didn't you?

He said under his breath, "So now I'm some kind of *monster man* who goes and shreds people up and doesn't remember doing it. Ah, that's fucking great."

Kyle adjusted the bill of his hat, then rubbed his wrist apprehensively. "God *damn it.*"

Like a far echo, he suddenly heard his own words, *monster man.* He'd heard those words before. *Where?*

When he considered those alliterative words, he realized why they'd remained in his subconscious. The housekeeper he'd walked in on at Yellowstone Lake Hotel—she'd said those words with such a sarcastic expression that they never left his mind.

Then, Fenn stopped in his tracks.

Oh my God, what if . . . Kyle remembered the TV program playing in the room when he found the housekeeper, and the scientist guy that she was referencing. He recounted the man's ranting and the crowd booing him. He remembered his batshit-crazy Native American creature theories.

A hot wave rushed through Kyle's body and a prickly feeling arose around his neck. His theories, the cave, the bones, the fanged skull . . .

Kyle looked in the direction of Nicole's house and sighed shakily.

A storm of emotion turned inside him as he made his decision. He needed this man's council. It wasn't a decision composed of absolute certainty or calculated clarity—far from it. But the feeling in his gut told him it was the only course of action he had. And if worse came to worse, he knew the Yellowstone mountains, knew their seclusion could act as a buffer between him and others if need be.

He steeled his eyes, pushed himself the opposite direction of Nicole, and headed directly toward the nearest truck stop.

CHAPTER 21

"THAT'S ABSOLUTELY RIDICULOUS. Kyle would never hurt anyone! Much less, someone he's never met. And what about the fact that his clothes were found shredded up?! You ever consider Kyle is probably a victim too?"

Nicole sat with her arms crossed at her kitchen table, glaring at two Blacksburg police officers seated across from her. Her eyes were sunken in as she hadn't slept in days, only dozed off randomly for ten or twenty minutes at a time. It wasn't long ago that she'd ran out of tears from mourning her mother. The same happened now, and her eyes were red-rimmed and dry, her temper a tad more volatile during this grieving cycle than the last. It seemed, by some sick joke, her spiritual contentment had been replenished only to be stolen once again.

The two officers were an unimpressed duo: an older man with a gunfighter mustache and a younger, dark-eyed officer who was silent during the whole interview, watching Nicole's every expression.

The mustached officer replied, "Ms. Bowman, no one ever said Mr. Fenn killed Officer Bonner or his mare. Mr. Fenn hasn't officially been listed as a suspect, only as missing, and he certainly could be a victim. We're just trying—"

"You said the ranger's horse was found dead with its neck removed. What the hell is that?"

"Look, maybe it was attacked by a bear after—"

Nicole interrupted again, her words measured. "You're suggesting a park ranger got murdered by someone, then a bear happened to come along and kill his horse right after? You do know how asinine that sounds, right?"

The younger officer adjusted in his seat and inhaled, tightening his eyes on Nicole as he listened.

The older officer flipped through his small notepad, ignoring her rebuttal. He continued. "We received some information from Tennessee—from Ashton. You're aware Mr. Fenn is from Ashton, correct?"

"Yes."

"Turns out, the day you say Kyle showed up in Blacksburg looking 'upset,' was the same day a woman was found torn apart in an Ashton soybean field. They're still looking for her killer. A Patty Feltner. Ever heard of her?"

She looked to the ceiling quickly, then back at the man. She said sarcastically, "Nope."

"Had Kyle ever talked about Mrs. Feltner, to your recollection?"

"No. Of course not."

The mustached officer's eyes quickly surveyed the room before leveling back on Nicole. He asked, "You said your mother passed recently. How, may I ask? Was this before Kyle arrived in Virginia?"

Nicole's chest bounced with a laugh. "Are you fucking serious right now?"

No answer.

"Cancer. You dumbshits." Nicole's face was blank. She looked deep into their eyes, searching for a shred of intelligence in either of them.

Nicole said through her teeth, "Kyle was a good man. *Is* a good man! I don't know where he is, but I'm more than happy to let you know when I find out. He's got nothing to hide. He wouldn't have done any of this."

"Why did the woman and her kids get attacked in the parking lot approximately two minutes after you say you last saw Mr. Fenn? Where is he? Why can't we find him?"

"You think I don't ask myself the same questions?"

The younger officer finally spoke up. "Ms. Bowman. We'd like to ask you a little more about your relationship with Kyle."

Nicole glared at him. She thought, *I want to slap the smugness right off your fucking face.*

"You two were, eh, romantic, correct?"

"What exactly do you mean?"

"I just mean, you know, did you guys ever . . ." He waved his pen in circles in the air, waiting for her to answer without him going further.

"What the *hell* does that have to do with anything?"

She rocketed from her chair. "That's enough. We're done here."

The two hesitated.

"We're done here, I said. Get the hell out!"

The officers reattached their pens and notepads to their uniforms and begrudgingly left the house. When they stepped outside, Nicole watched through the window as they entered their vehicle. They'd been in this neighborhood before—the disgust was written all over their faces.

Nicole returned to the kitchen and let her heart settle. This was the second time they'd questioned her since the night Kyle went missing. She'd tried going back to the hotel and helping the victims' family members and acquaintances search for the attacker, but the police told her not to go anywhere near them. The untrusting glares from the victim's families had burned into her skin and she'd never felt more in danger. It wasn't fair—she'd lost someone, too.

Besides, the police were scouring the mountains and Blacksburg for him doggedly. Surely, he would turn up.

Then the thought returned to her—what if whoever killed the forest ranger and attacked that family had done something to Kyle?

The anxiety was almost crippling, and her heart thumped in her chest. She looked at her hands that quivered like she'd had too much coffee.

What was she supposed to do? She was helpless.

Nicole checked her cell phone yet again. No calls. She was sure Kyle had his when he'd walked off.

He did act funny as he left her at the dinner table, a little like the day he'd returned—off-kilter. And his eyes, they had been tinted yellow. *What the hell was that about?*

She found herself in doubt. Nicole had dated losers before and wondered how she could have been so naïve. Was this any different? Could he really be one of those maniacs on TV? Will she be on one of those shows one day, saying what a nice guy the killer was, like they always do, then talk about how he tried to kill her? Was he hiding out right now, lurking, waiting for her somewhere?

The frustrating thing of it all—nothing added up. There were no answers to all this.

Kyle's letters were still stacked on the shelf next to her, unopened. There must have been at least a dozen.

She curiously opened one.

As she read through his letter, a sorrowful pain squeezed her gut.

Kyle wrote about their hikes together, recalling specific trails and moments. He wrote about the time they'd woke in their tent on top of Electric Peak—instead of popping up to catch the sunrise, they'd simply stared into each other's eyes as the rising sun slowly illuminated the walls of the tent.

The next part made Nicole's heart sink.

He told her he'd missed her and talked about the days getting darker and colder. He compared the weather to his days without her.

Nicole covered her mouth and wanted to cry, but the well was dry.

Please be alive, just somewhere alive, please, she pleaded.

THE RESTAURANT KYLE sat in was adjoined to a rustic resort, tucked away into a mountain draw in Gallatin National Forest, Montana.

"Your Buckin' Bison Burger, sir." The waitress slid Kyle's plate in front of him. "Medium rare."

The greasy and scarlet juices from the processed buffalo meat seeped off the patty and into the thick French fries.

"Thank you, ma'am."

As she walked away, he dropped his fake smile and resumed his study of the bar-restaurant's guests.

In the last few days, Kyle had found that semi-truck drivers were quite generous. They seemed to be lonely folk, and talkative—too talkative. He had to repeat the same story about losing his family in a car accident, then using drugs and failing to hold down a job. His lie was that he had a dishwasher position waiting for him in Yellowstone. The truckers said they admired Kyle's determination against such terrible odds, his willingness to work. Two of the drivers on separate occasions even slipped him cash without him asking for it.

Four hops between trucks had brought him here, to Aspen Hot Springs Resort, just north of Gardiner, Montana. On the site were a historical inn, cabins, and other lodging. A hot swimming pool fed by natural hot springs was visible through a window behind the bar. A handful of swimmers padded up to the sliding window, ordered beers, and took them back into the pool area. The steam ghosted up from the water into the crisp mountain air as the guests sank in neck-deep.

He'd visited the comfortably rugged location before while working in Yellowstone and had found that it was a hot spot, not just for tourists, but for the few residents of Paradise Valley—those who lived further outside Gardiner along the north-running interstate. Kyle remembered the housekeeper telling him that Dr. Donnan MacLeod lived in Paradise Valley the day he stumbled into her and her coworker slacking on the job.

Monster man. Those words repeated in his head.

Kyle needed an answer for what was happening to him. If anyone could explain Kyle's apparent curse, it would be Dr. Donnan MacLeod.

Kyle was still unsure about how to approach the learned professor even if he found him— *Excuse me, sir, I think a Native spirit in a lakeshore cave hexed me and it might have caused me to kill people. Can you help me?* He would have to trust on his life that Dr. MacLeod would help without going to the authorities.

Kyle wondered if he had the nerve to force the ex-professor to help. If it meant ever getting back to Nicole, perhaps he would do whatever he had to. Imagining what she was going through right now ate at Kyle. It was all he could do to suppress those speculations, along with the possibility that he really was the one who murdered Patty Feltner and a Virginia forest ranger.

Kyle's trucker hat was low over his eyes. He did his best to keep the unease from showing on his face, though his eyes continually searched the establishment and his hands were restless. He hoped there was nothing unusual about his appearance, except maybe that he was alone.

The sounds and aromas of his surroundings were oddly heightened and vivid to him. The scent of cash in the bar's register when it opened, someone's strong, flowery deodorant emanating from the kitchen, a musty scent rising up from the floor, perhaps from a crawlspace or basement. Even the scent of evergreens and gasoline from the few cars outside all mingled within his nasal cavity.

He could hear the otherwise-silent sprinkle of sand-like beads of silicone players were dropping on the table shuffleboard game in the back of the bar room area. A hissing noise came from beneath a bus as it parked, making Fenn turn his head. Outside and across a lawn, a wedding party held rehearsals, and a small girl hummed the notes that accompany the swaying lyrics, *Here comes the bride*. Kyle whispered to himself nervously, "All dressed in white."

Kyle took a large bite of the buffalo burger. After he swallowed, he dropped the sandwich back to the plate. He thought seeing a fresh burger and fries would reignite his lost appetite. It didn't.

He pushed the plate aside and pondered his next move carefully. He'd need to decide whom to make small talk with and how to make his way to MacLeod in conversation. Kyle measured which patrons looked to be locals, zeroing in on those who looked friendly and gregarious.

Suddenly, Kyle heard someone using Dr. MacLeod's name at the bar.

"He told me he'd be back after a while. He said he's got another speech to give over at Missoula—a real big one." Two men watched the aged bartender as he spoke.

A gentleman in overall bibs and a white Bullhide cowboy hat replied, "That man is always getting called up. There's always some important dig or something he's leaving us for. I don't believe he'll ever *actually* retire."

The always-informed bartender tossed his dish towel over his shoulder. "I guess that's the price you pay when you're as important as Donnie—when you're that smart." He lowered his voice secretively, "And when you make enough money to live in one of them *castles* out on Antelope Loop like him, I guess work comes first."

Kyle laid cash on the table.

He walked into the main lobby, plucked a visitor's map from a wide, wooden pamphlet display, then slipped out the door.

THAT NIGHT, WALKING in the dark seemed unusually comfortable to Kyle.

After a five-mile road hike from the resort and a mile walk down Antelope Loop, Kyle had spotted the estate's entrance, which had real flame lamps casting light up to the arching bronze letters: "MacLeod's Getaway."

MacLeod's property was still and silent in this secluded spot, and not a single light was on, inside or out.

Kyle moved like a cat around the garage and to the back porch. Creeping along the sprawling patio, he gently tested the back door.

It was locked.

A steel grill, however, helped Kyle climb to a small kitchen window that was unlocked.

He crawled through head first onto the sink and quietly shut the window behind him. Crouching on the marble countertop, he was taken aback by the lavish living room that opened up from the kitchen. Moonlight shot through the large windows and stretched across the wide lounge.

Kyle sat motionless and allowed his senses to survey the entire house like a barn owl in a hayloft.

The house was dead quiet.

He found a light switch and flipped it on, illuminating the impressive sight of contemporary wooden and granite interior. He'd never been inside a home so lavish. He flinched, though, when he noticed the taxidermized eyes of a mounted bobcat glinting at him. His gaze went from one mule deer head to the next, to the bull moose over the fireplace, to a triangular bison head with empty, dark eyes, in a succession of frozen animals that seemed endless.

Kyle ignored the feeling of being watched by the mounted beasts and focused on the task at hand.

He dropped from the countertop quietly and began to snoop.

It took Kyle more than thirty minutes to explore every room on each of the two floors, which were separated into two wings. In his modest upbringing, he'd never seen such wealth.

Though he'd confirmed the house was empty, he couldn't help but sense that something was off. He could detect an air of negativity hanging in the home, like smoke from an unseen house fire. The feeling gave him chills as he slowly opened each door.

Each room and hallway had some form of Native American artifact. He found authentic-looking arrows displayed in a guest bathroom and a decorative parka-like garment made of animal hide in a sunroom. Throughout the house were framed black and white photos of Native Americans sitting upright and sober, or standing in fields showcasing their rifles and horses.

In the master bedroom was an apparently cherished possession—a long head dress encased in a glass cabinet, alongside a spear decorated with feathers and dangling leather strips that reminded Kyle of Stephen Tyler's microphone stand. He thought it interesting that the king-sized bed of the master bedroom was only untucked at one corner, where just one person had slept. Kyle thought that surely MacLeod must have a wife, a lady friend, or even a male friend—somebody to share all this with.

When he eventually made his way through the second floor of the second wing, he found a small set of stairs that led up to a room by itself—a study.

By the looks of the study, Kyle assumed this was where Dr. MacLeod must have spent most of his hours when at home. A stuffed golden eagle with its wings wide and beak open, frozen in an expression of anger, commanded one side of the room. Below it was a broad desk with a dichotomy of items modern and classic: an early-nineteenth-century paraffin lamp, a USB multi-card reader, an antique cigar box, a Dell printer, a double handled Grecian jar, a hand-held magnetometer. Loose and untidy sheets of paper littered the desk. Boxes, placed sporadically about, contained rolled maps standing vertically on end. The study had an altogether refined appearance to it, like it could be the home office of Professor Indiana Jones, save the numerous stained coffee mugs and whiskey glasses scattered around.

The most peculiar items Kyle discovered were a projector reel and a file cabinet with wheels of film scrupulously labeled. The reel loaded onto the projector was labeled *Family Dynamics and Oral Tradition. Yellowstone Indian Interviews. May, 1911. (7 of 33)*. He flipped the projector's power switch on, and it started to operate, filling the room with a fast, mechanical flapping sound.

Kyle walked across the chocolate-colored wood floor and turned off the light.

On a bare wall was the black and white moving image of an elderly Native woman sitting at a table, her eyes cast down at her leathery hands. A young Native man was next to her, wearing an ironed shirt, vest, and tie. On the other side of the table, a white man with glasses at the end of his long nose spoke to her and took notes. " . . . and your great-grandfather, your grandfather—the men in the family—what role did they play in raising the children?"

As the Native man translated to the woman, the film showed the signs of its age, with vertical slivers appearing on the image and crackles in the audio.

When the woman finished her reply to the young man, he turned to the interviewer and said, "She says the men, going very far back, were simply warriors and hunters. A father took his young boy on the hunts. He taught him to make weapons and to process animals. These things he would teach him at a very young age. These things he did not teach to the daughters, only the boys."

"I see." The spectacled man jotted on a notepad in a very stiff manner. "Okay, tell me about tribal conflict. Can you tell me anything about warring tribes around Yellowstone? Maybe some stories handed down . . . "

The young man translated the interviewer's questions to the woman.

Her silver hair lay in a long braid over her chest, and she kept her eyes down when she made her response.

The translator spoke. "She says, once, when she was a child, her great-grandmother told her about a tradition. During each big moon, her great-grandmother's elders took all the children in close between large fires. They made great fires in a circle on these nights and did not leave until the sun had returned. They would tell the children great tales about the beast-men from long ago. The elders warned them about these creatures and told them to never forget."

The white man exhaustedly rubbed his eyes under his spectacles, looking exasperated. This was clearly not the answer he wanted. He replied, "No, I'm sorry. I wasn't clear. What I meant was, did your tribe fight with another tribe over territory, that you know of?"

The interviewer paused as he saw the woman look up at him. She had read his body language perfectly clear and looked just as fed up with the interviews as he. When she answered, her tone had stiffened. Her eyes had the glare of a grandmother scolding a foolish child.

The translator spoke for her. "The beast-men were spirit creatures, man eaters. They were created by the tribes to kill other tribes, and there were great battles. Many brave men fought and died protecting their people. She has never seen these things herself, but she believes the myths. This was very long ago."

Suddenly, the refrigerator's ice maker somewhere downstairs released a fresh batch of ice that startled Kyle and made his heart race.

He stopped the projector and sat at MacLeod's wide desk with his elbows on the leather arm rests. He steepled his fingers under his chin and stared at the film on its wheel. By the looks of what he'd just seen, Dr. MacLeod was, in fact, the man Kyle was looking for. Fenn decided now that if he had to force MacLeod to help, he would. He'd come too far, and he would do whatever it took to rid himself of this obvious curse.

Yes, Kyle told himself, *a curse. An obvious one indeed.*

Subconsciously, he'd just agreed that Patty Feltner and the park ranger weren't just murdered; they were taken by a beast, a beast just like the ones the old woman spoke of—the beast that Kyle had surely become. Kyle, in this moment, finally held a light to that suppressed realization, that subconscious knowledge that he was, indeed, a monster.

Even after traveling all this way, clear across the country, searching for the man who could help Kyle with his problem, Kyle had never definitively admitted to himself that this was real.

For some reason, Kyle's high school baseball coach came to mind. He remembered his coach's lecture one day about why players cry when they lose a big game. He'd said athletes cry when they lose a huge contest because they experience an identity crisis—they'd assumed, to a certain degree, that they were to be champion this whole time, and now they suddenly weren't. It was the sudden change in identity that caused the intense emotion.

An identity crisis, yes, but this was no game, and Kyle didn't find the tears.

He broke into a cold sweat. A powerful chill ran through his body and he felt he wanted to puke all over MacLeod's desk. He tucked his arms around his mid-section, feeling like he'd just fell through a sheet of ice.

He shook as he considered his victims. "Those people."

Kyle jolted up and paced around.

He walked over to the stuffed eagle and took in its angry expression. The bird of prey, the fierce predator, seemed to transfer a word to him: *Welcome.*

At the sink of the study's bathroom, Kyle filled a glass with water. As he drank it, he opened the mirror cabinet and combed through its contents: some ibuprofen, shaving items, and not much more.

He threw the ibuprofen down his throat with another gulp of water and splashed water on his face.

Kyle closed the mirror and studied his reflection for a moment, letting his heart rate slow. This was the face that was splashed all over the news in Virginia. They must have questioned Nicole about that night. She was the last person he remembered being with before his blackout and apparent murder. He sighed nervously at the thought of how much Nicole must be hurting right now. He couldn't contact her for his own safety—and for hers, if he really was this unpredictable killer.

But what triggered his monster? He couldn't put the pieces together.

Where was MacLeod? He needed him *now*.

Kyle yelled, "MacLeod! Dr. Donnan MacLeod! I need to talk to you. It's a matter of life and death!"

He waited a few beats.

His new ultra-hearing told him again that he was alone.

After a moment of thought, another realization hit him. Even if the professor could somehow banish the evil in him, Kyle Fenn could no longer be Kyle Fenn, not in this world.

He removed his hat and placed his hands over the crown of his head. He pictured himself with a burred haircut.

John.

Kyle rolled his eyes—too simple. "Okay . . . Kevin."

No, it can't start with a "K," he mused.

Hello, my name is Sam. Hey, I'm Sam. Nice to meet you, I'm Sam . . . McGillicudy.

McGillicudy? Seriously?

All right, Sam . . . Harris.

As he greeted his new self in the mirror, he noticed his eyes had a strange appearance.

He looked closer.

An eerie yellow color surrounded his pupils, intruding on his green irises. He reached for the light switch, turned it off, and dared to look in the mirror.

In the pitch black, Sam Harris saw his glowing yellow eyes looking back at him, piercing into his soul.

CHAPTER 22

MACLEOD WAS SCHEDULED to speak third.

The conference on Native American Archaeology and Heritage, hosted by The Archaeological Institute of the Americas at the University of Montana, started in twenty minutes. MacLeod was dressed in a tuxedo, resting in his ForeRunner in a parking lot outside a massive brick building with a clock steeple. The clock loomed over a columned and recessed entryway. A bronze grizzly statue was centered in the quad atop a concrete platform—the bear carried a heavy layer of snow on its back as it climbed daunting terrain. In its preserved pose, the creature looked back over its shoulder in MacLeod's direction, like Medusa had caught its attention.

MacLeod sneered at the ferocious beast, then tipped back his flask.

He'd made up his mind. He would release the RedMoon name in his lecture and uncover their dirty little secret. Once he was done, Wyoming law enforcement authorities would have their answers to unsolved murders and missing-people cases in the counties surrounding Dunoir, Wyoming, and cause for questioning the RedMoons. And with how much wealth their land contained in gemstone and oil, local connections and big wigs would be more than happy in seeing to their demise.

Donnan knew several scenarios could play out, all of which would benefit him and thrust him into celebrity and wealth. Authorities could force a confession out of one of them—likely a young one. The RedMoons would resist, only further insinuating their guilt. Investigators could obtain their DNA and match them to the murders, or the RedMoons could lawyer-up, in which case they'd have to enter a plea of temporary insanity as the evidence would be stacked so high against them, one could climb it and see all the way to Scotland.

The RedMoons were powerful, but for only one day a month. They were no match for bloodthirsty prosecutors and the firepower of the Wyoming State Police.

And above all, Donnan knew, this was how he got Sherri back.

She'd leave her job in Yellowstone, come crawling back to him, lusting for his newfound fortune and glory. He'd be at his house in Paradise Valley this summer, her teal-colored Volvo returned to its proper place in his garage, TV crews knocking at his front door while he and Sherri made love, rolling around on a bed of cash.

MacLeod found a pep in his step when he exited his SUV and strolled across the parking lot. Leaving his leather-bound notebook of Wahota-RedMoon research on the front passenger seat, he knew there was no need for it—all the information was there in his brilliant head. He nearly skipped his way toward the academic building, whistling and snapping his fingers. The frigid air of the Missoula sky was cold enough to freeze him like the grizzly statue, but he was warm with anticipation.

Midway through the lot, MacLeod quickly came to a stop. He'd gotten so good at repressing one particular memory that he hadn't even realized he was walking right past it.

How could he have forgotten? This was the same conference building where it happened.

MacLeod's heavy breath billowed from his face. His sallow eyes were fixed on the white stripes of the parking spaces. His gaze ran across the spaces and stopped at one beneath a light pole. Her teal Volvo was there, though only in his mind.

He gasped.

His mind replayed the event, in vivid detail—the shirtless valet driver laying over his Sherri, visible through the smears on the fogged window, smears being made by the soles of Sherri's feet.

The pure rage that he'd felt in that instant hit him again.

Then he remembered how his rage was crushed by what he had heard next—Sherri's moan. It wasn't one of pain, but of pleasure, and the sound shot through him again like a slug to the chest.

He collapsed to the pavement, landing directly on his tailbone.

"No. God, no."

AN HOUR AND a half after Donnan had dragged himself back to his truck and finished his fifth of Glenlivet, he stumbled into the auditorium.

A Native American couple were on stage. Members of the audience stepped up to a microphone located in the vomitorium between the first and second tiers and presented questions about Native American heritage and lifestyle. The couple took turns giving scholarly answers about what measures are being taken to address current indigenous issues, like poverty levels and depression.

Donnan swayed in the back entrance, listening, his eyebrows drawn together.

"Funding," the woman answered when asked about underlying problems with crime rates on reservations. "Plain and simple. It is reported by the National Institute of Justice that tribes only receive fifty-five to seventy-five percent of the resource base available to non-Indian communities, yet crime rate in Indian Country is between double and triple the national average for comparable communities. A comparable community by crime rate would be, say, Detroit or New York City, where there are four to seven officers per thousand citizens. There are few departments in Indian Country that have ratios of more than two officers per thousand. These disparities are astronomical, so you can see how funding is certainly at the root of the issues of crime, violence against women, and drug use among Native communities."

MacLeod shouted from the back, "Violence against women? Who says they don't ask for it?"

After a few strides down the descending walkway, MacLeod's coordination gave under his gathering speed, and he toppled face-first onto the thin, red carpeting.

The crowd stirred.

Pushing himself up carefully and finding his feet, Donnan pointed at the stage and bellowed, "You *women* are the scourge of the Earth." He continued forward, shouting, "Clear the stage, you blithering bawbags. The world is mine now."

A man wearing suspenders stepped in front of MacLeod, but met Donnan's right hook.

The man's legs buckled, and he hit the floor.

So did MacLeod.

To pull himself up, MacLeod placed his outstretched hand on a seated woman's breast.

After a quick scramble, he stood over the woman.

She shrieked in horror. To MacLeod's surprise, the woman smacked him across his bearded face.

Donnan smiled. "Well, aren't you a bonnie l'il lassie."

He dropped his trousers, raised his arms, and twirled his hips.

FIVE HUNDRED MILES south, Sid RedMoon's silver, flowing hair glowed in the shadows of a cave as he walked around the outside of a large circle of fires.

The cave was formed by an underground river, ages ago, where the flow had bottlenecked, hitting a less weatherable igneous layer before continuing through its crevasses. It resulted in a hollowed-out area large enough to play basketball in. This area was special to the RedMoons, a part of the land their family had to strive and struggle to own a few decades ago, despite having been there for centuries.

Inside the fire circle, more than sixty RedMoons were seated on another circle of boulders, facing each other. Sid spoke to them in the Wahota language as he casually circled the other side of the flames. His arm was draped over Phoenix's shoulders. "Just as the mother hawk soars over its nest, protecting its young ones, I walk the Wahota Circle and protect those within, with claw and blood. I bring the newest Wahota under my wing to the safety of our tribe."

His voice carried across the cave and bounced off the walls, which were hidden in the darkness. The firelight illuminated a ring of stalactites on the cave roof, making their moist surfaces glisten.

When Sid and Phoenix reached an entrance to the fire circle, Wymon handed Sid a burning torch.

Sid said, "We celebrate this day with our hearts. Today, a Wahota is no longer a cub. This day, I announce that a Wahota has earned his seat within the family."

Sid led Phoenix into the circle of family members to a mound of kindling and wood. The patriarch tossed the torch in, and the mound ignited, throwing light onto the cave walls and on the black-eyed faces of the family members, including the steely-eyed Wymon, his wife and other two children, and the bear-sized Vic with his wife and daughter. The other eight RedMoon subfamilies were Sid's younger siblings, cousins, and their offspring.

Standing behind Phoenix, Sid had his palms on the boy's shoulders. Phoenix stared absently into the fire. Sid said, "I present to all of you, with pride, a true Wahota, Phoenix RedMoon." Then, he whispered in Phoenix's ear. "You make me proud, Grandson."

Phoenix visited each member from inside the circle, exchanging hugs and handshakes with his kin. As he passed previous honorees of this ritual, they exchanged the words: "With claw and blood."

The greetings and exchanges between Phoenix and his family weren't celebratory at all, as Sid had just proclaimed. They were stiff, quiet, sheepish. Family members conducted themselves rigidly, as if they were being held at gunpoint. No one raised their voice too high, and their wary eyes rarely left Sid.

Once every family member had congratulated Phoenix, Sid said almost smiling, "It was at this time in the ceremony where our ancestors would eat from a roast of *gwich'in*. I think next time we shall have some."

The family gathered in front of Sid in a half-circle.

He walked over to a group of children and tickled one little girl's belly. Sid made pretend-antlers on the top of his head with his fingers and said, "*Gwich'in* . . . reindeer meat."

Returning to the big fire, his stone face returned. He glared at the adult members. "But, a lot of you never knew that. Too much of our past has been swept away, thanks to the lack of leadership amongst the families. We grow ever closer to assimilation with the white man, and I have become unsettled by it. The Wahota way of life is disappearing."

Sid approached Phoenix and stroked his head. "That is why I reinstated this sacred tradition after Father's death, this sacred honor that Phoenix, here, will hold for the rest of his life."

The patriarch returned to the big fire and began to bite off his words. "It is *shameful* that few of you have even heard the word '*gwich'in*' spoken. One Wahota word at a time, one tradition at a time, the leaders of our households have become complacent and corrupt. Knowledge of our forefathers is vanishing within our own ranks. We have a power that sets us apart from the rest of the world. Face it. You cannot deny that the Wahota blood is superior. Yet, you care not?"

He shook his head and gazed into the fire. He clasped his hands behind his back, and said, "From this day, I will decide who will be taught English. A Wahota child will be taught Wahota. I hope to see, in my lifetime, every Wahota speaking proper Wahota, and naming their children as such. I decree the same for our children's education. I will decide who needs an education from the outsiders and who does not."

Wymon and Vic kept their eyes on the ground.

Sid said, "These are things we will change. It is obvious I have been too lenient. As you know, Henry, my own son, has *betrayed* his family. He has opened my eyes to the lack of discipline under my leadership."

He snapped at them, "Henry is not to return. And should anyone, from this day on, decide to leave, they will be hunted and taken from this world. That is my decree."

CHAPTER 23

AT THE END of a second-floor hallway, in the east wing of Donnan MacLeod's mountain manor, a closet door opened, and Kyle stepped out, sleepy-eyed. The stairway over the door led up to the only third floor living space—MacLeod's study.

Fenn rubbed his face, then stood still.

He methodically turned his head to the sides, then up and down. *No one home. Big surprise*, he thought.

It had been eighteen days, and still no sign of MacLeod. Kyle had strategically chosen the wide stairwell closet for his sleeping space. If MacLeod came home in the middle of the night, he would likely head for his study, and Kyle would hear his footsteps. Also, the only way out of the study, besides the stairs, was out the third-story window, which meant MacLeod would be cornered.

Kyle went through his routine sweep of the house. Once he cleared every room, he ambled into the kitchen and poured himself some orange juice.

Looking out the window, Kyle sighed. Where was this man? How long would he have to wait? With as much money as MacLeod apparently had, he could be gone for the winter, posted up in some beachside condo, for all Kyle knew.

To pass his time, Kyle had spent most of his days rooting through MacLeod's study, learning about indigenous civilizations in North America—everything from how they fashioned hunting weapons, to average lifespan, to their agricultural practices. Not once, however, did Kyle find anything about "beast-men."

Other parts of his day were spent hiking along the mountainside that overlooked MacLeod's property. The view let him survey any vehicles approaching and gave him a better perspective of the house's dimensions. But most importantly, it let him feel like he'd gotten away from his problems, if only for a few hours. The air up there was magical. Up there he could feel Yellowstone, its valleys and peaks, somehow calling to him. There, he felt like all he had to do was hike through the mountain pass and disappear into the wild, leaving every worry behind.

Instead, he was stuck. He had terrible issues to resolve but was spinning his wheels, getting nowhere.

Worst of all, he thought as he looked out the kitchen window, was the state Nicole must be in. Did she mourn for him, thinking he was dead somewhere? Or did she think he was a murderer? He wished he had some kind of access to the Blacksburg local news, but he couldn't log into MacLeod's home computer and the news on his television was either world news or news about black angus cattle auctions in southwestern Montana. If he could just reach her, he'd tell her everything was all right.

He couldn't take it any longer. He said aloud, "Screw it."

Kyle grabbed the cordless phone from the wall. He looked at the keypad, took a deep breath, and dialed Nicole's number.

THE PHONE WAS ringing when Nicole pushed through the front door with Cujo by her side. "Hold on, hold on."

She dropped Cujo's leash, shut the door, and moved quickly to the kitchen phone. She transferred a staple gun from her right hand to her left.

She picked up. "Hello?"

Someone was on the line but didn't say anything. After a few seconds, they hung up.

"Hello?"

Rolling her eyes, she huffed in frustration. She wanted to kick herself for not having a caller ID installed on the house phone.

Cujo swiped past her and slurped at his water bowl.

After she set the staple gun on the table, she unzipped her coat and pulled out a stack of papers emblazoned with the word "MISSING." Kyle's face grinned from the top of the sheets. She'd cropped herself out of a photo where they stood side by side, the Grand Canyon of Yellowstone in the background, a few osprey visible as black specks within the sweeping canyon. He had a wide smile beneath his Red Sox hat, and his hair was lifted slightly behind his ears by the canyon breeze.

Nicole picked up the phone again and dialed.

"West Side Marriot, how may I assist you today?"

"Could I speak to room three twelve please?"

"One moment."

Nicole removed her coat with the phone cradled in the crook of her neck.

A woman answered. "Hello?"

"It's me," Nicole said.

"Hey, Nicole. How are you?" The woman's voice was weak.

"Oh, don't worry about me. I just wanted to check in on you. I just got in. I think I've got the entire east side covered. That just leaves the south. I'll start on that tomorrow."

"Bless you, Nicole."

"How you holdin' up?"

"As good as can be expected," the woman said.

"You keep your head up. I know it's got to be hard. It's hard enough on me, but you're his mother—I just can't imagine. We'll find him, okay? I promise. He'll show up. I know it."

"Thank you, dear. You're incredible. We appreciate everything you're doing."

"I wouldn't have it any other way."

"So, we decided on next Tuesday. If there's nothing by then, we'll be going back to Tennessee. All of our friends have been searching there, and we'll join in with them."

"Okay. Well, I don't want to take up your time. And Cujo's looking at me like he's hungry. I'll let you go, okay? I'll let you know when I'm done with the next round."

As Nicole said goodbye and hung up, the emptiness of the house bore down on her once again. She sat at the kitchen table and looked at Kyle's letters there. Nicole had been reading and rereading them to make it seem he was there, to help keep her positive. She'd also laid out every picture she had of him, looking at them every morning and night.

Nicole bit her lip as a thought crossed her mind.

Pulling a notebook from the shelf, she sat at the table and wrote back to him.

Words flowed from her pen, every emotion, every thought—she got it all out. She wrote of her regret for not letting him come to Virginia with her, for not stopping him before he walked away at the Mountain Lake Hotel dining room. She wrote about the flyers she'd been putting up and how she chose her favorite picture of him to use, about how much she missed him, about how much she cries, about meeting his mother and father who came to help look for him, about how great it will be when they find him lost but okay in the woods, and about the house they would buy together. Nicole wrote about how she couldn't imagine loving someone else as much as she did Kyle.

She wrote, *When we find you, will you marry me?*

CHAPTER 24

KYLE SAT IN the booth by the biggest window, gazing out from the quiet Green Goose Saloon in Gardiner. On the other side of the glass rose the landmark arch that marked Yellowstone's north entrance. From his seat, Fenn could see the arch quite clearly. The fifty-foot-tall stone monument stood as a majestic invitation to visitors—a stalwart structure that, through more than a hundred unforgiving winters, had stood proud, offering Theodore Roosevelt's words, *FOR THE BENEFIT AND ENJOYMENT OF THE PEOPLE*, engraved across its crown. The March sun sank and patiently took with it the lighter tans from the arch's basaltic boulders. Its hefty and rugged, yet dignified appearance was appropriately suggestive of the two million acres of protected land that waited behind it.

Kyle had hiked his way into Gardiner from Donnan MacLeod's house. On this day, he felt particularly edgy. Multiple weeks of staring at the walls of the professor's home had driven him into town for some normalcy. He would have to stay low-key, but it would be worth it if it could remedy his cabin fever. Plus, he wanted to find a non-descript postcard to send to Nicole. Maybe he could tell her something only the two of them would know, let her know he was okay, that he was working things out, and that it was he who called her and hung up. Her voice had filled him with a bit of hope, knowing she was all right. It also fueled his yearning to find MacLeod quickly.

He meant to get up and leave the saloon an hour ago, but he felt drawn to the window, and had forgotten about finding a postcard. A strong desire to be inside Yellowstone pulled at him, and he couldn't place why. It was more than just nostalgia. It had only been three months since he fled Yellowstone, and he was now back at its doorstep feeling somehow summoned back in.

He stoked an old memory in his head from when he worked in the park—on one of his first nights there, after picking up a calzone from the employee pub, he heard his first elk bugle on his walk home to his dormitory. The scent of the pine sap and buffalo droppings would accompany those walks through the forested trail. He recalled how the buffalo excrement had such smooth consistency that it created a perfect circle on the ground, like big buffalo crap pancakes.

Suddenly, Kyle broke into a cold sweat as an odd feeling rushed through him. His vision of the arch through the window faded in and out, like a camera struggling to focus.

But just as quickly as they appeared, the unusual sensations passed.

Kyle shook his head and rubbed his eyes. After a moment, he walked to the jukebox and searched the listings for something to lighten the mood, something to distract him. He dropped in the coins and punched in A206: Johnny Cash, *Folsom Prison Blues*.

He caught his reflection on the machine—the burr haircut he'd given himself with MacLeod's beard trimmer this morning and his grown beard did well at concealing his identity.

Before he could step away, the machine started. It played the wrong song. With an old cowpoke rhythm, *Shame on the Moon* by Bob Seger filled the old saloon. Kyle pursed his lips and smacked the machine.

"Whatever," Kyle said.

As he took up a stool at the bar, he noticed another bargoer; a large man with long, blonde hair, two stools from him.

The bartender greeted the man, "And how are you, Mr. Hatfield?"

The burly man raised a pointed finger. "What the fuck did I tell you?"

The bartender made an ugly face and inhaled through his teeth. "Shit, sorry."

The irked man ordered a draft beer, then looked at Kyle. He asked gruffly, "Hey. What's up with you?"

"What? Me? Nothin's up." Kyle adjusted a coaster in front of him, and made an effort to conceal his edginess. He chuckled and tried to lead the man into a more light-hearted exchange. "Why? What's uh . . . What's up with you?"

"You look nervous." He paused and engaged Kyle with a cold expression. "That makes me nervous."

"Look, man, I'm just here for a beer. All right?"

The man examined Kyle, starting at his feet and working his way up. Seeming pleased with his assessment that the smaller and unarmed Kyle wasn't a threat, he smiled and replied, "All right, Bud. I'm just fuckin with ya."

The blonde-haired man grabbed two peanuts and cracked the shells on the bar top with the meat of his hand. "What you doing in Gardiner? Don't think I've seen you before."

It hadn't crossed Kyle's mind what he would say if he were asked that question. "What am I doing in Gardiner? Well, I'm up, there's—I just, moved here."

He did his best to sell it. "I'm Sam."

They shook hands, and peanut-shell debris transferred to Kyle's palm.

Kyle nodded toward a pool table in the corner sitting under a hanging Rainier Beer lamp. "How about some pool?"

The man perked up. "You shoot for cash?"

"I would if I had some."

"Tell me about it."

BY THE END of the third game, the two had become good company. Kyle, after being secluded for a month, just needed someone to hang around with and to be a normal person again. Although the man had given Kyle sidelong glances the entire time, he had loosened up and even told him his name was Russell. Kyle put forth a story of being an insurance salesman—something he thought wouldn't interest Russell and lead to further inquiry.

The man also seemed to keep his own secrets, not telling him what he did for a living or much of anything else, except that he wasn't allowed to see his daughter enough. Kyle had the sense that, for the sake of a good time, both of them decided to accept each other for who they said they were and just enjoy some billiards and a beer.

Of course, it wouldn't have been a proper pool game if nothing were wagered.

Cigarettes were the price for Kyle's three losses. The antique cigarette machine was right outside the bar.

Russell sarcastically got the door for Kyle. "That'll be a big ol' pack of Marlboro Reds, thank you."

As they stepped outside, Kyle noticed the town was hushed. If it had been summer, like the last time he'd visited the town en route to Aspen Hot Springs, there would still have been a fair amount of traffic, more busy restaurants, western wear stores, and souvenir shops ringing up their final customers. But this time it was cold and desolate—there were no bustling crowds of travelers, and the citizens of Gardiner were settled in.

The saloon was at the town's edge, facing the moonlit beginnings of Yellowstone's vastness, like looking out into the enormity of an ocean from the shore. The full moon spread its glow over the park's northern ranges, highlighting the white snowcaps of the highest peaks. Somewhere in Yellowstone, Kyle thought, large beasts roamed the gray night, daring not to venture near gurgling mud pots or the geysers spraying up at the star-filled sky.

Among the sleepy silence, Kyle heard a flashing traffic light as it clicked and buzzed rhythmically.

"Yoo-hoo. Sam." Russell pulled his last cigarette from his pack. He gestured at the cigarette machine. "You going to settle up or just stare at the park?"

"Right, my bad."

Russell took a few steps away from Kyle and peered down the street as he smoked. "So, Sam. I gotta say, for a guy who sells insurance, how is it you don't have any money to bet on pool? Or are you just smart enough not to bet on yourself?"

Hatfield chuckled at his own wittiness and continued, "You should come out to Boiling River with me one night. We can hit on these two foreign chicks that are always skinny dippin' there."

Russell turned his head back to Kyle. "Sam?"

Kyle leaned on a blue U.S. Postal Service receptacle with both hands, grunting with pain. It was happening—again.

He raised his head to the sky.

The moon. It was the full moon.

The old woman from the projector film had said "on every big moon." *Of course! How could he have been so stupid?*

Kyle growled, "No! Get away from me. Run! *Now.*"

When he said the word "now," Kyle's bottom jaw jutted out with a *crack*. Sharp claws protracted from his fingertips, slicing into the metal container.

"What the *fuck?*" Russell backpedaled and reached for his pistol under his jacket. It was stuck.

MacLeod's jeans and collared shirt shredded off Kyle's body as he grew rapidly. His arms lengthened like long tree branches, and thin black hair sprouted over his body. Fangs and teeth jutted from Kyle's wide, steel trap of a mouth. His form arched its back and writhed as its legs extended.

The beast bent forward, placing its knuckles on the sidewalk.

It regarded Russell with rage, and snapped its jaws, like a crocodile warning a wildlife handler.

It lunged.

With one strike, slicing its claws diagonally across Russell's face and chest, it dropped Hatfield. It pinned Russell to the concrete and bit into his thigh. Hatfield tried to scream, but the creature placed its wretched hand over his mouth.

For a moment, it looked around alertly, its triangular ears independently rotating.

Hatfield's blood streamed onto the sidewalk from his leg. His eyes rolled back, and he went limp.

The wolf-man gripped Russell's ankle and dragged him down the sidewalk.

Hatfield's other leg folded underneath him as he was pulled along. His head bounced off the sidewalk cracks, then the curb as it hauled him into the darkness—away from the lights of Gardiner.

CHAPTER 25

WITHIN A COPSE of hunter-green Douglas fir forest that ran up a mountain draw, Russell Hatfield came to.

He let out a groan of agony, causing a hen grouse to flap away in half flight.

He lay beneath a foot of snow, chunks of granite and rhyolite, branches, and heaves of earth that were a combination of pine needles, pinecones, and frigid dirt.

With a powerful grunt, he pushed the debris away from his face, and reached out onto the snow-sprinkled ground. Gradually, he began to pull himself free.

He stopped halfway and rolled to his back. He placed his big hands over his forehead and winced. Another groan and he crawled his way out of the shallow and hastily dug grave.

Looking at the sky, Russell felt the side of his face. His hand traced the slash wound that ran from the top of his head, down the side of his goatee, across his collarbone, then chest.

As he sat up, he shivered violently and looked downhill. The Gardiner High School football field below accommodated a scrum of grazing cow elk. The stone entrance to northern Yellowstone arched behind it.

"Son of a *fucking* bitch."

His skin was blue, and his yellow locks were matted with snow and earth.

His thigh was gouged. When he saw the leg wound, he collapsed back to the cold ground and moaned. Breathing heavily, his eyes explored the baby blue morning sky.

"You mother fucker," he grumbled.

FOR THE THIRD time, Kyle woke up stark naked, not knowing quite where he was.

It took him a moment to realize he was in MacLeod's lofty living room fireplace. There was wood ash across his legs and torso and again, large quantities of blood dried to his arms, chest, and face.

In an instant, he knew whose blood it must have been.

In his mind's eye, he saw his beastly arms digging through hard ground and icy snow. He saw Russell's face, his blonde hair bloodied. Then, in another flash, he could see Hatfield's body half-buried. Kyle could see his own breath rolling out of him in swells.

Kyle stood and lurched out of the fireplace, pushing away the visions.

The cast-iron basket used for holding burning logs had been pitched to the other side of the room and busted through the glass coffee table, the half-burned logs and ash scattered about.

He crouched and gathered himself.

He and that Russell guy had just stepped outside. His memory was a blank around that point. But then . . .

"Shhhit."

That full, haunting moon he'd seen as they exited the saloon appeared in his mind.

"Oh my God."

Kyle looked at his hands. He curled his fingers in and out.

He shuddered like he'd just fallen into an icy lake.

I am a killer.

Too many people had been hurt. He couldn't do this anymore.

There was only one thing to do—run. Run to where he could no longer hurt people.

Then pray.

THE ADMINISTRATIVE PORTION of his work wasn't his favorite. Henry had spent the morning in a meeting with the Park Superintendent, Chief Ranger, and other District Rangers. Each District Ranger had given their monthly report, and not much had occurred, except for a Bombardier track vehicle used to shuttle tourists had broken down just north of Old Faithful, and the park service had come to the rescue. Although it wasn't much of a rescue—the resort company had already dispatched an extra Bombardier and mechanics out to the site when the headstrong Old Faithful District Ranger insisted that the park service would send their extra Bombardier. RedMoon could see that with the recent addition of three new districts and the subsequent hiring of District Rangers, competition and political scrum to make Chief Ranger, if not here, then at another national park, had already begun.

They'd also announced that on April nineteenth the roads within the park will be cleared and opened back up to regular vehicles for the start of the summer season. Henry looked forward to the date, when tourist traffic picked up and he could get out of the office more.

When he returned to his office from the meeting, he brewed his afternoon coffee, the prequel to his evening coffee, and went to his desk.

Hurrying through his emails from human resources about the new seasonal hires, and the options being weighed with the slightly higher budget this year, he clicked open an internet search bar. He typed in, *Donnan MacLeod*.

RedMoon had stewed over who this man was and wondered if he was the driver of the ForeRunner. He'd ran a check and did, in fact, see that MacLeod, who lived in Paradise Valley, had a green 2001 Toyota ForeRunner registered in his name.

His internet search results for *Donnan MacLeod* appeared on the computer screen.

He clicked on a YouTube video with MacLeod's name in the title: *Professor MacLeod is a nutcase.*

As Henry watched the video, he leaned to one side of his chair and sipped his coffee.

In the clip, MacLeod spoke about beast-men myths and lore of the indigenous people of North America and Canada. Henry leaned in when MacLeod presented his theory that an evil ritual was brought to the continent from a migrating tribe that came across the Bering Strait. When he went on to discuss a "Ritual of Three" involving the energy from geothermal activity, the full moon, and blood sacrifice, RedMoon flinched.

In the video, the crowd booed the stage.

When MacLeod clicked his projector remote and the screen behind him displayed the names, *Yohawnee* and *Wahota*, Henry shot up from his chair.

CHAPTER 26

A WOMAN IN a drab blazer sat across the desk from Nicole. The woman rapidly spouted, "This is your Affidavit of Title. Basically, you are stating that the property is yours to sell, there are no liens, you're not bankrupt—things like that."

Nicole simply nodded; the woman's voice was no more than a droning in Nicole's head.

Page by page, through a stack of documents an inch thick, Nicole laid down her signature nearly fifty times.

She shook her hand as it began to cramp up. *All this hoopla over a piece-of-shit house*, she thought.

Once all was signed, the mortgage broker gathered the documents into a neat pile. "I'll just need to make copies of these. In the meantime . . . " Looking up from the documents, the woman finally noticed Nicole's hearing aid. *Here it comes,* Nicole thought. The woman raised her voice slightly, "Oh, I'm sorry, I didn't notice your . . . "

"No, no, it's fine. I barely need it. It's nothing. I can hear you just fine."

"Okay, I'm sorry."

Nicole's voice was tinged with frustration. "Don't be sorry. It's fine."

"Right. Well, in the meantime, Barbara here has the other paperwork for you to sign as well. I'll be right back."

Like a well-oiled machine, the two women in pantsuits shuffled about, slipping papers in and out of folders, smiling like it was Friday afternoon and they had a Bahamas cruise that left in the morning.

Halfway through signing the second stack of closing documents, the second woman seemed to notice Nicole's defeated demeanor.

The second woman said in her southern accent, "It's okay, girl, just a few more, I promise."

Upon her last signature, the woman told Nicole to keep the pen, as it probably didn't have any ink left in it anyway, and giggled.

Nicole forced a smile in return.

"All right, hon, I'll run and make some copies, and we'll be all set, mmkay?"

Nicole nodded.

When the first woman returned, she handed Nicole a clipped bundle of papers encased in a plastic sleeve. "There you are, Ms. Bowman."

"Thank you."

The woman asked, "So, what's next for you? Are you looking to buy a home soon?"

"No, not for a while, at least."

"Oh yeah?"

"I'm taking my old job back, in Yellowstone."

"Wow, that sounds nice. What do you do there?"

Nicole said, "I work at Yellowstone Lake Hotel in the pantry section. I put together deserts and appetizers."

"And you get to live in Yellowstone? That's great. That seems *way* more interesting than what I do for a living."

People always said that to Nicole, and she was always annoyed by what it inferred. Traveling to a national park and working for a summer was too easy for your average young adult with no children. All it took was an ounce of adventure and maybe a Greyhound ticket. They were admitting outright that, during their young and new adulthood, they knowingly chose to be a slave to their profession, to college, or to a significant other, instead of simply venturing out, seeing the world, discovering things like working in a park—even for one summer. Yet they would never say that part out loud. It was either this, or they thought the idea of wasting time, playing around in a park was a joke, and she was being patronized.

"It doesn't start for another month." Nicole said weightily, "I can't wait to get out of this town."

"Ugh, tell me about it."

Nicole just smiled and thought, *I'd rather not.*

"Where will you stay until you leave?"

"At a friend's."

AS NICOLE SAT her luggage on the bed in Sandra's guest room, she could hear Cujo barking outside.

At the window, Nicole spotted Sandra's daughter rolling and tumbling with the golden retriever in the large backyard, as well as Sandra's barren cornfield and the sprawling forest beyond it.

Sandra had told Nicole that her husband would be sowing the sweet corn seeds around the end of May. Sandra described the sweet, dusty smell of the high stalks that would be there in August, but Nicole was never too intimate with such things where she was raised.

Nicole wondered how far along she would be with her grief by August. Maybe by then she would have some closure. Maybe the warm embrace of the Yellowstone mountains could help her come to accept that she'd lost her mother. And maybe they could help her come to accept that the search for Kyle was a lost cause, and they were right to have called it off. What kind of closure awaited her in August, if any, remained a cruel mystery.

CHAPTER 27

REMOVING HIS WIDE-STRIPED inmate scrubs and donning his tuxedo again felt amazing, but Donnan's desire for a pull of scotch was unspeakable, and they couldn't get the release process finished quick enough.

He stepped out of the bathroom and checked the blazer pocket—those ingrates had taken his flask. Or maybe it had fell out during the kerfuffle that he vaguely remembered.

When he heard a loud buzz and something unlock, he pushed through a heavy metal door and stepped up to a lobby counter.

The attendant lifted the box with MacLeod's possessions and set it in the window. The spectacled woman slid a business card across the counter. "You'll have to call a cab at this number to take you to the impound to retrieve your vehicle. First, sign these papers."

"I have to pay for a taxi? You're the one who took my vehicle. You're off your *fuckin'* trolley."

She eyed him over the top of her glasses and hovered her hand over the emergency walkie-talkie. She tapped the short antennae like Doc Holliday readying to draw, daring him to escalate further.

THERE WERE A dozen casinos within the Missoula area—a perfect storm for a freed and desperate Donnan MacLeod.

The shunned archaeologist swung his hotel door open and slogged in with a look of utter defeat, his eyes dry, his bowtie unclipped, his hair straight out from where he had tugged at it in the elevator. In under forty minutes, the casino downstairs had taken two-hundred grand from the crestfallen scholar.

At the desk, he pulled a bottle of Jameson from a paper bag and poured a glass.

Through the sliding glass door, he noticed the three-quarters-full moon in the dark plum sky.

He rifled through his computer bag and selected a thin hardback book, scuffed with age. It was maroon with silver lettering on the front that read, *The Rituals of Three.*

On the balcony, MacLeod plopped onto a chair and peered at the moon, the tiny red veins pulsing in the whites of his eyes, his mouth slightly agape like someone under hypnosis.

He took a swig from his glass, then opened the book to a bookmarked page.

He cleared his throat and began reciting the words in a Native American dialect. His recital was rhythmic, an incantation. The ex-professor spoke the words as if he'd read them hundreds of times.

After a few beats, he finally stumbled with a word.

MacLeod repeated it, trying to pronounce the word suitably.

He repeated it three times, correcting himself until it sounded right.

The Wahota language is so beautiful, he thought. *I'm going to miss it. Does one miss things when they're gone?*

MacLeod stood and leaned forward on the railing, staring at the lit street, five floors down. His face shrank as he let out a single whimper.

What will she think? Will she even care?

With that thought, he walked back inside and picked up his cell phone. When he noticed his laptop, he dropped the phone on the bed. MacLeod sat at the desk and fired up the computer, opening his home security application.

Her parking spot was as empty as always.

Well, Donnie boy, you had a good run.

As he reached to close the screen, he noticed something in one of the other camera feeds, the one in the living room.

His glass coffee table was shattered.

He looked curiously. Was that part of his fireplace lying in the middle of it?

Adjusting the zoom, he discovered it was.

"What in God's name?"

He rewound the footage over the course of a day, then two, without seeing any movement.

Eventually, something blipped. He stopped the footage and pushed play.

A man, probably in his twenties, was reaching through his pantry, stocking a backpack.

"Goddamn heathens!"

MacLeod rewound the footage further, and, as he passed through the nighttime hours, a large black figure squirreled around the rapid images.

He stopped the footage again and leaned in, his nose almost touching the screen.

After a few seconds, he saw the door to the back patio bust open, and a massive, black werewolf step through.

MACLEOD HAD CHECKED every minute of tape. The young man in his house had not been seen in the footage after the day he'd staggered out of the fireplace naked. Donnan hadn't wasted any time, nor considered the danger in driving drunk, and endured the five-hour drive home overnight until a sliver of sun topped the eastern horizon in his front windshield. MacLeod had traveled with intense purpose, like a man possessed. He'd dedicated his entire life to his craft, and he knew, doubtlessly now, that he'd discovered what no one else had.

The young man was his key to redemption, to fortune— or to something else.

During the ride home, his mind had reeled with the possibilities of befriending this infected person. The possibilities of what he could do with this individual disturbed even him—for a moment.

Before he exited his ForeRunner, he attached his holster and nine-millimeter to his belt and hid it beneath his jacket.

Cautiously, MacLeod entered his front door and yelled, "Hello? Are you here? Please, don't worry! I'm not here to hurt you! My name is Donnan MacLeod."

As he spoke, he searched the corners of the lavish living room, behind couches, in closets.

"I don't care that you broke in. Whatever it is, I can help you. It's safe to come out. I'm alone."

In the security video, the man had spent a lot of time in this living room area and the adjoining kitchen. Ideally, he'd be asleep at this early hour in the nearby guest rooms, able to hear his voice.

When MacLeod had entered, he recalled that one of the last things the intruder did was write something down on a notepad in the kitchen.

After seeing no signs of life in the living area, MacLeod tiptoed to the kitchen.

On the marble topped island was a message, shakily written:

Mr. MacLeod,

I saw you on TV. You're right about the beast men myths being real. Whatever it is, it's happening to me. I can't tell you who I am. I need you to tell me how to stop it. I'm going to the observation cabin on Turret Mountain in Yellowstone. If you bring the police, I'll know. I have your rifle. I don't want to hurt anyone else. Please HELP ME!

MacLeod cursed. He yanked open a kitchen drawer and withdrew a topographical map of Yellowstone, fingering through it until he found Turret Mountain and the nearby trails.

It would be a challenging hike.

MacLeod pushed his glasses up his nose and pondered as he reread the letter.

What in God's name would he do when he found him? MacLeod had checked the date that the werewolf was there, and it was on the full moon. There wasn't enough time to reach Turrett before the next full moon.

He considered the possible outcomes again. He knew what cured the infection, or at least what the legends claimed. But if he stopped the werewolf, there would be no proof he ever existed, no glory, no fortune. His pursuit at exposing the RedMoons was dashed by his own belligerence, his credibility destroyed—what was left of it anyway.

The home footage would be laughed off if he presented it. He wore a furry suit and ransacked his own house, they'd say.

Was it possible to capture this man and somehow record evidence of his changing? Slim chance, but possible. But then, that would mean he would have to commit a kidnapping and keep someone against their will—even assault him if necessary.

Was being back in jail worth it? He didn't have enough years left in his life to wait out those convictions.

Every direction he turned met a dead end.

Except.

There was one other option.

No, he couldn't do *that.*

Could he?

He involuntarily chuckled.

This was a sign. This was fate.

Wasn't it?

A depraved smile slithered across his face.

DONNAN'S SINGING VOICE disturbed the silence of a wide mountain meadow on his property. The sun had just fully crested the horizon, not yet lighting the west face of Mount Cowan and its fellow north-running peaks. He sang:

> *I will build my love a tower . . .*
> *Near yon' pure crystal fountain . . .*
> *And on it I will build . . .*
> *All the flowers of the mountain.*

MacLeod's eyes shined with a crazed light. His hymn was as clumsy as his feet.

Donnan sucked in his chest and drummed up the base from his ribcage, *Will ye go, lassie, go!*

Crashing through a barn door, Donnan and the morning light spilled into the abandoned structure. Woodford Reserve bourbon dribbled off one hand—a consequence of drudging across two acres of exposed roots and deadfall of forest with a shallow but full glass.

Only three times since moving in eighteen years ago, had he visited the building. Each time he did, he'd spotted the foul creatures and cringed—foul creatures he hoped were still there.

He clicked on his headlamp. Weathered boards that once contained horses were split and warped with age.

Carefully, he climbed the ladder to the hayloft.

In the loft, the beam of light from his head slowly climbed the barn wall as he looked up. As the circle of light met the triangular arrangement of the pointed roof and rafters, he could confirm the critters were still there.

Those hideous, fanged, furred, leathery-winged, night lurkers were still there, huddled next to one another—the aptly named Big Brown Bats, dozens of them.

MacLeod whispered, "*Will ye go, lassie, go.*"

Donnan decided he would help this infected man—not in a way the stranger would like, however.

MacLeod desired to see for himself what man changing to beast looked like, to feel the raw energy of spiritual power melding with a mortal body. It would be a look into the future, a preamble to the great history that Dr. Donnan MacLeod, World-Renowned Archeologist and Master of Anthropology, would write for himself.

CHAPTER 28

HENRY PARKED HIS Jeep in the same spot on Main Street near The Goose. Since discovering that this Dr. MacLeod and someone with a ForeRunner had been seeking him out, RedMoon had been purposefully keeping himself in plain sight around Gardiner—shopping for groceries at the same place and time, having breakfast at The Goose routinely. More times than not, he'd left his ranger uniform on when in town to help him stick out. He knew it would be easier to spin a web and just let the insect come to him.

MacLeod knew too much. The man had never mentioned the RedMoon name in the YouTube videos or in any research he'd published, still Henry knew the real danger MacLeod posed to his family.

RedMoon's black eyes surveyed his peripherals as he approached The Goose's front doors. The hard soles of his shining garrison work shoes clopped on the cold sidewalk. It was April, and although the air had lost its winter bite, it was still frigid this afternoon. The Gardiner streets held a strange silence as his breath rose in front of him in wisps of white steam.

A miniscule inclination within the recesses of his mind told him something was off, that his surroundings, this town—*something* was out of place. It was strange; he had this feeling each time he was near The Goose. Normally, he would shrug it off, but this time he chose not to ignore it.

He stopped and removed his hands from his pockets. He breathed deeply, closed his eyes, and listened to the stillness.

As he opened his eyes, he found himself staring at a blue U.S. Postal Service mail receptacle. There were five punctures in its side, spread out like someone with hunting knives for fingers had attacked the metal container.

"Oh, hey Henry, good afternoon." Frank pulled a rug outside onto the sidewalk. He followed Henry's gaze to the mailbox. "Yeah, that's nuts, huh? Vandals I suppose. It happened about a month ago. You never noticed it?"

"No." The fact he hadn't seen it before was slightly unsettling, and the possibilities for what could have caused it were unnerving.

Frank said, "I think there was a bad fight too that night. I had to wash the blood off the sidewalk—" Frank emphasized, "*again.*"

Frank held the door for Henry. "They raise 'em rough in this town, if you know what I mean."

RedMoon's work cell phone buzzed in his pocket. He raised his hand to Frank, and the bartender went back inside.

"Yeah?"

It was the office clerk. His new seasonal officer, whom he had no part in hiring, had called saying that he can do his meet and greet with Henry on Tuesday at nine.

"My seasonal hire called to tell *me* when to meet him?" RedMoon shook his head. "No. Tell him that time is no good. Tell him we'll get back to him." *When we damn well please*, Henry thought.

Henry looked at the sky and found the full moon as gray as the clouds around it. "Also, make sure the coffee is stocked. I'm working Hodges' third shift again tonight."

KYLE SAT AGAINST a wall, inside a National Park Service patrol cabin, with his knees tucked in against his torso. The small wooden structure sat atop the snow-covered peak of Turret Mountain in the heart of Yellowstone. Its sister cabins were posted at the apexes of the highest peaks and scattered miles apart throughout the park. Out in the deep darkness, these observation posts rode the backs of whales like Mount Washburn and Mount Holmes and were used in warmer months by park rangers to spot wildfires when fire potentials were high.

Kyle hoped the seclusion could keep him from doing horrible things to others. However, in a few weeks, the spring snow melts would begin, and eventually hikers would be taking trails up the mountain slopes, reaching cabins like his as their destination.

Kyle stared at the busted window on the opposite wall where he'd climbed through.

Outside, the wind carried a few sparse snowflakes in its blustering roar.

He had already felt the curse creep up as he caught a flash of a memory from one of the full-moon nights when he'd changed. The memory was two seconds of being batted in the chest by horse hooves. The feeling was intense, laced with a feeling of great fury, and over in an instant.

He had the urge to take off his clothes, knowing they would be shredded off anyway. If he were to wait it out for an undetermined amount of time here, he would have to be resourceful.

Just then, he felt his jaws ache at the back.

He started to rub them when suddenly his back arched, pushing him against the wall.

He felt a great squeeze around his entire torso as his body slid up the wall.

Frantically, he kicked off his boots and removed his jacket.

FAR NORTH FROM Kyle's location, two young women hastily removed their underwear in the dark and tiptoed into the steamy, hot Boiling River of northern Yellowstone. The bouldered river, located a few miles from the north entrance, was closed to visitors for the season, but that didn't stop the two adventurers who were working as housekeepers in the park at Mammoth Hot Springs Hotel & Cabins.

The girls were accompanied by a plump and dough-faced man who carried their things for them. He grinned politely and kept his eyes averted.

The girls submerged their soft bodies into a naturally formed hot tub created by an eddy at the bank of the river. Their pale bodies shown in the clear water with the help of the blazing full moon. They gave the man the signal to join them.

He removed his shirt and entered the river, cautiously maneuvering his heavy body over the slippery rocks.

He floated in front of them on his back, his toes, belly, and beard protruding from the dark water. The long-sloping ridge leading to Mount Everts paralleled his river. He rested a brown bottle of lager on his stomach as he stared up at the twinkling stars broadcast across the deep, navy blue sky.

The man sang with a beer-induced swagger, "*Is it any wondeeer that his face is red? Kaw-Liga that poor ol' wooden head!*"

The girls sat in the steaming pool and stared at him with curious and flirtatious eyes. They spoke to each other in a non-English language that was chock-full of *s* and *sh* sounds.

He laid his arm over a boulder and turned toward the two, letting the slow current role down his back and into his unsightly ass crack.

His confidence seemed to swell. "Hey there, naked ladies. I don't know exactly what it is you're discussin' over there. My Polish is, well, a tad rusty. But did I mention I know a little French?" He winked and tipped his bottle into his puckered lips. "You two ever heard of the phrase *ménage a—*"

The big-bellied man stopped and looked above the girls with a primal fear in his eyes.

A guttural and powerful growl rattled from the sloping hillside behind the foreign girls.

The man dropped his beer bottle, ignoring it as it drifted down the stream.

A massive beast with blonde hair, the head of a berserker wolfman, and dog-like legs, approached the girls from behind. It reached down and sank its claws deep into their eye sockets like it was grasping two bowling balls.

The man watched in horror as it dragged them ashore by their skulls.

They screamed in anguish and kicked and thrashed.

The tall beast chewed through the blonde's chest while the brunette squirmed in agony, trying to crawl away up the hillside.

She didn't make it far before the creature had finished with the blonde, then pursued her. It clamped down on the brunette's arm and jerked it clean off. When she tried to yell, it put its mouth around her entire head and crumpled it like a melon.

The wolfish beast quickly turned to the man in the water, blood dripping from its jaws, mixing with the straw-colored hair of its neck and chest. Its eyes were blood red.

Instantly, the creature plunged into the river and pinned the man to the boulder.

It placed its long hand over the drunken man's face while he flailed and splashed about.

The blonde beast jerked the man's body up onto a larger rock and slashed at his stomach with claws as long and sharp as its canines.

Chunks of whitish-yellow fat, the pink outer skin still attached, and sections of small intestines splashed into the mountain water and floated away under the Yellowstone moon.

CHAPTER 29

"WELL . . . LIKE A werewolf."

Kyle rode in the passenger's seat of his mother's car, with her behind the wheel.

"Honey, a werewolf?" she said doubtfully. She looked over at him with deep worry lines on her face and concern etched in her emerald eyes.

"Mom, I know. You have to listen to me. I've done some very bad things. I know it sounds insane, but it's true. And I can't stop it."

"A Native curse? Every full moon? Blood and guts?"

He nodded.

"Kyle, you're a grown man now, but you sound like when you were a little boy. You would tell me you were Cal Ripken Junior. Do you remember telling me you played shortstop for the Orioles? You collected all those mini Louisville Slugger bats and put them on your shelves."

She smiled warmly, as if remembering his pinchable cheeks.

"I killed people! I tore them apart! Are you hearing me?!" His voice boomed inside the compact car. He reached and tightly clutched her arm to demand her attention.

Frightened by Kyle's anger, his mother flicked on her turn signal and quickly pulled the car to the shoulder. Her gaze stayed on the steering wheel.

"Kyle, honey, I believe something is wrong with you. I just don't know what. I am here for you, but I just don't know how I'm supposed to help you. You're talking about having flashbacks, being a monster, and running around up in the mountains. You tell me you can't stop it. What am I supposed to do, Kyle?"

Her eyes began to pool with tears.

"I don't know." He released her arm. "I'm sorry. I just need you or someone to help me, somehow. I tried to find this man who I thought could help me, but I couldn't get to him in time. My changing is happening more and more. Lately, it's happening on more nights than just the full moons."

He eased the tone of his words. "That's why I came out here—so I couldn't hurt anyone. I'm afraid the next time I change, I won't change back. I think it's too late for me. I don't even know what day it is anymore."

"Honey," she touched his shoulder and turned to look him in the eye. She asked with a pitch of confusion in her voice, "Came out here, where?"

"What?"

"You said that's why you came out here. Here, where? Where are we?"

His mother's concerned face slowly vanished with the dream as Kyle opened his eyes.

Kyle lay on a snowy patch of ground. He blinked into the early-morning sunlight. Uphill from him was the observation cabin where he'd tried to trap himself.

Nearby, he could hear a constant roar as snowmelt waters burst into white flurries and cascaded over a waterfall—the initiating sounds of a Yellowstone spring.

He crept on all fours to a stream trickling nearby. The frigid liquid flowed from the highlands, polishing the calico rocks on the waterway's floor.

His reflection was an undulating image with a hairy outline and pointed ears at the sides of his head. Though it was a startling sight, a calming mood suddenly flowed through him. He listened to the sound of finches chirping and maple leaves brushing in the gentle breeze. Kyle suddenly felt like he was the tallest tree in the forest, swaying to a rest after the very last gust of a storm bent its upper limbs.

The predator within him dissolved, and he saw his own unshaven face and black hair at the tops of his shoulders.

His hands returned to their hairless and human state.

He was naked, and again unaffected by the cold.

There was no blood—anywhere on him. *Thank God.*

As he stared into the water, he'd never felt so alone. He wasn't himself and would never again be. Would he be strong enough to keep himself in seclusion forever? Had anything in his life prepared him for this?

No.

The stark reality that he would hide like this forever sat like a stone in his gut, turning over and over.

He was afraid most for his mother. Maybe she'd faced more hardship than he would in the years to come, not knowing where he was. And Nicole, she would be strong enough to move on, eventually. Wouldn't she?

The thing that stared back at him in the water's reflection a moment ago was part of him now, and there was no denying it. The young man finally understood the fear, the panic, the horror he must have caused his victims—what they saw seconds before their deaths.

Kyle sat back from the brook and began to sob. He wasn't strong enough for this. He wasn't made to withstand this kind of life. He wouldn't live like this. He wouldn't live—at all.

Stoically, Kyle rose.

He followed the stream toward the waterfall, feeling like a puppet on strings as he stepped through the snow and dirt at a slow march.

At a stone's throw from the edge of the waterfall, Kyle's path was blocked by someone who appeared from behind a lodgepole pine.

Kyle stopped and squinted.

He saw a Native American man. The man's emotionless face was painted black across his mouth and jaw, white across the top half. His eyes were gaunt and dead set. He was wrapped in a bison hide—the skin so large it covered his entire body and dragged behind him. The hide wasn't the typical brown-tan color, but a deep, eerie jet black. Its darkness wasn't like a reflective color Kyle could see, more of a translucent opening into an empty, colorless, void—like he could throw a rock at it and it would sail right through into nothingness. Above the hide, he wore a wolverine cap with bristling black and brown hair, and an eagle's tail fanned out at the back of his neck.

As the man approached, Kyle veered off course to avoid him.

The man adjusted, staying between Kyle and the waterfall.

It was clear he wasn't backing down, and Kyle would have to confront him if he wanted to reach the point of his escape from this world.

Kyle stepped directly toward him.

Swinging one side of the buffalo hide open, the native displayed a wooden staff with bushy marten tails and a small animal skull attached to the top.

The staff rattled as the man discarded it to the ground.

Kyle took another step forward.

Suddenly, the native's legs grew, sprouting beneath the hide, picking the skin off the ground.

The legs elongated, and dog-like paws formed at his feet, their claws piercing into the ground.

Kyle gasped and took a backward step.

A few seconds later, the man burst from the hide and cap and lurched forward as a sandy brown werewolf.

Kyle stumbled backward as the creature stared him down. Its eyes were a piercing yellow and locked onto Kyle.

Kyle lowered his eyes to deny what he was seeing. It was only his imagination, he told himself. A hallucination. Kyle concentrated on the ground in front of him as he continued to the waterfall.

The crashing sound of the toppling waters grew stronger as he neared.

Kyle imagined a tranquil pool at the bottom of the falls where his freedom awaited.

Suddenly, he heard rapid and heavy steps like the thudding of horse hooves trouncing toward him.

Kyle looked up.

His eyes were belly-high to the beast as it now towered in front of him.

Kyle took a step back to see the thing's face.

It had a wide, black snout that wasn't human or wolf, but a grotesque combination of the two. One side of the face was missing a patch of flesh, as if from a battle wound, that exposed dagger teeth, bone and part of an eye socket.

The wolfman hunched forward to show its teeth to Kyle.

It snapped its jaws and scared the life back into the young man.

Another slow step back, and the thing didn't pursue.

A few more steps and Kyle was relieved to see the creature lower to a crouched position and reign in its snarl.

Kyle knew it couldn't be real, but the fear was so great, the creature so vile, he didn't dare advance on it.

Out the side of his mouth, Kyle said, "What the hell are you?"

The snarl on its face returned, lifting its lips as it opened its mouth. It struggled to bring its lips together as it croaked, "*Bay—osh.*"

Its fine hair waved in the whirring breeze.

After a silent moment of surrender and resignation, Kyle turned and began a slow walk back up the mountain to the patrol cabin.

I'm out of my mind, he decided.

He looked back over his shoulder and the wolfish creature was gone—no tracks, no bison hide, no staff.

Goddammit, Kyle, get your shit together.

He didn't just see a werewolf—and it didn't just speak to him.

And MacLeod would come. He had to.

CHAPTER 30

NICOLE STEPPED BACK to examine her things packed tightly into the back of her Ford Explorer. The maroon bucket of bolts already had nearly three hundred thousand miles on it, and Nicole was not without reservations about adding another few thousand in the next two days. But she'd been through this before—the two had made the trip between Virginia and Yellowstone a dozen times. There was a sentimental value to the automobile—the machine seemed a luck charm and had seen her through a lot over the years. She was going to ride it until the wheels fell off.

This could very well be her last voyage west, she thought, at least for a good while. This return to the park could give a whole new meaning to the words "fresh start." What was once simply seasonal work and fun had accumulated until she became skilled at it, living that kind of life, adapting to that kind of environment, slowly severing her connection to her previous life. This time it felt more like going home than going on an adventure.

She could apply for the year-round positions and stay in permanent employee housing at Old Faithful or Mammoth Hot Springs. She could become a food production manager, a "lifer" as the seasonal workers referred to them, or move to nearby Bozeman, or Gardiner, Montana and find work there. Who knew—if she did settle in a town, she and Cujo could reunite and he could spend his golden years in the Rocky Mountains with her.

She kept positive thoughts like these alive—anything to give her reason to keep moving forward. It would be a rough go, she knew, no matter what she might accomplish in the next few years. There was no outrunning grief. Nicole wondered how long she'd mourn for her missing Kyle, and for her mother. The counselor in Yellowstone she'd seen after Annie-A was killed had told Nicole her grief would be there as long as she lived—it was just a matter of coping, and it would get easier in time. But how long when you've lost two within months of each other?

She heard Sandra call for her daughter and Cujo at the back porch.

It was time.

To distract herself, Nicole lifted the back hatch of the Explorer and eyed her packed items. She checked them off her mental inventory, the two most important items being a scrapbook of printed photos holding memories of Kyle and her mom, and in the front seat, strapped in with the seatbelt, her mother's urn.

She stifled the worry that she was giving up on Kyle too soon. In the recesses of her mind, she knew she'd likely be waiting around a long time only to have a corpse turn up one day and it would be his. This ordeal had turned her into a believer in Creation, and she prayed for his safety, whether it was here or in the afterlife. She had to believe that someone or something was listening, otherwise she'd lose it. Placing it in God's hands felt better than being defeated daily and accepting that horrible things had occurred.

When Nicole saw Cujo sprinting for her, she slammed the back hatch shut so he wouldn't try to jump in.

He had a punctured and wet frisbee in his mouth, which he showed her proudly. She stroked his smooth head as he playfully wagged his entire back half.

He had no idea she was leaving him again. Would he realize it tonight when she wasn't there? Tomorrow?

Nicole's throat swelled. She felt like she needed to say something to him, but she didn't have the words. Just, "'Bye, buddy. I'll miss you."

Sandra's daughter yelled for Cujo as she ran to them. When she made it to Nicole, she hugged her leg and said, "Goodbye, Miss Nikki!" She tugged at the other end of the frisbee in Cujo's mouth, and the two took off for the backyard.

Sandra strode over from the house, and pulled Nicole into a deep embrace, nearly squeezing the air out of her. When she was finally done, she adjusted Nicole's hair and straightened her collar.

"You going to make it, girl?"

Nicole slid her arm through a backpack strap and smiled bravely. "Yeah, I got this."

CHAPTER 31

HIS MIND SIMULTANEOUSLY searched the school playground for Maddie, who he hadn't seen there in three consecutive days, while considering all that had transpired in the past two months and what it could mean for him. On the radio, another update on the Boiling River victims' autopsies was being released—this time confirming that evisceration and loss of limbs had been involved. But Russell already knew that. The morning after the slayings, Russell awoke on his bedroom floor, his naked body decorated with blood from an unknown source, his head reeling. However, the flashbacks from his rampage at Boiling River had come to him, not at once, but in lightning-quick bursts—miniscule slices, until a terrifying sketch of what happened was played out.

Still, his memory of that night wasn't whole. There were sporadic gaps in time, between dashing across mountainous terrain with great speed one moment, to feeling his clawed feet entering the hot river, seeing his powerful reflection in the water, to looking skyward at the full moon.

He made the connection with that night and the night he met the stranger named Sam, who, under the full moon had changed into a monster and attacked him. The potential for what caused this seemingly full–moon-induced event should've given him concern, he knew, but it had a different effect on him—a dark sensation that showed in his now sunken face and reddish irises each time he glanced in his El Camino's side mirror.

Lost in dark thoughts, Russell ignored the buzzing of his cell phone on the passenger seat until it stopped. With a big inhale, he refocused on the playground. He grabbed his cell phone and saw the phone message alert icon. He dialed his voice mailbox.

Russell, this is Jim. Don't bother calling this number back, you'll get no answer. I just wanted you to be aware that Jill, Maddie, and I have moved to . . . someplace warm. Don't bother trying to track us down, either, because the restraining order, which you have nearly broken a dozen times, is still in effect, and Dad's attorneys are well aware of you. They're ready to respond if you try anything. They're some of the best in the country. So . . .

Russell could almost hear his smug smile as he paused.

Welp, you have a great day, and . . . welp, go fuck yourself.

LEAGUES BELOW THE ground where Dr. MacLeod knelt, a huge body of magma, like an evil titan, ached and stewed sluggishly as it had for ages.

He stayed a safe distance from the edge of Sapphire Pool, known in Yellowstone for its crystal-clear blue waters. With Kevlar grilling gloves, he threw a chained bucket into the two-hundred-degree liquid. Once it was full, he pulled the bucket up from the water and dumped it into another, larger metal bucket. It would need to cool before he poured it into the empty milk jugs lined next to him.

The convection of superheated water in the pool was a byproduct of processes deep within the earth. A spirit-like steam wafted from the water's surface, and a ring of gray sinter circled the body of water, which was twenty feet across. The pool had an angelic blue tint, though the water was colorless when extracted. The pool's bottom had no visible end, trailing off into the dark and deep abyss seemingly en route to the planet's core.

The feature was a death trap, despite its majestic appearance, and MacLeod was well aware of the water's flesh-rendering temperature. Pools like these had killed more than one tourist over the years, the color so alluring and inviting that onlookers forget to keep their distance. Only a few years ago, one man had died trying to save a friend's dog from the hot pool. Donnan couldn't imagine a more painful death.

There wasn't much about the park that MacLeod wasn't familiar with. He and the land of Yellowstone had been boon companions since his forced retirement from instructing and semi-retirement from field research. That's how he knew the track vehicles that normally carried curious passengers from Old Faithful Snow Lodge to this outlying basin had concluded for the winter season, meaning he could conduct his work unseen.

The man felt at home within the treacherous landscape and hardy creatures of the park, his purple sock hat warming his balding head, the cloudy breath rising in puffs around his salt and pepper beard as he pushed his portly body to its limits. He knew his Scottish roots but felt like maybe, in another life, he'd been a mountain man of the American West, suffering the winters to trade his hard-earned beaver furs at markets in the foothills of the Teton Mountains.

The real stories of the mountain men and their trading and skirmishes with the natives had intrigued him as a youngster, ultimately leading him to his profession. He cocked his head. *Just imagine the stories children will read about me when I'm through.*

Donnan retrieved one more bucket from the pool and set it aside.

Carefully, he filled the milk jugs and tightened their caps.

Stepping away from the steaming water, he held a jug up to the sky and admired it. Just as Jim Bridger might have looked lustfully at his pile of pelts, so did Donnan at the liquid in the jug—as if it were laced with specks of gold.

Donnan quickly checked his watch, then began gathering his equipment.

Time was ticking.

Tonight, the full moon would rise over Yellowstone, and he needed to be in place. There was no room for error and timing would mean everything.

THE BUZZING NEEDLE dug into Russell Hatfield's meaty shoulder, its mechanized tip slowly etching gray and black inks, creating defined craters and the foreboding face of a full moon. He watched in the mirror as the imprinted image of a cryptic skull gradually melded into the moon's surface.

He watched the blur of the needle tip, then glimpsed the skull-faced moon tattoo in the mirror again. Death was their destiny whether he delivered it or not, those Polish girls and that fat man. *Fuck them and their sheltered lives anyway.*

The tattoo artist wiped away the blood and ink after his final detailing.

He asked. "How many?"

Russell held up three fingers.

The artist began to streak the vertical lines that would make three tally marks below the moon.

As he saw the first mark being drawn, electricity shot through Russell, sparking the deep, underlying reason for all his rage. His tiny girl would have been the single factor to soften his ways, to give him reason to reign in his life of anger.

The second mark tore into his shoulder like a red-hot saber.

For the first time during the session, sweat beaded on Russell's forehead.

She'd been taken from him, the innocent girl, in an act of deceit and betrayal. Her childhood slipped by with each passing day without him in it. Would she even remember him when she entered womanhood?

The third tally mark sank in and Hatfield exhaled through his nose. *Fuck Jim Walters.*

Three tiny marks—how could three tiny marks be so painful for someone so powerful? he thought.

The word "powerful" triggered something in his altered mind. He suddenly recalled the lecture he'd given Frank on power, how it was an illusion, how it was fed by tolerance and inaction . . . a power like that of Jim and all the Walters.

CHAPTER 32

"PUT BOTH ARMS in the air! All right. Now, lift one leg off the ground!"

A group of children stood in a straight line, paying close attention to the voice ringing out overhead.

"Now, release the beasts!"

A metallic *bang* rang out over the stadium as a cattle gate swung open. Three calves darted out under the stadium lights, each with a red ribbon attached to its tail.

The announcer proclaimed, "The first buckaroos to get a red flag get a FREE Dairy Queen Blizzard!"

A crowd of a few hundred people, residents of Cody, Wyoming, the self-proclaimed "Rodeo Capitol of the World," cheered on the exuberant children.

It was dusk in the outdoor stadium. Large moths circled the beaming lights above the crowd, while all around them stretched the empty Wyoming prairie and foggy mountain ranges in the distance.

The metallic voice rooted them on through the speaker. "Go get 'em!"

Bethany stood in the middle of the crowd of children. At six years old, she was only chest-high to most of the kids, and when the releasing command was given, she stumbled to the dirt, her golden locks spilling onto her face.

The little warrior regained her footing and chased behind the other children.

As they ran amuck, the group looked like a school of fish flowing to one side of the stadium to the other, while little Bethany followed behind.

Bethany's mother cheered from the aluminum bleachers. Her personal bodyguard, a serious man in sunglasses and a button-up shirt, sat next to her while his colleagues patrolled the rodeo grounds, watching over Bethany and her mother.

On the other side of the facility, Russell Hatfield leaned forward with his hands on a chain-link fence, bending it with his weight, watching Monte Walters' wife and their daughter, Bethany, with dead set eyes.

Russell exhaled forcefully through his nose. *Where the fuck is he?* Nearly an hour in, and the Senator still hadn't shown up.

Russell could spot the security detail. The guards were unassuming in appearance, except for their earpieces and the obvious fact that they were never far from the woman and her daughter, even at a friendly rodeo.

Hatfield had seen the senator's wife on television, smiling blankly in the background while her pig of a husband lied through his teeth into press microphones. In those appearances, she usually wore high-end business attire, matched with her signature string of pearls. Now, she was in a Carhart jacket and denim jeans. The woman's concocted façade was like that of a pink chameleon, Russell thought, walking among flamingos, trying to blend into a peaceful crowd as if she weren't a cold-blooded reptile. What kind of creature could support such a crooked, oil-hungry power player like Walters, other than a slithering animal that squirms on its belly?

One of the guards opposite him seemed to take notice of Russell, so he pulled his rough hands from the fence and walked away casually, raising his head, looking moonward.

In the loose dirt of the rodeo floor, the Wyoming children continued to pursue the bovine beasts. A boy in a cowboy hat made a quick change of direction and ended up knocking Bethany back to the soil. He paid no attention and kept running as fast as he could in his oversized cowboy boots.

When Bethany lifted her head, her eyes shifted to the other end of the ring, where a single calf was alone, completely unseen by the other children—a cherry-colored ribbon attached to its swaying tail.

Movingly discretely, she got up and dashed toward it. Halfway there, though, when the herd of children caught on, they easily overtook her best pace and flooded passed her toward the last calf.

Bethany stopped running. She puffed with exhaustion and watched the other kids closing in on the last ribbon. The girl looked to the stands where her mother cheered her on.

Bethany resumed the chase, pumping her arms at her side, sprinting like her life depended on it.

But after just a few steps, a blood-curdling sound brought her and the other children to a dead stop. A thunderous roar came from inside the dark corral connected to one end of the ring. The bulls inside the corral frenzied about and slammed against the railings of their enclosures as dust rose from the commotion.

The rodeo crowd stood to see the riot.

Just then, a bull burst free from the enclosure. The raging animal toppled a light post which caused the stadium lights to shut off and sparks to burst from a nearby transformer.

A wide gate broke open, spilling bulls into the moonlit arena.

Among the moshing bulls was a blonde-haired wolf creature on all fours with blood-red eyes. It was so large that even on all fours, its head rose above the backs of the bulls.

The beast stood on its hind legs, and dispatched a deep and hellish howl that scattered the audience.

Through the darkness, parents in the crowd hurled themselves down the bleachers toward their children. At the same time, the children bolted away from the beast, running directly toward Bethany. They weren't fast enough, and the monster charged through them, mowing them down like a bowling ball through a lily garden.

It had blades for teeth, a massive chest, and its red eyes zeroed in on the fleeing girl. The beast was as fast as a thoroughbred quarter horse, dirt flinging behind it as its four clawed limbs propelled it forward.

A snarly growl laced each inhale as it sped forward.

Before the little girl's bodyguards could hurdle the livestock barrier, the creature had already snatched her body into its jaws, trailing her blood as it carried her off into the dark of night.

THE ONLY SOUND on the entire mountain at six o'clock in the morning was Nicole's heavy breathing and crumbling rock as she hung on for dear life. The last boulder she reached for was broken, and a piece had hammered her on the forehead when she pulled it loose.

Nicole could hear mother's voice in her head protesting Nicole's intrepid behavior. *What the hell are you thinking, climbing around on the side of a mountain . . . by yourself!*

Reeling from the impact, her sight blurred with a kaleidoscope view of late spring snow and the loose granite she now clung to. All four of her limbs were splayed out, and she stretched nearly vertical against the rockface. Warm blood trailed down the bridge of her nose, inciting her to whisper profanities to herself.

She'd started this day before dawn, hoping to catch the sunrise from a high point. She was only branching off the trail where she'd camped to scale up a few hundred feet— it shouldn't have been this hard.

Her fear then turned to anger at whoever had cut the trail and decided not to run it up to the peak. After all, this was Eagle Peak, the highest peak in Yellowstone. Why didn't they cut the trail all the way to its top?

Morons.

Think, dammit, think, she admonished herself. No time to waste being angry. She took a deep breath and surveyed her surroundings.

With one careful step after another, she hoofed her way laterally. After some careful maneuvering, her footing stabilized, and the slope slowly leveled until her hands were free at her sides.

Grateful to be alive, she left her spot of shame and continued her search for the perfect spot to catch the sunrise—the perfect place to say goodbye.

A modest ten-foot drop was all that remained between her and a manageable route to an overlook she'd spotted thirty minutes ago. She lay flat on her stomach, peering over the edge. She lowered, then released her pack slowly to avoid losing balance when she made the jump to the next ledge.

Nicole was still on her belly when she saw the pack roll toward the brink of the ledge below. The drop beyond that must have been six hundred feet or more.

"No, no, no!"

She scrambled to her feet in desperation and looked at the pack again.

It paused momentarily at the edge like a suicidal person standing on the balcony rail, their face devoid of expression. Nicole's face, however, held an expression of utter panic for her mother's urn tucked into the outer mesh pocket.

With desperate haste, she attempted to climb down but slipped. After a second of free fall, she slammed to the rocky ground, flat on her back, knocking the wind from her chest.

A great pressure squeezed her lungs, disallowing an inhale.

As she watched the starry sky, she waited desperately for what seemed like an eternity for her breath to return.

She focused on the full moon—holding onto its light, controlling her emotion, stifling the urge to panic.

Then, after a few more grueling seconds, the pressure released, and a rush of air returned to her. She pulled in huge breaths, thinking of how life seemed spiteful, taking her mother from her, then Kyle, *now this*.

She gritted her teeth, rolled to all fours, and pounced forward.

She dove for the pack without hesitation and grasped it just as it left the edge.

Simultaneously, she hooked her boot on a lodge-pole pine sapling. Her advance was halted, but not before her foothold slipped to a toehold.

Huffing with pure resolve, she wiggled her foot back to a more secure position, shimmied her torso. The irony hit her like a mallet—"don't look down" was the safety phrase for all time, yet where else could she look? So, she closed her eyes, pictured her foothold and nothing else. Meticulously, she pulled the pack up, and crawled herself back to safety.

A fallen pine made the ideal spot to lay and catch her breath.

When her heart finished pounding, she pulled out the urn and held it for sweet confirmation. Thankfully, there was still time to find a sunrise viewing point—to find the place where she would say goodbye to her mother.

Laying her head back on the tree, Nicole sighed and basked in the peace and stillness of the mountaintop. Around her, the alpine fog was thick. White patches of snow were scattered beneath the gray and cool, clouded air of the Washakie Wilderness.

Suddenly, she began to shiver for no obvious reason.

Out of the silence, a breeze moaned through the trees, sending a foul odor under her nose.

From the side of a house-sized rock to her left, a dark figure watched her. She felt its presence and froze.

Scared for her life, she slowly turned her head to look at it.

At the side of the rock wall, she could see fur and an eye, probably eight feet high, glowing yellow—the moonlight reflecting off its half-silhouette.

Though her instinct told her to be afraid and run, something deeper told her that it wasn't there to harm her. In fact, she felt an inner familiarity with the creature.

For no logical reason, she whispered, "Kyle?"

Nicole set the urn on the ground and slowly stood. With her eyes on the figure, she walked carefully to it, like she might approach a feral dog on the street.

When she came close to it, the figure suddenly disappeared.

She continued to the edge, then stopped and waited where it once stood.

She leaned forward to peer around.

Nothing.

She pulled back and sighed with disappointment. Her near fatal slip must be messing with her head.

Through the fog, a long, hairy forearm with claws swung around and slammed her skull against the rock, pinning her there.

Her feet dangled off the ground.

The black beast's powerful shoulder and enormous half-man, half-wolf head appeared gradually around the corner.

It bared its ravenous teeth as a growl revved in its throat.

Fury showed on its wide snout, and it discharged a deafening roar.

Under its brow, its deep-set eyes radiated with brindled bumblebee colors.

CHAPTER 33

WITH HIS DOUBLE-BARRELED Holland & Holland .700 Nitro Express elephant gun aimed at the patrol cabin's front door, Dr. MacLeod steeled himself, though his stubby hands trembled. The top of Turret Mountain was desolate and snowy this morning, even in May. The peak was miles from civilization and silent, save for the whirring of occasional frosty gusts gliding by.

A few miles north, Eagle Peak reached for the sky, its sprawling shoulders encompassing both eastern Yellowstone and a sampling of the Washakie Wilderness of Wyoming. To the west, Yellowstone Lake covered one hundred and thirty square miles, placing a great divide between the numerous mountain ranges, as though a vast meteorite had collided with the earth, splaying it open.

Twice, he lowered the gun, shaking out his hands. His bulky Kelty pack, which he carried through the backcountry, lay on the ground behind him. MacLeod pushed the front of his Washington Huskies stocking cap up his forehead, letting the sweat evaporate into a whirl of steam.

Repositioning his weapon, he approached the one-room cabin.

The wooden boarding had been removed from one of the windows, and the glass had been broken out. Wood splinters and a padlock still attached to a latch lay at the foot of the door. The door was slightly ajar, and the cabin was dark within. Tracks surrounded the immediate area and a patch of ground near the cabin was disturbed—soil and snow lumped and mixed together, like something had been digging.

MacLeod held his breath, then kicked in the faded oak door.

Kyle occupied the corner of the room, unclothed and resting on his shins and forearms. Black hair covered his back. His arms and legs were still long, making him look absurdly lanky. His slightly extended snout was hairless, and sweat covered his clammy skin.

He stared blankly at the cracks in the floor, breathing heavily, mumbling incoherently.

Donnan stepped forward. "Don't you move, laddie!"

Kyle swiveled his head toward MacLeod. His eyes were sullen, tilted inward, his cheekbones high and angular. He had an overbite, with sharp canines reaching down his chin.

He said with despair in his cracking voice, "Get it out of me. Help me!"

The professor supported his large-barreled weapon while reaching into his jacket pocket.

Kyle moved up to a crouched position, his hands flat on the floor in front of him. He jerked his head to the side and clenched his jaws, as if trying to keep his canines from growing.

He shouted, "Shoot me!"

"Stay down, I told you!" The shaky MacLeod pulled a water bottle from inside his jacket. He knelt and rolled it on the floor to Kyle, still keeping his gun trained on him.

Donnan stood back up, "You drink it and you drink it quick."

Kyle took the bottle in his bony hand and gave a quick look back at Donnan.

MacLeod exclaimed, his accent growing thicker, "I'm going to blast ya in three seconds if ya don't!"

Kyle uncapped the bottle and poured it down his throat. The liquid sloshed down his chin and neck.

MacLeod mumbled under his breath, "Christ, shit, this better work."

Suddenly, Kyle doubled over like a fastball pitch had pelted him in the stomach, dropping the half-empty bottle.

His right forearm grew five inches in an instant, and claws sprouted from his fingernail beds. He looked up at Donnan with pure hate in his bright yellow eyes.

MacLeod shifted his right foot back to brace for the gun's blast and waited.

As Kyle rose to his feet, he curiously looked down at his arm.

He raised it in front of him and examined it, front and back—it was human again.

Swiftly, Kyle shrank, his bones snapping back to their original formation with a sound like knuckles cracking. His face lost all scorn, and a wave of disbelief came over him as the hair left his back and his teeth flattened.

Donnan laid the gun on the single bed and scooped Kyle's clothes off the floor. "For cryin' out loud, put some clothes on." He tossed the bundle toward Kyle.

Kyle strenuously raised his index finger at Donnan. "You're him? You're MacLeod?"

"That's right." MacLeod's demeanor had cooled, and his accent wasn't nearly as thick. "Donnan MacLeod. Just call me Donnie."

When MacLeod said his name, a delighted smile stretched across Kyle's untidy beard, and he released a hysterical giggle that strengthened into a continuous laugh.

MacLeod's face opened, and he laughed madly with the young man. He sat down at a small fold-out table, catching his breath.

He removed his sock hat and asked Kyle, "So what's your name?"

Kyle lied, "Sam Harris."

"Sure it is," Donnan remarked. "Well, put your pants on, Sam. We have a lot to talk about."

MACLEOD MADE THEM instant coffee on a miniature propane burner as they sat at a scarred wooden table. The chubby man took a sip from his thermos cap and scratched his bearded chin as he continued filling in Kyle.

"I call it my 'muley cam.' It's inside the nostril of one of the mule deer in the living room. I have them all over the place. I can monitor my security system's footage online while I'm away. Lucky for you, I disabled my alarm system—my wife, she forgets the dammed code all the time."

Kyle nodded at this, though it was odd. No woman had come by the whole time he was there, nor did it seem like a woman, or any other person, had currently been living at the house.

"I suppose more attention should have been paid to locking and wiring windows, in retrospect. Nonetheless, I saw you walk around as the beast and destroy the place until you decided the fireplace was where you would bed down. Once the sun shined through all the windows, you changed back to your fleshy self. I timed how long it took you to change upon first light of day. I wanted to help you with your demon, but if I waited until you were already human to give you the drink, I wouldn't know if it worked. Catching you on the way down was the best time to test its effectiveness . . . to a degree."

Kyle chose not to inform him of the intermittentness of his curse, half-changing randomly without the influence of a full moon as of late. Not just yet.

MacLeod set his coffee aside and folded his hands. "And speaking of that—your changing . . . I have a lot of questions for you, my young friend."

Kyle looked up from his coffee. "Yeah, sorry about that."

"Oh, I don't care about the damage—*how* did you become a werewolf?" MacLeod's smile was giddy.

On the one hand, Kyle was pleased that he'd found his man, and that no convincing would be necessary to solicit his help. He was also overjoyed that MacLeod had sought him out without getting the police involved. But at the same time, he found it disturbing that the man could speak so lightly of Kyle's horrific condition. Maybe MacLeod had no idea about the things Kyle did.

It occurred to Kyle that keeping certain information to himself would be beneficial—but how much should he conceal? He would have to feel MacLeod out, give him just enough information for the professor to help him without revealing his crimes. After all, the man was still a stranger.

Fenn rubbed his face as he tried to think this conversation through. "Well, it was by Yellowstone Lake, there was this cave, and this big skull, and petroglyphs and pictograms—it's a long story. I think you need to fill me in on what the *hell* is going on with me first, and what was in that bottle?"

Kyle was surprised to find MacLeod with an ecstatic smile stretched across his face. Donnan clapped his hands once. "You found him? I always *knew* he would be near the lake."

"Who?"

Donnan exclaimed, "You *found* him!" His belly bounced as he hooted exuberantly.

MacLeod drew another sip of coffee and wiped his mouth. "Fair enough, my friend. I will tell you all you need to know, then you will tell me about this cave, yes?"

Kyle nodded and thought, *Finally, some answers.*

Donnan leaned back in his metal chair as it strained under his wide torso. He took a deep breath. "Well, Sam, you found the resting tomb of one particularly gifted shaman. The legend says a certain Native tribe in Yellowstone, known as the Yohawnee, had a shaman with remarkable talents—talents we would label as supernatural. He could summon demons, heal the sick, curse the wicked, do unnatural things that defied the powers of mortal man. His mother claimed he was seeded in her womb spontaneously. As he grew up and developed his powers, the tribe grew wary of him. He was seen as a freak. His life was that of an outcast, not banished from the tribe, but living on its fringes, in caves. It's said he performed a great miracle by reviving the chief's son after a gruesome wolverine attack, but still, they shunned him because of his other-worldly nature. As the story goes, he had no name, but the tribe called him *duhu ku'uta,* or Black Cloak, because he was always seen roaming the land wearing a dark bison hide, one as black as night. The hide came from a black buffalo he created. As this buffalo grew up, he became friends with it, could speak to it."

Kyle ran his fingers around the rim of his coffee, remembering his vision of the shaman and that ominous buffalo hide he wore.

MacLeod continued. "Anyway, a time came when another tribe migrated into Yellowstone from the north—

the Wahota. They are—sorry, were—a brutal tribe. They were gifted . . . "

Donnan paused suddenly. His eyes slipped away from Kyle and out the window. He cleared his throat, " . . . excuse me—in warfare, gifted in warfare, and they invaded the Yohawnee, nearly driving them out of the area. That is, until the unlikeliest of heroes, our Black Cloak, conjured a moon demon and injected it into himself. He performed a particularly dark blood ritual, one that involved sacrificing an animal under the full moon and taking on its liking. He chose a timberwolf and he became a werewolf—a *full-time* werewolf, since he was directly infected by the demon. From there, he went on to bite and infect his fellow tribesmen, who then only changed when the moon was full and at its strongest, fueling the moon spirit within them, thus producing your typical werewolves as we know them. Thinking of it medically, their infections were secondary, demonstrating only acute symptoms during the full moon like it is an antigen and their changing was the auto-immune response. The shaman and his werewolf brethren dispatched out under the full moon and ruthlessly slaughtered the Wahota, eventually driving them away."

"So, he was a hero?"

"He *did* save his people. And yet, he was still no hero." The window light illuminated MacLeod's blue-gray eyes. They were absent, blank like the lifeless eyes of a doll as he was lost in thought. After a beat, the ex-professor drew in a long breath like he had not yet inhaled since beginning the conversation, "Look, the great matter here is that the water works." MacLeod cleared his throat again. "I mean, the concoction I mixed, it works. It keeps the werewolf inside you away. And good thing, too. I didn't want to blow your head off, necessarily."

"You didn't know it was going to work?"

"The probability was high that it would work, however, I needed to see it do so with my own eyes. That is why I showed up at precisely the time I did. I would not be a true scientist if I held probabilities as certainties, now would I?"

Kyle confessed, "Actually, you don't know how lucky you were."

"Oh?"

"I've been here for . . . " Kyle peered through the open door, "well, two months now, I think, and I only remember being me about half the time."

MacLeod's eyes widened. "Of course, a direct infection. *Fuck* me." He looked thoughtfully through the doorway as well. "You're destined to be full-time, just like the shaman was. I suppose, just like some chronic infections, it takes time to build, the symptoms get more severe, more permanent as you go." Donnan retrieved another plastic bottle from his jacket pocket and forced it into Kyle's hands. "You keep these on you at all times. I have more. It is imperative that you stay near me—I am the only one who knows the recipe."

Kyle held the bottle. "So, what *is* this?"

"It's the end of Black Cloak's story. Like I said, they still didn't view him as a hero, despite saving them. The Wahota were gone and there was peace again. But it wasn't the

Yohawnee way to be violent, so they shifted gears—changed strategies. What you have in that bottle is what the tribe used to heal its warriors when they decided the killings, the werewolf gift, was unnecessary. They no longer had a need for the shaman monster and the poor guy retreated to his cave where his mortal body died."

"And I was the lucky one who found him."

"Speaking of that, was there any artwork or paintings, etchings perhaps, inside that cave?"

"Yeah. Like, mountains, paw prints . . . and eyes. There were lots of big eyeball-looking things."

"Warding off evil spirits. Probably arrows pointing inward at a dot too?"

Kyle was impressed. He nodded. "Yeah."

"Likely, the warriors entered after he died and decorated the place." MacLeod eyed the water bottle. "Look, you don't know how many years of research it took me to acquire that concoction. People give me dirty looks when I tell them how much of the folklore holds up. Those *twats*. I have studied Yellowstone indigenous heritage and history through its entirety. No one knows more than me. That is something I am very proud of. Now, you guard that bottle with your life."

Donnan scooted his chair closer and leaned over the table, his glasses fogging from his coffee's steam. He raised his eyebrows and said, "Talk about preventative medicine."

Kyle leaned back in his chair, crossed his arms over his chest, and looked out the broken window in contemplation.

MacLeod said, "This shaman wolfman was the most dominant creature to ever walk through Yellowstone, and that is saying something. They even gave the creature a name, once he was no longer human, no longer Black Cloak."

Kyle said with a sigh, "*Bayosh.*"

MacLeod was utterly dumbstruck, his mouth hanging open. "How do you know that name?"

Kyle stood and pointed through the doorway. "He showed himself to me down at that stream. At least some version of his self. He kept me from—" He stopped himself. That was too personal. Plus, it hurt to think about it.

Suddenly, something caught Kyle's eye—something horrifying. Out the back window, he saw a boot and an ankle protruding from a loose pile of dirty snow and sticks. He recognized the small tattoo near the ankle—a flowing feather wrapping its way through the word *Mom.*

Kyle darted to the back door, which was padlocked from the outside. He reared back and rammed his shoulder through it. The small door burst out into the mountain air like it had been rigged with C4 explosives.

When he reached the shallow grave, Kyle dug through the snow and debris like his life depended on it. As he dug and scraped, he wept desperately.

MacLeod stood back in the doorway, quietly observing.

When Kyle was able to remove Nicole's body, he pulled her close and cradled her. She had blood stains at the side of her head and down the length of her body. Her once light-brown skin was now ghostly pale, her lips blue. Crimson, dried blood saturated the side of her abdomen around several puncture wounds in the shape of a bite.

He screamed, "Nicole! My God, Nicole! Wake up, baby, wake up . . . " Kyle bawled and rocked her in his arms.

MacLeod asked, "Sam, who is—".

Donnan stopped mid-inquiry when the woman began to move and moan. She blinked, struggling to keep her eyes open.

"Look at me," Kyle moaned through his tears. "It's me, Kyle. Hey, it's me. It's okay, baby."

She began to cry.

He removed his thick coat and wrapped her with it.

MacLeod whispered, "Truly fascinating."

Without looking away from Nicole, Kyle addressed Donnan, "I've done this before. I've buried before."

Kyle lifted Nicole and rushed past MacLeod as he carried her inside. "Hold on, look at me. I got you. It's okay. You're okay."

Nicole sobbed, "Kyle?"

MacLeod studied the dug-up ground. He glanced back at the cabin and scratched the back of his neck.

He mumbled to himself, "Well, this complicates things."

CHAPTER 34

FOUR HIKERS SAID they'd found blood in the backcountry on Eagle Peak trail. They claimed to have seen it in an area where the trail hugged around a rock wall, and that they'd also found an empty tent not far from the sight.

Henry was the Chief Ranger's choice to handle the call. The four investigating officers would need to be on horseback due to the location's treacherous landscape. If there was work to be done on the mountainside on horseback, he'd told Henry over the phone, it was best done by a RedMoon.

Henry was happy to deal with the investigation, as long as he didn't have to sort out the hoopla with the local news. The hikers had gloated about what they'd found in an interview with three separate reporters. Between this latest news and the Boiling River incident only a few weeks ago, explained away as a gruesome grizzly attack, the media was in a full-on frenzy.

Chief told Henry he wanted a real assessment of this incident, if there even was one, before other Park Service officials got there, muddied up the scene, and found nothing worth a damn because they weren't as "acclimated to the mountain" as Henry.

After three hours of hoofing through the valley trail, then ascending toward Eagle Peak, Henry and his counterpart, Officer Hodges, rode their horses in silence. Henry rode a pinto horse, its hide a patchwork of large white and pecan splotches, and Hodges sat awkwardly on a khaki gelding, the officer's face grimacing from groin pain—a discomfort he'd grumbled about the entire trip.

For the past hour, the two navigated steep switchbacks, the view over the sprawling valley floor shrinking at every turn, their location growing ever isolated.

When they'd reached a series of cliff ledges, stacked on top of one another, Henry raised his hand and halted their convoy. The air was different here, he sensed.

RedMoon narrowed his eyes and opened his senses. He looked at his boot and tilted his head a moment, the plane of his wide brimmed ranger hat parallel with the mountain slope.

He waited a beat.

Hodges said, "What are—"

"Shut up." RedMoon's deep voice carried down the mountain.

Pulling air in through his nose, RedMoon steadied his gaze straight ahead and sensations came to him.

He felt something big rush passed him. It thudded, panted, carrying a load. It was something enormous and filled with fury. Its rancid odor lingered on the mountain, and it stirred up something deep within Henry's core like nothing he'd felt before.

Henry steered his horse to an area just thirty meters from the trail and looked at the ground.

He saw large, bipedal indentions in the ground where the thin snow and pine needles were forced into the mud. The tracks continued up the ridge, running south—the opposite direction of the grid coordinates where the hikers claimed they found the blood.

RedMoon nudged his horse's flanks with his heels and stepped off to follow the tracks northward.

Hodges looked around and threw up his hands in frustration. "Where are you going? Do you want me to follow you, or . . . ?" His gelding followed Henry. "Okay, we're going with him. Here we go. Who needs the trail, am I right Sea Biscuit?"

As Henry followed the tracks, they came upon a trail of blood. Meandering the mountainside, they followed the tracks and blood for two miles.

Hodges followed behind, struggling several times to get his horse to move—he'd click his tongue at the horse, and it would respond by burying its muzzle in the snow and rooting for blades of grass.

Eventually the tracks and blood led them back to the trail and then to the rock face. Henry checked his GPS tracker. Sure enough, these were the coordinates Chief had given them.

RedMoon dismounted his horse and examined the rock wall. A blood splatter was imprinted on its surface near a corner, approximately five to six feet from the ground. The blood was a few days old by Henry's estimation. He could picture the creature stalking on one side of the corner and the victim approaching the other. He instinctively swiveled his head to the nearby limb of a Douglas fir. A long strand of honey-brown hair clung to it.

Searching the ground where the blood was thickest, he saw something similar to a jellybean in shape and size, but flesh toned.

He squatted and pinched it out of the bloody dirt—a small hearing aid. It fell apart in his hand.

"Hodges."

"Yeah, Boss?"

RedMoon opened his mouth but rolled his eyes first. He turned back around the rock corner and scowled at Hodges.

"Sorry, District Officer RedMoon."

Henry sighed—he'd told Hodges dozens of times to simply call him Henry. "Did you run the plates on that Explorer at the trailhead like I asked?"

Hodges fumbled at his small notebook. "Uh, that's right. A ninety-three Ford Explorer. Belonged to a Nicole Bowman in Blacksburg, Virginia. Twenty-seven years old."

Just then, RedMoon spotted a hiking pack leaning against a fallen tree beyond Hodges. Henry lowered his gaze and thought for a few seconds.

"Hodges, you head back to the trailhead and lead the others in when they arrive. I'm staying to secure the area."

"But that's like thirteen miles."

There were answers Henry wanted, before the "real investigators" arrived. There were things he didn't want them to find, like bipedal tracks. Henry wasn't notified of the Boiling River fatalities until after the scene was locked down. He wasn't able to search and get a feel for what really happened there. The authorities had labeled that event a grizzly attack, but Henry had a terrible hunch they'd misdiagnosed what really happened that full-moon night.

Henry said, "You'll be fine. You're a . . . " Henry looked away, hiding his face under his hat. His voice was nearly inaudible as he lied, "You're a great rider. I'm sure you can find your way and lead them back. I trust you."

Hodges beamed with pride. "All right, you got it, Boss."

THE CLOUDS MELTED into the purple sky, and the sky into the mountains, until the entire horizon muddled into the same sleepy, dark state. Once the sun had tucked itself away behind the western ranges of Paradise Valley, the foot-to-ceiling windowpane at Kyle and Nicole's noses had been painted black, except for a multitude of stars dusting the sky. The couple had watched the dusk's shifting shades in silence, saturated with one another's presence.

Nicole lifted the tail of the flannel shirt MacLeod had given her and pulled back the bandaging on her side. She told Kyle, "Look."

All that remained from her bite wound were five small puncture sites with barely visible scar tissue—mere blemishes.

Kyle's shoulders collapsed, and he exhaled. He tenderly grabbed the sides of her head and kissed her brow. The swelling and discoloration at her temple was long gone, and her soft, light brown complexion had returned. Seeing her heal so rapidly helped dull the pain of regret and unease that weighed in his gut.

Only days ago, Kyle had pulled Nicole from the shallow, snowy grave his wolf form had dug for her, and Nicole's resilience within the horrific circumstances astounded Kyle. He witnessed her courage as she'd suffered through a range of emotions, from enduring the aching pain in her head and wounds, to turning pale when he explained the curse to her, referring to it as "the infection," to her peering stoically through the window as they drove to MacLeod's estate, to waking up in a panic in the middle of the night after finally falling asleep and squeezing Kyle tightly; shivering, scared out of her mind.

Still, despite the horrible things he had to tell her, she managed to raise a half smile to him again and again, letting him know that she was still there, that she wouldn't allow her fears to overtake her. He was inspired by her durability, how she allowed the emotions to come, then pass, then come again, and still fight.

"MacLeod's Getaway" was a lighthouse and sanctuary for the two as they faced their new and grim realities together. They were in a stranger's home, yes, but above all else, they had each other again. With the knowledge that Kyle's counterpart was by his side came the hope that anything was possible. Kyle only hoped that Nicole truly felt the same way, though she had stated as much, bringing light back into his bleak world, offering a half-dozen times the words, "Kyle, I need you."

It was difficult to wrap his head around the fact she held him faultless, telling him many times that it wasn't he who killed, that he was doing everything he could not to hurt people, that she knew Kyle would never intentionally hurt her, and that everything would work out, somehow.

Kyle and Nicole had shared thoughts last night, analyzing their situation, strategizing over their future. The bizarre liquid mixture MacLeod had given them worked, and they would depend on it for the rest of their lives. The two of them had been partaking in the drink, consuming a shot every four hours as instructed by Dr. MacLeod, since their reuniting at Turret Mountain. Nicole still "took her medicine" despite the assumption that her infection was secondary, and she only had the full-moon nights to fear.

As far as civilization was concerned, Kyle was a wanted man, and Nicole was missing. It was only a matter of time before MacLeod figured out the former. Obviously, Nicole would soon be searched for by the badge, but MacLeod oddly never discussed her predicament. They thought it strange that the professor never offered her the phone to call home or anywhere, although it wasn't something they had requested or wanted anyway.

Kyle had his own apprehensions. MacLeod's motives were as murky as the dead, black eyes of his stuffed mule deer. Perhaps MacLeod knew more than he should. The Scot could have easily assumed that Kyle had killed before coming to his house, but never asked about that either. Had MacLeod found it in his heart to help the two of them out of pity, knowing Kyle was not at fault? Or maybe MacLeod was so fascinated by their infections that he was willing to hide them from the law. Was it possible his scientific mind wanted to lock them up, study them, dissect them? Kyle had seen crazier things in the past year. Maybe it was any combination of these hypotheticals. Each of his theories was not without substance and hung in the air above Kyle like a fog, awaiting resolution.

Kyle said softly, "How's the headache?"

"Completely gone. I've felt great all day."

She raised a hand to feel her head, and her fingers brushed her ear. Pushing the tip of her finger into her earhole, she whispered, "Oh my God."

"What?"

"My hearing aid."

Nicole turned her head as if searching for something with her eyes not directly focused on anything. She repeated, "Oh my God."

"Are you okay?"

"I can hear. I can hear just fine. I hadn't even noticed." She looked at him, her mouth agape, eyes wide with a look of both pleasant astonishment and fright.

They embraced and pressed their foreheads together. He knew they would have to hold on to moments like these, considering the challenges they faced.

Kyle said, "We're gonna make it."

Nicole starred up at him with brave eyes. "I think I'll take my mother's name. Kelly."

Kyle replied, "And your last name?"

He secretly hoped she would say "Fenn."

She smiled up at him. "Harris."

Kyle looked skyward through the window at the winking stars. "Sam and Kelly Harris. Yeah, I can live with that. But you don't look like a Kelly."

"Oh, really? What do I look like?"

"An angel."

MacLeod stood behind his bar at the other end of the immense living room. He set out empty water bottles and began filling them with the liquid from the gallon jugs. His voice volleyed off the walls of the large corridor. "I would ask you two to get a room, but I am afraid I have already accommodated you with one!"

He paused his bottle filling and gathered two CamelBaks, common hiking equipment meant to keep people hydrated as they trekked through the wilderness. They resembled small backpacks, but were actually bladders fixed with flexible hoses that could be sucked on like a straw. A big smile stretched across MacLeod's face as he waddled to Kyle and Nicole.

As he handed the hydration systems to Kyle and Nicole, he said, "Has the happy couple ever used these before?"

They nodded.

"Yes, yes. I know, it may be overkill, but it sets my mind at ease. Try them for a while anyway, won't you? Especially you, Sam."

Nicole said, "It's not overkill. We're glad to have them."

Kyle accepted the offer. "No problem, Doc."

Nicole adjusted the straps on the CamelBak and said, "You're too kind, Mr. MacLeod. We're lucky to have met you. Thank you."

MacLeod straightened his face. "Well, no need to thank me. I brought you here to murder you."

Nicole and Kyle stared at the stocky man, speechless at his sudden cold façade.

Donnan snorted, "I'm just fuckin' with ya. Just because you are werewolves doesn't mean we can't still joke a bit, aye?"

Nicole said, "I knew I liked you, Mr. MacLeod."

"It's *Donnie*. I will not tell you again." He rubbed his hands together, "Now, I do, however, want your blood. Come with me."

Donnan turned and continued speaking as he walked, "I will need to draw venous samples from you regularly to check your mercury levels. I want to be sure that I'm not giving you too much of the liquid solution. If you are to stay in my care, I will require regular monitoring."

Kyle and Nicole followed behind.

Kyle said, "When we're done, we need to talk about finding Hatfield. He needs to be stopped. We can help him."

There was a hitch in MacLeod's step as Kyle made the suggestion. Without turning his head, he said, "Of course. Yes, we will have to address that."

CHAPTER 35

AT SEVEN IN the evening, drinking coffee as black as his hair, Henry sat outside a corner coffee shop in Gardiner, his coal-black Stetson shading his steady eyes. He was off duty, but he was still dressed tight, his denim button-up shirt pressed and tucked neatly into his snug, black Wrangler jeans. His lean figure tilted back in the dainty chair, one ankle resting on the other knee, his elbows on the armrests, pushing his broad shoulders up to his ears. He stood out among the passersby streaming the sidewalk, selecting the next boutique or outdoor apparel shop to browse.

Henry had yet to explain this Dr. MacLeod's reconnaissance of him, or rather, his reason for it. What did he want from Henry? It seemed MacLeod's secret visits had ceased after the night he approached his ForeRunner. RedMoon's two-day vigil outside MacLeod's Getaway a few weeks ago had turned up nothing: no one, not a single light flickered on or off, and no vehicles had gone in or out.

And what did the archaeologist-turned-alcoholic make of the killings at Boiling River? If MacLeod was privy to knowledge of the RedMoon family, surely he would be suspicious of the three slayings, not misguided by the "common knowledge" that it was a bear attack. It was within the ballpark of that time, Henry remembered, that MacLeod had seemingly abandoned Henry's trail. Was he afraid of Henry? If RedMoon could just find MacLeod and speak with him, he could find out exactly what MacLeod knew of his family. Henry could approach him and use the persuasiveness of his uniform to pitch the lie that the Boiling River and Eagle Creek affairs were the works of a rogue grizzly and that whatever he may have heard about the Wahota-RedMoon legacy was nonsense.

Henry was in a jam. Although he'd parted ways with his family, he would always feel obligated to protect them—everyone but Sid, anyway. Henry understood too well that the RedMoon secret could never get out, that it would undoubtedly be their demise.

Other aspects puzzled Henry as well. There must have been a link between the missing woman at Eagle Peak and the melee at the Cody Rodeo, where the senator's daughter went missing. Witnesses at the rodeo were reporting things that didn't match up against anything a grizzly or other wild predator would do, and public interest was becoming a little too magnified for Henry's comfort. He was perplexed by the idea of linking the two events—Eagle Peak and the rodeo did, after all, occur under the same full moon. Was it possible for a RedMoon to cover that amount of distance in one night?

Henry wished to confront his family, but he needed more evidence first, a sharper plan of approach, and a better understanding of which RedMoon would be carrying out these gruesome attacks if that was the case. It wasn't like his father to venture far in his bloodlust, and it was unbecoming of the rest of them, so this being a RedMoon act was highly questionable.

There was, Henry thought, one other prospect, an answer to all this, but it was so farfetched that he snickered at himself. Those tales were nothing but concocted stories to scare the children—a way for RedMoon mothers, fathers, aunts, and uncles to get back at the young ones for all their rambunctious behavior.

Henry laughed again at the thought and lifted his coffee mug to his mouth. He sipped, then frowned. The beverage had gotten cold while he'd lost himself in contemplation.

He signaled to the waitress.

She whisked by with a hot pot.

Henry shook his head, "No, could you please fill me up when you brew a fresh batch?" He was well aware of his fussiness, but he couldn't help himself.

"Sure thing." She turned on her heel, and he stopped her.

"How long will that take?"

"I'll start a pot right now."

"Thank you."

As she strolled off, a dark emotion suddenly hit Henry like a truck. He sat straight up, and surveyed his surroundings. A feeling of pure evil, or hate—something Henry couldn't place, had instantly surrounded him.

Just then, a green Toyota ForeRunner at the intersection in front of Henry blared its horn.

An angry man with long, blonde hair and a goatee approached the front of the vehicle. His eyes were red around the irises, like they bled internally. In the backseat—a woman with honey-brown hair.

NINE HOURS OF patrolling Gardiner was sure to turn up Russell Hatfield, or at least some sign of him. Kyle and Nicole rode in the back as Dr. MacLeod drove them through the clean, tourist-lined streets.

Hatfield had presumably been changing and killing in recent months. As Kyle had theorized, it would explain the slain trio at Boiling River and the Cody Rodeo attacks. According to witnesses, both incidents involved a "blonde beast" rampaging about on two legs.

In their efforts to spot Hatfield, they had scanned the Green Goose Saloon several times and walked into all of the other restaurants dotting the main streets. They hoped to recognize his long, sandy-blonde hair and hefty figure somewhere amongst the May crowds, but so far, no luck.

MacLeod, who was more or less cooperative in their search despite being visibly reluctant, came to a stop at a red traffic light and huffed, "Are you sure he never mentioned where he lived or worked? Nothing?"

"No, he just said he went to The Goose a lot. Like I said, he told me he was a truck driver, but that was it." Kyle grew weary with the search and said with resignation, "Look, I can come back tonight by myself and try to catch him at The Goose."

MacLeod vehemently interjected, "I would not attempt it—not alone. And it is best to meet him in daylight with bystanders around." MacLeod gestured toward the sky. "It is dark enough already."

Kyle asked, "Then what should we do? Keep this up every day till we find him? What if he spotted us already? Hell, what if anyone's spotted us? We can't be out in public like this."

MacLeod said, "You are right. We should leave him be."

In light of MacLeod's gutsy actions on Turret Mountain, Kyle thought Donnan would be up to the task and willing to help thwart the infection from spreading further, from taking more lives.

When Donnan looked back, Kyle shot him a confused look, his eyebrows bent, "Are you scared, Donnie?"

"Well, yes. The killings that he seems to be involved in are brutal—like he enjoys it. I don't trust him. With you, I had the advantage of desolation and the security of my elephant gun, but not in this situation. I know there are weeks until his next full moon, but a murdering werewolf is a *murdering werewolf.* The man is off his trolley."

Nicole suddenly sat up in her seat.

She asked stoically, "Uh, guys? Is that him?"

When Kyle looked through the windshield, he saw the ominous, bulky man striding across the asphalt in front of them.

"That's him!" Kyle shouted.

MacLeod whimpered, "Oh dear."

Kyle reached into the front of the cab and slammed on the horn.

Russell turned his head and peered into their vehicle with bloodshot eyes, his gold hair framing his gruff face. He spotted Kyle and pivoted his broad body toward the Toyota.

At once, Kyle exited the ForeRunner and approached Hatfield. "If you want to know what happened to you, get in the car."

Looking down at Fenn, Hatfield said with sly sarcasm, "I'm sorry. I have no idea what you're talking about, Mr . . . ?"

Kyle felt a surge of confidence he'd never felt in his life. He felt like he could reach out and grab Russell by the collar and hurl him to the ground—like he was about to.

Fenn stepped closer and growled, "Get in the car."

Strangely, Hatfield backed away, his jaw slouching. He seemed to shrink before Kyle.

Russell adjusted his belt unnecessarily, then started for the back door.

Kyle grabbed Russell by the tricep. "No, get in the front seat."

MACLEOD HAD BEEN pacing the length of his bar, giving Russell a brief history lesson, the reasons for Russell's curse, and all that had led up to their current situation. Russell was quietly seated at his barstool, sipping at the beer MacLeod had offered, listening intently to MacLeod with a cryptic look.

Kyle and Nicole also sat at the bar, occasionally interjecting details to help MacLeod explain everything. Kyle had sat purposefully between Russell and Nicole and was monitoring Hatfield's every move.

"That's why you woke up, half-buried, not ripped to pieces. You were chosen, or spared, however you wish to look at it. Like I said, I refer to it as an infection, because that is exactly what it is." Donnan beamed with pride. "And I have the medicine for it."

MacLeod paused, waiting for Russell's reply.

When Hatfield stayed quiet, MacLeod rolled his shoulders and said, "Look at your face—so *doomy and gloomy.* You are a miracle sitting right before my eyes—all three of you. This is a call for celebration, not gloom."

He danced over to a cabinet with a glass door and removed a liquor bottle, handling it cautiously as if it would explode if shaken. The twist lid crackled as he opened it and set it on the bar near Nicole.

She asked, "What is it?"

"A Highland Scotch, aged fifty-three years."

Hatfield let out a soft whistle. "Goddamn," he said huskily.

Hearing him finally break his silence gave Kyle some relief, though he remained guarded.

MacLeod said, "It's been awaiting a special occasion. What better occasion than this?"

He carefully filled four shot glasses with the brown liquor.

Nicole suddenly slapped the table, causing a jump out of both Kyle and Russell as they leaned on the wooden surface.

"He's right, loosen up. We might as well get used to each other. Sure, this sucks, and we're probably stuck with it for life, but I for one am not going to mope about it."

Kyle smiled, though he could tell she was still trying to convince herself of her own words.

Nicole pinched one of the shot glasses with her fingertips and downed the aged scotch. Hatfield distributed the remaining three shot glasses amongst the men, and MacLeod poured.

Russell and Kyle shared a glance, and with a short nod from Kyle, agreed on peace for at least one shot.

They raised their shots quickly and drank, then set glasses back on the bar top.

Kyle hid his wince.

MacLeod quickly poured himself another and indulged.

For a quiet minute, the likely reality that Hatfield had murdered willfully, which had not been addressed, filled the room like a woolly mammoth, its enormous tusks idling overhead.

Hatfield still swirled the Scotch in his mouth. He tilted his head back, swished some more, closed his eyes, then swallowed like he wanted to taste every year it had aged.

Russell stroked his hairy chin in deep thought. He gave a protracted sigh and finally spoke, "So I'm guessing that you guys have some ideas about what I've been doing on full moons. I'm also assuming you know about the crazy shit that's been going down around here—that guy and those two Polish bitches who got killed at Boiling River, the thing people say they saw at the Cody Rodeo."

He had the appearance of a dim-witted biker grunt, but laid out his profanity-littered words with plenty of forethought and calculation.

"The answer to the question you're not asking me is no, I didn't kill any of those people. I only have a few flashbacks of those nights. Most of them are of killing Angus cows or chasing down deer. Besides, any other memories that may or may not have come to me are my own damn business."

He grabbed the bottle and poured himself another shot. "With that being said, and as far as you know, I haven't done anything wrong. And that's all that will be said about it. Same goes for Sam, or whatever his name is, and whatever he's done. If my name gets mixed up in the same conversation with all of that crazy shit, I'll know exactly who talked."

Russell made these threats without looking Kyle in the eye. He drank the shot and filled the other three shot glasses.

"I think we understand each other. And now, Doc here is going to tell us the recipe so we don't have to depend on him. Ain't that right?"

"I will not. It would not be wise. I will not risk overdose. We have not tested its strength pre-change, only at the tail end of it. No, no, much more research is needed before I can formulate the precise mixture, how much to take, and when, in order to get maximum efficiency—these types of things."

MacLeod's shirt had ridden up, and suddenly taking notice, he hastily pulled it down over his belly. "Now, I'm going to offer you a place in my home—all three of you. I will need a significant amount of time before I am comfortable letting you go with a fully effective recipe. Until then, my home is your home. If anyone should ask me, which they never will because we will remain out of sight, you are former students whom I have invited to stay for a length of time and carry my supplies for me on my digs. I will play the old-man card and say you work all the gadgets for me as well. I will say you're helping a fossil like me keep his home, giving him company to make his days a bit brighter. Furthermore, for the sake of science and establishing a solid remedy, any past transgressions on any of your parts will be null and void."

"Not a *bad* plan," Kyle said, "but why are you helping us?"

"If I were to release you into the wild and the infection became an epidemic, I would not want to be on the wrong side of history, being the one who could have stopped it and did not. And if I gave you over to authorities, well, I can't imagine what the government's scientists might have in store for the likes of you."

Nicole asked, "Are you sure, what about when the moon is full? Are you going to be safe? Do you really trust the drink that much? No offense, but I'm not sure I trust it completely yet."

"None taken. I knew this would be a concern, and I have drawn up a plan for that as well."

Hatfield spit, "Oh, this should be good."

MacLeod said, "Luckily, the previous owners of this land were farmers. I have an empty silo just across the property there. I will begin reinforcing it to contain you on the full moon. Of course, I do not believe it to be necessary—only precautionary. I am certain you will only endure one long, boring night listening to the crickets.

Kyle said, "All of that doesn't sound too hard."

MacLeod moved his eyes over each of them. "Do you agree to let me help you?"

Russell replied, "No. I don't agree to shit. I might be drinking your stuff when the time comes, but that's it. You ain't stickin' me in no goddamn silo, and you're not getting any of my blood."

"That is perfectly fine, Mr. Hatfield—to each his own. I only wish to help, and you are free to come and go as you please."

Turning to Kyle and Nicole, MacLeod said, "I'll forget anything that I might have heard back at that ranger cabin regarding your identities. However, if someone were to ask you tomorrow what your names were, what would you say?"

Kyle answered, "I'm still Sam. She's Kelly. We're the Harris's."

MacLeod asked, "And what do you do?"

Nicole said, "College kids, helping you with your research." She looked around the immaculate yet dusty living room. "This place could use a woman's touch, anyway."

Kyle knew they didn't have much of a choice, knowing that they were doomed to kill without MacLeod's help. He put his arm around Nicole's shoulder. "Yeah, Donnie, I think you're stuck with us."

"Let us make our pact official, then," MacLeod said.

The three of them consumed the Scotch shots that MacLeod had prepared a moment ago. Kyle opened one of the plastic bottles filled with the remedy and topped off three shot glasses, then placed them in front of each of the changelings. "I guess some of this wouldn't hurt either, huh?"

Kyle and Nicole took down the drink like a couple on spring break, but Hatfield left his.

Kyle said, "Come on, it just tastes like mineral water."

Russell got up from his bar stool. "You're all out of your fucking minds." He took the scotch bottle and walked toward the front door.

"Where the hell are you going?" Kyle asked.

"Home."

"We have a truck, you know," Kyle said sarcastically.

Russell slammed the door behind him.

Donnan said, "Let him go, let him go. He is a creature of the night now. We have done what we could for him. It is up to him to decide. I am more at a loss for the scotch. That was just downright rude."

MacLeod was right—it would be a waste of energy trying to convince Hatfield to stay. What could Kyle do, kidnap the man? Russell said it with his own mouth—he'd drink the miracle drink when the time came. Kyle had to worry about keeping himself in check and protecting Nicole. She would be safe here with him in this luxurious fortress, safer than if Hatfield were around anyway.

CHAPTER 36

WHEN KYLE AWOKE at seven-thirty in the morning, he noticed Nicole was not by his side. He clumsily got to his feet and went to the doorway where he heard the gentle clinking of glass at the end of the hall.

He padded through the wide corridor, then into the kitchen with a sleepy sway and squinty eyes where he found Nicole, washing wine glasses at the sink. The first rays of dawn's light shot through the window and bounced off the riveted brass plating of the fume hood near her.

Kyle knew Nicole harbored anxiety about the upcoming full moon and assumed that was why she was up. She had told him that she had faith the solution would work, but a distant worry in her mind told her that there was something awry. The feeling of being watched also disturbed her from time to time, she'd said. Kyle reminded her of the cameras, but she insisted it was more than that. Kyle told her it was just nerves, though he had the same inkling at times.

"Hey. You're up early again," he said.

"Yeah. I couldn't really sleep."

She finished drying the wine glass in her hand and hung it upside-down in a rack overhead. "These things are all spotty. I thought I would tidy them up."

He pulled a glass from a handcrafted elm cabinet and filled it with water. "What's got you up this morning?"

"I couldn't stop thinking about Mom's urn and how it will probably end up with my worthless uncle. That is, if they find it."

"Maybe we can sneak up Eagle Peak one night, see if it's still there."

She put down her towel and locked her arms around his waist. "That's sweet, but you know it's too risky."

He couldn't argue.

She said, "It's just, the closer we get to the full moon, the realer it gets. Not that it isn't real enough already, all this."

Kyle wanted to reassure her. "That drink—when I swallowed it, it was like throwing a bucket of water on a campfire. It was amazing."

"So, you remember being that, um, *Bayosh*, before drinking that stuff?"

"Barely. Like I said, I only have flashbacks of a few seconds at a time."

She perched herself on a kitchen stool and straightened the items on the island as she thought through something. Finally, she said, "Do you ever think that maybe you have some kind of control whenever it happens, or is it all him?"

That thought had occurred to Kyle any time he reflected on the night in Tennessee—how his beast went after those coyotes. His flashbacks had showed him how he'd taken them down. Why would *Bayosh* have randomly targeted them, if not somehow under Kyle's control. He hated those coyotes and what they were doing to Scanland. Was it foolish to think his will persuaded or guided *Bayosh* at one moment or another?

Kyle opened his mouth to bring up the coyote question but stopped himself. He'd decided from the start that he wouldn't tell her about Tennessee. She'd said she didn't hold Kyle responsible for the things that had happened, the things his wolf must have done, and there was no need to test that. Instead, he asked, "Control? Why do you say that?"

"Kyle, *Bayosh* chose to infect me. Why wouldn't he just kill me? Was that you telling him to spare my life?"

He didn't want to state the obvious and hurt her feelings.

She said it for him. "Yeah, I know, he buried Russell too—I just like to think that you saved me because I'm special, I guess."

They shared small smiles.

Russell was another worry. Kyle thought he would be all right with the fact that he let Russell go, but like Nicole said, —the closer they got to a full moon . . .

Kyle had seen right through Russell's lies the other night at MacLeod's bar. There was a peculiar connection Kyle felt to Hatfield, like he could interpret his emotions, his moods, like watching the inside of a lava lamp morphing shape, changing colors. He detected a disturbing sense of recklessness and a hunger for power surrounding Hatfield.

Just then, Donnan walked into the kitchen in his bathrobe and house slippers. He opened the refrigerator and pulled out raw steaks wrapped in deli paper.

Observing Kyle's eyes closely, MacLeod waved the meat under Kyle's nose. "You see?"

"See what?" Nicole asked.

"Raw meat is inches from his nose, and there is not so much as a wink or a single drop of drool from the boy. And the yellowing of his irises appears to be restricted to approximately two to three millimeters."

He tossed the block of meat into the oversized basin-sink, causing a loud *bang.*

MacLeod said, "I couldn't help but overhear your discussion, and I think I can shed some light. May I?"

Kyle said, "You could hear us? Where were you?"

Donnan pointed at the half-bathroom at the front of the hallway, shrugged, then tightened his robe. He helped himself to a stool. "The control question—yes, it is my belief that it can be controlled over time. But we dare not test that belief, yes? Now, I venture to say that it was *Bayosh's* decision to bite and bury whom he did. You see, when the moon-demon *Bayosh* took the half-wolf, half-man physical form, he took on wolf-like characteristics. So naturally, I believe he is again trying to establish a pack. Wolf packs, as you may know, have a hierarchy, a job for each member. *Bayosh* is obviously the Alpha—he leads, he calls the shots, he gets what he wants and if he does not, someone will pay dearly, as evidenced by Mr. Hatfield's submission to Kyle at Gardiner. Russell, to me, seems like *Bayosh* selection as the protector. Oftentimes, the largest member takes on the role of protecting the pack, being the first one to charge into battle with a rival pack, and will be the one to enforce the rules of the pack at the dinner table as well—a bouncer, if you will. It appears that *Bayosh* has misjudged Russell's character, though, as there is too much aggression and dominance within him to fill this role appropriately."

MacLeod nodded at Nicole. "I would wager that you can guess what role he chose you for."

Kyle smiled and raised his eyebrows suggestively. "He's got good taste at least."

Nicole rolled her eyes.

Donnan rose from his stool and went to the refrigerator. He opened the door, and lingered for a moment, taking stock of the refrigerator contents. Finally, MacLeod pulled out the orange juice. "Anyway, I need to tell you to be careful if you do leave to find Mr. Hatfield. I just don't trust the man. This kind of power in the wrong hands can be disastrous."

Nicole asked, "So you think Russell did those things, killed those people?"

"Without question. However, our biggest concern is making sure 'the Harris's' are safe. Russell will choose for himself his own destiny. And speaking of your safety, I have great news. My work on the silo is well ahead of schedule. I will warn you, it is an intimidating sight. It may be best to wait until the day-of to show you the inside. I don't want to spook you."

Kyle said, hoping to ease Nicole's worries, "But like you said, we won't really need it anyway—it'll just be crickets."

"Yes, of course," MacLeod said. "Merely a precaution."

DISTRICT RANGER REDMOON roosted on the hood of his cruiser and focused his binoculars downhill toward Donnan MacLeod's grand mountain home, zooming in on the three figures in the kitchen. This morning, he'd snuck out of the office right after he brewed a pot of coffee and filled his thermos. His mug was on the hood next to him, its steam drifting up into the new morning air under the brisk, azure Montana sky. His position was just off a dirt road that skirted a patchy aspen and cedar forest surrounding the massive house.

Life had returned to MacLeod's Getaway.

That one chance sighting of the ForeRunner and the four individuals in the streets of Gardiner had led Henry back to this ridge, spying more intensely the occurrences on MacLeod's property. The information he gathered was not for the National Park Service or any justice system, but for his own curiosity and the safety of his family. That one possible scenario he feared might explain it all was inching closer toward reality the more he dug.

Henry easily recognized MacLeod from the YouTube videos and his driver's license photo.

It was the couple in the back who required a bit more research.

The woman's mixed complexion resembled his missing female from Eagle Peak. An internet search for "Nicole Bowman" had uncovered a twenty-second news video of her behind a microphone begging anyone with information about her missing boyfriend to please come forward. She'd given his name at the end; Kyle Fenn from Ashton, Tennessee. He was the man who went missing from Mountain Lake Hotel the same night a national forest ranger was slain in the adjacent mountains.

Henry discovered that Kyle Fenn, twenty-three, was featured in several sports news articles in Tennessee covering his heroics on baseball diamonds for the local college. The strapping young southerner was pictured diving for a flyball, swinging a bat with measured intensity, walking into home plate distributing high fives above his head. Henry had also read more recent back issues from the *Ashton Chronicle*, scanning for news in the days immediately following the most recent full moons. Once he found the article about the brutal disembowelment and murder of Patty Feltner, things started to add up.

Without a doubt, the man who'd exited the ForeRunner and forced the larger man into the vehicle matched Kyle Fenn's physical profile and appearance to a T.

But who was the larger man? A local perhaps. Certainly not a tourist—too rough.

Henry scratched his chin as he pondered that fourth individual. Lowering his binoculars, he looked at his chest and almost jumped. He'd forgotten that he was just at work this morning, that he was still in his uniform and using his patrol car. If spotted, he would certainly draw attention.

You're starting to let your guard down, he thought to himself. He had scouted and searched too tirelessly, knowing there were mere days until the next full moon night—the night he would have to make a monumental decision, if his theory turned out to be true.

Henry quickly got back into his cruiser and drove in the opposite direction of MacLeod's estate. As he drove away, Henry again thought about the man who had crossly met Kyle Fenn in front of MacLeod's Toyota. So far, he had not been able to locate nor identify the man. Despite walking through Gardiner several times, he simply couldn't spot him. Given the small population of the town, he knew he couldn't go asking about him either, risking his anonymity.

It itched at him—who was he, and why was there a strong sense of anger, even evil, about him? Henry wanted to place all suspicion on Fenn, and it would have been easy if not for this peculiar and hellish figure of a man.

Pop!

The sudden sound was similar to that of a tennis ball being whacked by a racket, only more powerful, and he thought for a second that it was a distant rifle shot.

Henry didn't stop—if there was a shooter, stopping would mean death. Patting himself, he checked for bullet wounds. He was intact.

Suddenly, the front of his car began to wobble and pitch, then bounce slightly. In his rearview mirror, Henry saw spike strips stretching across the narrow road, with several spikes missing.

He hit the brakes, and came to a sliding stop. There was abrasive hissing from his front tires as he stepped out. Henry silenced the microphone on his lapel and moved his eyes over the wooded mountainside paralleling the road.

He listened intently for any movement.

There was no sign of life.

He took stock of his options. There was one spare tire under the trunk, but he doubted the can of Fix-A-Flat would hold for the second tire. If it didn't fix the punctured tire, he would need a dammed good alibi when he called Hodges to make him drive all the way to Paradise Valley with a spare.

CHAPTER 37

EACH OAK BOARD around the outside of MacLeod's shed had finally been saturated with a Jacobean-colored wood stain. The quiescent, open air of the bright day comforted Kyle as he admired his work. Chores like these helped Kyle clear his mind so he could think through his problems more accurately.

As he applied the stain, board by board, he'd contemplated ways of making Nicole feel more at home, and how to better search for Russell if he decided to look for him.

The hush surrounding Kyle was interrupted by the occasional sound of MacLeod welding inside the silo a few acres away. A few finishing touches and he needed to see to the chains, he'd said, giving Kyle a bit of apprehension. It was necessary, though, and they needn't be stingy with measures of precaution. Kyle and Nicole had decided to stick to the plan, to trust MacLeod's process as everything he suggested had worked so far.

Kyle couldn't deny the strangeness in MacLeod, and that he wished there were other options, but there really weren't. As long as he had "the drink," as they were now calling it, they needed to be in MacLeod's proximity. They'd eventually have the recipe for themselves, but letting MacLeod science it out first was wise. The most accurate dosage needed to be figured. Kyle would be remiss if he and Nicole struck out on their own with a half-concocted recipe that ended up hurting Nicole. He'd never forgive himself.

Kyle placed the brush over the mouth of the bucket of stain. Next to the bucket was a tin sign. He stepped back to view it again.

Kyle had found the antique sign inside the shed a few hours ago. It contained an illustration of a yellow Model 706 National Park Bus, those used in Yellowstone as early as nineteen-thirty-six and phased out around the mid nineteen-sixties. These automobiles had fascinated Kyle when he'd worked in the park, and he'd spent time reading up on them. At one point, there were nearly a hundred of them carrying tourists around Yellowstone. He considered the bus's double-clutch operation and how the sounds of jamming gears must have echoed off the mountainsides and reverberated through the sweeping, geyser-riddled valleys. The machine's appearance was a peculiar one. The yellow bus had black, protruding wheel wells, a flat windshield, square windows, detached headlights, and a tall steel grill that dominated the front end. Its nature was that of a tuxedoed butler with his large nose upturned.

Kyle grasped his hammer, which lay on the ground next to the sign. When he stood up, he had a distinct feeling that someone was near. He could feel their presence as sure as a slap in the face.

Then he could smell them.

He heard the crunching of footfall, but it seemed to be coming to him from inside his head, as though it was broadcast via a tiny speaker in his ear. Still, he somehow knew exactly where the noise emanated from. His eyes moved directly to the turn of the building.

Kyle crept to the corner, cocked the hammer over his shoulder like a baseball bat, and peeked his head around.

There was Russell waiting for him at about eight paces away. The weighty man had his right hand out in front of him, exposing his upraised palm to Kyle and the other hand at his mouth, making a *shh* gesture.

Kyle lowered the hammer. "What the *hell* are you doing?"

"Hey, be quiet. Just come over here." Hatfield waved him over.

"You wanna tell me where you've been?"

Once they were out of view of the house, Russell said, "Look, there's some heavy shit you need to know about."

"What shit? Why aren't you here taking your medicine? You should've been here taking the drink this whole time."

"First off, don't call it 'medicine.' Who knows what the hell it is? Second off, *you* might need to drink it every day, but not me. I'm a secondary infection, remember?"

Hatfield's eyes continually observed their surroundings as he talked. "Did you know you had a Yellowstone ranger casing this place?"

"What are you talking about?"

"I took care of him. He won't be coming back soon—not in a marked car anyway."

"Russell, I've lived here for a good while and haven't seen anything like that."

Russell said roughly, "Yeah, but you haven't been looking. You've got your head so far up MacLeod's ass, I doubt you can see the sun shining. Don't you see what he's doing? He's using you."

"Using me?"

"That drink—he's going to *sell it.*"

Kyle thought, then said, "Then why would he be helping us? Where would be the demand if there were no werewolves out spreading the infection?"

"He let me go awful easy, didn't he? And he knows damn well we don't know who all we could have bitten and buried during those nights. The infection could be everywhere by now."

Kyle ran his hand through his straight, black hair. "Look, I think you're acting a little paranoid. I think the infection is getting to you. Why don't you just come inside, have some of the drink, just try it."

"I know it works. You're not listening—"

Kyle interrupted, "It's not just working, it's working *miracles* for me—no voices, no flashbacks, I can sleep." Kyle slipped the hammer into his pocket. "And why are you sneaking around? No one's going to hurt you."

"The goddamn park ranger. He's shady as fuck. The way he acts—it's like he's alone in this, like it's personal. I can't put my finger on it. I don't like him. I hate him—I can . . . feel it."

Russell surveyed the area again, his crimson-tinted eyes darting over the nearby prairie, up the forested hillside, then back to Kyle. "Plus, I don't want MacLeod knowing I'm around. I don't want him to know where I live, my phone number, nothing. I'm telling you, it's not safe here, and you can't trust MacLeod."

"You know, Russell, I thought about how you've acted and the things you've allowed to happen. I know it had to have been you at Boiling River. No one wanted to ask you questions, but I will. Were you at the Cody Rodeo that night? Don't lie to me."

Russell only responded with silence, which was enough of an answer for Kyle.

A vertical crease developed on Kyle's brow between his eyes. He felt an intense desire to put his hands around Hatfield's neck, but he restrained himself. Kyle tried reasoning with him. "Russell, I know you can feel the power that this gives you. I've felt it myself, trust me. But you can't go around letting it hurt those you don't approve of. Now, I don't know if our conscience is in there somewhere when we change, but either way, someone gets killed if we don't stop ourselves—and you know that."

Russell replied in a serious tone, "Boiling River wasn't my choice. If there's anyone to blame for that, it's you. I didn't know it was coming. But I realized after, that we can fix injustices in this world. We can take down dirty, piece-of-shit politicians like Senator fucking Walters. You know . . . criminals, scumbag rapists, murderers . . . "

Kyle raised a hand to cut him short, clasped Russell by the collar, and forcefully drew him in. "You need to stop and listen to yourself. Did you forget, or did you just *choose* to forget about the little Walters girl? She was six years old. Was she a criminal? A scumbag?"

Russell didn't fight back, only said, "I was there for the senator. He never showed. Besides, what about you? I'm supposed to believe your hands are clean? Give me a break."

Kyle averted his eyes with a moment of guilt. After a few seconds, he thrust his face back into Russell's. He inhaled heavily through his nose, his voice an angry whisper. "I'm telling you, if you go down this path, innocent people will die because we don't have control over it."

"But what if we found a way to control it? Did you ever think about the potential in that?"

Kyle shoved Russell away and looked at him with disappointment. "I'll tell you this one time. You be here before the full moon."

Without an argument, Hatfield simply gave Kyle a helpless look and walked away. He made his way toward the nearby evergreens, his dirty yellow hair slowly disappearing within the darkness of the forest.

CHAPTER 38

THE MOON WAS but a sliver away from fullness, and Dr. MacLeod's great destiny only one day from manifestation. It was nightfall, and Dr. MacLeod moved through the dark barn with a purpose. Everything that had happened over the past month and a half was perfectly aligned with his master plan—*and why wouldn't it be*? he thought to himself. He deserved to have a successful campaign of it. He'd put in the work, studied the past, discovered its secrets and treated them with the utmost dignity. MacLeod had spent the better part of his life intimately connected to the histories of past cultures, while others denied it and greeted his theories with utter derision. The tables were turning, the odds leaning in his favor, and he would soon receive his rightful reward.

As he reached the opening in the back of the barn, he conceded that even this presumably daunting task had gone down without the slightest hitch.

The portly Scot clicked off his headlamp and sat an occupied dog cage on the ground, along with a long-handled fishing net.

The cage had been Sherrie's, for when she travelled with Mr. Phibbs, the terrible little rat of a dog she loved so dearly. The metal-barred enclosure banged and thrashed fitfully, the animal inside violently flapping, striking the walls in desperation. It dispensed a rapid and high-pitched chattering that was barely audible. MacLeod removed the welding gloves from his hands—the same ones he'd used at Sapphire Pool—and quickly draped a small blanket over the cage.

The outbursts de-escalated to a jostle every few seconds, then finally the creature became motionless and silent.

Cradling the cage, MacLeod traversed through scattered copses of lodgepole pine and spruce until he came to the metal silo he'd been preparing.

Before clicking his headlamp back on, he eyed his house, which was about a soccer field's distance from the silo. Between the silo and the house was a long hay field framed by sparse woods.

"The Harris's bedroom light was still on. *Good*, he thought, *still watching their ignorant movie—some stupid Disney movie about woolly mammoths and cave men*. MacLeod thought it pathetic of them, watching a cartoony flick with the lights on to subdue their anxieties about the night to follow. Their generation watching far-fetched movies about the geographical past instead of truly knowing it, doing the digging, putting in the effort that a real relationship with history requires, was an outrage.

And they were the ones with the gift. *What a waste.*

But he would fix all that.

MacLeod turned his headlamp back on and unlocked a wooden storage bin at the side of the silo. Swiftly, he took stock of his preparations: the elephant gun, its heavy rounds as big as whole dill pickles in a metal ammunition can, a charged, battery-operated spotlight, the loaded Smith & Wesson nine-millimeter, a full can of gasoline, and a fold-out camping chair.

He relocked the bin and aimed his light at his welding work. There were two exits from inside the silo. One would have been this access door a few feet off the ground, which he'd welded shut over the last week. He gave it one last look-over, appreciating the fine work he'd done.

The other exit was a ladder that descended the inside wall of the forty-foot tower from a side opening at the top. With the turn of a crank at the top, the ladder folded into itself and locked into place beneath a catwalk that stretched across the top.

That part needed no modification.

The timing had to be tomorrow, the day of the full moon. The logistics of locking the couple in the silo earlier would've been impractical—carrying supplies to them to keep them alive, monitoring them twenty-four hours a day. Besides, they were so foolishly cooperative that an early lock up wasn't necessary. Yes, he could have killed her, captured him, and waited for his change, but that all added up to too much risk, too much effort.

Conversely, he had no interest in killing Kyle and capturing Nicole to watch her change—he wanted to witness a primary infection, to feel *Bayosh*'s presence. MacLeod had initially viewed Nicole as extra baggage, but as time went on and the plan became more complete, she was now regarded simply as a bonus viewing. Once he realized he had his dogs by the leash, he knew all he would have to do is put them in their cage without their water before that beautiful glowing ball in the dark heavens called forth greater creatures.

There was great confidence within Donnan, also, that their destruction by gun and gasoline would be easily executed. They had to die if he was to be successful in his new skin, if he was to be the apex predator. If they were free, every man, woman, and child would end up a werewolf. That would make his new life of dominance much more difficult, make his plans for grandeur likely impossible.

CHAPTER 39

"NAH, THEY'RE NOT very heavy." Kyle turned down MacLeod's offer to help carry the two cots and blankets. If there was one benefit to his infection, it was the upgrade in physical strength and heightened senses. Kyle would give the gifts back in a heartbeat, though, if it meant none of this ever happened.

Looking at the ominous silo that would contain them tonight left no doubt in Kyle's mind about what dwelled within him, and Nicole. It would take this lofty, cylindrical prison made of bolted metal panels to stop their bad sides, should they come out.

Seeing MacLeod carrying two-gallon jugs of the drink helped calm his nerves as he crossed the field toward the silo, with Nicole on one side and Donnan on the other.

Kyle lightened the mood as they approached the stairwell that climbed up the side of the structure. "Honey, did you remember my nuts?"

Nicole wore a backpack stocked with flashlights and snacks. She smiled. "Yes, dear, I remembered your nuts."

She was taking this day well. Kyle knew it must have been nerve-racking for her, but she was a fighter. He just needed for this night to be over, for them to come down these stairs tomorrow unscathed, and move forward knowing that they had a handle on this thing.

Nicole stepped to the silo wall and gave a knock. The rap echoed inside the metal enclosure, then slipped away into its great emptiness. "I think it'll work." She had a book in her other hand. She held it up, said, "It'll add to the mystery."

The novel was a crime thriller by C.J. Box that she'd told Kyle about. The story took place in Yellowstone and reminded her of the "good ol' days", she said. He knew it was her way to escape their insane reality, even for a short while, and he hoped dearly it would comfort her tonight.

Kyle threw his chin at MacLeod. "Hey, maybe next time Donnie goes to town, he can pick up the rest of the series for you."

"Consider it done," MacLeod said as he began to ascend the stairs. "Right this way."

When they reached the top of the metal staircase, Donnan opened a small door and entered.

Nicole followed, then Kyle, who hunched slightly to get in. The June sunrays lasering through the entrance were the only source of light inside the structure.

They stood on a metal catwalk that reached to the other side. The roof overhead was conical. When he looked down, Kyle saw a concrete slab at the base of the darkness. There were dozens of haybales stacked all around the perimeter of the concrete floor and a layer of straw, perhaps six-inches thick, spread about.

Donnan said, "Yeah, that's hay. I don't know, I just thought it was better than a hard, concrete floor. I know you're not animals." He grinned.

The catwalk was so high, Kyle thought it would take about three seconds for one to fall all the way to bottom. It was a frightening height and the walls looked impenetrable. Its penitentiary feel was exactly what they needed.

"Well, it's cozy," Nicole remarked, her voice echoing in the cavernous chamber.

"Does it come with room service?" Kyle asked.

MacLeod was too busy to acknowledge the joke. He was already halfway down the ladder that hugged the inside wall.

When MacLeod reached the bottom, he shouted, "Just drop the cots. They are Army issue. They can take it; trust me."

"All right. Watch out." Kyle did as asked, and after a few beats, they toppled onto the layer of straw. *Yep, about three seconds.*

It took Kyle and Nicole a couple minutes, though, to scale down.

As they arrived, Donnan was stretching out the chains.

Nicole sat her bag down and began to assemble the cots. Kyle helped her, then laid out the blankets.

MacLeod handed them each a jug. "Now, as we discussed, the chains are short enough to keep you separated, in case your wolf sides do not agree. It is one-hundred-alloy chain. The tensile strength is incredible. If these won't hold you, nothing will."

There were two chains, one on either side of the silo floor in the low light. Each ran through two ringbolts embedded in the concrete below the straw, and there were shackles at both ends.

MacLeod lifted one set of shackles. "Come now, you first, Sam. Let's get on with it. No sense in delay."

Kyle kissed Nicole on the cheek, lifted a cot, and carried it to MacLeod's side of the silo.

MacLeod locked the steel bindings to Kyle's right wrist and left ankle. Kyle noticed the gaps between the locks and his skin. They were loose, but not so loose that he could free himself.

"The free space is for you to grow into." MacLeod said, noticing Kyle playing with the shackles.

As he walked to Nicole, MacLeod swung the shackle keys and began to whistle.

Nicole allowed MacLeod to secure the locks on her wrist and ankle.

It was what Donnan *didn't* do next that sent a frigid chill down Kyle's spine.

Once Nicole was bound, MacLeod said nothing and commenced in climbing the ladder.

Nicole shouted after him, "How much longer till the moon's up?"

But he didn't answer. MacLeod simply scaled the ladder, cranked it up the wall and, pulling a small chain, attached it to the bottom of the catwalk. He stuck the keys in his front pocket and exited the small doorway at the end of the catwalk.

Kyle saw Nicole look at him with concern. "Kyle?"

Funny, he didn't see her mouth move when she said his name. It was a little dark, but he could still see her face clearly.

He didn't answer her.

She did it again, "Kyle?"

Nicole definitely hadn't moved her mouth that time. Her eyebrows pinched together, and she cocked her head.

What is this? Kyle thought.

Nicole said aloud, "I don't know."

He thought, *Did you just—*

She nodded.

In the most bizarre way, he could feel her thoughts. And she could obviously feel his. Instantly, he sensed her anxiety that something wasn't right, that she could feel a sudden presence that wasn't of this world—an evil, perhaps.

He thought to her, *Shh, listen.*

Kyle could hear MacLeod descending the ladder, the sound of the keys sliding against each other in his pocket, even his breathing—sounds a normal person shouldn't be able to hear. He noticed Nicole's eyes following every step

MacLeod took as he reached the bottom and circled the silo behind Kyle.

Wow, she can hear him, too.

Nicole nodded again. *Yes, I can.*

Kyle asked in a whisper, "What's happening? I've been drinking the stuff all day. Have you?"

"Yeah, I had some just a minute ago," she said. *There's something near. I can feel it,* she thought.

I feel it, too. Kyle looked out the opening above—dusk was setting in. *It's like I can smell it.*

IN DUSK'S FADING light, Henry RedMoon waited at the wood line on the opposite side of MacLeod's house. As he eyed the back entrance, he muttered to himself, "No, it can't be." The unmistakable and growing ire he felt on this day, and the inclination that an ancient enemy of the Wahota was nearby, said otherwise. Disdain crawled under his skin and rattled his nerves. The feeling confirmed what he didn't want to believe—that the legend of *Bayosh* was true, and he'd somehow returned. But which one was he? Fenn, MacLeod, the big blonde man, the Bowman woman? His bet was the blonde man by the evil presence he felt when Henry had seen them in Gardiner. Were they all infected? Maybe none of them were *Bayosh*, only his changelings.

And where were they? He hadn't seen them in several hours, and night was closing in. They couldn't be far.

The choice was clear to him—Henry would stop this creature. He would do what he must to protect his family. If this curse made its way south, the RedMoons would be in terrible danger.

Regretfully, Henry removed his clothes and placed them together at the base of a tree. He found a spot that had ten feet of clearance all around him, and he took a knee. He placed his knuckles to the forest floor, and his eyes turned dark as night.

RUSSELL HATFIELD'S EL CAMINO rolled its way up MacLeod's long driveway. He put it in park, stopped the engine, but felt the need to leave the keys in the ignition.

For Maddie. He kept his daughter at the forefront of his mind. She was the only reason he was here. After much consideration, he'd decided that maybe it was best to keep his power chastened. How long—how many times could he deliver justice and get away with it? If he were ever found out, he would be imprisoned, killed, or locked away and studied, and Maddie would be without her biological father altogether. There was still a far-reaching possibility that, with enough time proving to be a "productive member of society" without any strikes against him, a court might eventually grant Russell partial custody.

There was something off, something as he stepped out of his vehicle. He left his hand idling near his side arm as his senses tingled. For the first time in his life, goose flesh prickled his forearms. There was an aura of anxiety in the air around him, cut with an undertone of utter hate.

MacLeod's ForeRunner was parked in the driveway next to the El Camino.

Russell peaked in the back and spotted a tiny dog cage with a towel covering it. One end of the cage was exposed. He looked into the darkness inside and saw the eye shine of two impossibly small eyes.

"What the fuck?"

He circled the truck, peering through the windows. On the front passenger seat was a dark maroon book, its silver lettering read, *The Rituals of Three.*

Russell entered the house and thought about yelling their names but didn't. Instead, he felt inclined to snoop.

MACLEOD'S BREATH WAS labored as he climbed back up the staircase and reentered the silo. He carried a red gasoline jug, a handheld spotlight, and a green ammo can. He had a camping chair strapped over his shoulder, and his Holland & Holland double rifle rested in the bend of his arm. On his belt was a holstered pistol.

After setting the gas and ammo aside and unfolding his chair, he wedged the spotlight in the overhead railing and snapped it on. The light cascaded down on the two captives.

It nearly blinded Kyle as he tried to find MacLeod. The light was too bright to stare at him directly. He could only make out MacLeod's shadowy figure in his peripherals when he looked away.

"Hey, you sure you need that rifle?" Kyle asked.

MacLeod sat in the chair and set his feet on a rail. He didn't answer.

Nicole asked, "Where'd you get the chair? Can we get one of those?"

No answer. It was pointless, Kyle knew, but they needed to get him talking.

Growing impatient, Kyle asked, "You really think these chains will work?"

MacLeod answered his question by breaking open the elephant gun and inserting two of the giant slugs. He closed the gun and put the barrel on the railing, still holding it in his hand.

Nicole screamed, "MacLeod!"

Kyle saw MacLeod's head turn to her.

She lifted the jug, took a swig, then glared up at him. Without taking her eyes off him, she held the plastic container straight out and tipped it upside down. The water rushed out.

Kyle could feel her intentions. It was a statement, a line in the sand.

She dropped the empty jug to the floor and yelled into the light, "Cut the shit, MacLeod!"

Donnan spoke, "They'll work long enough—those chains. Long enough for me to see what I need to see. And you can pour all the water out; I don't give a shit. It's only mineral water, you *morons*. I stopped giving you the drink two days ago"

Kyle demanded, "What the fuck is going on?"

"Do you believe in fate, Kyle? Yes, your name is Kyle, isn't it?"

His attempts to scare MacLeod weren't working. *Play good cop*, he thought to himself. Or was it Nicole thinking that?

He ignored what MacLeod had said, forced a laugh like it was just a joke. He said, "You know what, Donnie, on second thought, you're right. This isn't necessary. I trust the drink. We don't need to do all this. Let's just go inside and see what else you got behind that bar. Let's forget all this and make it a margarita night, huh? What do you say? Let's go have a bevvy."

MacLeod replied, "It was fate that brought you to me. It is I who should have your gifts. Why else would I have studied my whole life and obtained the knowledge to call it forth? Why else would you have stumbled into my house? Fate!"

Kyle gave a light laugh. "That's great, Donnie. How about those keys now? Can you just drop them down?"

"Have you ever wanted to fly, Kyle? I will. And you're going to help me."

MacLeod reached into his vest pocket and withdrew three small lavender-top tubes filled with blood. He stared longingly at them and said, "You already have."

Nicole shouted, "What the fuck are you doing? We don't want to be in here anymore. Let us out, now."

"Sorry, dear, but you're never leaving this silo."

"You can't just keep us chained up in here forever." Kyle chuckled. "This is a joke, right? That's a good one. You got us good. I admit, I was scared there for a second. Come on, let's go get a drink. Man, I sure could use some scotch."

"No, Kyle. There are greater things than scotch, greater things ahead for Dr. Donnan MacLeod."

"Let us go, goddammit! This isn't funny!" Nicole screamed furiously.

"Am I *laughing*?" After a moment of silence, MacLeod let out a single laugh, like it had snuck up on him. He said, "You've got a mouth like my dear old Sherri. She was a bloody fucking whore."

Kyle recalled Russell's theory. Of course, it all makes sense. "Is this about selling the drink? Look, we'll cooperate. You can test the dosage, keep testing our blood, whatever you need. You can work it all out, get what you want, and when you're done, we'll leave. You'll never see us again. We won't say anything. We can't. We need to be as far away from the cops as possible."

"No, my feeble-minded friend. I cannot sell it. Are you kidding me? I would have were-people hunting me down the rest of my days. They would capture me, torture the information out, then remove my head so they could have the leverage. If you only knew how simple the remedy is. My God, it is so simple."

He shifted his weight and slid further down his chair. "I've been making the switches for weeks now, you know, giving you mineral water instead of the drink. Turns out it is approximately two days before I start seeing the yellow return to your eyes, and indeed, I can see them from here—you are ripe for the moon all right, just as I planned. Oh, and speaking of magical liquids . . . " MacLeod stood from the chair and grasped the gas can. "Here comes the marinade!"

He walked to one end of the catwalk and poured the gasoline over the rail. Kyle jumped back, but not before the gas poured down the right half of his body.

"Goddammit MacLeod! I swear to God, I'll fucking kill you!"

MacLeod danced across the walk and did the same to Nicole.

Her shoulder and one side of her head caught a stream of it. She reached for her blanket to wipe the gas off her.

Kyle stopped her. *Don't do that. We may need those to put out the flames.*

MacLeod sang, "*And we'll all goo tagether, to pluck wild mountain thyme, all around the bloomin' heather!*"

Kyle doused his blanket with the mineral water, then threw the jug to Nicole. "Quick, wet your blanket."

She frantically sloshed the water onto the blanket, her hair half-soaked with gasoline.

"*Will ye go, Lassie, go!*" His song was a dark lullaby, calling Kyle and Nicole to their death. "*Near yon pure crystal fountain, and on it I will pile, all the flowers of the mountain!*"

The melody sank. Kyle could feel Nicole's deep fear and sadness at what was surely their end. The sorrow was remarkable, painful. His eyes started to swell with tears.

Then, like a trigger, Nicole's despair turned to fire, anger, defiance.

She started to softly sing, *"Will ye go, Lassie, go."*

Her voice slowly raised in volume. MacLeod's off-tune singing came to a sudden stop.

"And we'll all go together, to pluck wild mountain thyme, all around the bloomin' heather!" Nicole had the voice of a Scottish angel sent here from a faraway fantastical land.

Right then, Kyle sensed the same dark presence he'd come to recognize—it was Russell.

Kyle sensed that Nicole knew it too.

It was brilliant—she was singing for Hatfield, calling to the pack's protector.

"Will ye go, Lassie, goooooo!"

RUSSELL'S PACE QUICKENED as he searched the huge home. The sky was darkening, and very little light was now coming through the windows. There was an urge in him. He was worried, but for what? *Someone needs me, desperately.*

Near the end of one wing, he stopped. Someone had left a stereo on. The sound seemed to be coming from behind a door atop a small staircase

Russell sprang up the steps to find the door was locked. Before he knew what he was doing, something compelled him to slam his shoulder into the door. It loosened. He gave it one more charge and burst through. There, he found himself in a grand study. *This must be where the old man works*, he thought.

A leather-covered notebook on MacLeod's desk caught his attention. He opened it.

The first page had two columns, one titled *Yohawnee*, the other *Wahota*. His blood-colored eyes read the body on the *Yohawnee* side. The information described a Yellowstone tribe and their ability to change to wolfmen. It also said they were invaded by the Wahota.

MacLeod never mentioned this.

Under *Wahota*, the text explained the invaders, how they originated from Kamchatka Peninsula of northeastern Russia, how they used a predator native to that land as their totem animal. Instead of a wolf, in a sacred ritual, the Wahota sacrificed a—Russell heard it again, the singing.

There was no stereo that he could see.

The windows—something drew him there. Hatfield hurried over. It was there he saw a silo in the distance. He smelled MacLeod, somehow, knowing he was in there. Sam and Kelly were there too—they were in trouble.

NICOLE'S VOICE GREW powerful and wild.

"The summertime is coming, and the trees are sweetly bloomin'!"

The sound of her voice swirled around the rounded walls of the silo, collecting back into themselves, amplifying into a beautiful, ceremonious concert. Her eyes were now yellow-rimmed. Her voice wailed with wolf-like undertones.

Kyle could see MacLeod's face as he moved away from the light. His face was expressionless, his eyes entranced like he was mesmerized by a Siren's song.

"HEY!" RUSSELL BOUNDED through the waist-high grass, closing in on Donnan and the silo. He reached for his pistol.

"Shit!" MacLeod dropped the gas can and ducked behind the side of the entryway. Fumbling with a lighter, he lit the end of a rolled newspaper. A good head of flames quickly grew, and Donnan held it over the railing, hesitating.

After a beat, he said, "Aye, fuck it!" and dropped the igniter. Then he hastily dropped the gas can behind it.

The lit newspaper landed near Kyle, and the floor erupted into flames. The gas can landed just behind the flames after bouncing off the wall.

Nicole screamed, "No! Kyle!"

Kyle covered himself with the wet blanket and moved back as far as his chains would allow. He yelled. "Where's the gas can?"

"It's on the other side of the fire. Kyle, it's really close!"

MacLeod drew his pistol and jumped out onto the staircase, firing at Russell. He aimed for the first two shots, then fired without looking as he nearly stumbled down the steps.

Kyle told Nicole, "Get down!"

Hatfield returned fire. Suddenly his leg buckled beneath him as he finally felt the two rounds that had zipped through his femur. He hit the ground rolling.

MacLeod reached the bottom of the stairs and took off across the field, disappearing into a line of cedar trees.

THE SCENE ON the other side of the house played out in Henry's mind as he listened; the singing, the shots from an elevated position, the return fire, a man tumbling, another running through the trees toward the house, a fire building inside a metal structure.

Henry's heart pounded. His muscles tensed. His four canines sprouted, and his lips curled back.

RUSSELL'S CHEST EXPANDED, and his shirt ripped at the seams. His eyes went completely red, and anger surged through his body.

NICOLE LOOKED AT her hands. Thin claws slid from her nail beds.

Kyle said quickly, "Listen, as soon as we get out of here, I want you to run to the study, as fast as you can. Barricade the windows and door. Bust the glass out of his gun cabinet and load up anything you think you can. There's more of the drink in the garage. I'll get it and meet you in the study."

Nicole nodded.

Kyle's cot was fully engulfed in the fire now. He leveled his tone. "You're about to see a full-on werewolf in like a half a second. It's going to be huge." He anxiously squeezed his hands. "I've seen my reflection before. It's going to scare the shit out of you, but remember, he'll help us. Be strong."

Kyle heard her think, *Don't worry, Kyle. You got this.*

He screamed, "Russell! In here! Hurry up!"

Heavy footfall rapidly approached the outside of the silo wall, like a boulder rolling downhill.

Something slammed into the silo wall near the fire, like someone chucked an anvil at it, leaving a large indention.

The thing slammed into the same thick, metal panel again, and the sheet broke from its bolts on one side.

Wicked, clawed fingers spidered their way through the gap and yanked the sheet back. It pulled again and again until the sheet curled back like the top of a tin can. The new, gaping hole allowed a gushing wind to circulate in, fueling the fire, bringing forth an almost explosive *whoosh* that instantly heightened the flames.

Behind the dancing fire, Kyle saw the thing he knew was Russell's beast crouch down and step inside.

It sprung through the flames, landed on all fours, then stood.

Kyle could feel Nicole's spirit shudder with fear and revulsion. He too trembled, and fought for his breath.

Straw-colored hair lightly covered most of its skin except for parts of the face, hands, and chest, which were all a sickly pale hue. Its clawed and bloodied hands were formed like that of a man. The forearms were extended, vascular. The arms and torso were also that of a human, only three times a normal man's size. The waist was relatively small, giving the creature a V-shape, rather than a barreled appearance. Its legs were like a wolf's, bending back halfway down, and long—remarkably long.

Its breath was loud, like a horse—the head, massive and twitchy. Blonde hair covered its head between its pointed, slightly arched ears. Its mouth was like a pit bull's—wide, muscles bulging at the sides, containing a mass of menacing, jagged teeth. Its blood-red eyes moved from Kyle to Nicole, then back at the hole it had created, like it was thinking.

"Russell!" Kyle raised his chained wrist.

It snapped its head toward Kyle.

Kyle said forcefully, "Get us out of here!"

In just two strides, the beast was in front of Kyle.

The wave of heat and wind from the creature's charge nearly knocked Kyle to the ground.

It bent forward, and Kyle turned his head.

Russell's wolf grabbed the chain near Kyle's wrist with both hands and bit down. Moving the chain to the back of it jaws, it gnawed, then cut through. Kyle stared up at the hulking creature as it moved to his other side, then bit through the ankle chain.

Without being told, it proceeded to Nicole and freed her. As soon as her second chain was cut, it shot back through the flames and out of the silo like a hound that had caught the scent of a fox.

Kyle listened. MacLeod's ForeRunner was leaving the valley, heading south. Russell was running north.

Where's Russell going? Nicole thought to Kyle.

MOCHA-COLORED FUR with black flecks sprouted across Henry's entire body. His torso expanded, followed by his head. A snout with pronounced canines formed from the front of his enlarging skull. Dagger claws, as long as Army bayonets, shot from his fingers and toes. His legs bulked to the size of tree trunks. The crunching of his body expanding was rapid and globular. The hair on his arms became long, while the hair on his chest and legs was shorter, revealing robust and tensed muscles. The muscles in his neck, chest, and shoulders became so brawny that his head looked too small for his body.

In just a few seconds, Henry's Wahota gift, coupled with the full moon, had produced a titan of a man with a barreled ribcage, hulking arms, and the head of a Russian brown bear. He stood as tall as an African elephant, chest out, with inky black eyes zeroed in on Russell Hatfield's werewolf state as it charged at him.

Henry opened his jaws and out came a roar that shook Sheep Mountain and stampeded its way through Paradise Valley. The feathered black hair that ran from his forehead to his back in a mohawk vibrated from the powerful sound waves.

Kyle and Nicole were nearly at the house when the roar came. They instantly ducked below the high grass. Kyle could see Russell's golden body streaking across the wood line in the direction of the colossal sound. He snarled and flung soil as he sprinted on all fours.

Nicole put her hand over her mouth to conceal her scream.

Russell disappeared behind the house, and the noise of an incredible battle disturbed the silence—massive bodies colliding, grappling, growling, gnashing of teeth, tearing of flesh, and painful groans and whines.

Kyle could also sense woodland creatures, nocturnal animals that hadn't been awake yet, now scurrying for cover, or high tailing away.

Nicole darted for the house. "Come on, we're running out of time!"

Bursting through the front door and into the grand living room, they split from each other—Nicole to the study, and Kyle to the garage to fetch the last of the drink.

As Kyle exploded into the garage, he thanked his lucky stars to find the drink still stored in the refrigerator there. There were six individual water bottles and a one-gallon jug left.

He guzzled as much of the drink as possible, then tucked a few more bottles under his arm for Nicole.

The sound of the battling beasts came closer to the house. He peered through the garage's back window.

There Russell and another, larger beast grappled for position in the glow of the back-porch light. Russell was on the hairy creature's back, his teeth sunk into its unnaturally large trapezius muscle, while the unknown creature had Russell's forearm in its mouth.

Russell's blonde hair was now pink from the spilled blood, and he had slicing wounds across his face and abdomen. Russell's attacker didn't look in much better shape either, with shreds across its upper body exposing pinkish-yellow subcutaneous layers.

Using its superior size, Russell's opponent was able to shake the werewolf loose. It wrapped it arms around him and charged forward, pinning Russell to the ground.

Kyle shrieked, "No!"

To Kyle's dismay, the creature raised its head and locked eyes with him. Its head was that of a mad, wicked bear.

The memory of Annie A's bear attack hit him like a train at full speed. Its eyes and expression were calculating, sending a primal chill through Kyle's very bones.

"Holy *shit*!"

Fenn ducked below the window and gathered himself. He adjusted the bottle in his armpit, then scurried back inside. Before he got to the study door, he reached out to Nicole with his mind. *It's me. I'm coming. Let me in.*

When he reached the door, he could hear Nicole on the other side pushing MacLeod's desk out of the way from where she must have placed it as a barricade.

He entered and tossed her a bottle. "Here! Drink it quick." His heart raced.

Kyle noticed Nicole's canine teeth were already protruding over her bottom lip, and her light-brown irises had brightened.

She asked, "Are you sure we should drink this? What if we need to defend ourselves?"

Kyle saw the three shotguns, two rifles, and four handguns she'd laid out on the luxury leather sofa. He picked up a shotgun and started loading it. "Just drink it."

Nicole raised the bottle to her lips and began gulping it down.

Kyle set the shotgun on the hefty desk and pushed it back in front of the door.

He turned back around, and her canines had retreated.

THREE HOURS LATER, three fires blazed around Donnan MacLeod.

He was shirtless and down on both knees.

His eyes were void of irises and pupils, or even whites. They were beady, black, and covered in an outer membrane that flickered in the firelight.

Two porcupine quills pierced the skin of his chest. Thin, leather strings attached the quills to two straight pine branches stuck in the ground like posts.

Empty venipuncture tubes lay at his side, and Kyle Fenn's blood churned in his stomach.

At his back, the gushing waters of the Yellowstone River toppled headlong over Lower Falls at the Grand Canyon of Yellowstone. The full, silvery moon shone brightly in the clear night sky overhead.

The book he'd been reciting from, *The Rituals of Three*, was still open before his knees, but he looked straight on and continued chanting in the Yohawnee tongue.

Without missing a beat, he grasped the little dog cage and tossed it into the fire in front of him.

The bat inside banged and thrashed. It squeaked and flailed in agony. Within seconds, its skin sizzled, and it curled its wings in as all its muscles contracted.

Suddenly, MacLeod rose without effort, as if an unseen being was lifting him by the armpits.

He planted his bare feet in the soil and stepped forward, his shoulders relaxing.

He pulled to one side, and one quill ripped from his chest, taking flesh with it. He pulled to the other side and the other quill did the same.

Beneath the fresh wounds appeared patches of black, leathery skin.

MacLeod continued to walk straight ahead, the mud pots boiling around him, sporadic geyser sprays in the distance, hailing his arrival.

His pink flesh fell away from him in wedges, then clumps, then sections, to reveal glistening black muscles lined with thin, brown fur.

He stopped chanting when his jaw protruded, and small fangs sprung forth.

PART III
COYOTE AND BADGER

CHAPTER 40

KYLE AND NICOLE made it through the night without sleeping and without morphing into werewolves. At last, the light of a Montana sunrise slipped through the blinds and illuminated the Brazilian walnut floor.

"Hey. You hangin' in there?" They lay beneath MacLeod's desk, huddled together. Kyle stroked the side of Nicole's head. His other arm cradled a twelve-gauge shotgun.

"Yeah. I'm a little stiff." She stuck her fingers under the shackle on her wrist and rubbed.

"I can't lay here anymore," he said.

"Me either."

Kyle helped her up and put the Remington against the wall near the other guns. He planted himself in Donnan's desk chair.

Nicole arched her back and yawned. She looked at Kyle with her sleepless eyes. "So, are you going to tell me about what you saw last night?"

Nicole sat on the desk and faced him.

"There's something else out there. Something fought with Russell, and it was winning. Nicole, this thing was enormous. I thought it was a bear, but it moved like a man.

It must've been eight feet tall or more. It looked me in the eye. It's something else—something like us."

Nicole asked, "When do you think MacLeod's coming back?"

Kyle ran his fingers through his hair and rubbed his face. "I don't think he'll be back. Now that he knows Russell's on to him. We have to find MacLeod, though. We still need that recipe."

"But what if he does? What if he finds out we're still here and goes to the cops? What if he tells them he was attacked by Russell and we broke into his house?"

"I don't think he would. It sounds weird, but I felt something in him last night. It was like he wanted to just throw it all away—his life, everything, like he was about to do something terrible."

"Thank God Russell decided to show up last night. We wouldn't be here if he hadn't."

"Speaking of him, I need to go take a look out back, see if I can tell what happened. I'm worried about him."

Kyle played at his wrist shackle, then rose from the desk chair. "Then we can see about getting these damn things off. I know MacLeod's got plenty of power tools."

She slung a rifle over his shoulder and handed him the shotgun. "Don't forget these, Rambo."

He tried to merge minds with her again. *Are you doing okay? I mean with the claws and the teeth last night—didn't freak you out?*

It didn't work. No connection. Must have been a full moon thing.

"You doing okay? You know, with last night?"

"You mean how I could read your mind? Yeah, what the hell was that?" She squinted into his eyes. "Doesn't seem to be working anymore."

"No, I meant did your . . . " He couldn't think of softer words, "your teeth freak you out, or your claws? I'm sorry I couldn't get you to the drink faster."

"No, I'm fine. Really. For a second, I actually thought it was pretty cool." She looked at her fingers where the claws had been. "But then I remembered, you know, the whole 'I could end up murdering someone' thing, so . . . "

"You're a real piece of work, you know that?"

NICOLE WATCHED FROM the high window as Kyle reconnoitered the property. After a few minutes, she looked back over her shoulder and thought about the small library, the desk filled with documents, the projector.

Nicole decided to do some reconnoitering of her own and searched the study. Last night was the first night she'd even seen this room. The high shelves of aged books caught her attention first. The many volumes must have gone unused for years, as thick dust covered their spines. *Probably all for show*, she assessed.

Then, she noticed, right where she had sat a moment ago, on MacLeod's desk, was a leather-bound journal. *Now, that's something worth looking at.*

She searched the journal and learned of the once warring tribes, the Yohawnee and Wahota. It laid out how the Yohawnee were native to Yellowstone, but the Wahota weren't. It read:

> *. . . and thus, with certainty, I know that the Wahota lineage has its roots in Asia. It is these people who, in their native land of modern-day Kamchatka Peninsula, specifically the mountainous regions nearest The Valley of Geysers, used a sacrificial ritual by fire to give themselves the likings of the Russian Brown Bear under the influence of the full moon, a gift that the Wyoming descendants still possess to this day. The Wahota migrated over the Bering Strait, south through Canada, and into the Greater Yellowstone area. It was there, while under attack by the Wahota, that a Yohawnee shaman conducted the same ritual to create werewolves.*

As she read on, it was hard to distinguish between what MacLeod was documenting as fact or what was his own theory, his words beginning geographical in nature, structured logically, then trending toward sporadic, subjective statements that would otherwise seem manic had she not experienced the things she had—statements like, *The RedMoons are the Wahota, the Wahota are werebears, they have the ability to shapeshift at will under a full moon.*

She said to herself, "Were-*bears*?" MacLeod had informed her and Kyle about the Yohawnee-werewolf-*Bayosh* storyline, but not *this*. He wrote that the Wahota invaded the Yohawnee, using the full-moon nights to *bring slaughter to their doorstep, which was returned in kind.*

MacLeod credited his theory with his decades' worth of research and fieldwork, which included specific finds that he had documented elsewhere.

What was this Ritual of Three? she pondered. *Three what?*

And who the hell were *The RedMoons*?

She got her answer at the bottom of the page:

> *The Wahota*
>
> *Sid RedMoon, Self-Employed, Horse Husbandry, Horse Trader*
>
> *Sid 65, Larinda 67*
>
> *sons Wymon 34, Vic 30, Henry 27 (Yellowstone Park Ranger)*

Her research was abruptly interrupted by a muffled scream.

Nicole ran across the backyard to where Kyle knelt. As she took the last steps toward him, she raised her hands to her mouth.

On the grass in front of Kyle, Russell lay on his back, naked. His head was tilted to the side, the inner workings of his neck and throat exposed like a classroom science prop, except glistening real. His skin was pale yellow and his body stiff. A ghostly blue surrounded his open, glazed eyes.

"Oh my God, Kyle!"

She knelt next to Kyle and they embraced.

He choked out, "He saved us," as tears streamed down his face. "Goddammit! I should've been out here."

"We'll bury him. We'll do right by him. It's all we can do."

He looked Hatfield's body up and down, a storm of emotion playing across his face.

Kyle stood up. "No."

"What?"

"We can't. He stays here—as is. They find him in a shallow grave, what's that look like? No—one day this will all come out. This will at least be the one thing people will know I'm not guilty of."

"Kyle, what are you talking about?"

"We didn't do this! I didn't do this!" He began to break. "I never asked for this! I didn't do anything to deserve this!"

He kicked Russell's side "You stupid fuck! You just had to go and kill people and draw attention, didn't you? That's what this is, isn't it? Goddammit!"

A second kick barely nudged the man.

Nicole wrapped Kyle up and walked him backwards. "All right. It's fine. It's okay. We can leave him. Whatever you want. It's okay."

They both sat down in the lawn.

The young couple sat there silent until Kyle calmed.

Wiping tears from his face, he said, "You're right. We can't just leave him here."

"Okay," she said softly. "I'll find some shovels."

Nicole got up, turned to the house.

Something became clear to Kyle as he looked at the man.

He *was* responsible for Russell's death.

Kyle said, "Just one shovel. I'll do this. I'm the reason he turned in the first place. He'd be alive if not for me."

CHAPTER 41

HENRY'S BLACK JEEP Wrangler left a trail of dust in its wake as it made its way down the single gravel road leading to the RedMoon Ranch. Their huge mountain property was spread below a south-facing mountain ridge overlooking smooth hills and a placid, windswept valley.

Henry's two brothers, Wymon and Vic, waited for him outside the gate in Carhartt canvas jackets and white straw cattleman hats. Their disdain for him showed on their faces as Henry exited the Jeep and approached them.

Wymon's son, Phoenix, was there behind the entry gate, holding the reigns of three tan geldings.

"Phoenix? How are you, buddy?"

Henry could almost feel his heart breaking as the boy stared blankly at him. It seemed the coercion of Wymon and Sid had soured the boy's sentiment toward Henry.

Or was it something else? Surely Sid hadn't made him carry out the tradition yet. He was just a boy. If Henry found out . . .

Wymon spoke in a deep, powerful voice. "State your business, *brother*." He was a spitting image of Henry, and were it not for Wymon's longer hair and more severe facial features, the two could've been mistaken for twins.

Henry demanded, "I need to speak to Father. Get out of my way."

Wymon huffed, "Why would I let you do that? You left our family . . . for what? Did you find a good life out there among the snakes? I heard you were a full-time cop now. You here to *arrest us*?"

"It's about the legends. I have something you all need to hear. Now, step aside and open the gate."

Wymon stepped forward, grabbed Henry by the collar, and threw his elbow across Henry's temple.

Henry fell to his knee, and Wymon removed his hat.

Henry charged, scooped his brother by both legs, and drove him to the ground.

As the scuffle ensued, dry dust clouded about as if a buffalo were rolling in the dirt.

Vic removed his hat and walked toward the dust cloud.

Henry emerged.

Vic swung at his younger brother.

Henry parried, slipping the strike and catching Vic in an arm throw. It took Henry an extra second to get his hulking brother airborne, but he was successful, and when Vic hit the ground, the air exited his lungs at once.

"Enough!" The gate opened, and out sauntered Sid on a painted stud, a rifle in his lap.

Henry could feel the usual abhorrence that had always surrounded his father—it radiated from his dark spirit like a rancid stench. Henry needed to inform his father that he'd fought an enemy of their ancestors in Montana, or at least a version of it—that the legend was true, and that there could be more of them out there.

Henry said, "There you are. Look, we need to talk."

Sid clicked his rifle off safe and aimed it at Henry. "You will not speak in my presence."

Vic and Wymon got to their feet and dusted themselves off.

Sid said, "Take him to my horse barn. Keep him there until the next moon."

Sid kept his firearm aimed at Henry's chest as Vic and Wymon took Henry and his Jeep onto the property.

The patriarch and Phoenix closed the gate and led the horses in behind them.

Sid said to Phoenix, "Take heed, Grandson. This is what happens when you betray your family."

"YOU CAN'T BE serious, Wymon. Don't be stupid. Open this door and let me out."

Henry's hands were bound. He sat in straw, looking up at the corner of his enclosure. Outside, he could hear the rumble of distant thunder.

Wymon busily finished installing a roof over the horse stall that was now Henry's temporary holding cell. Thick oak boarding comprised the bottom half of a sliding door, while steel bars constituted its upper half, starting at about chest height.

Wymon hammered at the last remaining board as he shouted down to Henry, "He'll never compromise with you. You knew that."

As the last board went into place, what little light there was now came through the steel bars. Henry could feel the swollen, dark thunderheads portending the looming storm.

Wymon leapt nimbly down from the top of the show stall, hammer in hand, his long ponytail ribboning down after him. He dusted off his jeans and stared at Henry through the bars.

Henry stood and drew near him. "Look, I have some information that affects the entire family. Please, just let me explain what has been happening. We are all in danger, brother."

"You betrayed us, Henry," Wymon said with contempt. "You spit in our face the day you left. You disgraced our whole way of life, our proud heritage. You left and joined *them.* You chose to be a part of that world of greedy and spiritless men. They destroy land, consume all, kill all. They betray each other over wealth. There is no true loyalty out there. No honor."

"And killing defenseless people in the name of loyalty to Father . . . that makes you better than them? That gives you honor? He has warped your mind, Wymon. Don't you see that?"

Wymon furrowed his brow and tightened his grip around his hammer.

Despite Wymon's stone façade, Henry could sense a flash of confusion deep within him—a hint of good still lingering within that needed but a spark to show him the obvious truth.

Henry said boldly, "I killed a Yohawnee wolf, Wymon. Just a few weeks ago, in Montana."

After a moment of thought, Wymon chuckled, said without looking at Henry, "And tell me, brother, how many drugs have you been using since you left? Huh? Maybe some stuff you confiscated from some Yellowstone tourists?"

"*Look at me,*" Henry shouted in a voice that rattled his enclosure.

Wymon turned sharply to stare at his brother.

"Do I look like I'm lying? Wake up, Wymon. You know me! The legends—they're true."

Wymon hesitantly glanced outside at the gathering storm, then back at Henry.

Henry continued, "Look at me and tell me I'm a liar. You know better."

"I don't know what to believe anymore, Henry. My hope for change around here died a long time ago." He dropped the hammer to the dirt. "And you—just yesterday, you were dead to me. Now, here you stand before my eyes. You tell me you killed a Yohawnee wolf, something that hasn't existed in thousands of years. They were just stories from Grandfather, told to him by countless grandfathers before him. Just stories for children."

"They're not, Wymon, and I'm living proof. And speaking of children—what about Phoenix? Think about his future. The Yohawnee infection could be spreading as we speak. He'll be fighting this spread the rest of his days if we don't stop it now."

Wymon turned away, casting his eyes to the ground.

Henry stared at him for a moment, surprised at the way he suddenly backed down. Then it hit him. His suspicion was valid. Henry could read it on Wymon's face—Sid had made Phoenix kill.

"Wymon, you let him put Phoenix through confirmation?"

Wymon's lip quivered.

"He's just a *boy*."

When Wymon didn't answer, Henry began to pace inside the stall like an animal. "Think about what you're doing. Don't be the one who could've helped save our family and didn't. If not for me, then for Phoenix. Let me out so I can talk to Father."

Just then, the first raindrops began pattering against the tin roof.

Wymon simply sighed and wiped his brow with his sleeve. "You'll be here until the next full moon, Father says." He checked to ensure the lock was in place. "It doesn't look good for you."

A wave of thunder rolled across the mountainside.

As Wymon turned away, Henry said, "I just told you I took out a Yohawnee wolf, and you think *I'm* in danger? You should've seen its hideous face when I took its life. It was the easiest fight I've ever been in."

Wymon ignored Henry's words as he exited the open double doors.

Henry chuckled. "You still have a lot to learn, my brother. Soon you'll need to choose whose side you are on. Just remember that."

As Wymon left, Vic approached and took up his guard post inside the barn entrance.

Henry shouted, "Vic!"

The big man looked at Henry, then back at Wymon as he walked off.

"Vic, you know this isn't right."

When Vic returned his gaze to Henry, his eyebrows sank on the outside and he had a nervous quiver at the corner of his mouth. He lowered his gaze and turned his back to Henry. Throughout his life, Henry knew Vic was the one with the biggest heart, but at the same time, he had a terrible habit of always doing what he was told. Henry said tenderly, "Vic, come on."

Vic stepped back outside the threshold, and the rain began to come down on him in sheets. He leaned his back against the outside wall, letting the rain soak his entire body.

CHAPTER 42

THE STUFFED MULE DEER stared blankly ahead as Kyle looked up at it. He lifted a shotgun above his head and raised the middle finger of his other hand, showing off for the camera tucked inside the animal's nose. He pulled the tiny camera from the cavern of the buck's black nose, laid it on the floor, and crushed it with the butt of the gun.

"It looks like he wanted your blood for this Ritual of Three thing." Nicole had MacLeod's research laid out on the kitchen island. "He claims it brings together the energy from three elements to bring about a spirit demon. It uses the energy from strong geothermal activity, the full moon, and blood. Black Cloak sacrificed a wolf in his full moon ritual, and drank the blood of an infected Wahota, thereby transferring to him the ability to change. The Wahotas were able to perform the same ritual on Kamchatka Peninsula, because it's a geothermal hot spot, and naturally they chose the biggest predator there for their form—a Russian Brown Bear. He claims the Wahota's first were-bear, the full-timer, their version of *Bayosh*, died before they reached Yellowstone, though he's not sure where."

"And he says the Yohawnee drove these bear guys out of Yellowstone? How?"

"*Bayosh*. He was full-time. That was the advantage for the Yohawnee."

Kyle searched around the living room, looking for more cameras as he thought. "But then, whose blood did the Wahota have to drink to get their own shapeshifting ability?"

"Yeah, it gets weirder—from a *bandurrai*. Deep into his rant here, he says it's what he will become. He says, "and I'll be unstoppable, and no one will be laughing then, and I'll take that bitch, Sherri MacLeod, straight to hell with me.""

Kyle narrowed his eyes at her. "A what, again?"

"A *bandurrai*. He said it was an evil creature that once walked—and flew—over the earth, like a bat. It was pure evil, and its only mission was to kill all of mankind. He thinks the Wahota somehow got its blood and carried out their Ritual of Three. He says its origin is unknown. He doesn't know if there were more of them, or if it was linked to a certain ancient people, just that it is further evidence that "evil always finds a way". It's as far as he'd gotten with his research."

She pulled her hair back into a ponytail and tied it. Sliding her hand back under the journal, she continued, "This *bandurrai* took its victims by removing their heads. I guess when it's your job to kill every human being on the planet, that would be a pretty efficient way to do it."

Kyle walked to Nicole, frustration tightening his words. "So, let's recap! We have *were-bears* hunting us—they live in Wyoming. MacLeod has our blood and is going to turn himself into some goddam evil bat monster so he can kill everyone . . . *and* he's the only one who knows the drink recipe that can keep *us* from killing everyone."

"Well, yeah. That pretty much sums it up. Oh, and we only have a few bottles of the drink left."

"*And* there's a dead body up in the hills here."

She said in a soothing voice, "Babe, come here."

Kyle walked over and joined her at the kitchen stools.

She rubbed his back and gave him a look that instantly calmed him. "Come on. Let's keep it together."

"Yeah, I know. But how long till they come looking for Russell?"

"Maybe never. Why would they have any reason to connect him with here? Unless they break into the garage and find his car under the tarp, I don't think anyone will know he was here. The only one who knows is that 'were-bear'."

Kyle walked wearily to the fridge. "And what about these RedMoons?"

"That's what I'm curious about. They obviously found some connection with MacLeod and the Cody and Boiling River killings."

"I think they knew it was Russell and just followed him out here." Kyle picked up a package of turkey meat but set it back on the shelf. He knew he had to eat something, but trying to figure everything out was upsetting him. Right now, he'd rather punch a hole in every one of MacLeod's walls than have lunch.

"Or maybe they finally heard about MacLeod's ranting lectures." Nicole chewed her pen. "They . . . why wouldn't the whole gang have shown up here if they knew? Why just one? It says here every RedMoon male can change on the full moon if they choose to. It says their option to change may be the result of hundreds of years of honing their gift."

Kyle looked at the journal and pointed at Henry's name and ranger title. "There! That's it! Russell told me a Yellowstone ranger was casing MacLeod's house before the last full moon."

"And you didn't tell me about it?"

"Well, I just thought Russell was being paranoid."

Nicole rolled her eyes. "MacLeod wrote that this Ranger Henry RedMoon is the only one known to have left and lived outside the RedMoon family ranch. You think the ranger who was watching us is this estranged RedMoon?"

"It has to be. We need to find him . . . "

"Why?"

Pointing at Nicole's research, Kyle explained, "If MacLeod's going to use the geothermal energy for his stupid ritual, he'll do it inside the park. Hopefully, he hasn't changed himself already. RedMoon can help us find him if he hasn't. We need that recipe."

"Alright. Just, hold on. Look me in the eye and tell me you believe MacLeod can *actually* change himself into evil Batman?"

Kyle tried, but couldn't. "Right. But, he'll probably try to."

"Besides, do you think Ranger Henry's up for helping the eternal enemy of his ancestors? What exactly is in it for him if he helps us?"

"Me not taking out his whole family. I'm the new *Bayosh*, remember?"

"Hang on. Didn't you say, 'Never point a gun at someone unless you intend to use it'?"

Kyle didn't answer. He didn't want to turn, and they both knew it. Even if he did, he could never live with his killings.

Nicole said, "We need to think this through." She rubbed his arm. "I'm still willing to bet MacLeod has the recipe written down somewhere in this house, somewhere we haven't looked yet. Let's just keep looking for it—it has to be here somewhere. And maybe MacLeod or RedMoon will try and come back, maybe not. Either way, we're armed to the teeth. We'll be ready for them."

"I guess I can't argue with that."

She said, "We still have enough drink left. I say we give it until after the next full moon and wait to see if either of them comes back. If RedMoon shows up, we'll make him help us—he'll also want that recipe to exist for his family's sake and his own. If he shows up on the full moon," Nicole sarcastically threw up her hands, "we'll fill him with lead. But he didn't try to kill us last time; so, I don't think he will now. If neither come back, then we'll have the extra time to prepare for whatever plan we come up with next. A good plan. At that point, if we haven't found the drink recipe, we can get the ranger to help us find MacLeod who probably won't be evil Batman."

"I love how smart you are."

"I know."

THAT NIGHT, SHERRI'S route from the employee pub to her dorm included a short hike on a foot trail that joined an access road skirting the guest cabins. After a quarter mile on this road, she would follow another quick forest trail that brought her home.

She stepped out onto the old pavement, carrying leftover pizza, feeling particularly pretty this night. A man she'd played darts and shared pizza with was a square-jawed, handsome horse wrangler from the other end of the village who'd told her how pretty her hair was and said he'd like to take her riding sometime. With a slight alcohol-induced sway to her step, she gushed over what she would do to him the next time she saw him. She'd almost invited him to her dorm tonight, until his buddies showed up and started playing competitive pool. The middle-aged divorcee decided to let him be, for now, as it had been a long day. He looked like a handful who'd required a lot from a woman her age. He had to have been twenty years younger than she.

Besides, there was plenty of play back at the dorm—the Ukrainian kids who ran the buffet line were always easy work. She thought they were probably in the dorm lobby playing ping pong right about now, liquored up real good, ready for her to prey on.

The heels of Sherri's sexy cowgirl boots made a horse-like clopping noise on the lonely, empty road. The blacktop was old and weathered from the extreme snowy winters. There was a single streetlamp casting a circle of light onto the curving road, and a yellow veil against the wall of tall evergreens behind it.

In the stillness, she tried to decide which young foreigner she would pull into her room tonight—perhaps even one of those Romanian girls, the black-haired beauties. Anyone with a pulse would probably do tonight.

Sherri stopped and looked around. She was suddenly uneasy.

Gradually, she could hear the sound of rhythmic and heavy thumps, like something was pounding on the ground in the nearby forest floor.

She stepped back as twigs snapped and the underbrush rustled.

The noise grew closer, the timber crashing and the sound of deadfall being trampled, sending her a dreadful warning.

Then, bursting through the wood line, two bull bison charged at her.

She screamed and dashed out of the road.

They raced by with heavy nasally breaths, hooves beating the pavement, grunting. Sherri ducked as the thousand-plus pounds of fur and meat rushed through the small street, just feet away. She peaked up to see the glistening of their damp, black snouts and the glints of their onyx eyes. The beasts were so solid and moved which such speed that they seemed like Army tanks rolling full tilt into combat, spearheading a blitzkrieg.

Fortunately, the animals seemed not to notice her as they sprinted down the road, then back into the woods.

Sherri's heart raced and her hands quivered. She was dismayed to find her pizza had fallen from her grip, and two slices lay in the pine needles at her feet.

She picked up her soiled food and placed it back into the box.

"What the hell was that all about?"

She returned to the road a little on edge, hoping another random stampede wouldn't happen again.

Maybe they were on their way to the pub, just got off work. She chortled at herself.

Just then, she heard a sound like someone shaking out a heavy rug.

She surveyed the cabins.

There was no one in sight, and no lights were on in any of the small wooden structures.

It was dead quiet.

She continued on, feeling drawn to the safety of the streetlight. She heard it again, the rug-waving sound. This time, it came from above, veiled within the darkness.

"Hello?"

She took another step, just hoping to get to the light of the streetlamp. But just before she reached it, something fell from the sky, into that very pool of light.

Just before reaching the ground, the thing projected enormous wings out to its sides, the length of a school bus, catching itself in the air. Two human-like legs descended, and it landed gracefully on the road.

Sherri froze and dropped the rest of her pizza.

The thing walked below the streetlamp with an offbeat stride, its wings half-cocked. Its feet were like hands, the fingers curled under so that it walked on the knuckles. Its entire body was so dark, its presence so malevolent, it was as if the devil's shadow had been stood upright, given wings, and summoned to hunt the living.

She mumbled incoherently, trying to scream for help or say anything. The sight of it paralyzed her. She couldn't discern its face but could see white fangs in its open mouth.

Its long-fingered hands, tipped with curled claws, hung below its knees. It had enormous and pointed ears flattened to the sides of its head, reaching back, the tips nearly touching.

It emitted an unnerving, chittering sound as it closed in on her. A long, forked tongue slipped in and out of the being's mouth like a writhing serpent.

Sherri slowly kicked her cowgirl boots off and turned. When she began to run, the winged thing bounded forward.

The black creature sprung once more, then spread its leathery wings and rose into the sable sky.

Sherri's socked feet padded against the crumbly asphalt as she ran, and she began to sob with despair.

A second later, it appeared above Sherri, batting its immense wings. It dove and clutched her with its hands and feet like an owl plucking a vole from the ground, then lifted her.

It propelled them skyward with one beat of its wings.

There was the rug wafting sound again, then silence.

The abrupt hush hung in the air for a few beats, then . . .

Sherri's body splatted to the concrete with a sickening crunch, crumpling into a crooked heap.

The creature returned, landing on top of her. It rolled her carcass over with its slender, bent fingers.

The hellish being pulled Sherri's head back and opened its jaws. Below its upturned nose, a steaming spray, the color and consistency of egg yolks, squirted from its mouth, sizzling as it hit Sherri's throat.

The dead woman's skin melted instantly, the liquid cutting through her scalene muscles and cervical bones. When it melted through the trachea, the air from her lungs escaped and produced a brief hissing sound.

Using its teeth to gnaw through her neck, the creature pulled her head completely off. It clutched former Mrs. MacLeod's wavy-haired head in the talons of its feet and launched itself into the vastness of the Yellowstone night.

CHAPTER 43

KYLE WALKED IN and locked the door behind him. As quietly as he could, he engaged the safety switch on his slung bolt-action rifle and moved it to his back. He loosened his jaw and listened for Nicole in the upstairs study.

She wasn't there.

Kyle pulled a walkie-talkie from his front pocket and squeezed the talk button. "Hey, where are you?"

She replied, "In the downstairs den, in the west wing."

She was far from where she said she'd be when he left to check on Russell's stone-covered grave.

Kyle asked, "You all right?"

"Yeah, I'm fine. Come down here."

As he traveled to the other wing, he moved with caution, peering around corners. They had kept to the study and east wing mostly so far. Unfortunately, twenty-four days had passed without any sight or sound of MacLeod or Ranger Henry, but that didn't mean he could let his guard down. They also hadn't found the recipe or any evidence of one, either.

A thought crossed Kyle's mind—maybe she'd found it, the recipe. Maybe she was looking at it right now, some kind of short list jotted down on a sticky note like a grocery list, something simple that they could easily find at a drug store. They could whip it up on their own and keep it near, always, never to change again.

Then we could get the hell out of Montana.

The thought gave him a zap of energy, and he moved more quickly, imagining their freedom.

Once he reached the staircase and began to descend, he asked, "Any luck with finding the recipe?"

She didn't answer right away, and when he entered the den, he didn't see her.

Then she said from an adjacent room, "No, haven't found it. Be there in a sec. Hey, do me a favor?"

"Yeah?"

"Will you make me a Captain and Coke?"

"Uh, sure."

He went to the small bar in one corner of the low-lit room. It seemed every area of the home had a small bar nearby, or at least some sort of arrangement including a tiny sink and a cabinet or tray stand stocked with liquor bottles.

Laying the rifle on the bar, he opened the cabinet doors below it. He retrieved the rum, then the Coke from a miniature refrigerator. Pulling two glasses from an overhead cabinet, he poured the cocktails. As the glasses filled, he noticed the pool table with leather-tasseled pockets at the far end of the room. There was a broad stacked-stone veneer fireplace in one wall, a fire crackling in its belly, framed by an audience of three couches.

Kyle said, "His grave's still intact. Doesn't look like anything has disturbed it."

She didn't reply.

"You know, I get the feeling they ain't coming back. Seems like either one of them would have come back by now if they meant to. We need to start thinking about what we'll do after the full moon. Time is ticking." Still no response. "Nicole? Nikki, babe, what's goin' on over there?"

Nicole stepped out from the spare bedroom. A snowy-white mountain goat hide was wrapped around her shoulders. Her light ocher hair was flipped to one side, covering her right shoulder. Only her sleek, bare legs showed—Kyle's favorite part of her. Her eyes were lazy and sensual, and she smiled sweetly at Kyle.

Kyle raised his eyebrows. "Hey there."

She tiptoed over to the pool table and leaned against it. A gap between the fluffy fur revealed the caramel skin of her chest and belly. She opened the fur just enough to reveal a little more to the entranced Kyle.

She said, "I miss you, Kyle. I miss being with you. Come over here. Let's forget all this craziness, all this death and destruction. Let me just hold you again."

A smile grew on Kyle's face that nearly touched both ears. He scooped both drinks and strutted over to her.

Nicole pointed a remote at the stereo system and a sultry song with a Spanish guitar commenced.

Kyle sat both drinks on the table's edge on either side of her. He reached his arms between the fur cape, lifted her up by her bare backside, and sat her on the table. "Well, I think I need to take you to the . . . " he struggled to find his swagger. "I'm gonna get that—uh, I'm about to—"

Nicole planted her lips on his.

She laid back onto the table, sending the billiard balls rolling.

CHAPTER 44

THE GRAY-BLUE haze from the moon blanketed everything around Sid RedMoon atop his painted stallion as he slowly made his way toward the horse barn. The moonlight highlighted the shine of his silver head and the white patches of his horse. His stern face showed no emotion as he approached the bright light within the barn.

A shirtless Henry paced in his holding cell.

Vic guarded the barn opening in front of Sid, and Wymon secured the exit on the other side of the building.

Vic stepped aside, and watched Sid stop at the entrance when Henry spoke.

"Father, we need to talk. I know you think I betrayed you, but you've never been in this kind of danger. It's about the legends, about *Bayosh*," Henry pleaded as he watched his father dismount from his horse. "His spirit exists. I found a turned man near Gardiner last moon. He came straight for me."

Sid slid off his boots and set them neatly next to his horse.

Henry continued, "I killed him. I protected the family. It means *Bayosh* is alive. And who knows how many more might be out there? They've killed twice already. I saw the murder scene in Yellowstone with my own eyes."

Sid scoffed, "How do you know you didn't kill *Bayosh* himself?"

"Do you even remember the teachings?"

"You dare lecture me about the teachings of our great family?"

"I know it wasn't *Bayosh*, because *Bayosh* changes his host body permanently. Only those he bites change by the moon. Not only that, *Bayosh destroyed* our people. He drove them from Yellowstone to here. No single Wahota can stop *Bayosh*—not me, not you. You have to hear me! Once he and his changelings catch wind of us, they'll come, blinded by bloodlust. They can't stop it; the curse will turn them against us. Do you hear what I am saying? Do you find no truth in what I tell you?"

Sid said calmly, "Yes, I do."

Sid removed his shirt and unbuckled his belt. "I believe all of it. I only can't believe that you thought you could walk back into our gates and take over." He sneered. "You actually think you have what it takes to lord the Wahota? I swear to the Creator, if you want lordship, you'll have to take it from me."

"Father, this is your last chance. This is my last offer for peace."

"I honor your challenge. Tonight, I will decide who is lord."

Henry had to concede to himself that he, in fact, *did* come to take over, and though he knew it would likely come to violence, he promised himself he'd give peace a chance.

Well, he had. There was no peace, nothing of the sort, within his father's heart. He said to his siblings, "Wymon, Vic, you will not step in. You hear me?"

His brothers' faces were blank.

Vic and Wymon slowly turned into the darkness and vanished.

It only took a moment, Sid's changing. Then into the barn light stepped Sid's version of a Wahota bear.

At the center of the barn, Sid's head knocked the hanging light. The fixture teetered and flashed, flinging the light in circles, illuminating all the hidden corners of the barn.

Henry saw flashes of his father's beast as it moved through the wide breezeway. He could hear its thudding steps drawing closer.

When the light stopped spinning, Sid was opposite Henry's cell with a snarl on his thick snout. He was enormous and hairy, his limbs bound with layer upon layer of muscle. His fur was thick at his back and thinner at the chest and abdomen. A run of long, silver hair started at his forehead, streaked between his hairless, rounded ears, and fell down his back.

Sid punched his long claws into the dirt and leaned forward like a defensive lineman.

"I was eight years old. She was my best friend, our neighbor from over the ridge. Do you even remember her, *Sid*?" It was the first time Henry had ever called the man by his name. He squared off with his father on the other side of the stall door. "Do you? She was eight years old."

Rage burned in Henry. From the moment his father had forced young Wymon to mercilessly kill the little girl in the name of tradition, he knew the time would come when he would have to change his family's ways—he just didn't know it would require physically removing Sid from power. But the RedMoons were nearing a disastrous brink, and Sid had to be dethroned. The time had come.

Henry grabbed the stall door by its bars. "She was *eight—years—old!*"

His claws ejected between the bars like switchblade knives.

Sid pulled his front claws from the dirt and bluff charged the stall, full tilt, stopping just short of Henry's door. Sid swiped his claws across the dirt in front of him.

Henry's body exploded into shape, and in a snap, he removed the half-barred stall door.

He hurled it at Sid, and it broke in half against his body.

Sid stumbled back and Henry bluff charged at Sid, stopping within spitting distance.

The Wahotas faced off, both whuffing and grunting lowly, mouths drooling, their shoulders tensing, their fierce claws readied at their sides.

Both lowered their heads and clacked their teeth.

Sid's clawed feet dug into the earth, and he bulldozed straight through Henry, rolling him across his back.

Henry jumped to his feet, and the two swatted at each other. They exchanged heavy blows for a few violent seconds. Fur and skin chunks littered the ground around them, and the blood began to stream down their faces and chests.

The bear-men backed away a step. Both had taken damage, but the excessive wounds on Sid's neck and shoulders revealed who had the superior striking speed.

Henry lowered to all fours with a natural movement as his arms were considerably longer than his bulky legs.

Sid did the same.

As they circled each other, each bellowed and moaned. The tears in their shoulders and faces were already healing. Sid had lost a claw on his right hand, though, which had been stepped on and lay imprinted in the mud.

Henry returned to a bipedal stance, then lunged for Sid.

Sid stepped aside, and Henry crashed into a stall, partially collapsing its wooden wall.

Sid reached for a nearby tractor tire and hurled it at his son.

The flying tire sent Henry all the way inside the stall. Straw from the upper level and dust showered down into the hole he'd made.

Sid grunted heavily as he watched the dark opening. Considerable patches of flesh and fur, missing only a few moments ago, had filled in on his neck and arms.

The challenged patriarch ducked through the hole and entered the stall to find it empty and a large opening through the outside wall.

As Sid emerged from the hole, Henry was waiting in the grass—as a naked human. Sid's beast could only stop in disbelief, its onyx eyes studying Henry with a look of confusion.

Henry raised a shotgun and fired two blasts into Sid's upper torso. The third took off Sid's cheek.

The shots had no effect, and Sid's ruthless eyes stayed focused on his son. He charged. Henry rolled to the side, and Sid barreled past him.

Sid turned back to Henry and raised to his hind legs, towering over him.

Vic was there behind Henry. He tossed Henry a Mauser M98 rifle they used to put down sick horses. Henry aimed and fired. The round entered and exited where Henry thought Sid's heart would be.

Sid dropped down to all fours again. Frustration left his snout in the form of nasal huffs. He paced with exhaustion and seemed near the point of collapse.

Henry stepped over to his beastly father and backed him up against the side of the barn with the muzzle of the Mauser.

Then, a Kubota tractor fired up and filled the night air with a constant rumble. Attached to its front was a three-pronged loader used for lifting thousand-pound round hay bales. Wymon sat at the wheel.

Wymon shifted it into gear, and drove toward Sid.

Henry stepped aside, and the prongs skewered their evil father. There was the muffled sound of bone breaking and organs bursting, then a defiant roar that quickly fell flat. Sid gurgled as dark blood oozed from his jaws, and he took his last breath, staring Henry in the eye.

THIS TIME, WHEN they took to MacLeod's study, they boarded the windows and door. Nicole slept on the couch, which was pushed to the middle of the floor while Kyle sat in the desk chair next to her, the Remington across his lap. He'd kept a fire burning all night.

Plastic bottles of the anti-werewolf drink, the recipe still unknown, sat at Kyle's feet.

A peaceful and reassuring sunrise once again brightened the windows.

With the full moon gone and no sign of a were-bear or MacLeod, it was time to carry out their plan—a slippery and dangerous affair that still worried Kyle, but they had no other choice.

In the next few days, he and Nicole would seek out Henry RedMoon. Kyle would play the role of Sam Harris, and Nicole that of his wife, Kelly. They'd continue their roles as MacLeod's assistants, who knew about Henry's fight with the blonde werewolf. They would ask him who this werewolf was, and somehow find a way to ask if there was a cure for such werewolf-ism. If the answer was no, they'd inform RedMoon of MacLeod's missing status and ask for his help finding him. From there, they could only hope that MacLeod had not already successfully carried out the Ritual of Three and morphed permanently. What they would do in that scenario, who knew?

There was another risk they faced with this plan; if RedMoon were to not believe them, not cooperate, or see through their lies, well . . .

Let him lash out, Kyle thought as he stroked the butt of the rifle. Nicole would be safer without this RedMoon werebear around anyway.

Kyle was through with half-measures. There was no time left for slogging around. If RedMoon didn't help them, that would be his own demise. Kyle would just have to scour Yellowstone himself until MacLeod showed up, or he'd threaten every known archeologist, anthropologist, *whoever*-ist, until he got his answers.

This time, as the morning rays slid across MacLeod's study floor, Fenn watched the door, utterly resolute. His gaze was steel, his heart undaunted.

All of the major events of his life—from getting removed from his baseball team, to finding that cave, to becoming a werewolf, to endangering Nicole—had carried him to one finite conclusion.

He was done running.

Kyle would no longer duck his problems; he would not flee or waver. Never again would he be weak-minded, as he was when he'd decided to jeopardize his baseball career— when he'd watched Annie-A get slaughtered right before his eyes and did nothing—when he'd run from Yellowstone, taking his curse with him to his family, then to Nicole—when he'd gone into the park instead of continuing to seek out MacLeod, further endangering Nicole—when he'd passively trusted MacLeod instead of forcing the recipe out of him like Russell would have—or when he'd cowered away while Russell fought to the death for him and Nicole.

No, never again.

To reach Henry, they would be forced to head straight into the heart of Yellowstone—the place where *Bayosh* nearly took control of Kyle. Old Kyle would have surely looked for an easier way around, causing more harm than good, but not this time.

For the first time in his life, Kyle knew he had a real purpose, something to accomplish with life-or-death consequences attached. This was no time to be shy or meek.

The great urgency and cruciality of his success somehow brought a confident calm over him—an intense focus he'd only felt at times walking up to the plate, being the last batter with a chance to win the game. In those moments, on baseball diamonds, when it was all or nothing, he'd never wavered—not once.

This would be no different. He would summon that strength, that intensity. His task at hand was perfectly clear: Get that recipe from MacLeod or whomever, protect Nicole, and survive.

CHAPTER 45

A CIRCLE OF fires lit the Wahota ceremonial cave, and although some of their faces were painted with angst and others jubilation, the overall prevailing sense between the limestone walls was joy, Henry sensed. Hope had returned to the RedMoons, and it lingered over his family members like a blessed fog.

One by one, the RedMoons entered the circle and took their places at the ring of sitting stones. As they funneled in, there was a low murmuring of voices amongst the group.

Henry was in the circle's center, greeting each family member as they arrived. He was distinct from the rest, as he was the only one with his black hair cut short. Wymon and Vic stood behind him, arms crossed behind their back, faces stoic.

Some members, particularly the elders who had lived many years under Sid's reign, met Henry with a strong embrace. A few RedMoons, those most distant from Henry's immediate family, while compliant, still seemed to harbor reservations and greeted him with only brief nods, avoiding eye contact. The children in the group seemed either disinterested or confused, and quietly followed their parents to their seats.

When Phoenix met Henry, the young man threw his arms around his uncle. His joy was real, Henry knew, but when he released his embrace, the boy's emotionless face and his words unveiled a great guilt within.

"I am sorry, Uncle Henry," the boy said, his wet eyes glistening in the dim light.

"You have not wronged me, Phoenix. I am the one who is sorry. I never should have left," Henry said, placing one hand on the boy's shoulder to comfort him. Phoenix sniffled once, opened his mouth to say something more, but then closed it and moved toward his seat.

"Mother refused to leave her room," Vic said to Henry, his deep voice echoing off the cave walls.

"She can remain there as long as she likes. Make sure she is taken care of night and day. I'll visit her myself when the time is right."

Henry motioned his family to have a seat. "Please."

He took in the faces before him. There was so much to say, so much to establish. Their faces were rough and solemn, yet not joyless. His heart ached with pride for these resilient people. What potential they had if they were only steered in the right path. Henry couldn't wait to begin their journey, to be their beacon of light toward a new, stronger foundation and foothold in this world.

"Brothers and sisters, nieces and nephews, aunts, uncles, cousins—this is sudden. Such a thing has never happened in our family, as far as I can recount. There is a ceremony for this kind of thing in our texts, but we will not use it today. I'll explain in a moment why this is not a time for ritual. As you know, our father, our leader, is gone. He met me in a challenge, and I took his life."

Vic spoke up, "And Henry will lead us."

Wymon and the elders gave their nods as the family's eyes turned to them.

Vic continued, "We all knew something would have to give, one day. Henry was the only one with the courage to do what needed to be done. He also understands the outside world more than us. He will keep our heritage strong, but he knows that we need to look outward, and he knows how to do that. If we are to remain in this world, we must adapt. It is how our family has survived for so long."

Wymon stepped forward. "We will take Henry's lead. He is not the man Father claimed him to be—he is a good man. Father was devoted to his family. He was an intelligent man and did his best to keep us safe. But he was also cruel and mistaken in his ways."

Henry glanced at Phoenix who had his eyes toward the flickering shadows on the ground.

Wymon continued, "Grandfather witnessed to me, late in his life, that something had changed within Father, that evil was not always his way. I have a deep feeling that something happened to him. I believe something spiritual, something dark, had a hand in it. I can feel it in the wind, when I listen to the spirits, that his change was a sign of something worse to come. I have felt this for some time and feared it was the prophecy coming true. Henry, here, has confirmed my suspicion."

Henry said, "Before I get to that, I want to tell each of you directly . . . " His eyes scanned the circle. "You are free."

He paused for a moment to let his words sink in, then said, "You are free to go where you wish. No one here will stop you. No longer will a RedMoon male be forced to find a female companion from the reservation, nor will a RedMoon bride be forced to stay here; you are not slaves, not RedMoon property. You are free to seek out your education among the outside world again, all of you—not just the few. In fact, I encourage it. We will learn the ways of the outside world and integrate where necessary before they begin to see us as a threat. They have the resources to remove us whether we like it or not. The wealth that runs through our land, our abundance of oil and gemstone, is too great, their greed too powerful, and it is only a matter of time before they seek it out. We *do* have rights. We must know them, and understand how to protect ourselves."

Henry folded his arms behind his back. "I hereby nullify Father's restrictive and fruitless decrees. Every RedMoon man, woman, and child has a right to take their life in whatever direction they see fit. Every one of you has the right to love whom you choose. We will rebuild our household with love and compassion for one another as a free people. This family's love for one another is so powerful, there is no need for a dictatorship. I am honored to make decisions that our majority cannot decide on its own, but I do not foresee this being necessary. I have only one restriction for as long as I am the head—you will not use the Wahota gift under any circumstance unless it be for the protection of the family. This is a restriction I will abide as well. Anyone who changes for any other reason will be eliminated, for they willingly become a liability to the family in doing so. Am I understood? If anyone challenges this, speak now."

There was a quiet consensus and even a smile or two. Some of the elders embraced one another, or held hands.

"Now, as I said, we must not rejoice. A different time is upon us. We've all heard the legends—how our ancestors traveled through Yellowstone and encountered a great evil. They warred with the Yohawnee there, who summoned the moon-demon *Bayosh*. This creature nearly wiped out our bloodline. We have all heard the stories, and many among you have passed them on to your young ones. Who knows the entire truth to the wolf creature myths? No one, perhaps. However, I will tell you that *Bayosh* is as real as the very rock you sit on. I can tell you this, because I have met one of his changelings . . . and I ended its life."

The family stirred.

He continued, interrupting their fuss, "I know it was only a changeling because it changed by the full moon."

There was more grumbling.

"I am ashamed that it took this encounter for me to come back and fight for all of you against Father."

Henry walked around the inside of the circle as he continued, wanting to see all of their reactions, to look them in the eyes as he drove home this reality.

"It came for me. I could feel its hatred for my very blood. This means the spirit *Bayosh* has resurfaced, somehow, and taken on a host human. Now, I am not asking you to believe me. I hope I never have to prove myself, because if any of us were close enough to see *Bayosh* in the flesh, I fear there would be a great loss of life. *Bayosh* was brought forth, created with a purpose—to kill Wahota. Now is the time for us to come together and find a solution, for he will surely come for us. We need to be prepared for him and any changelings he may have created."

A woman's voice, weak but unyielding, interrupted Henry. "I know when a storm will come and when a mare is pregnant. I don't need a white man's almanac to tell me when a harvest will be fruitless. All the same, I know when a Wahota is lying, especially my own son."

Larinda RedMoon stood at the cave entrance.

All eyes turned to her. The entire group was silent.

The matriarch walked closer and took a deep breath.

She said solemnly, "Henry's claims are not conceived to fool us—they are not lies. Henry was never a liar. And I felt his battle with the wolf man in my heart. We *will* follow Henry. We will no longer kill for sport, nor let isolation become the death of us. The Creator has delivered a true leader to our people, and a son back to his mother."

CHAPTER 46

OUTSIDE THE FISHING Bridge General Store and Diner, in the center of Yellowstone, dozens of tourists strolled about the sunny, pine-scented day, ice cream cones and shopping bags in hand. Children giggled and screamed as they raced across the log building's expansive porch. Parents in hiking boots looked over park maps on the hoods of rented SUVs. Ground squirrels and chipmunks took their turns darting across the walkways and the thinly grassed lawns, scooping up the bits of food and scrap the humans left behind, then vanishing from sight. Down the road, five vehicles had accumulated roadside and were taking photos of a scrum of elk that had neared the small highway. A thick bull elk in the center of the group, with its regal and broad-sweeping antlers, was the focus of attention.

On the general store's front porch, Kyle and Nicole monitored the area for any sign of a ranger patrol car. They knew what RedMoon looked like from newspaper clippings found in MacLeod's study, so spotting him wouldn't be difficult. And while finding Ranger Henry was top priority, not being identified was just as important. To remedy this, Nicole wore a toboggan and Kyle a baseball hat, both emblazoned with MacLeod's alma mater University of Washington husky heads. Sunglasses also helped to conceal their identities, and Kyle couldn't help feeling a bit ridiculous in the get-up.

Fortunately, his journey through the park thus far had presented no additional physical or emotional side effects, as far as he could tell. Them travelling through the geothermally charged park on a limited supply of the drink, rationing it out for Kyle as best they thought necessary, was a tad nerve-racking and felt like they were deep sea diving with one small tank of air.

The couple had hoped that driving MacLeod's own Mercedes might bait him in if he were around, but it hadn't. There was no sign of him, so far, at the rest stops, restaurants, hotel lobbies, pull-outs, trail heads—no green ForeRunners anywhere. The hotel and cabin clerks that were kind enough to query a booking for a Donnan MacLeod turned up no sign either. Nicole had suggested they at least search for Donnan until the Fishing Bridge location, then make the telephone call if there was no MacLeod.

Kyle stepped over to the payphone half-booth, and dialed the ranger headquarters number from a business card he found inside the gift shop.

Nicole kept watch.

A man's voice picked up, greeting lazily, "Park Service, Officer Hodges. How can I help you?"

Kyle laid on a thick north-Midwestern accent. "Yes, how are ya? My wife and I are here from Wisconsin for the week, and our first day here we had an accident. A deer ran straight out in front of us, and by golly if I didn't just jerk our RV right off the road!"

"Yeah, that'll happen. Is everyone okay?"

"Yes, yes. We're both okay, don't ya know. The fender took a hit from a few little trees, but we're all unscathed." He let out an exaggerated laugh, then said, "So, ya see, I just wanted to thank the officer who helped us. He left so quick I never got the chance to thank him. So, and this is silly I know, but I just wondered if I could tell him thank you for getting us back on the road so quickly and being such a nice gentleman, ya know? I didn't get his name, but I'm pretty sure the name on his uniform said RedMoon, or something like that . . . "

"Well, you must be referring to District Ranger RedMoon . . . Henry. Dark hair, dark eyes? Pretty fit . . . "

"Umm, yes. Yes, that would be him."

"I'm sorry to tell you, but he no longer works here. He resigned just a few days ago."

Kyle paused for a moment, the news taking him by surprise. "Oh, darn it. Any reason he resigned? He seemed to really enjoy his job."

"He said he had some family affairs to tend to. Wish I knew what that meant. I miss him already." The ranger paused a second, then confessed, "Uh, sir, don't tell anyone I told you that. Forgot I ain't supposed to really talk about it. If you want, I can see if they'll relay a message to him. If you just give me your name and numb—"

Kyle hung up the phone and sighed.

Just then, Nicole peeked over his shoulder, "Any luck?"

"He resigned. Just like a couple days ago, they said."

"Shit."

"He stated he had family issues. Nicole, I think he went back to Dunoir."

Nicole placed her hands on her hips and stared down at the floorboards.

Kyle watched two kids fight over a stuffed buffalo toy as he thought. He said, "That would make sense. Wouldn't you go to your family if you'd just found out a werewolf curse had returned and could endanger them—even if you didn't necessarily get along?"

She nodded.

He winced, "Well, this complicates things."

Kyle began to consider strategies for visiting the RedMoon Ranch versus a continued search for MacLeod within the park. They did have the address, and it was another couple hours' drive away. But would that be a waste of time? Could they possibly find MacLeod on their own?

Nicole said softly, "Honey." She was in front of a newspaper stand, looking spellbound as she read the front page of the *Billings Gazette* through the glass. "Things just got worse."

Kyle joined her side and read aloud, skipping over the words, " . . . autopsy reveals cause of death as *decapitation* . . . the third headless victim in as many weeks . . . body suffered internal injuries consistent with a fall, though was found on a clearing of flat ground."

He continued reading silently with his lips moving, then said, dumbfounded, " . . . finally identified as *Sherri*

MacLeod, estranged wife to Dr. Donnan MacLeod, world-renowned archeologist." He stepped back. "Ssshit! Nicole, *decapitation*—"

Nicole replied defeatedly, "Yeah."

A man and two small boys walked by as they entered the shop. Kyle waited for them to pass, then lowered his voice. "This happened last week, before the full moon." He lifted his hat a bit, then rubbed his mouth. "He pulled it off, the Ritual of Three, the night he ran away."

"How can you be sure?"

Kyle straightened his hat. "Would it surprise you, after all we've seen? The man was able to keep us from turning. I don't see why he wouldn't have the resources to make the opposite happen. No, he's turned, all right. I'm not doubting my instincts anymore."

With her eyes wide, Nicole whispered, "Oh my god, our license plate. MacLeod's probably wanted now. We need to get out of sight."

Kyle said, turning to the Mercedes, "Come on, I know a trailhead a mile or so from here where people park. We can get a new plate there."

As they left the porch, Kyle said, "We're going to Dunoir."

THE WYOMING BREEZE lifted the ends of Phoenix's jet-black hair as he pulled the string back on his compound bow. Henry instructed, "Don't forget to breathe. Keep your chest out."

Phoenix was focused, his eyes steady. With the subtlest of motion, he released his arrow and it impaled a beech sapling that was now wider than a horseshoe.

Henry pushed his black Stetson to the back of his head. "Good. Again."

Phoenix drew another arrow and set the nock in the nocking point. He inhaled, raised the bow, and pulled back the string in one fluid motion. He exhaled slowly.

Just as he was about to release, Henry dangled a long stick behind Phoenix's head and stuck it through his hair.

The arrow sailed wide.

Henry cast the stick away. "What happened, nephew?"

Phoenix felt at his head, brushing out his hair.

Henry snickered. He said, "Bugs are getting bad this summer."

Realizing his uncle's tomfoolery, Phoenix swiveled toward Henry and made a motion as if he were going to raise the bow at him. Henry said, still smiling, "Whoa. Never point a weapon at someone unless you intend to use it."

Phoenix's grin quickly faded as he looked over Henry's shoulder and down at the valley below.

Henry followed his gaze. A white Mercedes approached their estate on the single road that led into their property. Dust clouds billowed behind as it traveled.

Henry said, "Phoenix, ride back to the house. I'll meet you there in a while. I want to scout for signs of white-tail. I'll be a few hours. If I'm not back by dinner, just save me a plate."

Phoenix nodded, mounted his horse, and turned down the trail.

Once the boy was out of sight, Henry's face hardened.

He straightened his Stetson on the crown of his head, mounted his saddle-less Przewalski horse, and charged down the mountain draw.

ABOUT ONE KILOMETER away from the house, Kyle and Nicole spotted Henry and his horse on the open road.

Kyle slowed the vehicle so he could measure up the statuesque man in his cowboy hat, button-up shirt, and vest. Instantly, Kyle felt threatened, though the man just sat there. A vague sense of hatred toward him washed over Kyle, but he shook the feeling off.

Kyle stopped the car. "All right. This is close enough."

"Is that him?"

"Looks like him. I want you to stay here."

"But Kyle—"

"He's unarmed. Come on. Get behind the wheel."

They both exited and met in front of the car.

Kyle said, "Look, if something bad happens, just turn around and go."

"Yeah, that's not happening."

As he looked at her, he knew he wouldn't win that argument. "Like I said, he's unarmed. Everything will be fine. Just keep the car running—I gotta go now."

Kyle felt at his shirt, ensuring MacLeod's nine-millimeter was still hidden in his waistband, then immediately stepped away.

Nicole pouted, "I *love you too*."

WHEN KYLE WAS within pitching distance, Henry had already dismounted.

Kyle raised both hands slightly. "I suppose I should introduce myself. My name's Sam Harris. I was wondering where I could find Henry RedMoon, if he's available."

"No, you're not."

Kyle gave a curious look. The man was sweating, curling his fingers into fists. He was trembling, slightly. Kyle could feel the man's loathing radiating behind his coal-black eyes.

"You're not Sam Harris; you're Kyle Fenn." Henry raised his finger at the Mercedes. "And she is Nicole Bowman, a missing person for a few months now. I might ask you what it is you're doing with a missing person, driving what seems to be a stolen vehicle, since it's registered to a Donnan MacLeod of Gardiner, Montana. Not to mention the murder you're wanted for in Virginia."

Kyle looked at the ground. Yep, it was Henry RedMoon, all right.

This wasn't playing out the way he'd hoped. This guy, in fact, knew everything.

Fenn looked back at the man and again sized him up. The lean and hardy shouldered RedMoon wouldn't be an easy fight, that much was certain. Still, Kyle could feel himself inexplicably welcoming a fight. He held fast.

RedMoon seemed to be reigning in his hatred as well, by the way he clenched his jaw, bit off his words, and narrowed his eyes at Kyle. Indeed, this Henry wanted to fight, sure as the day was long. But why? Could he tell Kyle was infected? Kyle knew the answer to that question as soon as it formed in his mind. *Yes, that's it—he can sense it.*

Fenn looked RedMoon in the eyes, daring him. "Now, now, Henry. Take it easy. We know a little about you, too, and your family, thanks to Dr. MacLeod's research." Kyle smirked, "And you killed Russell Hatfield."

Henry didn't respond.

"Saw it with my own eyes from MacLeod's garage window. Security cameras caught it too. You changing and all."

Henry glared at the Mercedes, then back at Kyle. He still didn't reply.

Kyle knew he had his dirt on this Henry, but Henry had more on Kyle. And, they were still on RedMoon land. Why didn't he advance on Kyle? Something held him back. What was stopping him? Maybe RedMoon was smart enough to know that Kyle could be armed. He was a lawman, after all.

Fenn chose his next words carefully. "Look, I'm here because we need your help."

RedMoon suddenly said, "And it seems I need yours. I want to know what your connection is to this Hatfield. Was he the one who took Ms. Bowman that night at Eagle Peak?"

"Why?"

"I know it was Hatfield who killed those folks at Boiling River, and the Cody Rodeo, but Eagle Peak—that was something else. Wasn't it?"

"How do we know it wasn't you or someone in your family on either of those occasions? Or for that matter, the recent beheadings in the park," Kyle said.

"Don't play that card. That wasn't us and you know it. In fact, I think you know a lot more than you let on. I fear you know about all this, more intimately than you want to—the murders in Tennessee and Virginia have you written all over them. I think you know what I'm getting at, don't you, Mr. Fenn?"

Kyle paused, knowing that this conversation had come to a tipping point. He would have to tell him. Their plan to deceive their way to a cure for their curse was dead in the water the moment RedMoon stated their real names.

This was fight or flight.

Kyle said forwardly, "I'm him."

RedMoon widened his stance, tightening his fists at his sides.

"*Bayosh*—his spirit imprinted itself on me in a cave at Yellowstone Lake."

Henry took a charging step forward, but immediately caught himself when Kyle raised his shirt tail, exposing the pistol. Kyle said, "Now, listen. Be smart. *Bayosh* finding me was all an accident, and I don't want the goddamn curse. I've done everything I can to stop it. That's why I've come here—to ask for your help—to see if you know how to get rid of it."

RedMoon's chest rose and fell.

"But make no mistake, I'll put every one of these rounds through your chest and head without a second thought if you come at me." Kyle gestured at the car behind him with a turn of his head. "I'd do it a thousand times over if it meant protecting her. She and I are together in this, and if you hurt me, that's no good for her."

Henry looked behind Kyle. He said, "I think she can protect herself just fine."

Kyle gave a sideways glance toward the Mercedes to find that Nicole had exited the car and stood behind her open door, the shotgun trained on Henry. "Jesus, Nicole!"

RedMoon asked, "If you are *Bayosh*, why aren't you changed right now? According to legend his spirit changes the person permanently."

"MacLeod gave me some kind of potion that keeps me straight. But he's gone and it's running out. Like I said, we need your help."

RedMoon walked back to his horse and put his open hand on its muzzle. He threw his hand in the direction of the ranch. At once, the horse whipped its tail and trotted that way.

Henry returned to Kyle, walking toward the Mercedes. He raised his hands, said, "Come on. I know a woman who may be able to help."

Kyle withdrew the Smith & Wesson and followed behind.

RedMoon said, "We need to hurry. I can resist the persuasion of my curse, but it's taking everything I have not to try and take your life. If I were a younger man, I don't know that I could control the hatred I have for your blood. You were right to bring the weapons."'

"Where are we going?"

"She lives on the rez."

When they reached Nicole, Henry said, "Hello, Ms. Bowman. Good to see you're alive."

CHAPTER 47

AT THREE O'CLOCK in the afternoon, MacLeod's Mercedes left RedMoon Ranch and cruised toward Elk River Reservation in western Wyoming, a few miles northeast.

Henry was behind the wheel, and Nicole and Kyle sat in the back, still armed.

They had briefed Henry on the entire situation; how MacLeod researched the Wahota and Yohawnee and claimed to have found Wahota bear bones; how he'd concocted a mysterious drink just so he could keep them alive to view their changing, then kill them; how they needed the recipe; how they were sure MacLeod had become a *bandurrai* and was beheading people inside the park, choosing his wife as his first victim. Kyle told him about the cave and the petroglyphs and of how he'd infected Russell. Kyle never mentioned how he infected Nicole, although if Henry had been at the Eagle Peak scene like he said he was, he should have deduced as much.

After a bit, Henry spoke about the woman they were going to visit. "I was at a rez party. I was with Vic, one of my older brothers. It was his turn to find a bride. The RedMoons never forced the women to come with them, but they may as well have. Our family is wealthy, so it wasn't hard to find a young female trying to survive rez life who would come to the ranch. Anyway, I was on the back porch, at this party, when I saw a fire burning in the distance. I went to it, and there was an old woman there. I sat and spoke with her. It turned out she knew me by appearance, knew I was Wahota. She told me so many stories about my family's history. She was the kindest, most interesting person I've ever met."

Henry had a distant look on his face. "I remember she gave me coffee. It was the first time I ever had coffee, now that I think about it."

He inhaled and continued, "She said she used to teach at the university but came back to live on the reservation to help where she could. She is very educated, very knowledgeable of tradition and myths. Pray that she can help us."

It was comforting to Kyle to hear him say "us."

He noticed Henry rubbing his neck vigorously, and knew the ex-ranger fought hard against his hard-wired detestation for Kyle's blood. Fenn was familiar with the feeling; it was not unlike fighting the urge to urinate, trying not to think about it and to hold it as long as humanly possible. He wondered if he hadn't been consuming MacLeod's drink today, would he be able to hold back his hate for Henry?

Kyle asked, "Is it me? Are you still hanging in there? Anything I can do to help?"

Henry said, "Yes, you can just . . . stop talking. That would help."

Kyle raised his eyebrows to Nicole and grinned.

Once the trio had entered the pothole-ridden streets of the reservation, Kyle noticed a change come over RedMoon. As they made their way through "the rez," Henry continually sighed and rubbed his mouth with his hand. When they passed certain buildings, he'd slow and peer at them anxiously. They drove by a rusted water tower, a graffitied laundry mat, groups of youths loitering at places of business with nothing to do, someone burning a couch near the sidewalk of their dirt yard.

Kyle watched Henry's eyes through the rearview mirror. He could read the uneasy concern in them. Kyle said, "You don't like this place?"

"The place, no. The people, yes. Every time I come back—I don't know. It's like I expect it to be better, at least a little. But it never is."

Nicole asked, "Are all reservations like this?"

"Too many are."

HENRY PULLED INTO the gravel parking lot of a one-level building. A banner sign overhead read; *GROCERIES OPEN 8-8*. A whiskey bottle and beer cans littered the concrete below it.

Henry said, "The store makes more money off of liquor sales in one weekend than it does selling food in an entire month." He shook his head. "It's a terrible reality. But alcohol is only the beginning of the problem around here. The poverty level is sky high. See that door? That's the grocery. This door here, that's the civic center, slash town hall meeting place, slash gymnasium, slash post office, slash classroom for 'what to do when your husband gets out of prison' classes."

RedMoon killed the engine, and the cab was silent. At the corner of the building, a group of teens stood in a semi-circle around two girls no older than fourteen. One finished a Colt 45 malt beer and slammed it against a dumpster. The other, a heftier girl in a white tank top, attacked her as a few older teenagers rooted them on.

Henry reached quickly for the door handle but stopped. He looked ready to charge out of the car and neutralize the situation.

Instead, he stared down at the floor of the car. He removed the keys from the ignition and said, "There is so much wrong here. Our people shouldn't live like this."

Grabbing his Stetson from the front passenger seat, RedMoon opened his door and said, "Stay here. I'll be right back.'

As Henry walked to the entrance of the building, he eyed the lawless young ones. They returned his glares with vulgarity and unpleasant gestures.

"G FIFTY-EIGHT." The caller grabbed the spherical cage by a handle and cranked it forward, the wooden bingo balls chaotically toppling over each other.

Smoke filled the rundown public hall. Middle-aged men and women sat huddled at the flimsy tables, hypnotized by the numbers as they scanned the tickets before them.

Henry walked through the seated crowd, searching the participants' faces.

Finally, he spotted someone and approached them.

The woman sat alone, tipping her ink-filled dobber upside down, scanning her many paper cards. Her long, gray ponytail cascaded over her shoulder, down to her chest.

"Mary LittleOwl?"

"That's me," she replied without looking up.

He sat next to her and removed his hat. He asked, "Do you remember me?"

She interrupted him with an uplifted dobber as the next number was called. She dobbed here, dobbed there.

He said, "I don't want to intrude, but can I bother you a minute, ask you a few questions?"

"But I'm in the middle of a big pot."

"Ma'am. My name is Henry RedMoon. I met you years ago."

The woman on the other side of Mary perked up when he said "RedMoon."

Mary beamed up at him with sudden amazement. Her lips moved as she played at her gums in thought. Her eyes widened, and her eyebrows raised. "Take my purse. I live three blocks away."

She raised her arm for him to lift her.

THE SLOUCHED AND shrunken woman hurried as quick as an aging woman could, arranging the kitchen table, setting out cups for coffee, starting the coffee maker. "Sit, sit!"

She spoke to no one in particular as she moved about. "All my life they called me crazy for delving into my great-grandmother's stories. Even as a professor, they rolled their eyes at me. Those *ridiculous* tales of *Bayosh*, the werewolves, the Yohawnee battling the Wahota in Yellowstone—if they were all nonsense, then why is a RedMoon showing up out of thin air asking for me and my help? My failing mind could be fooling me right now, on my way out of this world, yes. If so, I may as well enjoy it." She laughed gently to herself.

Her three visitors sat at the dining room table as she brought them their coffee.

"It's good to see you," Henry said. "I don't know if you remember, but I met you one night, many years ago. There was a party right out here—"

"Huh? My hearing is not so good."

He raised his voice. "A party, right out here. I came and talked to you."

She furrowed her brow. "Yes, of course you did! How could I forget? Don't be silly." She smiled excitedly like a little girl, looking at Kyle and Nicole. "Who are these two?"

Kyle had already given her their fake names in the car. *It must be her failing mind*, he thought. He felt comfortable, now, telling her their real names. "I'm Kyle. This is Nicole."

"Oh, that's better now." She winked.

Clever, Kyle thought.

She sat and interlaced her fingers. "So, what is it you wanted to ask me?"

Henry said, "It's about the legends."

"You should know more than I do. You're a RedMoon, a Wahota. No one believes me when I tell them about your people."

RedMoon said, "Specifically, we want to know about how *Bayosh's* curse ended. We've heard rumors before about an elixir maybe, some kind of medicine that could kill the curse. Is this true?"

"No, nothing can kill it."

Kyle and Nicole shared a look of worry. LittleOwl watched them with her small eyes.

She said, "It can't be killed; you can never extinguish evil completely. To do so would be to play God. There will always be a balance. But luckily there was something that could keep this evil curse at bay, even if temporarily. After the Wahota traveled south, the Yohawnee changelings stopped themselves from changing by drinking the water from the Sapphire Pool when *Bayosh* wasn't watching. It didn't matter how many times *Bayosh* tried to turn more Yohawnee, they would just gather more of the water. Of course, *Bayosh* wasn't smart enough to figure it out, and after a long time had passed, he went into a cave, it is said, somewhere in Yellowstone, abandoned by his people. It's a tragic story, really. A Yohawnee shaman allows a moon demon to enter his body, to change it indefinitely to half-wolf, protects his people from the Wahota, then dies alone in his cave, forsaken because his bloodlust was too much. Almost makes me sad, that story. But like I was told repeatedly in academia—it's just a legend."

Nicole asked, "The Sapphire Pool? The geothermal feature in Yellowstone?"

"Yes, the Peace Pond. Its water has the power to heal. That was where tribes would go to make peace treaties, as well. Any two enemies can meet at the pool and swear peace, and it will be. Many know that there are portals where evil flows between this world and the other, but few people know of one like this—one of peace, love, and friendship that trumps all other forces. I've been to the feature myself. There's a serene presence there. You only have to open yourself to it. It is powerful stuff."

Henry asked, "What did they mix with this water to give it healing power?"

She sipped her coffee, licked her lips. "Buffalo urine."

Kyle said, "Excuse me?"

Nicole shifted in her seat, again sharing a concerned look with Kyle.

Henry glanced at the couple and seemed on the precipice of bursting with laughter.

Kyle asked, "Did you say, buffalo urine?"

She slapped the table and chortled. "Buffalo piss! No, you dumb-dumbs, they didn't mix anything with it." She giggled so hard, she passed wind.

Henry couldn't stifle his laughter.

"Look at your faces! You look like my students did when I'd fool with them."

She caught her breath and took another sip of coffee. "The liquid is an element of good, blessed by the spirit of the earth itself."

Kyle said, "Sorry, we were told it was a mixture. I think we were lied to."

"Bamboozled, were you? Hornswoggled? By whom, might I ask?"

Nicole said, "A guy named Donnan MacLeod."

Mary LittleOwl's smile flattened immediately. "*Dr.* Donnan MacLeod, the fat, Scottish archeologist?"

Henry asked, "You know this man?"

"Yes, he was a student of mine in North Carolina, the most brilliant of all my pupils. I've been following his story as of late. He's really taken a fall." Her eyes suddenly met them with suspicion, her eyebrows pulling together. "And I hear his wife was just found dead. How is it you know Donnie?"

"You could say we had a run in with him," Kyle said. "And we think he's behind her murder."

Mary turned her head to the window. Her hazy, well-traveled eyes glistened by the light of the blurry panes.

"The beheadings . . . my goodness. He performed the ritual, didn't he? I could always feel a darkness behind his obsession with that book, with the *bandurrai*. How terrible. How . . . true, the legends, all of it."

A silence gripped them.

After a pause, Mary said, "The water won't help him. Nothing can. My dear boy, sweet Donnie, what have you done?"

Kyle covered her hand with his. "Don't worry, Ms. LittleOwl. I'm going to stop him—*we* will stop him."

She said gloomily, "Only thing worse than a moon spirit is a moon spirit raised through blood ritual. That's what the first Wahota bear was, what *Bayosh* was, and what Donnie has become."

She bent down to scratch her cat's chin, then lifted the orange feline and placed it in her lap. She gestured at Nicole with her bony finger, "I hope you're not going to be involved in all this, you know. This, stopping Donnie."

Nicole asked, "Why is that?"

Mary was astonished. "You really don't know?"

Nicole's smile widened. "Know what?"

LittleOwl looked at Nicole's abdomen, then back at Nicole's face. "I've been around the better part of ninety years, so believe me when I say this." She cradled her cat like an infant and rocked it. "You're pregnant, lady."

THE MERCEDES ROLLED on the main highway exiting Elk River Reservation.

Kyle recounted what LittleOwl had told them. "So, MacLeod was pulling our chain. There's no recipe." He rode in the backseat with Nicole while Henry drove. "Why would he make that up?"

Henry's black eyes gazed through the window and scanned the dilapidated housing. He said, "He needed you to depend on him, so he lied. If you knew that it was only the water from Sapphire Pool that you needed, you wouldn't need him. It kept you from leaving. He must have really wanted to see you change."

Kyle said firmly, "If I hadn't let MacLeod take my blood, there wouldn't be more people dying right now. I swear to God, on the next full moon, I'm going to kill him."

"Guys," Nicole said.

"Careful," Henry said. "You're going to need help."

"Hey, guys," Nicole said.

Kyle replied, "Your kind and mine don't mix on the full moon, remember?"

Henry said, "I have a plan for that. And I'm also going to ask that you stop talking again." "Right, my bad," Kyle said.

Nicole shouted, "Guys! Are we just going to act like Mary didn't say I was pregnant?!"

Henry said without a hint of sarcasm, "Oh, yeah, you're definitely pregnant. Older Indigenous women like her can tell that kind of thing."

Kyle locked eyes with her and shook his head. He mouthed the words, *No, you're not.*

A SPIRIT-LIKE steam gently wafted from the pool's calm surface like a jacuzzi. There was a dual nature to its appearance, Kyle thought. On one hand, the water in Sapphire Pool was crystal clear, quiescent, with a color of blue that is surely envied by the angels. Yet, despite its heavenly appearance, he knew the water was around two hundred degrees Fahrenheit. Its waters must have seeped up from the very depths of hell, he proposed. He could see the inside walls of the pool, but as he looked into its depths, there was just a hole at the bottom—nothing beyond it, just a deep blue abyss.

Dual nature aside, the pool was literally a life saver for "The Harrises." Kyle had never cared much for the geothermal features when he worked in the park. He never imagined he would be so mesmerized by one, or that one would be a portal through which peace traveled one dimension to another.

It seemed like a dream, yet there it was in all its blue glory.

Kyle, Nicole, and Henry leaned on the weathered bannister of the wooden walkway that ran across Sapphire's edge. Next to them stood Wymon RedMoon in his ranch attire—Wrangler jeans, button-up collared shirt with a bolo tie and vest. His long, braided black hair was just about the only thing that differentiated him from his brother, Kyle noticed.

After leaving the rez a few hours ago, Henry had them drop him off at his ranch and told them to meet him here at the Sapphire Pool—the Peace Pond. They were going to squash this ancient feud, once and for all.

The group quietly waited, viewing the pool from just a few feet away as dusk nestled in. The tourists had mostly gone for the day, returning to their campsites and lodges.

Kyle could feel the power of the pool, and he noticed it in Henry's eyes as well, the moment they'd approached the geothermal feature. Mary LittleOwl was spot on—there was a peaceful magic here, almost a high he felt when he opened his senses to his surroundings. Moments ago, Henry had even shaken Kyle and Nicole's hands for the first time. This was going to be something special.

"Right over there." Henry tipped his chin toward a tree line close by.

Nicole agreed. "Looks like the perfect spot."

NUMEROUS STARS POPULATED the cloudless night sky. The glow from a small fire bounced off their faces.

Henry's black eyes stared contently into the flames. "This place is special. There is a great calm all around the pool. The spirits are happy here." He tilted his head skyward and closed his eyes.

The group was hidden just out of sight at the far side of the pool, in case any straggling sightseers came by. As darkness had fallen, Sapphire's blue hue had disappeared into a thick blackness. The steam, though, was quite visible—ghostly as it ascended, dissipating into the sky.

They had gathered by the fire in their chosen spot to make their peace official. The Wahota blood and the spiritual power and influence of *Bayosh* would no longer be at odds. In fact, they would be allies after the ceremony, Mary had said. Not even a demon moon spirit such as *Bayosh* could overrule such a pact. So long as the portal and liquid remained, peace would rule between them.

Kyle had a newfound appreciation for Henry. Behind his rough exterior, the man was remarkably kind. Henry could just as easily chosen to kill Kyle, but he sought peace over blood. He'd also decided to take part in Kyle's campaign to stop MacLeod. Kyle admired Henry's good will and his courageous, dogged pursuit for right over wrong, good over evil.

Henry pulled a long pipe from his bag. A small bowl was perched on one end of the wooden shaft while a few long feathers dangled from its center. He guided it through the smoke rising from a mussel shell on the ground in front of him.

Wymon sat next to him, lightly beating a rawhide drum and chanting. Henry's eyes closed as he drew a puff and exhaled through his nose. He said, "We recognize the Creator and send our prayers."

Nicole reached out as he passed it to her.

"The tobacco smoke rises to the sky and delivers our message of peace to the spirits and the Creator. The Wahota, Kyle Fenn, Nicole Bowman, anyone infected with the *Bayosh* curse—let it be known, there will be peace between our curses, between our kinds, from here forward."

Nicole quietly smoked and passed the pipe to Kyle, who did the same.

When Wymon received the pipe, he exhaled deeply, letting the smoke obscure his face and swirl around his head.

He handed the ceremonial pipe to Henry, who continued. "It is known that some predators in the natural world can coexist. They can hunt together. The coyote and badger. They are known to hunt in unison for the prairie dog. Our spirits hunt together like the coyote and badger."

Kyle whispered to Nicole, "Yes. I love badgers. I want to be the badger."

Nicole shot Kyle a disgusted look for his interruption. Through her scowl, Nicole added a correction. "Clearly, you're the coyote."

Kyle didn't understand.

She said under her breath, "Just zip it, would you?"

Kyle looked at Henry and caught him rolling his black eyes as they reflected the dancing flames.

"Just as the coyote," Henry pointed to Kyle with his pipe then to himself, "and the badger hunt symbiotically, so will we. We will not let such evil exist in this beautiful place."

Henry set the pipe aside. "There's something else." He turned to Nicole, who sat next to him. "I have something of yours, something you left at Eagle Peak."

Henry pulled an urn from a leather pouch, the Renaissance bronze glinting from the flames.

Nicole put her hand over her mouth and burst into tears, weeping joyfully.

"As a token of our friendship, a token of trust, I return this to you. The Creator has woven our paths together to have closure for you, Nicole. I didn't let the government take possession of it. I didn't know why the Creator wanted me to hide it—now I know."

Before he could hand it to her, she crawled over and embraced him.

He gave her the urn.

She said, "I don't know what to say—you don't know how much this means to me."

She cradled it, went to Kyle, and wept into his chest.

CHAPTER 48

"SO, THAT'S WHEN I decided to take action. That's why I work for Bear-B-Gone." PeeWee gestured toward the T-shirts displaying the logo, fifteen of which he proudly sold today. "Yep, it wasn't enough he had to take my Annie from me last year, but now, he's goin' around killing at will. And they can't find him anywhere. I think they could do a better job looking, though. I think they're too busy following their serial killer, or rabid wolves theories. It's a griz. There's no doubt in my mind."

PeeWee told his story to two tourists from inside a wooden booth in an abandoned parking lot, just off the road near Canyon Hotel. He rang up the young couple for their two cans of bear spray rentals. "You're doing the right thing. Keep my story in mind when you're out there. You can never be too careful, so keep it on you at all times. I sure as hell do." He flicked the metal canister on his hip, making a *tink-tink* sound.

The tourist couple thanked him and went back to their SUV. When their vehicle left, the parking lot was officially empty, save for PeeWee's small pickup. A lamp post flickered on with a buzzing sound as night quickly approached. The warm air cooled, and the sous chef-turned-bear attack prevention activist threw on his zip-up hoodie.

He returned to his stool, flipped his ponytail to his back. He returned a guitar to his lap and played as the sun snuck behind the horizon, giving way to a gray hue settling over the parking lot and adjacent pine forest. He loved helping customers, educating them, preventing further loss of life, but liked to be alone at this time of his busy day. There lingered a sweet calm with sunset and he listened to his lonely tune echoing off the forest wall. He thought about Annie, like he usually did at this time, and channeled her beautiful spirit and let it flow through his hands and into the smooth, sad melody radiating from his instrument.

After some time had passed, and when the songs eventually made his eyes tear up and throat swell, he stopped playing.

He checked his watch. It was time to leave fifteen minutes ago.

He sighed, gathered his things, and padlocked the booth door and sliding window. As he walked to his truck, his footsteps on the weather-beaten pavement were a lonely rhythm under the parking lot lights. "Okay, Annie-A, another day in the books."

He looked up at the night sky, just knowing she was one of those stars looking down on him with that warm smile and flowing red hair. He whistled the song Nicole had sang along to that night at the fire, the last song he would ever play for Annie before she was taken.

His whistling had an echo in the distance, and he thought maybe it had slid into the canyon and was ricocheting off the yellowy walls that some claim were the inspiration for the park's name.

That's when he heard footfall within the dark forest that butted up against the parking lot. The sound was less than a shout away. He stopped and listened. Branches snapped as something heavy traveled nearer.

"Hey, somebody there?"

He was already unholstering his spray can. No bear was going to take this cowboy—no way in hell. He heard a single flapping sound, like someone opening an umbrella.

It's the wind, he thought.

PeeWee turned around and continued to his truck.

He nervously began to sing again, this time a bit quieter.

The umbrella noise came again from behind. Then there was the sound of something scraping, sliding over the blacktop like someone roller-blading.

With lightning speed, PeeWee pivoted around and drew his bear spray.

A hideous creature shaped like a man but with the wings of a bat glided over the asphalt, dragging its decrepit, clawed feet, like a hang glider about to come to a stop.

PeeWee screamed his war cry as he removed the safety cover and squeezed the trigger.

A thirty-foot shot of capsaicin zoomed straight for the monster.

It opened its mouth and delivered its own spray, a stream of yellow, steaming juice that lasered through the bear spray and splattered PeeWee across the neck.

The bat-like creature flexed its wings forward one flap, rising it high into the air.

PeeWee dropped the can and fell to his knees. In agony, he gripped at his throat, and screamed, *"What the fuu—"* His curse was interrupted as his vocal cords seemed to quit—the air exiting the growing hole in his throat as a raspy exhale.

He could still inhale, but the air came through his neck, along with blood and yellow fluid. His mouth still moved as he tried to shout at the demon, but nothing came out.

He began to sway.

The being gave one more beat of its wings, then folded them back like a peregrine falcon and dove at PeeWee. In one swift motion, it swooped over PeeWee, spread its wings, and sank its claws into his torso. It pushed off the ground with its feet and lifted away like a great condor.

As the bat beast soared away, high above the park, PeeWee's consciousness was allowed seven final seconds. A claw penetrated one eye, but the other eye viewed the Grand Canyon of Yellowstone under the light of the stars, the yellow radiance of the sheer canyon walls, the hunter-green and navy-blue patina of the high forests. He heard Annie calling to him, heard the rush of the waterfalls below. The last sensation he had before fading was freefall.

His twirling, lifeless body, hurled downward at a great speed, disappearing into the heart of the canyon.

CHAPTER 49

"HE'S NOT LIKE anyone you'll ever know," Wymon said of his brother, Henry.

Nicole and Kyle joined Wymon and Phoenix at a roughhewn dining table in one wing of Wymon RedMoon's home. Kyle admired the fireplace at one end of the long room. It was comprised of stones of widely varying shapes, sizes, and colors, seemingly thrown together at random. Phoenix had proudly identified the components to the couple earlier—the smooth spherical ones, the size of cantaloupes, were from the river, other chunks were chalcopyrite and limestone, and interspersed throughout were magnificent pieces of quartz-filled rosasite, garnet, and elegant, emerald Wyoming jade.

Next to the fireplace was a bed with a patchwork quilt. On the other side was a stack of hides—deer, beaver, and a third kind that was pronghorn antelope, Kyle guessed. The worn wooden floor creaked with every step, and the entire room had a scent of wood smoke. Three windows, side by side, presented a stretched view of a horse prairie, sage-dotted rolling hills, and a gentle, far ridge capped with patches of white aspen and juniper trees.

The RedMoons were a people of the land, not monsters. His preconceived notion of a wild, blood-crazed tribe living off the grid had been quite misconstrued. Wymon had formally introduced the couple to each of the RedMoon homes, and Kyle felt that a collective vibe of redemption resonated on the ranch. Even now, as Kyle could see through the windows a view of mingling horses enjoying the beaming sun, the feeling within the walls of Wymon's home was one of relief and optimism.

Wymon explained, "He's a lot like our great-grandfather, Henry is. He understood the difference in keeping heritage and absolute segregation. Great-grandfather required each of us to have an education. That is, until Father forbade it under his rule. I cannot deny, I find the outside world, your world, to be a cruel one, and full of greed. But the Wahota must adapt to it, understand its ways, if we are to survive it. Our father, Sid—he led our family down a dark path. No one really knows how evil found its way into his heart. It took Henry busting my head before I would admit we needed to stop Father. Henry had the guts to stand up to him when no one else would. I look at young Phoenix here, and I now see light where I once saw a dark future."

Phoenix held a smile on his face while he listened to his father.

"Again, we can't thank you enough for letting us stay here," Nicole said.

"There is no need to thank us. Henry has named you as family. I can see why. You are good people. You fight for good, like Henry."

Wymon stood and pushed in his chair. "Like I said, Phoenix and I are just down the hall. Dinner will be starting soon. I will let you know when it is ready. So long as I am second head of the Wahota, you will always have a seat at our table."

Phoenix joined Wymon, and they left the couple to their room.

Once the door was closed, Nicole said, "He's been gone three days now."

"He'll be fine. Henry knows what he's doing. He'll find MacLeod. I promise."

Nicole circled the table to stand at Kyle's back. She began to rub his shoulders. Kyle knew she always did that when she was nervous.

She said, peering out at the ridge, "We only have two more nights until it's full."

"Don't worry. Everything will work out. We're going to make it through this."

"So, we kill MacLeod, keep drinking our medicine . . . " She looked at their stockpile of milk jugs full of the Sapphire Pool water, a cache that had taken several nightly trips into the park to retrieve. "Then what?"

"Correction—Henry and I will kill MacLeod, not you. Two pink lines meant pregnant, remember?" He turned his head and placed his cheek on her stomach. "You're not allowed to change."

"Of course I'm not going to change into a werewolf while I'm pregnant. I'm going to help you, though. I need to make sure you don't screw this up. The baby needs its father."

Kyle grinned.

She said, "I'm asking, what then—after we finish with MacLeod?"

"The RedMoons were eventually able to control their gift over time. Maybe we can find out how and learn to control our own."

Nicole sighed. "Not long ago, I would have said that sounds ridiculous, but after all the crap I've seen, the stuff we've been through . . . I don't know, anything's possible."

Kyle stood from his chair and threw his arm around her shoulders. "But don't worry about all of that. Right now, just let me do my thing, and then we can sort all that out."

While Nicole had expressed her apprehension for the full moon, whose appearance loomed ever-closer, Kyle welcomed it. He yearned for the moment he could kill MacLeod. In a way, the act was a reckoning, a means for him to right his wrongs. He sought to prove something—not necessarily to the world that had given him this great burden, but more to himself. Kyle would change on the full moon, control *Bayosh*, and use that power for good. For once, he wouldn't flee from the incredible task in front of him. The knowledge of being a soon-to-be-father, instead of steering him from danger, had ironically motivated him further to make this happen. What would he tell his son, or daughter, years from now, when they would ask what he did to stop this *bandurrai* that still lived, hidden in some remote location, visiting humans in the night and taking their heads?

And the fact that Nicole was actually supporting him in this told him that she understood—that she knew Kyle had to take the plunge, to seek out his own redemption. Not to mention, her grace under fire with the sudden knowledge that she was with child; the woman was incredible.

Nicole hugged him and said softly, "I'm proud of you. You didn't ask for this, but you've faced this curse head on. You're doing everything you possibly can. Like you said, let's make this one thing go right. Then we move on to the next problem, one at a time. Let's kill this son-of-a-bitch."

The door opened, and Henry stepped in.

"Henry. It's great to see you." *Alive,* Kyle wanted to say.

He placed his Stetson on the table. "He's at Lower Falls, in a den near the top."

"What did he look like?" Nicole asked.

He gave them a dead look, opening his mouth slightly, but not speaking. He sat, put an elbow on the table, and put his fist to his mouth.

Kyle asked, "Is everything all right?"

Henry glared gravely at Kyle. He said, "We need to be ready. Our plan needs to be flawless."

Crossing his arms, Kyle pondered, then asked, "In a den, you say?"

Henry answered, "That's right."

Then, Henry said, "Oh, and there is something else. Another person went missing. Some employee named PeeWee."

CHAPTER 50

IT WAS DAYLIGHT'S last hour.

On a high, plateaued cliff, Kyle knelt in an open clearing.

With yellow-rimmed and undaunted eyes beneath the bill of his hat, he sneered at the opening to the vile creature's den.

Behind him, sixty thousand gallons per second rushed over the edge of Lower Falls into the Grand Canyon of Yellowstone. The Yellowstone River gushed headlong, toppling, filling the air with a ceaseless roar. The river was an endlessly working being, a tireless entity that smoothed boulders and cut valley floors. The waters hurriedly passed by, indifferent to Kyle and the beastly donnybrook that could ensue at any moment.

The den was narrow—a dug out, dark slide of a hole beneath a long slab of rhyolite. The den had the appearance of a large, half-closed eye in the side of the gently sloping hill. Sporadically placed blue spruce spread across the hillside, but a clear area of flat land separated Kyle and the den, reaching out to his left and right as if he were a pitcher on the mound and the den were home plate.

It didn't matter that the setting sun made the empty, slender hole even harder to see into, and that Kyle hadn't been able to spot any sign of movement over the last forty-five minutes. When Kyle had first approached, he had caught the slightest of shadow, a subtle black on black maneuver within the hole. The movement he saw, combined with an eerie and malicious presence he sensed under the rock, was more than enough to convince Kyle that MacLeod, or rather the form he took, was coiled within.

It waited for him, Kyle knew—waited for the dark of night to use to its advantage.

Or so it thought.

Nightfall and the rising of the bloated full moon was to Kyle and Henry's advantage, should they need it. The darkness would also be to Nicole's advantage as she waited behind a thick pine to Kyle's left, right where first base would be. The entire time, her eyes were fixed on Kyle, her hands gripping a twelve-gauge shotgun, her CamelBak's bladder topped off with the Sapphire water.

Henry was behind a fallen tree, in an area to Kyle's right, exactly where a team dugout would be situated.

Kyle began to breathe deeply. Then his breaths quickened.

He focused on the pine needles on the ground at his side.

The veins bulged in his neck and spittle flung from his mouth as the name came out involuntarily. "*MacLeod!*"

His nasally huffs increased like a locomotive gaining speed. He removed his hat and his dark hair fell across his chin.

"*MacLeod*!"

He snarled at the slender hole. His jaw buckled, and his canines and upper teeth grew into points, giving him an overbite.

The full moon swelled as the stars pierced through the deep burgundy sky.

Kyle thrust his arms out to his sides, and razor-sharp claws splay from his fingertips. He rose to his feet and his legs extended, bursting through his jeans.

Just then, a folded, black wing and a dark, leathery leg emerged from the hole.

Human skulls spilled out and rolled a few rotations down the slope. The clean, white bone of the craniums where flesh had been rendered luminesced in the moonlight.

The *bandurrai's* head appeared. The look of its bat-like face was that of pure malice.

Its fanged mouth vibrated and chittered.

As Kyle's limbs lengthened and his muscles expanded, his vision morphed from a cast of nightly blacks and grays into a view of heat signatures—the ground a cool blue, the rhyolite layer a lighter lavender. The winged being was a cold, deep-purple hue in Kyle's sight, except for a column that glowed orange and yellow within its throat and chest.

A forked, fleshy strap of a tongue tested the air, in and out, as the rest of its body scuttled out from the den.

As it started to stand, Nicole suddenly shouted, "Hey! You piece of shit! You the one who killed our friend?!"

She'd jumped the gun. Henry was supposed to draw attention and engage it first.

Kyle's voice came as a husky growl, "No!"

Nicole cocked a slug into the chamber and fired.

The shot hit the creature in the leg, and it staggered back, seemingly more surprised than in pain.

She chambered another slug.

The creature pivoted away and opened its wings.

Before it could launch, Henry aimed his Mauser and blasted the demon through its wing, leaving a gaping tear.

It shrieked like a banshee.

With an awkward effort, the *bandurrai* was able to lift off the ground with its injured wing, though it dipped off-rhythm like a moth.

It turned back in Nicole's direction, and she fired into its abdomen.

The round seemed to have no result except to infuriate the creature.

Its beady eyes locked onto Nicole and it flew at her.

Henry dropped his weapon and sprang forth. He threw his arms forward, and when they hit the ground, they were fully clawed. His canines became railroad spikes, and within seconds he was sprinting on all fours, all eight hundred pounds of him, leaving his clothes behind in tears.

As Kyle sprinted to Nicole, a tremendous revelation came to him. He was fully changed—and he was in control.

He easily switched to a running form that utilized his hands as well as feet, propelling himself forward like a racing greyhound.

What *power* he felt, what *strength and speed*, what *rage*.

The *bandurrai* dove at Nicole, but Kyle intercepted with a tremendous leap. At once, he sank every claw into its skin and pulled it to ground.

As they tumbled, it spit its venom at him, scorching his side.

It sprayed again, this time hitting the side of Kyle's head, melting half his pointed ear. The pain was immense and further emblazoned his fury.

A mountainous roar boomed from Henry as he bounded for the *bandurrai*.

The *bandurrai* lifted Kyle by the scruff and shot skyward.

Henry missed.

The demon bat flapped its wings with great effort as Kyle swatted and thrashed. It gained speed as it flew in the direction of the falls.

Nicole fired and missed.

She yelled, "Henry, the cliff! He's going to drop him!"

The Wahota bear was a juggernaut, barreling toward them with remarkable speed.

Henry jumped and drove his claws through the *bandurrai's* leg.

The three fell from the sky and rolled in a great entanglement of hair, claws, and fangs, gnashing and slashing and biting. Wild sounds, elemental and fierce, accompanied the flinging of fur and spilling of blood as the cloud of violence slid across open ground toward the cliff's edge.

And then . . .

. . . over they went . . .

. . . leaving Nicole with nothing but the roar of the rushing waterfall.

A MILE DOWNSTREAM and four hundred feet lower in elevation, at a bend in the river, Kyle fought for his life. One second, his muzzle would breach the surface, gasping for air, the next he'd be well below water, silvery bubbles streaking in every direction, taking a beating from the large boulders. It was a rollercoaster, a back and forth between the sound of rushing rapids and openness when he surfaced, to the garbled sound of undercurrents as he sank. He was strong, but the current was stronger, and it was impossible to achieve a grip on the smooth rocks or slippery timber. With every crash against the mountain stone, his strength was taken away. His condensed body was too heavy, pulling him down as he kicked and clawed and swallowed more and more water.

Kyle had smartly reserved his energy, knowing this could be a long drift, but after so long, it was clear he no longer had that luxury. Reaching the surface became overwhelmingly difficult.

With the last surfacing, he'd called out to Nicole, although only in his mind. It seemed as if she had received his cries and was shouting back, *I'm coming.*

But it wasn't her voice he heard, rather her aura he felt. Was it only his imagination—his mind fading, instinctively concocting warm experiences so that he could die in peace?

Right before he slipped below the surface again, he spotted something.

There, on the bank ahead, was a man.

Kyle sank back down. He slammed against another boulder, this time hitting him in the lower back, sending his body cartwheeling under the rapids. The pain shot through his back, and he swore he felt something break.

Seeing the figure on the bank inspired Kyle to dig up one last effort, and a last effort it would be as he was utterly depleted.

Kyle locked his jaws tight and held his breath.

If death wanted this breath, it would have to take it from him.

Kicking and flailing as best he could, he swam to the surface and gasped deeply.

The man was there—it was Henry, in waist-deep water, holding out a branch.

This time, instead of letting the current pull him back under, he conjured an energy within his last thread of life force. He paddled desperately, his long fingers batting the river's surface. His dog legs scrambled frantically until they finally met stone, and he could keep his snarled nose above water. The next breath he took was so deep it burned his lungs. He planted his foot on a boulder and propelled his head and shoulder free of the river.

"Grab it!" Henry demanded, shaking the branch at him.

One last lunge and Kyle clutched it with both hands as the current took the rest of his body.

Henry anchored the other end while the current forced Kyle out of the rapids.

When the river flow no longer played on his body, Kyle went limp and lay in the shallow water on his back.

His flank and the side of his head still burned from the *bandurrai's* venom. He had excruciating pain in his ribs and leg where he was sure the fall into the river had fractured if not snapped them.

His energy was wasted so, it was taxing just to blink. The pain was overwhelming.

Kyle could see Henry in his peripheral. He was shouting, but Kyle couldn't make out the words right away.

With a moan, Kyle rolled. He pushed himself up, then collapsed to one knee.

Henry's voice started to come through, " . . . and his blood trail leads up here into these woods. There is no time; I have to catch him before he gains distance on us. You will heal. When you do, come for us!"

With that, Henry morphed back into a Wahota bear as he exited the water and took to the forest.

Kyle hung his wolfish head. He encouraged himself: *You'll heal. You'll heal.*

From here, the once overbearing noise of the falls was but a slight static in the distance. The moon was at full tilt now and shined as bright as a streetlamp.

The pain spiked in his ribs again. He gritted his lethal teeth. *Breathe, Kyle, breathe.*

THE BLOOD TRAIL took the Wahota bear up a few hundred feet in elevation through a mixture of thick pine and blue spruce forest. He stopped his sprinting pursuit every few minutes to stand and put his black nose to the wind. Gradually, the woods thinned, and odd geological formations surrounded Henry. A cream-colored mud stack resembling a crawfish hole towered nearly two stories high, with boiling hot runoff dribbling from the top. A wet slope of earth rose seemingly from nowhere with rust coloration sliding down its southern face. Expanses of steaming water, some as big as Olympic swimming pools, dotted the horizon at random. Mud pots bubbled nearby. A lone geyser in a clearing spat and sprayed as if peeved by the Wahota's presence.

The otherworldly valley was silent except for blusterous gusts that washed against patches of birch and pine, sending dead twigs and pinecones to pelt the ground.

Something thudded behind Henry, and he halted.

He twisted around and cast his eyes from one tree to the next. His big head surveyed the tops of the trees, the bases. He sniffed the air again, but his nose was drawn to the forest floor before him, to an aspen log.

A splatter of blood trailed across its white bark.

He followed.

The splatter thickened.

Soon he was putting his nose down to pools of blood, inhaling deeply. Henry increased his speed, grunting with anticipation. He sprinted now on all four limbs, his steps thumping and crushing everything in his path.

RedMoon vaulted a fallen tree, then another, and raced down an embankment, his nose to the wind now. When he reached the bottom of the hill, his feet plunged into a mud bog, catching him mid-stride.

Churning his legs, he attempted to escape, but the bog would not surrender its grip.

Henry extended his massive arms to reach dry land, but he'd landed too far in. Once belly-deep, he stopped sinking. Whuffing and moaning, he jerked and thrashed to no avail.

He roared in anger, shaking the elevated valley's foundation.

His roar was met with the hellish shriek of the *bandurrai*.

Just ahead of Henry, the onyx-colored creature limped forward. The wing that had been shot was now broken, hanging catawampus.

The bat-faced being thrust its head forward. A fresh wound sliced from the bottom of its veiny ear, across its sharp jaw line. The egg-yolkish liquid seeped from its mouth.

As it neared, the *bandurrai* crouched, putting its gnarled knuckles at the bog's edge. Its bottom jaw detached and opened as it postured to spray.

Henry roared in defiance, and it hissed back.

As the hiss started to gurgle, two clawed hands gripped the base of its leathery wings and tugged them backwards until they snapped.

The demon writhed.

It turned to its foe with its yellow spray ejecting.

Kyle slipped his head from the stream and clutched the *bandurrai* by the throat with one hand.

The spray stopped at once, and the creature struggled for air.

Kyle could feel the vocal cords vibrating in its throat in a thwarted scream.

The monster put its arachnid-like hands around Kyle's throat and jabbed at his stomach with its toe claws.

Kyle curled his lips, squeezed harder, and the resistance stopped. The slits on its nose pulsed and spasmed under its beady, soulless eyes. There was nothing of MacLeod's liking left at all on the creature's blackened, demonic face, no hint of him at all on its contorted expression.

Its convulsing mouth seemed to breath the name, "Fenn."

When the wicked being went limp, Kyle clamped his jaws around the back of its neck. He jerked and shook the rag dolled body in a savage fashion.

Lowering the *bandurrai* to the ground, Kyle placed both hands on its back and pulled its head free.

He tossed the head to the side, and it rolled into a mud pot. It sank sideways into the boiling earth, one pointed ear at a time, the unholy screaming expression never leaving its face.

As Kyle spit the blood and traces of yellow grime from his snout, he noticed Henry still lodged in the unforgiving mud.

Kyle hurried to his friend.

By the time Kyle realized he was knee deep himself, it was too late, and he joined the Wahota in the bog, immobile and helpless.

AT DAWN, NICOLE continued her frantic search of the riverbanks. Several times on the overnight journey, she found her claws had snuck out and hair had started to grow on her forearms, prompting her to drink more Sapphire water from the spout of her CamelBak. Though the drink kept the baby in her womb safe from her transformation, she had not gone without temptation to allow her curse to take over and aid her in finding Kyle.

But not changing was the one promise she'd made when they put this plan together. She wasn't in Kyle's original proposal for the attack on MacLeod, but when she took the shotgun hostage and refused to give it up, insisting she would fight at their side no matter what they said, Kyle complied and made her promise not to transform. Plus, a bit of a guilt trip helped her case when she brought up PeeWee and her desire for revenge on behalf of her friend. She didn't know if Kyle budged because he understood her argument or simply because he knew how stubborn she could be.

After hiking one side of the river for two miles, she had finally found a location where she could safely traverse the water, then take her search back in the direction of the falls on the other side.

She had spent the entire night carefully descending into the canyon, then trying to find a sign of Kyle or Henry—the whole time toting the Mauser, twelve gauge, and the survival pack with ammo and other items they'd prepared.

The exhausted girl's trudging pace was frighteningly weak an hour ago when she'd spotted the blood trails and two very large sets of tracks. The find had provided her with a second wind, and she powered through, alert now and reinvigorated with angst.

After meticulously following the tracks for what seemed like forever up a forested slope, she came to an area where the woods began to clear. Soon she found herself among the strange geological formations. The smell of sulfur was rank in the air. This was one of those areas park rangers warned tourists about—the reason why you never go off trail.

More cautiously now, the weary woman moved forward, following a single track. She had her head down, connecting one footprint to the next, taking at least four steps to its two.

She heard a groan. Then, "Hey! Over here!"

Nicole was taken aback by the scene laid out in front of her.

The *bandurrai* lay headless, its yellow goo spilled around it, its wings a crumpled mess.

Just feet away, she spotted Henry half-sunken in the ground with mud covering his body and hair. He faced the other direction, looking over his shoulder at her, his upper buttocks exposed above the mud.

Kyle was near him, half-sunken and muddied up as well. However, his face was grotesque, and thin strands of hair hung in patches around his body. He still bore his deadly teeth and claws. The moon was far gone, but the strength of his direct infection obviously wasn't. He was absolutely stuck, and there was no fight left in him.

She grinned and began to giggle with a mixture of relief, joy, and hysteria. The pair looked like beaten dogs who'd been left outside all night in bad weather.

The Great Coyote and Badger, she thought.

She retrieved a bottle of Sapphire pool water from her pack and tossed it to Kyle.

He had difficulty handling the bottle, trying to remove the plastic cap. When he couldn't successfully twist it off, he sliced off the neck with his claw, then poured the entire bottle into his blunt snout.

It took Kyle four breaths to shrink, shed, and retract his pointy projectiles.

Henry and Kyle were too bushed to speak.

Nicole unloaded the guns and set them aside.

She plopped down onto her rump and crossed her arms around her knees. They were a sad and naked sight, she mused.

She smiled, said, "Well, boys . . . I hate to pry . . . "

EPILOGUE

Nine Years Later

AT THE EDGE of an alpine meadow, Kyle rested on one knee, leaning his elbow on a lodgepole pine. Beneath the bill of his hat, Kyle's eyes were unflinching as he steeled himself.

He said in a calm voice, "Phoenix."

A formidable grizzly bruin trotted down a hill in Phoenix's direction, its head high, eyeing the twenty-four-year-old RedMoon.

"Walk over to me very slowly. Don't look behind you," Kyle said.

A confused Phoenix abided and walked to Kyle. When Phoenix was safely behind him, Kyle stood, and without making any sudden movements, squared off with the charging bear, and stepped forward.

When it was close enough for him to hear its breath, Kyle started to walk more briskly.

The grizzly still charged, its claws tearing through the ground.

"*Hey.*"

No affect.

He yelled again with more force, "*Hey!*"

The bear planted its front paws in the dirt and came to a sliding halt in front of Kyle. The air from the beast's momentum raised Kyle's dark hair off his shoulders.

It stood and towered over him.

Phoenix raised his bow but didn't draw. He stepped to the side, allowing for an unobstructed shot at the animal. Kyle sensed his movement, and said, "Don't, Phoenix. We're alright."

Kyle lowered his hands, took a step forward.

He clinched a fist, and cursed the animal, *You're not taking this one, you son-of-a-bitch.*

It groaned and whuffed, then took a minute to test the air with its nose; first to the east, then in Kyle's direction.

Submitting to Kyle's gaze, the bruin lowered to all fours, turned shoulder and sauntered off.

CAMERA FLASHES AND reporters' questions flooded into the station as Police Chief Henry RedMoon opened the front door.

He shut the door behind him, silencing the crowd outside, and hung his Stetson on the coat rack.

Officer Wymon RedMoon shoulder-leaned against a bookshelf at the back of the station lobby, coffee in hand.

The now short-haired man raised his mug to Henry in a saluting fashion. "Well done, Chief."

Henry gave his brother a nod and stepped into his office. He sat down and replayed the press conference in his head, hoping his speech sounded right. The monthly conference consisted of the usual: a percent drop in drug and alcohol-related deaths, fewer violent crime arrests, the announcement of a new committee—this one to spearhead reservation graffiti cleanup. The increasing press over the years was a result of an immense amount of positive change that he and his limited officers created on the reservation, despite inadequate funds. He had gained national attention, and other reservations even sought to model his method of law enforcement, though it baffled them how he was able to rid a community of so much crime in so little time.

It didn't end as a routine press conference, however, as Henry publicly announced his candidacy for county mayor. His success at Elk River was substantial, but without political support, bulking up law enforcement would be impossible.

There was still much work to be done.

At his desk, Henry pulled out his cell phone and called the RedMoon ranch. Nicole picked up, "Well hello, Mr. Mayor."

He leaned back in his chair. "I take it you saw that?"

"We got the news on right now. Kyle's out hunting with Phoenix, though. I can't wait to tell him."

"How are the boys?"

She peaked through the kitchen blinds. "Just runnin' around the barn like wild animals. The usual."

Henry chuckled fondly. His six-year-old son, Elliot, named after Henry's great-grandfather, made him a proud man. Kyle and Nicole's nine-year-old, James, was Elliot's other half, and every day on the ranch was an adventure for the two, Henry knew. He pictured them sword fighting or throwing mud clods at each other in the barn at this moment.

Henry was also proud to offer Kyle and Nicole a place at his home. It was meant to be temporary until they could figure out how to live on their own, under the radar, but they folded into the family so well, there was no rush to leave, and the years flew by as they watched their kids grow. The couple became excellent ranch hands for Henry, and their gratitude was immeasurable. And of course, their supply of water from the Sapphire Pool was always well stocked to keep the wolves at bay.

Nicole said, "Larinda says hi." She was waving at the phone from a rocking chair in the living room.

"Tell her I have that elk meatloaf recipe for her. Maybe she can whip that up this weekend."

"I will. We'll celebrate your candidacy."

"Fair enough. Hey, have you seen the news about the park?"

"Yeah, the tremors? Sounds serious."

GEOLOGISTS FROM AROUND the world had made emergency flights to Yellowstone earlier in the week. They set up observation tents around seismographs and took measurements at sites throughout the park. One group was particularly interested in the western valleys and the Sapphire Pool. The spectacled scientists and all other visitors had been moved away and restricted from the pool.

Just this morning after a strong tremor, the pool had emptied. All that was left was an eerie hole in the ground, its slimy walls slipping down and clogging the bottom.

OUTSIDE, ELLIOT AND James romped through the horse barn. The hole in the side from Sid and Henry's battle had been repaired and painted over. They walked by each stall, explaining why which of the horses were their favorites. Though three years younger, Elliot was already a foot taller and fifty pounds heavier than James.

The barn's frame jostled subtly as a seismic surge rearranged the underworld. Geothermal features within Yellowstone and the region began to spurt and spew. Mudpots boiled vigorously.

Hot pools surged—some emptied.

Just then, horse dung loudly thudded onto the ground, and Badger's muscular rump released a noisy puff of gas.

Elliot was the first to succumb to laughter.

"Ewww. He *is* just like you, *Eli*." James sprinted away giggling, and Elliot lugged after him.

The nimbler James leapt onto a hay bale, "Anyway, Coyote is the fastest. That's why he's the best horse. He could beat Badger in a race any day of the week."

With James' help, Elliot stepped onto the same bale. It was time for the first of their daily contests.

Elliot steadied himself, "Ready?"

James nodded, "Yep."

Together, they counted, "One . . . two . . . three!"

The End

ABOUT THE AUTHOR

GREG MARCHAND is a Medical Laboratory Technician, Western Kentucky University Alum, U.S. Army veteran, and former Yellowstone sous chef currently living in the "Crossroads of America" state of Indiana. The colorful and contradictory people he has met in his lifetime inspire his stories, as do his fascination with the bizarre and his love for the mysteries held within mother nature.

When he's not cursing medical laboratory instruments for a living, Greg is often downstairs hashing out his tilted stories, P90x-ing, and struggling to learn banjo. Occasionally, he emerges from his man cave to cook for his wife and stepson, and to take the dogs down to the river.

Join Greg Online

BookBub	**@gregmarchand**
Facebook	**@gmarchauthor**
Instagram	**@gmarchauthor**

WWW.RHETASKEWPUBLISHING.COM

Made in the USA
Monee, IL
03 July 2021